MW01680766

TO LIVE, MARY REEDE MUST BECOME HER DEAD BROTHER, BUT TO LOVE SHE MUST BECOME HERSELF; HER STORY IS AN ODYSSEY WORTHY OF HOMER.

About two hundred yards off, our pursuer ran up her colors, a black flag bearing the curious device of a white skull in its center, with crossed white swords beneath.

"John," Candy said, "I've sailed with such in years past, and there's just a chance that I may know some of her crew. When they board, stand where you can be clearly seen, with your hands by your side — in plain sight — show no resistance at all. They'll be very hard sorts, and it's certain there'll be some who will stand ready to cut you down to drown in your own blood."

At that same moment there was a puff of gray smoke from her forward gun, followed closely by the dull thump of its report. A jet of water leaped from the surface of the sea some hundred feet or so in our path ahead.

A brightly clad figure stepped up by the forward shrouds onto its rail, and raised a speaking trumpet.

"Heave to! Heave to!" came a voice across the water, "Come into the wind till ye stay, and back your sails. We mean to board you for inspection. Heave to Damn ye!"

"... a man forced against his will to serve a pirate 'republic' and a pirate, who lived 300 years ago emerge here full blooded, historically viable ... a richness to the detail ... that is compelling."***—Rev. Dr. W. Gary Hayward, Covenant Evangelical Church, Barre, Massachusetts.***

"N. C. Schell's riveting novel tells the story of the pirate Mary Reede ... it's Mary's ... stunning defiance of gender expectations, her struggles at the edge of morality and her brave embrace of a dangerous love that gives this story its thunder and modern urgency. Everything about this novel, its eccentric characters, its consistently fascinating, spectacularly written action sequences and its powerful, resonant themes, screams to be made into a television series ...."—***Laura Harrington, Actress & Screenwriter, Hollywood, CA.***

"... a masterly crafted tale. From beginning to end, I could not put it down."—***Paula Warner, Sunderland, Massachusetts.***

"Very polished and dramatic ... attention to detail is phenomenal ... a great piece of work"—***Patrick Dunn, Manchester, New Hampshire.***

"I started reading and couldn't stop. I'm not much on reading either..."—***David Kettles, KY.***

"... how I love the story! I really wept at the last chapter ...."—***Maureen LePain, FL.***

"One sentence and I truly couldn't put it down. I am spellbound by the story ...."—***Richard Booth, MA.***

"... I just loved it! I wanted more. I guess that's the next book."—***Esther Kaddaras, AZ.***

"Just wrapped it up. This is great!...."—***Paula, MA.***

"Thank you for your book. It is a marvel."—***Elizabeth Dunn, NH.***

THE BALLADE OF MARY REEDE

Twilight of the Buccaneers

N.C. Schell

Moonshine Cove Publishing, LLC
Abbeville, South Carolina U.S.A.

FIRST MOONSHINE COVE EDITION AUGUST 2017

This book is a work of fiction. Names, characters, places and incidents are products of the author's imagination or are used fictitiously. Any resemblance to actual events, locales or persons, living or dead, is entirely coincidental.

ISBN: 978-1-945181-18-4
Library of Congress PCN: 2017949827
Copyright © 2017 by N.C. Schell

All rights reserved. No part of this book may be reproduced in whole or in part without written permission from the publisher except by reviewers who may quote brief excerpts as part of a review in a newspaper, magazine or electronic publication; nor may any part of this book be reproduced, stored in a retrieval system or transmitted in any form or by any means electronic, mechanical, photocopying, recording or any other means, without written permission from the publisher.

Front cover image public domain, cover design by Moonshine Cove staff.

For My Grandchildren: Harper, Ellery, Charlotte, Heather, Spencer, Noah, Devyn, Marcus, and of course Colton & the '*Pookaroo.*'

About The Author

I was born in Lebanon, Pennsylvania on September 17, 1944. I make no apology for being a big dumb Pennsylvania 'Dutch' country boy. I am the product of an abusive marriage and a broken family. I spent a nomadic life with my father, who was a kidnapping parent. I grew up unsupervised on small town streets.

My work life began at eight years old collecting bottles for their deposit, and shining shoes Fridays and Saturdays in a barbershop in Sebring, Florida—demanding work in that age of black shoes and ubiquitous white cotton socks. I have lived at the rough edge all of my life. My lessons have all been learned the hard way. My father, for all his faults, taught me to read very early using comic books.

I discovered historical novels at the age of nine, when I found a copy of Paul I. Wellman's *The Iron Mistress'* on a shelf in our rented rooms. I read it, and discovered the magic that happens between the mind, and the written word. Shortly afterward I also discovered public libraries. Libraries, along with Shirley Industrial School For Boys, and '*Classics Illustrated,* have been the primary sources of my early education.

My companions and teachers through many years have been Kenneth Roberts, C. S. Forester, Paul I. Wellman, Fredrick Marryat, James A. Michener, Louis L'Amour, Richard H. Dana, James Clavell and Patrick O'Brian.

I have endeavored to write an historical novel of a sufficient quality so that I may greet them in the Elysian Fields with my head held high.

Read more about the author's interests and writing approach at his website:

www.maryreede.com

Foreword

My life took an interesting turn when a concise, strident letter to the editor appeared in my local newspaper. It was one of those letters that compelled me to thank the author for taking the time, thought and courage to raise the level of civil discourse and challenge orthodox thought. After exchanging notes we met at a pub, shook hands as kindred spirits and began building a friendship around our shared love of realism and the creative spirit. We are both artists. I recreate worlds with paint and brush; Norman has dedicated his life to recreating them with music and words.

There is something timeless about a wooden table and a glass of ale in a darkened pub. Our friendship developed across a table in such a pub. I found myself a captive, looking across our ales at a man with gray eyes and a savvy smile, a story teller. Norman had me leaning across that table to better hear his tales from the early 18th century. We both relished our roles. Norm shared his stories of love and adventure from far away seas, centuries ago. His stories included one about Mary Reede, one of the most remarkable women to have graced the earth. A woman that history has never treated fairly. A woman who has been trivialized, but in fact was resourceful, valorous and decorated. A woman that Norman had, over time, come to know personally.

It was only because fate had placed her in the path of piracy that any of us know of her at all. Norman related all that history had to say about Mary and then went on to tell me about what he had discovered to be the truth. Norman's reconstruction of Mary's world and her life was so vivid I was certain that somehow, he had been there. Should the articles of Jack Rackham's republic ever surface it wouldn't surprise me to see "N.C. Schell" among the signatures.

Through the voice of a proud and decent man, a ships carpenter, Norman will take anyone who dares to join him to the pirate republic that brought Mary Reede a small measure of distorted fame. You will experience first hand the disciplined, colorful life of a tiny, floating, democratic state at war with all flags. Furthermore, you will finally meet the real Mary Reede, one of history's most remarkable women and until now, one of its most unappreciated and misunderstood. Rest your elbows on the table, take a small sip of ale, lean in and bend your ear to N.C. Schell. Our muse will set the record straight in a way you will never forget, telling us of an ingenious hero who traveled far and wide.

William B. Sillin
Sunderland, Massachusetts, 2017

Acknowledgment

Donald, Dorothy, and Esther Morrissey who rescued me from the bulrushes, and gave me a new life. William Sillin and Jeffery Crandell who kicked new life into an old man.

The Ballad of Mary Reede

Prologue
Summer 1752
The New England Hills

A young man came north along the river to visit me three days ago. He came well mounted, and leading a pack-horse. He was dressed much in the Abinaki fashion and wore leggings and a hunting shirt made of smoked deerskin as soft as velvet and a wide flat brimmed hat. He came up from his family's home in Gloucester, leaving early and heading west. "I'm headed out to the Mohawk Valley," he told me, "or maybe further on, to the Ohio country." He brought me greetings, and presents, from an old shipmate.

I recognized his father in him right off, although he was built upon a larger frame, and was more robust in appearance. His father Merit was retired from the sea now and his two elder brothers Andrew and Phillip took over the family business trading along the coast from Gloucester south to New York, and north to Arundel. They sailed two fine vessels he told me, a fast Jamaica built sloop named *The Spanyard*, and an Ipswich schooner named *The Lilly*.

This son, Nathaniel, the youngest, felt no call to the sea however, but was drawn to the deep forests, and to the great solitude. He was a keen eyed lad, alert and sanguine and he seemed to know his way around the business he was going upon.

That first night after we'd eaten and talked a bit, he brought out a small cedar chest from the duffel he'd unloaded from his packhorse. "My father sent this to you," he said. "He told me to tell you that the contents might affect you some, and for me to warn you thus. There's a letter from him inside that will explain everything."

Filled with curiosity, I knelt before the little chest and unbuckled its straps. The chest was well fitted and lined with tin, it held six wrapped dozens of fragrant Cuban cigaros, and a blank ship's log book, two fine steel quills, a bottle of India and a Spanish dagger. The scent of the cigaros washed up and brought me a wave of memories. At the sight of the dagger however it was as if a ghostly hand had took it up and cut me to my heart, so powerful was the emotion that seized me. I must have been visibly shaken, for the boy quietly arose and left me alone in the cabin.

I composed myself some and removed the letter, which was rolled around the hilt and tied in place with a long blue ribbon. There was no mistake about the dagger, eight inches of blue brown Spanish spada two inches wide. Two inches of its length being a thick choil bound with German silver wire. Its hilt was the tip of a narwhal tusk, worked so as to have a slight bulge up close to the choil. It was a design that was old when Rome was a village. I was still shaking inside as I began to read.

Dear mate,

I sent down to the islands special to get these cigaros for ye. The younger senhour Vazquez says they are the best Cubanos he knows of. His father — that being the Jorge as we know — had a scrap with a surly sort of a fellow — hailed from Manteca — fellow as used to serve John Barnett. Anyway Vazquez says the fellow made the mistake of pulling this blade on the old man, and that the fellow will have no further use for it where he is now. Young Vazquez sent it north with the cigaros, he said the old man wanted it passed on to the proper owner, which I have now done.

I've sent the pens and such along to ye in the hope that ye'll start to write your story down.

It's been a long time now, mate, and I think the living are down to thee and me, and the Viejo Vazquez of course, but his family's straight traders now and he don't give a damn what ye write. I always thought it a story as wants the telling. Since Roberts went under all the great pirates are gone, just a batch of penny thieves and cutthroats now. When we sailed there was still some as could make the world take notice.

The real point of this letter however, John, is that the family has talked on it and we would like ye to come down to Gloucester. We'd like ye to take charge of our boatyard for us, we want to do some building of our own vessels. There's the smell of another war coming from the old country and my oldest boy Andrew wants to build a big fast topsail schooner for privateering. The whole family is in complete agreement on this. Ye'll have yer own place and be well taken care of, and ye'll have plenty of time as well to write the story. The door and our hearts be open to ye, John, and all hope to see ye come.

The note was unsigned except for a little stick drawing of a hanged man. I sat for a time after I'd finished reading, and then I went out and joined the boy on my porch.

We sat together there each night of his visit, smoking the cigaros and watching the long drowsy twilight settle on the river. The music of the waters and the forest filling the dusk as the fall of night come on. He was good company for an old man, a bright cheerful and attentive lad, filled with funny little stories, mostly concerning his father's dealings through the years.

He had inherited all of his father's sense of justice and fair play, along with his total mistrust of any civil authority or worldly power as well. He asked me a lot of questions about his father's and my adventure together in the Caribbean. He had heard the story before, but he seemed to take a great pleasurable satisfaction in my accounting of the familiar story though different eyes.

"My father's right you know," he said the last night he was here. "It's a most unusual and exciting story of adventure that you have to offer. I hope you will write it as he's asked you to. I've read Captain Johnson's famous history of the pirates, and the story as he relates it seems sparse and dry. It leaves you wanting to know more of the people involved. I know that he left much of the detail out, in order to protect you — and some others — but the time is ripe now to set it down so that it is not lost."

On that first day I closed up my workshop and we went for a ramble north along the river.

I could see that he was a skilled woodsman, he being quiet and watchful even as we walked for pleasure. At dusk he called and bagged a fine fat turkey, which we roasted that night. He carried with him a wonderful rifled gun that he said was brought up special for him from Lancaster, in the Pennsylvania colony.

The rifle was as long as he was tall; it had an octagon barrel with a fire seasoned tiger maple stock, and browned steel lock and furnishings — a very business like piece. The workmanship was unadorned but very fine in all particulars, and it was marked with the gunsmith's etching on the top of the barrel by the lock. *Jakob Schell, Maker, Mount Joy Township, Pennsylvania 1751.*

He was justly proud of the piece, and later showed me some prodigious shooting. He easily hit the head-sized knot on a Beech tree, a hundred and fifty paces off, three shots in a row and in right smart time as well; although the process of loading a rifle gun is a sight more particular than ramming home a cartridge into a musket.

We fished together the second day and caught a half dozen of fat trout. We rolled them in corn flour, and fried them with salt pork crackling and onions. We ate them with corn bread and dandelion greens and washed them down with my dandelion wine. Life is good here on the river; I live in a garden.

I was some affected to see him go, and I think he felt something like it as well for he took his time in the preparation. I gave him a jug of maple syrup, and a jug of my wine for the trip, and we embraced at parting. After he mounted, he turned his horse to face me, and backed it away a few steps, showing himself to be a horseman, not just a man on a horse.

He threw me a knuckle to his forehead — sailor fashion. "That's from my father," he said, "He hopes you'll come to Gloucester — or else go to hell," he chuckled, and "he says there might at least be no black flies there, as he thinks old Ned wouldn't want the competition." He turned then and rode down the hill past the Beech that he'd peppered. He turned and doffed his wide brimmed hat to me a last time before disappearing into the forest at the bend in the trail.

I went back into my cabin and opened the little chest his father sent. I took up the Spanish dagger and sat there with it in my hands for some time, my thoughts drifting back through the years to the Caribbean, and to her. Around noon I heard someone calling for attention from my workshop.

I thought about him throughout the remainder of the day. How different he was from the generation that his father and I came from. He was born in this land, and he felt the full force of the freedom this New World has to offer to the bold and restless, as a birthright. There was no trace in him of the deferential and servile attitude that marked the first settlers; seeped as they were in the class structures, and hereditary authorities of the Old World.

He was like some young Scythian warrior, resourceful and cunning, completely self reliant, confident of his skills and owning no man to be his better — most especially because of birth. I reflected that soon an entire race of young men like him would populate these colonies. I wondered to myself how long a people like them would serve a king who was an ocean and more removed from them. I stopped work early and enjoyed a cigaro on my porch overlooking the fields and the river.

That night I dreamed of her again.

The dreams come when they will; I do not dwell in the thoughts and thus invite them — though I'll admit that recent events might have spawned this one — rather they seem to come to remind me, to twist at my heart.

In the beginning of the dream it is so real to me that I think I have awakened from another dream to find her still with me. Later in the dream I always lose sight of her somehow, and then the sad and fruitless searching begins again. I awake with a start, always deeply affected. Sometimes I will urge myself back to sleep trying to recapture the dream, it never works.

The dreams are both a joy, and a pain. In them I can walk again beside her, and feel her name upon my lips but in them I must lose her once more before I awaken.

The next morning I walked for a while along the river, and then sat down to begin the story.

Chapter 1
Laying the Keel

The boy's visit, the greetings and the gifts that he'd brought, opened up an old wound deep inside of me; and so the story I will relate is, in its way, like a sliver of fine white quartz which needs to come out for the wound to fully heal. A tale of my own experience will illustrate the point I wish to make.

In the summer of 1724 I marched north to Norridgewock with Captain Jeremiah Moulton, as much to escape the king's press gangs scouring Boston as for any other reason. We traveled up the Quinnebec by whale boat and on the 12th of August I took part in the great fight above the falls, which broke the back of the eastern Abinaki nation.

I took no part in the mutilations that occurred there however, for such things are blasphemous and unchristian. They are an affront to any civilized man, and they diminish any cause, however just. It shames me still to have witnessed Lieutenant Jacques take the scalp of the priest Father Rales. The lieutenant's courage and resourcefulness was buried for me in the memory of that act. The heat and the fear of battle can do terrible things to a man.

Near the end of the fight, as I was ramming home a fresh load into my musket, I took an arrow under my right arm. It came in at a sharp angle, struck a rib and burrowed under my flesh so that the point was sheltered in the lee of my shoulder blade. I reached back under my clothing, and broke the shaft off about an inch from the entrance wound before continuing with the business at hand.

After the fight, the attending churgion pronounced the wound a minor one and drew out what remained of the shaft. The head of the weapon remained however, and continued as a small lump under my flesh for nearly twenty years. The churgion offered to remove it after the more serious wounds had been attended to, but his hands were filthy and I wanted none of his cutting. The entrance wound left behind a ragged puckered pink scar that itched me from time to time, but caused no discomfort beyond that.

One day, all those years later, I was washing myself when I noticed that the small pink scar had become very irritated and red, and that a fresh scab had formed in its place. It caused me some right fierce itching over the next day, and that night as I washed I picked at the new scab in my scratching. It fell away, and with a little rush of clear liquid a sliver of milk white quartz popped out of me as though spit. I have it still, in my wampum bag. It is an inch long, and about half as wide at the base, tapering to a sharp point — like a little ship. The scar now is ragged and white, and hard, and the wound at last fully healed.

So too I think it is with wounds to the heart, or to the spirit. They may heal over to all outward appearances, yet deep down, under the flesh, they remain a living thing. The scent of the cigaros, and the sight of the Spanish dagger, caused the unseen pink scar over my breast to inflame and itch. The writing of this story — in its fullness — will serve I hope as the scratching of the scab. With luck its telling will be as cleansing and fulfilling to my heart's wound, as the birth of that little sliver of quartz was to my body's.

My name is John Tanner. When my tale begins I was a ship's carpenter. I have not followed that trade since returning from Norridgewock. I was mustered out as a corporal, and moved here to the river below Dummer's fort shortly afterward, onto land given me in grant for my services in that campaign.

For some years past I served the fort, and the general, in all manner of joining. Now I make my living in the building of small boats, bateaux, barrels and barns for any who will it. My livelihood has been good, as the little town below the fort has grown to the point of incorporation. It is expected to be named for Colonel Brattle who owns a royal title to the land, but who has never been here to my knowledge.

Now I am most used to the building of vessels, so I will approach this story concerning the twilight of the buccaneers in the way I know best. I know a vessel to be a living thing, and like it I think a story is a living thing. They are both so because of those who live within them. Now for a story, as also for a vessel, there needs be a starting point, a foundation upon which to build. In the building of a vessel this is the laying of the keel.

The keel of a vessel is like the spine of a living creature, for upon it the ribs are racked, the hull is hung, the frame is filled, and the decks are laid. Only then does the crew of the vessel come aboard to play their parts in the living whole. Now as I am the one who is about to tell the story of that which once I lived, I seem to be the keel. So then upon this keel I will build the vessel, which will carry the crew, and their story.

I was born in Bristol, England in the September of 1694. I am the only child of fine people. My father's name was Joseph, and my mother's name was Sarah Tweedly. They owned a small public house at the foot of Claire Street, not far from the Christmas Stairs, under the sign of the Rose and Thistle.

My father was that rarest of all Englishmen, a paid down veteran of twenty years service in his majesty's navy. Ten years of his service as captain of the foretop. My mother having spent these same years in service as chief cook to the dukes of Somerset, they having known each other all the while and silently trothed the time. Their love for that time mostly confined to the letters that each cherished.

My father was paid down in 1692, when his ship the *Renown* was brought into dry dock in Portsmouth roads. His having been badly wounded in the action that preceded the need for dry-docking, he was invalided out of service and not rotated onto an out bound vessel, as is the custom even to this day.

Released from hospital he quickly cashed out, and in his own words "legged it out of Portsmouth as fast as I could, with no look behind me, nor to either side, till I could smell the sea no longer." He had lived a frugal life in the navy, and between his back pay and the prize monies owed him, came back to Bristol with two hundred pounds. His first stop was at Somerset house, where I am told he invaded the kitchens, swept my weeping mother up onto his shoulders and carried her off the property and straight to Saint Mary Radcliffe to post the bans. To its eternal credit the house of Somerset dowered my mother handsomely and with its assistance and patronage the Rose and Thistle came to be.

My parent's house was a clean and decent place and no rowdyism was permitted. The food my mother served had been fit for a duke's table and so enjoyed a reputation as which brought the best sort of naval officers, mariners and merchants to our tables. It is these men who fed my youth with the desire to see the world. It was there that my heart was set for the sea. It was there also in my tenth year that I first met a thirty-two-year-old, sharp-tongued 'black Welshman' named Charles Llewelan Johnson.

He was a sparingly built man who stood with an habitual slight forward slump to his shoulders.

His short cropped hair and deeply set eyes were as black as coal, as were his eyebrows, the mole that graced his left cheek close by his mouth and the mustache that he maintained contrary to all the social fashions of the day and place. His face to the world was one of iron self control and a fiercely independent intelligence.

Only those who came to know him best knew of the great whooping humor that beat beneath his official face. He dressed very plainly and favored dark woolens of a simple cut with no adornment save a small blue velvet ribbon on the facing of his coat. I was witness many times to the doors this ribbon would open, and to the fawning attention of the officials he came into contact with, this all as a result of his personal accomplishments, and not of birth.

In 1686 he had sailed on the '*Cygnet*' with Dampier as a boy of 15, and returned with him in 1691 from the Indonesian islands as a wealthy young adventurer of twenty-one. He had been instrumental in the affairs of the Merchant Venturers Company of Bristol for at least ten years when I met him and was a well-known and very successful investor.

I never knew him to actually exercise the office of captain of any vessel on which I sailed with him; he rather exercised the authority of a commodore. As supercargo and chief steward of the company of investors his authority as far as the course and condition of sailing was absolute. Though beset on several occasions by Corsairs on his frequent voyages into the Levant — including once on my second voyage with him — no vessel upon which he sailed had ever struck its colors. Indeed on the voyage I've mentioned we sank a large Tunisian galley, and inflicted severe casualties on another. Our company's sense of elation at our victory was tempered by the knowledge that most of the oarsmen chained below on the sinking vessel were Christian slaves. I can still hear the lamentation of their wailing from the sinking vessel if I allow myself to dwell on that fateful hour.

The friendship that developed between the captain and my father seemed odd at first, they being such disparate seeming men. My father so tall and blonde and Saxon, and with the boisterous personality of a man of war's man. Captain Johnson slight of stature, dark and almost sinister looking at first glance, and seemingly much quieter by nature. The bursts of rollicking good-humored laughter that punctuated their quiet discussions at the back booth of the tavern always set my mother to shaking her head.

My parent's house being well known and successful, my education was assured, and carefully seen to by both my mother and my father. My mother being insistent that her son would be literate and have at least a nodding acquaintance with the classics, and my father equally insistent that I be prepared to hold my own in a world he knew to be populated by hard men. And thus I attended the Cathedral school of Mary Radcliffe to please my mother, and the school of pugilism, quarterstaff and wrestling under the tutelage of Frank 'thumper' Woodley to please my father.

Woodley was a Yorkshire man, an ex drover who had retired undefeated from the ring. His having held to all comers at the St. Bartholomew's and Scarborough fairs for three years running, till indeed there were no further challengers. He was a short and very broad man, with massive powerful arms and shoulders, a stomach and chest like some great barrel and legs like the stumps of young Oak trees. His hair cropped next the scalp in the boxer's fashion. In due time he and my father and Captain Johnson became tablemates and my mother's head shook all the more vigorously for it.

On my thirteenth birthday I was called to sit with these three at the back table, my mother too was in attendance. I was given a tankard of small beer and when we were all comfortable with one another I was asked if I should like to go into an apprenticeship under the sponsorship of Captain Johnson. The nature of which was designed to allow me to pursue my desire to join the maritime world that surrounded me, while insuring that I would go to sea as an artist, or as a warrant officer should I be pressed or enter into the King's service. I would be sponsored into an apprenticeship with master shipwright James Evans at the Albion yards, and at twenty be taken into my journeymanship as a carpenter's mate aboard a vessel in service to the interests of Captain Johnson. He would warrant to me a master's papers within six years if I would warrant diligent service to him for that same time.

So on Plow Monday of 1708 I entered into the Albion yards as an apprentice and into first learning the skills, which have sustained me all these years. Master Evans was a gentle and considerate man as well as being a very skilled shipwright and a patient teacher. My relationship to him quickly became as that of a favored nephew to a kind uncle. My regard for him grew not only out of my admiration for his skill, but also for his forthright honesty in sharing every skill and hard won secret with me. His regard for me — as he said when we parted — grew from my obvious love for the art that he loved.

Under his instruction I found that I had been given a wonderful gift for the working of wood. The comment was once made by another master in the yards that the wood seemed to work like butter in my hands, although I think my hands strangely gnarled for their having worked with butter all these years. Words fail me to express the swelling of my heart the first time ever a vessel that I had helped to build slipped down the ways and into the Avon. She was a 300 tonne brig christened *'Rachel.'*

At my mother's insistence the rounding of my education continued through tutoring as a condition of my apprenticeship, while other areas were accounted for by the constant attentions of my father, and Master Woodley. My days were very full indeed through the six years I worked the yards.

My twentieth birthday came during the year in which the first George was crowned. After the riots, which had claimed two lives in celebration of his coronation, Captain Johnson and Frank Woodley came to the Rose and Thistle early in the evening. My father of course was overjoyed to see his boon friends arrive, however my mother, though very fond of both these fine men, was less enthused for she readily surmised their errand.

The captain came, as she anticipated, to call me away from my home and her arms and into the broad world. I also learned that Frank Woodley had been taken into Captain Johnson's service as companion and bodyguard, and that thus my relationship with him would continue into the foreseeable future. I was delighted. A month later I was aboard the captain's 400 tonne bark the *Elizabeth Galley* out of Deptford, bound for Palestine and the great spice markets of the Levant.

The *Elizabeth* was as much warship as she was trader, being heavily armed with twelve pounders and carrying a crew of over a hundred men. There is no harm to say now that the vessel was used most often for the carriage of very important and valuable cargoes, in specie, goods, or personages, and carried quickly and with great security. She was known as a fast vessel; and as she was equipped as a galley with twenty sweeps she need not fear the unpredictable winds and frequent calms of the Mediterranean or Baltic seas. It was under the power of these sweeps that we savaged the Tunisian galleys that day.

I made three voyages with the captain between 1714 and 1719, twice to the Levant and once to the port of Boston in the Massachusett Bay colony. While the voyages through the Mediterranean were more exotic and certainly more adventure-some, the little port of Boston so won my heart that it was to Boston that I was glad to flee when the story that I am building came to its, now as I see it, inevitable end. I hid myself there for three years working as a cooper before the march to Norridgewock that I have told of.

During each voyage the crew was called by divisions to daily drills with musket, pike, axe, cutlass and pistol, every man aboard was also made ready to step into service of the main guns as needed. On each of the two voyages, prior to entering the middle sea, we laid-to off Biscay for several days in order to drill and service the guns, and burn up powder.

The rattle of musketry and the thump of the guns brought us the attention of passing vessels on several occasions. In the end all hands entered the Mediterranean accustomed to our weapons and well drilled in the defense of our cargo and lives. So as I have related it all came to good use for us on my second voyage east, and thus by it a great cargo of Ivory, silks and spices valued at over two hundred and fifty thousand guineas — any pirates dream — arrived safe at London.

Shortly before my birthday in September of 1719, about a month after our return from Genoa, Captain Johnson sent for me and informed me that he was having my master papers drawn up. My service and attention to detail over the past years being rewarded as he had warranted. He also mentioned that my steadiness and effectiveness in the late combat off the coast of Africa had been noticed and remarked upon by all the officers present, and so entered into the vessel's log. We agreed that I should remain in his service, and that when the master carpenter's berth on the *Elizabeth* should become available it was mine. He assigned me then as master carpenter aboard — as he said — "an old acquaintance" of mine the brig *Rachel*, which I had helped to build. I was told to go home to Bristol to visit my parents, to carry his heartfelt greetings to them and report to Mister Evans in the yards.

In December of that year the *Rachel* sailed up the Avon to enter into dry dock. She was to be scraped, re-caulked and well tarred.

An inner bulkhead was to be added all about her hold and racks built in preparation for a cargo of cloth goods, wines and furnishings; and a trysail mast was to be stepped to the deck just aft of the main. The brig then became a snow, or as is most times remarked by sailors, an hermaphrodite. The vessel would thus enjoy some of the sailing properties of a bark, being able to climb a little closer to the wind on a reach, and with increased handiness in light winds.

On February the first of 1720 work by the yard on the *Rachel* was nearly complete and she was tied up to the quay to be fitted with her top hamper, she would carry not only topgallants but also royals.

One month to the day later the *Rachel* was ready for sea again and her officers made their appearance. I was introduced to Captain Andrew Lovewell, a large booming man with a round red face full of good humor, and fitted with no guile. His first mate was Granville Chisholm, who looked more like a Clark than a beached lieutenant in his majesty's navy. He was a fine seaman and a gentleman by his nature.

The *Rachel's* second mate was a far more colorful character. He had been born Jeremiah Jasper, but answered to 'Jingles' by reason of the six large gold rings that he wore down the outside edge of his right ear, which rings did in fact jingle. He told me that he added one each time he crossed the line.

Work in earnest had already began on the provisioning and loading of the vessel, by prior arrangement with the yard and with several chandlers, as the crew of the *Rachel* signed the log two days later. The vessel was scheduled to sail on or before the first day of April, with a stop in the Canaries to meet the *Elizabeth* and ship aboard further cargoes bound out from Portugal. The goods we loaded aboard in Bristol consisted of best Bristol sail, fine lightweight woolens, linens and cotton calicoes.

In addition there were a number of high quality English furnishings as would bring a touch of home to the colonial officers of Jamaica, which island we were bound to. In addition to the Stiltons and Cheddars bound for the gentry of Jamaica there were also shipped aboard a dozen large wheels of Wensleydale cheese. These being the much sought after first spring cheeses fragrant of the Alder buds that poke up through the snow early on to tempt the cows. They would later be much prized by their eventual owners.

The crew of the *Rachel* consisted of two watches of six men each, called as on all vessels the starboard and larboard watches. The starboard watch was under the direction of Mister James Stevens as boatswain of the vessel. A dark and dour veteran of the privateering trade now cast ashore as peace reigned for a time. He was a gunner by profession and had no love for this merchant service. He seemed at once happy to have a berth when so many of his past mates had none, and yet sour at the berth he had. He was — nonetheless — a diligent Able rated seaman. Each watch then mustered an additional four ordinary ratings and one landsman or 'waister.' Six men so bound together are considered a mess.

The yeoman of the sheets for the larboard watch was Able seaman Agamemnon Jones. He answered to the name Candy, as given by his shipmates some twenty years before. His having won the name, as he related it, by his having been caught scraping candy slivers off the captain's sugar loaf while serving as the captain's steward. It earned him twelve laid well on, he told me, and a one-way trip to the top sheets.

Candy had the look of a boxer about his forehead, nose and ears. Captain Lovewell told me one day that Candy and I had a mutual friend in the 'Thumper," so when the occasion came I mentioned my student relationship with Master Woodley to Candy. It pleased him to tell me that he too considered himself a student of the Thumper, differing in that his lessons had cost him teeth, a once beautiful nose and a certain ringing in the ears that does not go away. He laughed with me and the stories began to flow.

Candy and I remained close friends and mates till he cast off. We sparred together often to keep in practice. Old as he was I should not have liked to have come to blows with him seriously.

In addition to the vessel's regular crew Captain Lovewell, in a gesture of Christian charity the like of which I have seldom seen — and the recompense he received for it neither for that matter — brought with him two young men of fourteen or fifteen years or so, whom he had found on the edge of starvation on the docks of Liverpool. Jonathan Peters and Noah Harwood by name. When first I saw them they were a pitiful sight indeed, scrawny and filthy, like stick figures covered with rags and shoeless, already missing teeth, shameful reminders of our fallen state.

Later, holystoned, decently dressed at Lovewell's expense and having several solid meals of bully beef, peas, cheese and ships biscuit in them they joined the crew as ship's boys charged to help out when and where-ever needed and to learn the trades of the sea. They were willing lads, mindful of their salvation to a new world. They seemed to thrive in the new found discipline and regularity of shipboard life, decent personalities emerged from the rubble and they soon gained the favor of the hands. Peters went to the starbowlines and Harwood to the larbowlines.

On March 30, 1720 Captain Lovewell called the crew together and gave us the conditions under which we would sail. He had, as he said, purchased and inspected all provisions personally and could assure us that they were all of best quality. Beef, pork, cheese and peas, oatmeal and butter plus those small additions as would sweeten the voyage. He informed us that all the officers, himself included, would eat the same rations as the crew. There would be Church of England services and plum duff every Sunday.

Although he did not approve of the practice personally he would accede to the traditions of the sea and serve out a two for one grog ration with supper. He added that he did this as well to have some privilege to remove in case a malefactor should arise, as he would tolerate no starting, striking, or flogging aboard his vessel.

At the turn of the middle watch that very night we rode the tide down the Avon to the Severn and then out into the sea.

Two weeks later we made our rendezvous with *Elizabeth* off the Canaries. We transshipped from her a great quantity of kegs of Madeira, Masala, Oporto and Sherry as well as cheeses, olives and smoked sausages from Italy and a quantity of silks and spices from the Levantine.

The seas kept a moderate chop throughout the transfer of goods by longboat from one vessel to the other, making for harder work for the crews but eliminating port duties for the investors. As ships carpenter my duties kept me below in the hold seeing to the stowage of the cargo, so my opinion of the difficulty of the work is from my observation of the exhaustion of our crew at the end of the day. Along with the officers of the *Rachel* I was invited to dine as a guest of Captain Johnson aboard the *Elizabeth* the evening before we parted company.

As it happened Candy Jones also served as coxswain of Captain Lovewell's Gig and as we came alongside the *Elizabcth* whose face should first appear at the rail but that of Frank Woodley. These two immediately upon seeing one another — with no outward sign of recognition — began to belabor each other in the way that strong men will do. Commentaries came fast and furious upon each other's hair, or the lack of it, skill with a Gig or the lack of it, along with general ugliness and questionable birth, these sallies led to great mirth on the Gig and on the deck of the *Elizabeth.* When we had at last all come aboard the vessel there was more in the way of misty looks, great back thumping, flipper smacking and embraces all around. Familiar smiling faces appeared all about me and I was filled with the great comfort a man may feel surrounded by jolly mates and true. As is customary in such times, the crew of the Gig was taken to their mess as guests of honor by the starboard watch; there was a great spotted dog that night.

The officers of the *Rachel* and I retired below to the great cabin. Captain Johnson was in a very expansive mood and greeted all of us most personally and warmly. It was all business that evening over our dinner of Lobscouse and boiled baby. The talk of Captain Lovewell's course, cargo and last minute directions regarding disposal of our cargo, was interspersed with news of general interest to the merchant seaman. Conditions were also apparently much improved in the Caribbean as regarded the depredations of pirates since Woodes-Rogers had brought the King's pardon two years past.

Captain Johnson was famously interested in pirates and attended as many trials as he was able. His relationship to the Admiralty was such that all doors and records were open to him, and he had also collected much in the way of detail and anecdotes from interviews with men who were scheduled to hang the next day.

He entertained his guests that evening with stories of the great pirate idealists Misson and Tew, Howell Davis and Avery, and their pirate republics on the island of Madagascar. He was able to shock even these hard and seasoned men with the vile and savage crimes of such villains as Lolonais, Braziliano and Lowther. He spoke with a reserved — but obvious — respect of both the one called Black Beard, and the one he called the 'great pirate Roberts." Both men, he ventured, who under different circumstances might have been English naval heroes; both men were fearless, bold and cunning as well as master seamen. Roberts he went so far as to call a 'great leader of men," on a par with Hawkins and Drake.

I had a brief privy conversation with the captain before our party shoved off. He asked of my parents, I assured him of their health and their expectation of seeing him when next in Bristol. He told me that upon my return from the Indies that I was to report to Master Evens again. He had plans to build a fast little clipper, as he called it, and wished the two of us to work together on the vessel. He gave me plans for it, just a little sketch really but clear in intention, the prospect of such work to come set my heart to racing. It was one of the great fortunes of my life to have the favor and the trust of such a man, it was reward enough in itself, and my love of my work made it all the sweeter.

The vessels parted the next dawn, with the thump of a salute from the *Elizabeth* answered by the feeble pop of our four pounders in reply, this much to the disgust of Stevens.

Under all sail, with studding sails on the mains and tops, the *Rachel* was a sweet swimmer.

We logged at least a hundred and fifty miles each day and on most came closer to two hundred.

Altogether it was perhaps the finest sailing weather that I've ever seen, even where the captain expected the doldrums the wind, though fitful, remained. Our rations were, as Lovewell had promised, best quality. Our two ship's boys were growing more stout and hearty by the day; all agreed that they earned their keep. The *Rachel* was a happy ship, something all sailors remember for the rest of their lives.

And so by all of this as I have told it, it happened that I was at the larboard rail of the *Rachel*, ten leagues or so southeast of the Turks, at six bells of the forenoon watch on June 22, 1720, when the first cry came from the main top. "Sail ho! Well away three points off the larboard quarter." The cry occasioned no particular alarm as these were frequently traveled waters, their being the gateway to the Windward Passage and thus to the waters of the Caribbean.

However, when at two bells of the afternoon watch, the same cry came from the top accompanied by the opinion that she was the same sail as had been logged earlier, the mood of the deck hands quickly changed from their normal indifference to the presence of deck officers as they went about their tasks, to an alert and apprehensive attention to their actions.

At this report Chisholm sent young Peters below to fetch the captain and climbed the shrouds himself for a better look. After a few moments in observation he called for Candy to join him in the tops. A very few minutes later Captain Lovewell came on deck. Upon Chisholm's invitation he too climbed into the tops. They four remained in the tops observing and talking till after the fourth bell of the watch. This conference was not lost on the crew working the deck. All hands kept to their duties, as all knew nothing of the vessel in question would be seen from the deck.

Word of any occurrence out of the ordinary travels quickly in the closed society of a vessel under sail. In as little time as it takes to tell of it the larboard watch began to drift back onto the deck in the most casual of manners, as if they had noticed the ocean and sky for the first time earlier and had come back up to the weather deck to admire them.

When the captain returned to the deck he summoned all hands to the waist. We were informed that the vessel seemed to be shadowing us and that we were now to take steps to evade them. The *Rachel* was brought to a new heading which would take us cleanly away from the other vessel. Our new course would eventually bring us through the Florida straight bound to the north coast of Cuba, a perfectly natural course for a merchantman to take. The watch at the top was given over to Candy.

Two hours later, at one bell into the first dogwatch, Candy called the captain and Chisholm aloft.

When Lovewell returned to the deck he was pale. He called the crew together at the waist once again and informed us of what the older hands already knew. We were — without doubt — being followed by the other vessel. He ordered that we should make ready to sail in complete silence and with no lights after dark. And that we should make ready to bring all the top courses down as if heaving to for the night and then come about briskly to our original heading during those darkest of dark moments just after nightfall.

All steps were to be prepared now so that when the sudden tropic night came we could act quickly and in concert. I was ordered to construct a tall frame to the stern of the longboat and affix a large ship's lantern to it. I was to step a short mast well forward, rigged for a small storm royal, and a sea anchor. The decoy was so constructed and tied off to the starboard quarter of the *Rachel*, being thus hid from view of the other vessel.

The vessel that was stalking us stayed well off on the horizon, she remained hull and mains down but kept us just in view from her tops, which now we could plainly see. All the sea dogs aboard us knew well that when we dropped our tops and lighted the stern lantern — as if coming to for the night — the other vessel would move in closer and then send boats to board and take us in the middle watch of the night. Thus it was imperative that our dissimulation and wearing off under reduced sail should happen quickly and smoothly in the blinding dark just after nightfall. With any luck we would have several hours of sail before the ruse was uncovered.

When the last point of the setting sun sank below the horizon, and the final flash of its light swept across the sea, the stern lamp of the decoy *Rachel* was lighted. Then under reefed main and fore courses alone, the vessel itself slipped carefully and silently away from the lamp hung from the frame on the longboat, and away into the dark cover of the night.

Chapter 2
The Black Flag

At the start of the middle watch — midnight — Captain Lovewell ordered all hands aloft to make sail and I was called up, along with the cook, to stand to the sheets at the waist. As Captain Lovewell acted on this voyage as both the ship's purser and super cargo, and as there also being no churgion aboard, the cook and I were the only idlers — as those who keep no watch but are called to work from dawn to dusk are noted in the log — left to call up.

The wind was fair for us, well off our starboard quarter, and when the line was cast at the turn of the watch we logged seven knots and a fathom. It is dangerous sailing to run so full in unfamiliar waters but the captain's urgency to leave the wolf behind us was shared by every man aboard, and so we cracked on all sail. I returned to my bunk shortly after all of our tops were set.

There was no ringing of the ship's bell for the changing of the watch. Save for the creak and groan off the vessel, the soft slap of bare feet on deck and the hiss of the sea there was no sound to disturb the watch sleeping below. I awoke with an uneasy start as men padded past my berth to answer the morning watch. I could feel instantly that the vessel had lost considerable way, and its pitch and yaw told me that we were coming up wind now and just coming onto the starboard tack. When I came up onto the main deck I was immediately struck by the change in our sailing condition since I had gone to my bunk. The wind had backed dramatically and the *Rachel*, according to Jingles at the helm, was now fighting to maintain four knots — without accounting for what seemed considerable leeway — into a light but steady wind off the bow.

I found the captain with Candy at the larboard rail peering intently into a dark and mist-shrouded sea. They cocked their heads a little now and again, as if listening for some distant sound. It was still some little time till dawn, and I surmised that they had been up throughout the night straining to hear something off in the distance, something whose presence they could only sense. As the watch coming up passed the waist, the captain spoke briefly with the men going aloft.

"Stevens, I want you at the main top gallant, you're to keep a sharp lookout on our larboard beam, just aft of the mains, and well out. I agree with Jones that we've not shaken the other vessel. Our ruse, I fear was not sufficient to lead them off our scent. Any noise — any light — anything at all I want you to call out immediately."

Turning to greet the mate coming up at the change of the watch, he gave several terse commands in quick succession. "All hands are to remain on watch Mr. Chisholm, and away aloft, I'll want every scrap of stun'sail laid on." He studied the top courses for a moment. "Helm, bring us a point into the wind."

"A point to windward, aye, Captain," sang out Jingles. Lovewell observed the action on deck for another moment. "Step lively now men," he called out, then turning to Candy he said, "Take your watch and see to setting the studdingsails on the mains, we have the weather gauge on whoever's out there, maybe we can still put some distance between them and us," he spoke again in a sort of after thought, "I'd some hope we'd shaken them in the night."

There was hurried activity aloft, and on the deck as well. The reefs were taken from every sail; they were allowed to fill and sheeted in. As the helm came up, and so brought us a point closer to the wind, there was a slight sense of increased way. I doubted that the *Rachel* would top six knots in this reach, even with her royals and staysails set. The wind was steady now off our starboard bow, not the best sailing point for a brig, and we were as close hauled as possible. The trysail stepped aft the main earned its keep here and added as much a full knot to our way in these conditions.

As Candy and his party hurried past me to set the studdingsails for the main course, he paused long enough to speak quietly, and quickly. "John, I know they're out there. Just before the wind backed so on us it veered — just for the moment you understand — and in that moment I'm sure I heard the sound of music come across the water from our stern. I can feel the presence of another vessel in our lee, and so can the captain. They've been staying just out of our ken — off our beam — running with us since two bells of the middle watch I say. They're much closer now, maybe half a league or less off the larboard quarter. I fear we'll have unwelcome guests by the forenoon watch lad. Stick close to me if I'm proved right."

In the tropical latitudes the sun both rises and sets with dramatic quickness, and there is little of what people in the northern latitudes call twilight, or a "glomming" in the evening, or of a first light just before true dawn. After a first muted flash of light, a mist shrouded and milky dawn set upon us just after three bells of the watch. The mist lay just off the water and it limited our range of vision from the deck to less than a cable length. The day promised to remain overcast and thick. And as a pearly light and the cry of gulls filled our world a hoarse excited shout came from Stevens at the main top.

"Sail ho! Two points abaft the larboard beam, half a league or less and closing fast."

I ran to the rail, joining several other men who were working at the waist, each of us straining to see from the deck what could then be seen only by the watch aloft. Captain Lovewell stepped back to the bitnacle and called up to the lookouts aloft.

"What do you make her to be?"

"A big topsail schooner, covered with sails, carrying t'gallant on her main even. And she's closing fast now," cried Stevens, "she's inside a mile, and closer to the beam;" there was a pause, "she's coming hard into the wind now… runnin' full and by — and picking up speed — she seems to climb straight up the wind by God…good Christ she's a swimmer!"

"I see it! I see it!" young Harwood, standing next to me cried. Following the pointing of his arm, I could just make out a ghostly shape flickering in and out of sight through the thinning mist. The other vessel seemed like some great dark hound — now seen, — now unseen, coursing through the mist at the edge of our sight and straining to come up before us to cut us off. A chill of goose flesh ran across my shoulders and up my neck. I realized that we had entered into a grave and dangerous circumstance, and that we had no chance of out sailing the terrible fast hunter closing on us out of the dawn.

There was nothing more to be done of course, we had all sail on and were running as close hauled as our vessel could sail without going into irons. I estimated our speed at four or five knots — a fine enough speed for a loaded snow sailing up the wind on a larboard tack. But we were a draft horse running from a courser.

A half hour later at the fifth bell of the watch the stranger could be clearly seen, less than a quarter mile off now, already forward of our larboard beam. She was like a black dart cutting through the sea. A large sleek schooner carrying gaff tops on both her masts, though the spars to alter her rig were clearly visible. She indeed carried a topgallant on her main. With her staysails and jibs set, she seemed to be carrying a cloud of sail on forward.

It was clear that she could run several points closer to the wind than we. As if to add to our disadvantage the wind backed again, giving her the weather gauge on us as well. The *Rachel* came briskly to the larboard tack; else we'd have surely stayed. The other surged forward and began to close in earnest. I felt Candy come up beside me as I watched our pursuer cut through the sea. He leaned onto the rail and heaved a deep sigh.

"Well John," he said, "We've only some little time now before we're brought to. She's standing for the sweet trade there's no doubt, and we'd best make ready to be boarded. When they come aboard make sure to stand out where you can be clearly seen, with your hands by your side — in plain sight — and show no spirit of resistance at all. They'll be very hard sorts, and it's certain there'll be some of them who will stand ready to cut you down to drown in your own blood. Stay close to me when they come on board.

"I've sailed with such in years past, and there's just a chance that I may know some of her crew. If they're a pack of cutthroats, out to leave no witnesses, I might talk us out of harm, and onto her crew — able ratings and carpenters being sometimes scarce in their trade. Watch out for the first ones to come aboard us though," he warned me, "they'll be the hardest lot she has to offer, and they'll crush any sign of a fight from the crew."

As we watched, the stranger closed the gap between us. When she was about two hundred yards off, she ran up her colors. On her foremast a dark red ensign, like a bloody spot on the close gray morning. On her main, a black flag bearing the curious device of a jawless white skull in its center, with crossed white swords beneath. I heard a sharp intake of breath, "Well I'll be damned!" said Candy with some emphasis.

At that same moment there was a puff of gray smoke from her forward gun, followed closely by the dull thump of its report. A jet of water leaped from the surface of the sea some hundred feet or so in our path ahead. As my gaze returned to the pirate vessel, a brightly clad figure stepped up by the forward shrouds onto its rail, and raised a speaking trumpet.

“Heave to! Heave to!” came a voice across the water, “Come into the wind till ye stay, and back your sails. We mean to board you for inspection. Heave to Damn ye!”

As if to punctuate the command there was a second roiling puff of smoke, and a second dull report. This time the ball whistled over our heads, and there was a loud boom from the main course. Looking up I saw a ragged oblong rip across the bunt of the sail, from which point it began to split down toward the deck and to luff and flutter in the wind.

“The next one’ll be into the hull,” Candy said, “and if that don’t bring us to, why then he’ll run in at us — real hard — like as though to ram us, give us a couple of whiffs of grape shot or langrage to clear the deck, and then send a pack of howling hell dogs in amongst us. At least so Johnny Rackham would do, and those are his colors on the main. Straight in, and get on with the business to hand, that was always Calico Jack Rackham’s way.”

I’ve never seen a grayer face than the one on Captain Lovewell, nor a wider set of eyes, as he leaned over from the quarterdeck, and called forward to the mate. “Bring in all sail Mr. Chisholm, back the main topgallant and the fore top. We cannot outrun them, and a fight is out of the question. I’m bringing us into the wind.” His voice cracked but remained steady. He turned to the helmsman, “Jingles, go below and fetch up the cook, have him douse the galley fires, there’ll be no breakfast this morning.” He then took the helm himself, and brought the bow of the *Rachel* into the wind until her sails could no longer draw. At this the sails backed against the mast, and the vessel lost way so quickly that some of us were jarred nearly off our feet, and we were in stays, or in irons as sailors call it…dead in the water by any name.

The same hurried activity which had brought us to full sail only an hour before now brought in all sail except those two ordered by the captain to remain backed. As we had come into the wind and lost our way, the pirate vessel surged beyond us. I watched as she beat into the wind to come about. There was no doubt that she had some fair hands on board, for she did so as neat as you please, crossed our bow with all her gun ports open, and came down on the wind to our starboard beam. Her topsails were smartly furled, then her main sail was lowered and flaked, and she maneuvered closer to us on just her foresail, forestays and jibs. She seemed almost to dance in the sea, and to hover on the wind like a bird of prey.

She then brought in all sail and hove to about fifty yards off, and we found ourselves looking down the throats of six cannon. I could make out quick movements along her deck, but her crew stayed low under her bulwarks, offering no clear sight of their numbers or activities. The same bright figure that had hailed us before now appeared again on the rail one hand on the shrouds to steady himself, and one hand on the speaking trumpet he raised to his face.

"I'll have the captain as my guest if you please." he called out, "Bring your papers, sir, and your crew and cargo manifests, step lively now, we haven't all day." He turned to glance over his shoulder, spoke something to those behind him, then turned his attention back to us and continued, "I'll give you to the end of this song to have your oars in the water captain, after that I'll be forced to pepper you with some encouragement."

We then heard the skirl of pipes, joined by a Fiddle, a Bodhran and a Fife. The instruments broke into a spirited rendition of "Men of Harlech." In spite of our bleak prospects and the dangerous circumstances I found myself briefly humming along, for the song was an old Welsh battle hymn that my mother loved, and that she would long ago hum to lull her fretful child to sleep.

"He's a marvel is, Johnny," broke in a voice behind me, it was Candy, "an arch pirate with a sense of humor. He always keeps a little band aboard. He got the notion from his days sailing with Charlie Vane, who fancied it. There's some pirates as will keep a musician or two on board just to help pass the time, sailors fancy it to make the work lighter. Other such will use a fiddler to lull prey they're closing on into thinking its a pleasure boat coming up, but Rackham? He presses good players whenever he can. He makes 'em work at it too. You'd think he was an admiral of the fleet, so as he fancies — wait till you see."

He listened appreciatively for a few moments. "We'll be all right now though I think John, Rackham's no butcher like Low — nor a bully like Teache was — there'll be no violence as long as we keep in sight, and give him no cause to loose his dogs. It was Jack I last sailed with, before I took the King's pardon. He'll likely put us through a few hoops before the day's out, but no one will come to hurt if we do as he says. Judging from the squawk of those damned pipes, and the way those topsails were handled, my guess is that I'll be seeing more than a few old gallows mates soon enough."

The *Rachel*'s jolly boat was lowered from the stern as he spoke. Lovewell ordered Jingles and two of the deck hands to climb down, unship the oars and make ready. As Lovewell lowered himself, clutching his portmanteau, onto a thwart, the band on the pirate vessel stepped briskly into the final chorus of the song.

"Excellent time, Captain," came the voice from across the water. "Have a care with those manifests if you please, sir, it would be most unfortunate were you to let them slip over the side...most unfortunate indeed. Have your crew stand by to receive visitors, make damned sure they understand to give my men no trouble, or they'll live only long enough to regret it. Come and cross between us now, across and forward to my cathead if you please, sir."

As our jolly boat pulled away toward the pirate vessel, Captain Lovewell called out to us to remain calm, and to allow the boarders no occasion for violence. As he was doing so, I saw a longboat come out from around the bow of the other vessel, and pull strongly toward the stern of the *Rachel.* Their course being one that took them carefully clear of coming in between our two vessels. The menacing black throats of the pirate's cannon thus free to instantly sweep us with iron from stem to stern should the need arise.

I counted six men manning the sweeps as the pirate's longboat approached and another half a dozen besides the coxswain seated on the thwarts. They pulled hard and came up under our bow well before our own boat had reached the other vessel. There was the scrape and thud of hooks as they made themselves fast to our stern, followed by the clattering sounds of armed men, and their grunting and cursing as they climbed up over rails, and onto the quarterdeck.

One lead man came up at the head of a party on either side of the quarterdeck, and they were as disparate a set as can be imagined. One was very short and barrel shaped, hatless, and with wild black hair done up in stiff thick braids on either side of his face, like drooping horns. He had a fierce black beard, the end of which was clenched between large white teeth held in a broad grimace. He wore a stained leather waistcoat, and a heavy leather petticoat kilt, with a broad black belt over all.

The squat dark pirate's waistcoat was open enough to show that the wild black hair covered more than just his head and face. He carried a long handled boarding axe and four pistols hung from leather straps slung over his shoulders; two other pistols were thrust into his belt. He had all the look of a maddened highland bullock about him, one held only just in check.

The other was tall and slender, clean faced, and very well featured, a very handsome face.

His eyes were squinted against the sun — but watchful — and his lips were a thin wide line. He had short-cropped light blonde hair, the color of white sand or new sails. He wore a short blue jacket, its brass buttons freshly shined so that they glowed, and a jaunty dark red knit cap with a tassel. He carried a cocked musketoon leveled in our direction, a cutlass on a hanger and a brace of very fine looking pistols tucked into a broad scarlet sash. His long white duck pants were tied down at the ankle and he was, as most of his companions proved to be, barefooted. He was smiling and friendly looking, but alert.

He gaze rested on me for a moment and a most surprising change came over his countenance. His eyes grew wider and his mouth seemed to relax — as if he were about to speak. For myself I was afraid that some movement of mine had raised an alarm in him and that I would be shot down. I extended my arms to either side, showing my hands empty. As a carpenter my sleeves were already rolled up for my days work so I showed him no weapon neither place to secret one. His reaction to my smile and extended arms was also curious for I saw the flicker of a smile on his otherwise grim face and he motioned me to the mast — though the barrel of his weapon was pointed at the deck and never directly at me.

The short feral one turned his head slightly, never taking his eyes off of us, and called down to the last of the others clambering up behind him with a harsh and mocking voice. "Step up lively mates, there's 'naught to fear on this scow, only a gaggle of common lubberly swabs up here, come from the bilges onto the deck to bid us a good morrow."

The other swept the deck with a sharp look, and his leveled firelock, and spoke up with a soft voice, and a cheerfully matter of fact tone. "Gather up about the main mast now lads, and keep your hands where I can see them, an honest tar has nothing to fear from us this day."

In little more time than it takes to tell of it, the deck of our vessel was overrun by heavily armed men; all dressed much alike in duck slops or petticoats, loose shirts with waistcoats or jackets of divers description. They scurried the length of the weather deck cutting loose every piece of running gear we had, saving only that which allowed us to keep our bow into the wind. It would be several days' work of splicing before we had regained control of our sails. Assuming we'd ever take control of our vessel again.

We were herded up tight to the main mast, and ordered to sit around it facing out. The short little barrel like fellow who had first come aboard set four men as a deck watch, one at each quarter. His tall blonde shipmate took two men below decks, to do what we could not know. One man went aloft on the main as a watch, and one took station by the helm. Two others stayed forward to mind the sheets on the backed sails. We were ordered to tuck our legs in close to our chests, and to put our hands upon our knees where they might be seen. The mate and the boson were called, and set down separately aft.

The fierce short one then took position, with the last man at his side, on the quarterdeck facing all the rest of our ship's company. The two mentioned officers seated at his feet. "This vessel is now in the hands of the brotherhood of the coast and subject to its laws. Ye are to stay silent until you are called upon to speak, and any man of ye who attempts to hinder our actions by way of mutiny will meet with an ugly death." He leaned over and roughly poked both Chisholm and Stevens with the boarding axe he brandished. "I'll invite these two misbegotten poxy bastards here to think I'm lying." He laughed.

Candy had been standing a little behind me, keeping his face averted from the direct gaze of the ringleaders while still following their directions to keep his actions in plain sight. After we'd sat down together he spoke to me in a very soft whisper, almost a hiss really, not moving his lips at all and looking slightly away from me the whole time.

"The short one is Mike Magoon," he said, "fancies being known as Black Mike, he sailed with Teache for a bit and he's just as violent and crazy as Teache was, although not altogether as much of a thinker. He's a bad customer all around, and will bear close watching. I know him enough to know that he'd as soon slit all our throats and dump us over the side as break wind. I never liked sailing with him. He's a murderous dog all the way to the bone of his black heart. The taller one now, the one who went below to check our cargo and secure below deck, is Mark Reede — he don't like being called Mark though, prefers just Reede — right firm about it. He's a mate of mine from my last trip with Rackham, and the one who would have handled their topsails so smart. He's a quiet sort, not a ruffian, keeps to himself and is always real proper and polite about the business — civil about it ye might say — don't let his quiet ways fool ye though, I've seen him in a scrap or two, and I can tell ye he's the very devil himself in a fight."

"What's going to happen now? What will they do with us?" I whispered.

"Rackham and his quartermaster will be going over the ships manifests with Captain Lovewell. They'll figure it to the last farthing you may be sure. I think they'll like what they find. Them that smuggles will give these fellows a good price for this cargo, and I've found that happy pirates are — on the whole — a lot more sociable than otherwise. When they've finished with the books they'll be coming over to join us. Then I think you'll get to see a real show."

From across the water came the eerie skirl of the pipes again, building to a very high and piercing pitch and then the Bodhran joined with a rapid pattering beat. The fiddle player added a slightly discordant drone — very like the music I had heard in the Levant — like the wailing cry of a human voice. The fife then filliped a sprightly little jig melody on all of this, and all played to a very quick beat. There was the pop of several pistol shots and the sounds of howling laughter and a queer rhythmic thumping.

"I think the captain will be getting his dancing lesson about now," said Candy softly.

Chapter 3
Calico Jack

We waited in that position, seated circling the main mast and enjoined to quiet by our captors, for what I think was an hour or more. As there was no longer the ringing of a ship's bell to mark the half hours of the watch, I've no certainty except that it was a long and nervous time. It was as though time had stopped for our vessel. There was no sound of a watch from the pirate craft either, and I took this as an omen, we had been swept up into another measure of time altogether. The measure that pirates keep.

As men will, when put into a state of forced inactivity, there slowly came the hushed murmuring of guarded speech as men tried to comfort themselves by contact with another. I knew it was impossible that our captors were unaware of the quiet speech, but on the whole I thought they cared little. They stood off from us, each of them armed with cutlass and pistols while we were unarmed. Their officer, for lack of a better term, the one Candy had identified as Magoon had stayed mostly on the quarterdeck with the man at the helm. As my position had me facing forward the vessel I had no direct knowledge of his whereabouts until, having just remarked quietly to Candy the presence of an Albatross circling over the pirate vessel, I turned my head slightly toward the right to see him looming over me.

"Are you about making a mutiny here you great pretty bastard you?" He shrieked a hellish blasphemy at me as he grabbed my hair and my shirt in great tarry paws and yanked me up into a position half seated and half erect. I was very much off balance and helpless in his grasp. "Trinket!, you lazy sod," he said at a short bug eyed wretch leaning against the gunwale, "I told you to keep these bilge rats quiet, now this one's started up a ruckus over here." The one he called Trinket replied with a loud rude noise made through his pursed lips. This drew titters from my shipmates but did my position no service.

"It's nothing of the sort," I started, but got no further in my protestations for he kneed me viciously in the chest, struck me across the face with his closed hand, and threw me out of the circle of my companions and head first up against the starboard rail, where I collapsed into the scuppers.

Stunned, I had no opportunity to rise in my defense, I think now that it was just as well, before he was full upon me, smelling of sweat, moldy leather and sour rum. He leaned his full weight onto me with his knee deeply and painfully jammed into my loin and rammed the barrel of a pistol hard into the back of my left ear. I heard the lock snapped back.

"Belay that damn ye, and put it up, Mike," I heard a voice behind us say with a commanding tone. "You know the captain's orders on boarding as well as me." Magoon used the barrel of the pistol and his knee to jam me down hard against the gunwale before turning, with a snarled oath, to face the source of the voice. "Bugger the captain and bugger you, Reede, this one's making trouble and I think blowing his brain across the deck will keep his mates from following a bad example."

I sat back against the gunwale with blood running from my nose, and from behind my left ear, to regard this turn of events. My blood was up for I have never accepted rough treatment from any man but am disposed to return in kind and with interest. Reede, whom I knew had just saved my life, stood off about five long paces with the cocked musketoon he carried pointed down at the deck midway between himself and my tormentor. His legs were spread slightly. I could see him to be in a tense and poised position, although his general air was that of a man counting parcels. He did not confront Magoon's eyes directly, I noticed, but rather looked placidly at the hand that held the pistol.

"Damn your eyes, Reede, one day you'll interfere with me the once too often for your health." Reede took a step forward, his eyes turning to slits, and opened one side of his wide mouth to speak, as he did so a cry came from the man sent aloft earlier as a watch.

"Captain's coming over, and the other's dressed for the court. Time for the court"

I slowly got back onto my feet there by the rail, and looked over at the pirate vessel. I saw a second longboat pulling away toward us. It carried a full load of a dozen men or so, in addition to our three shipmates and a strange figure all dressed in white and wearing a tall white head gear of some sort.

Our captors quickly started to rearrange matters on the deck. We were all brought toward the quarterdeck, and then seated in two rows across the deck facing aft. Three of the pirates, whooping with glee, seated themselves on the quarterdeck rail facing us and began a strange ritual of dress up. They placed what might once have passed for white neck cloths over their heads, and secured them by tying them fast with cord under their chins. Some of their mates brought up pieces of tarred tarpaulin from our hold, which they placed about their shoulders in some semblance of a robe. They preened and made much ado over each other's appearance. Each of them was given an oar from the *Rachel's* Gig, which they held in the vertical as they at last settled comfortably onto their perch.

Magoon returned to his post at the bitnacle with our officers, and Reede came to our front and faced us. The two men forward had come to the waist after the watchman's cry; one of them now sat with the strange group on the quarterdeck railing, the other went to the starboard rail to greet their coming commander. The little pop eyed pirate whom Magoon had called Trinket sat with the three at the rail. The watch in the main top stayed where he was. There was no human sound except the sniggering of the three oddly made out men rocking portentously on the rail.

"McGinnis," Reede said to a stout and bluff looking dark haired pirate, "why don't you go to the rail and tweet that little whistle of yours for Jack. You know how he loves it when you tweet him aboard."

"Damn it Reede!" the man McGinnis returned in a huff, "it's a bleeding pipe I keep telling you, a boatswain's pipe not a damned whistle, damn it. Hoys and Bumboats are as use a whistle. This is being the true dog's pizzle and thus a pipe." He moved — still sputtering — to the rail.

After a few minutes there was the sound of a boat bumping against the hull, and one of the men at the rail tossed down the boarding ladder. The man McGinnis stepped up and then proceeded to pipe the pirate chief aboard as he stepped up from the rope ladder to stand upon our deck. Several other of the pirates, having stolen similar pipes from other prizes but lacking the art of it, joined in aimless but for volume and creating a shrill and raucous discord — very like an admiral of the fleet just as Candy had said.

The man who stepped lightly onto the deck was the brightly clad figure, who had called out to us across the water. He stood a little over the middle height, well made and broad in the shoulder. He was dressed in a coat of many colors, being made of swatches of gay calicos. Underneath was a bright yellow waistcoat, and broad red striped pantaloons — all fashioned from the light cottons which gave him his odd name. He wore tall red Spanish leather boots, and a broad brimmed finely plaited grass hat, like those favored by the island planters; its brim was swept up raffishly in the front.

He carried two pistols hanging on bright purple ribbons across his body in the pirate fashion, and a Scots short sword with a basket hilt. He had a long; some would call it horsey, face with prominent upper teeth. He was not really a handsome man, but he had a curiously innocent friendliness about his face, a sort of boyishness that rendered him pleasant enough to look at and renewed my hopes for our safety. I learned later what a ladies man he was, with wives and bairns all over the Caribbean. So it would seem that the fairer sex found him pleasing enough indeed. My introduction to the world of this colorful and dangerous breed of men had begun.

Although he for all appearance had paid no attention whatsoever to my comrades and me, I knew that he had swept us with his eyes as he had come aboard. He turned to the three figures seated on the rail. His lank straw colored hair fell over his face as he swept the broad brimmed hat off his head with a flourish, bowed deeply with an extended leg, and saluted the three perched on the rail with all the aplomb of a courtier.

"All hail the worshipful magistrates of the court of free men and brethren of the coasts. I've come hither as required by the articles with all of the papers, reports and persons that your worshipful lordships may require. I am the court's most humble servant. May it so please the worshipful court."

The three perched on the rail, laughed, thumped their oars on the deck and sang back in a ragged but gleeful unison. "All hail the worshipful captain and commander, and thank'e for the prize we're sure." This was greeted with the pirate's usual signs of approbation with which I was to become familiar.

There was a general hooting cheer, and then the clashing and thumping of weapons from all the pirates on board. Their wild howling echoed by the crew of the longboat as they clambered on deck with Jingles and our other men in tow. Collins and Fairchild, the two oarsmen, were ordered to join us who were about the mast; they were very pale and quiet. Jingles was roughly pushed up to the Bitnacle and seated by Stevens. As he settled down to the deck I saw the one named Magoon reach out and catch the gold rings he wore in his ear. There was a sudden jerking movement and a roar of pain from Jingles as Magoon tore the rings away. Jingles' shriek of pain was lost in the general uproar on the deck, save to me and others of the *Rachel*'s crew. I will tell you a chill went through me at the callous meanness of the action.

I was astounded to see that the strange white figure I had observed among their company was our Captain Lovewell. He had been stripped down to his shirt; a short cape of sail linen was draped over his shoulder and pinned in place with a sail maker's awl. A brimless high white peaked hat was pushed down to his ears, his face was drawn and as white as his coverings and I could see that he was shaking as if chilled.

When the roaring and the thumping and the hooting died a bit the central figure on the quarter rail — which I now understood to be these rogue's parody of an admiralty court — thumped his oar three times and cried 'oy yea, 'oy yea, 'oy yea. The other two answered his call in kind and a surprising manner of attentive silence fell upon the pirates.

"In the matters before this worshipful court as pertains to the dancing of the once captain of this vessel, how says the right honorable captain commander?" the one seated amidships asked.

"I regret to report to your lordships that the once captain of this vessel proved quite disappointing in the matter of the dance, his being a great lumbering ox of a fellow really. The spirit seemed willing enough, with some prodding from our house of lords of course," This brought on a general fit of whooping laughter from the pirates, "but alas," he continued, "the flesh was really quite weak ... I'm sure your lordships take my meaning."

"Let's hang him then," squeaked the little bug-eyed judge, the one called Trinket, who was seated to the larboard, and then he thumped his oar. The other two did not thump in agreement to this. However, there was a burst of raucous laughter from the pirates, along with catcalls and scattered cries of "Aye hang the rat" — "Let's see him dance on air then. We'll need stout cable lads, that one's a broad slab bottomed scow." Captain Lovewell's fear-filled discomfiture was pitiful to behold.

I think I understood clearly in that moment that we were as much entertainment and distraction for these rogues and thieves as we were prey. This was their theater — we were their theater — and we were at once audience and players, spectators and victims.

Their coarse humor was found in the outrageous, the irreverent and in mockery. Right cruelty lay just below the surface of certain of them. I had no doubt at the time, and after much time and thought have none now, that had things gone otherwise shortly captain Lovewell would have indeed been hanged.

"I'm afraid," Rackham said with another bow, "That hanging will only marginally improve the prisoner's dancing skills m'lords. In the fellow's defense, if it so please the worshipful court, I will report that the once captain of this vessel was most punctilious and correct in his papers and reports to your worshipful lords' most humble," he bowed especially low, "and obedient servants.

"However, in the inspection of the cargo manifest for this vessel Mr. Corner and I were astounded to find goods being transported to the benefit of highly placed military and civil authorities in Jamaica, including none other than Sir Nicholas Lawes, lord commander and governor of the island. This leads us to suspect that the once captain of this vessel is no friend to we the brethren of the coast. So it please the court."

"Aye, but what of the prize then, Captain?" asked the stout and dour faced judge seated to starboard. "It is first the brass then the steel." His fellows on the bench took up the cry in a spirited manner, with a general thumping of oars. 'The brass, the brass first what of the brass, what of the prize?"

"Aye, what of the prize? What of the prize?" came a roaring chorus from the assembled pirates.

This accompanied by the general roaring and thumping I had already come to expect at each step of the play.

"I'm pleased to report to your lordships, and to the honorable brethren of the commonwealth," — with this Rackham turned to sweep his hat in an inclusive gesture toward all of the pirates on deck, "that the right honorable quartermaster Mr. Corner and I are in agreement that the prize is a fair one, and that when the account is settled it should bring something near to one hundred gold guineas per share." His men of course greeted this report with great jubilation. The little pipes shrilled their discord again.

"The court is well satisfied with your report in this matter most honorable captain commander," said the tall serious judge in the center, "and would now like to look into the matter of the once captain's relationship to the authorities mentioned and look also to his treatment of those poor servants whom he is paid to sweat for farthings to the gain of the rich and the powerful."

Shouts of "Aye bring him to book," and, "We want an accounting" broke out generally among the pirates as muskets and axes were thumped on the deck, and swords and axe heads were clashed together. They started up their queer hooting cheer again as well. "Let's hang him then." Squeaked the little bug eyed Judge Trinket, with a thump of his oar. Again his fellow magistrates did not thump.

Captain Lovewell's gray face turned upward toward heaven, and his eyes slowly closed as his body shook with a heaving sigh. I knew that he was praying. My heart broke for him, for I knew him as a gentle and a Christian man, who in no wise deserved this torment for his life.

Rackham turned toward us who sat before him now in stunned silence. He regarded closely, in turn, the face of each man as he walked slowly to the center of the deck.

"Which men here have suffered flogging or caning at the hands of this once captain, or his once officers?" he asked, "Speak up lads, you have nothing further to fear from them, you are in the hands of the brotherhood of the coast now, and the day of your justice is at hand."

There was not a stir from any of those seated facing him, for indeed no man there had ever been flogged, let alone caned by Captain Lovewell or his officers, though several I knew had suffered such on other ships, and by other men.

"Which of you then has suffered any blow at all, or been started, or hazed by any once officer of this vessel?" Rackham next said.

There was once again general silence from the crew of the *Rachel*, for Captain Lovewell had made it clear to all who signed aboard his command that no such practices were allowed aboard. Indeed no punishments beyond the loss of the two for one grog or extra duty — never to a point that could be called hazing — had ever been given out to any man, and the loss of the ration only twice — and to the same man.

"They are full of fear of these dogs," came Magoon's voice from our rear, "how will they know to bring charges against their keepers, when they have been struck and beaten into craven submission like helpless cattle? I agree with Trinket, let's hang the bastard and be done."

“Aye, there is nothing lower than one who’ll strike a helpless man” Reede offered mildly.

I tell you, I could feel the passage of that verbal dart go past my head to strike the bully; the sharp intake of breath that I heard from its target bore witness to its effect. I saw clearly that there was no love lost between these two, and that rather a deep-seated enmity was present. I knew as well that only a very quick and dangerous man would dare to bait the one they called Black Mike.

“I’ve a complaint to make if it please the court,” it was Potter, the ordinary of the starboard watch who had twice lost his two for one. Magoon’s face brightened. “On two occasions he removed my rum ration and give me extra duty to boot.”

This was greeted as you may imagine by howls of protest at the inhumanity of it and cries for poor Lovewell’s blood for sausage from the pit.

Rackham quickly broke into the moment before Magoon could do more than begin to sputter. “Shipmates, friends, and most worshipful members of the court of free men, if the case indeed may be made that we here are dealing with a terrified crew, driven to a trembling silence by their fear of these once masters, then all the more we must have the truth of the matter. I know of one man among their number, whom I have observed, who is well known to some of us as a boon companion. He is one not given to fear of any man, and he is one who is as truthful as he is skilled at his craft and fearless in a fight,” He stepped closer to us, and pointed to my friend. “Agamemnon Jones, stand up so that your old mates may say hello, and tell us, of a truth, whether or no there is a case to be made against these once masters.”

Candy slowly raised himself from the position he had held for the past hour of more, groaning a bit as he did so, for he was no longer a young man. “Good morrow to ye Jack,” he said, “and lads, good morrow t’ye all.”

There were several surprised shouts of recognition from members of the pirate crew, and general comments of approbation and agreement of the qualities pointed out by their captain. The little bug-eyed judge on the right positively whooped with glee, and thumped his oar upon the deck. “By God it’s good old Candy Jones, and still in the flesh, we’ll have the truth from him sure enough, and then we can hang the bastards and be gone on our way.”

"Jack, lads, worshipful members of the court," said Candy, "Some of ye know me right well, and know that two years past I took the kings pardon for my crimes. From that time to this I've sailed with Captain Lovewell — who gave me a berth when others would not — and I tell you that I have never seen the man lift a hand against any seaman, nor ever allow any other man under his command to do so. He is a fine Christian gentleman, and has done nothing to warrant the outrage of this worshipful court."

"You've heard the witness of a known and stouthearted mate on behalf of the prisoner's treatment of the men in his charge," said Rackham, "What say ye then members of the most worshipful court?"

There was a brief hushed conference among the three seated at the rail. It was evident that the little bug-eyed judge was still hopeful of a hanging, but in the end he acceded to the other two in the matter before them. The one seated amidships stood to pass the judgment reached.

"It is the judgment of this most worshipful court of free men and brethren of the coasts that the prisoners at the bar are free of guilt as to the mistreatment of those men sailing under their orders, and are herewith released from fear of their lives. It is our further judgment that they, and their employers, are to be fined to the value of their cargo for the cost of time and powder in bringing them to heel in order for judgment to be so passed," the three oars thumped in unison, "God save the court, the brotherhood of the coasts, and this commonwealth."

This pronouncement was met with noisy acclamation by the pirate crew — though there were renewed protests over the grog ration — and was accompanied by a fierce thumping of oars, axes, muskets, and pikes upon the deck. Captain Lovewell was taken aft to join Stevens, Jingles and Chisholm seated at the bitnacle. They were allowed now to turn and face their crew. None looked well.

The pirate magistrates now quickly doffed their robes and periwinkles. The one called Trinket stepped quickly over to greet Candy, thumping on him about the back and shoulders with great feeling. Small though the fellow was, no more than an hundred weight to the whole package, there was an air of real power about him that surprised me. After a brief visit he then went aloft to relieve the watch. The other two pirate judges having already joined their shipmates in the plundering of the *Rachel.* Several others of the pirates, including Reede, stopped now to talk briefly with Candy.

Their conversation was friendly, and there was a general relaxing of the tensions, which had commanded our attention through the morning. There being no doubt however that all of us were carefully watched as regards any possible spark of resistance. I remember Reede looking hard and straight at me for a moment before turning.

"John Tanner, ship's carpenter, step forward if you please sir," said Rackham, "Reede, fetch your mess and join me below decks, we have a cargo to inspect and shift while there's a calm sea."

Chapter 4
Forced

It is no easy task to transfer cargo from one vessel to another at sea, and we were about its completion the whole of that day, through the night, and into the morning of the next day. The pirates drew their craft up close beside the *Rachel*, secured by grappling hooks and stout cordage. Rackham put me to rigging a suspended gangway two fathoms wide between the two vessels, out of cordage and planking torn up from our orlop deck. When it was built and secured to his satisfaction, another wave of men — perhaps twenty strong — swarmed over onto our decks and the process of shifting the *Rachel's* cargo began in earnest. We were all, and I include Captain Lovewell, put to the task. The work of shifting cargo from the *Elizabeth* to the *Rachel* two months earlier was as nothing to this labor.

The sea was calm throughout the day, but even so it was a hair-raising trip across the open space separating the two vessels. The bumping and groaning of the vessels moving against each other at the waterline was a constant reminder of the unpleasantly deadly prospect of falling between them. Members of the pirate crew removed our cargo from the hold to the orlop, as they desired. Our men then brought it topside and to the far end of the gangway. At that point the pirates again took charge and moved and stowed the goods aboard their own vessel as they saw fit. The work of transferring the main cargo, and the water barrels, and foodstuffs was supervised by the man Magoon. Our crew was in such a terror of him after his attack on me that they made much quicker work of unloading our vessel for him than they ever had for Chisholm and Jingles in the loading thereof.

No member of our crew was allowed to step onto the other craft. There were very pale faces among our crew that day because of the trip across the gangway. Even surviving the possibility of being crushed between the hulls of the vessels gave them no comfort, for it is a little known thing but true, that few seamen know how to swim. Most actively resist the knowledge. The sailor's reasoning being that if your vessel founders, swimming will only prolong unnecessarily the inevitable. An hour or so of frantic and terrified paddling, availing nothing in the end.

The one named Reede, along with a small group of men, was given the task of ferreting out all of the cabins of the *Rachel* for valuables. Clothes, weapons, utensils, personal items of every sort were appropriated; from our hold the powder and shot, the flints, cordage and spare spars, our lumber and sails, all were taken. The *Rachel* was systematically stripped of everything save her paint.

As the sun seated itself upon the western horizon, the pace of the unloading was increased and our crew was pushed very hard. All hands having had nothing except water and a few bites of hardtack throughout the day. The bulk of the pirate crew now returned aboard their own vessel, working to finish the stowing of our once cargo into their hold. When the last light had faded we of the *Rachel* were all gathered again to the waist, a careful head count was taken and we were brought to an attentive silence by a profane order from Magoon.

His growling was wasted upon us however, for we were as spent as any group of men could be, having done several days of work in the course of one. A cold supper of rum and ship's biscuit was brought to us by our captors. As simple and bare as this meal was I think I have never been more grateful for food, and the rum of course provided a very welcome lift to our spirits. Aboard the pirate's vessel it appeared that richer fare was being served for two of that crew brought over for us a large wedge of the Wensleydale cheese that had been bound for the Governor's table. One was the fellow McGinnis who played the boson's pipe. It was a kindness that I well remember, although the cheese was not to my taste.

Our officers were removed from us and taken into the mate Chisholm's small cabin. A guard was placed at the door. The rest of us were moved into the forecastle and guards were placed on the deck above us. It was evident from the sounds over our heads that swivel guns were being readied on the railings both fore and aft. It was wasted effort on the pirate's part for our men collapsed into exhausted heaps about the cabin. Now the forecastle can be a damp and a musty room with no real comfort in it, for in it all the weather gear and such are stowed, it is the work shed of a vessel. A few stools and narrow benches along the bulkhead are the best it offers.

Amid the snoring heaps of filthy and sweat streaked men, as I slipped into an all too brief unconsciousness, I remember seeing that Stevens sat close by the ships' boys Peters and Harwood, and he seemed to be encouraging them in this trial. I remember the sound of wild shrill music from the pirate vessel, and a howling and a roaring…it seemed to fade quickly away.

I cannot imagine what hour it was when the hatches were thrown back with a crash and Magoon and several others came roaring into the cabin, it seemed that I had only just closed my eyes. "Up ye lazy lubberly sacks of shit!" he yelled, "The wind is changing and there is no time for rest."

No overt blows were struck but the crew was roughly pushed and prodded out onto the weather deck. Nor Lovewell nor the officers were spared this final great push of effort, though it seemed plain that our captain was on the verge of collapse. The wind had veered and was now coming directly on our starboard beam, placing the pirate vessel in our lee. The wind was pushing the *Rachel* against the hull of the other vessel so that the constant rocking and grinding of the hulls sounded like a hungry moaning, and the gangway that connected the vessels was heaving up and down something dreadful to behold.

Happily the lighter burdens predominated as they were the things our captors had set aside in order to get the heavier items stowed away aboard their vessel first. There was as much material tossed in sacks across the distance between the decks as there was transferred across the gangway by ashen-faced seaman. The pirates working among us were just as stupefied with fatigue as we were, perhaps more so as they seemed to be working under the influence of an excess of gaiety from the night before. The difference however lay in the fact that they were heavily armed and were very surly, short tempered and quick with a curse or a shove with us.

As the first aurora of dawn came from the eastern horizon the last of the spoil was thrown across to the pirate vessel. The one called Magoon then strode over to our bitnacle and with two great blows of his boarding axe smashed it to pieces. We would have no compass to guide us now, as well as having no food nor water and several days of frantic work to get steerage on our drifting vessel.

Reede and the pirate captain came up from the hold onto the quarterdeck. They stood well aft by the taffrail and shared some quiet discussion with the little bug-eyed judge. Rackham spoke briefly, and with some warning I thought, to our officers. As the bulk of the pirate crew jumped and leaped and swung across to their own deck amid wild shouts and laughter, Rackham stepped forward to the edge of the quarterdeck and addressed our assembled crew in the friendliest of terms.

"Lads, you have had a trying time I know, but our visit together is about to come to an end. It is our custom at these times of parting, to offer the freedom of our company to any of you who have a heart to join us in freedom and equality." He drew the Scots sword and plunged its point into the deck. He laid one hand atop the other upon its basket hilt and leaned forward upon the weapon. He looked before him onto the deck for a moment, gathering himself it seemed. Then he lifted his gaze, and slowly swept the assembled crew of the merchantman with the most penetrating and commanding look imaginable.

"We sail as a commonwealth of free men." He began, "we are all bound together in a solemn partnership all for the benefit of each, and each bound to the benefit of all. As a free commonwealth of equals we bear allegiance to no flag, nor sovereign, except that of ourselves. In so doing we have as much right as any people on earth, for every people, every tribe and nation of men exists only by the exercise of its own will to do so. In the world we have together spurned, all of those tribes and peoples and nations have without exception, fallen in thralldom to the will of the strongest, cruelest or richest among them.

"These then have bullied and fancied themselves into kings and princes, dukes and barons — and they took to themselves the power to pass lands and riches and rights and power to their drooling piss-pot whelps. And by so doing they perpetuate their riches, upon riches, upon riches to their heirs till there be no more riches for others, and the lash must be used upon their enslaved brothers. — Damn their eyes.

"Now lads, this is all done to the purpose of enforcing their will upon their fellows, men like yourselves, men who are their equals in all but entitlement of birth…or sovereign riches." He looked skyward with great drama and in a loud voice quoted an old, old verse. *'The lord who from the earth made churls, from that same earth made he the earls."* Rackham returned his attention to our crew and said in a soft voice "The worm knows not brothers — on rich and poor alike he dines. Now friends, the riches themselves have no thought, and they care not whose purse they rest in. Riches may be taken by the bold — and riches with boldness together make for strength. And strength in the end is liberty.

"Now brothers where do all these riches that the cruel fops of privilege wallow in come from?

"You may well ask it brothers. Their riches come from the sweat of those who are held in bondage to them by armed force, or by the foolish habits of a servile mind. Their riches come in the end from you yourselves brothers they come from your toil and sweat, and from your father's toil and sweat, and from his father's toil and sweat. They have been stolen in fact from all those who starve and freeze and groan and sweat to wrest a little comfort from an unfeeling world. Riches my friends are always stolen, and they care not by whom." He paced to the windward rail, looked out to sea, and then turned to speak again.

"Today you have seen those hirelings set over you brought to trial on this deck by we who today hold the power to do so. I warrant, and some of you will know it first hand to be true, that they were given a hearing far more fair this day than any of you would have had by any court in the world. We judged them solely on their treatment of you — who are their servants — and it was you alone who saved them from the stern hand of justice by a dependable witness that they had done you no ill. Yet friends there is still an ill to come, for you will sail again, and sweat again to make another's ease. Or you will plow or gather or grind for another master who will hold your life and body — will that one be as kind?"

He worked himself up into a fine passion through the course of this speech, and now he pulled his sword out of the deck, and held it across his open hands. From the rail of the pirate vessel there was loud murmuring of approval and a shout of encouragement from the rogues gathered there to watch as their commander brought their great play to its climax.

"Here is the cutter of ropes, and of whips, and of chains my brothers." He sang out and flashed the bright blade over his head. "Who among you will join our company in the brotherhood of the coast, and with one act of his will, free himself from the shackles of a world which despises him? A world where ye may be starved, or beaten, or flogged or hanged at the will of men who value only the profit that your bowels may bring to them. A world where you may be cast into deadly combat with others of your class, all for the glory of some rag upon a stick, or for the advancement of some sweating prig in a cassock or in Ermine. We here are all humble men as ye, born to fight and sweat and groan and die. Join our company, and do all these same things but for your own, and not another's gain. Come up now brothers, and step forward, the hour is late and we sail hence, at war against all flags."

Three men came to their feet and stepped forward. The two once starving boys from the docks of Liverpool, Jonathan Peters and Noah Harwood, they went up as lambs, led to their doom by Parker Stevens. The three were greeted by lusty cheers and a crashing of weapons from the pirate crew. Rackham directed them to stand behind him, and once again prepared to address the *Rachel's* crew.

There was a cry of real anguish from Captain Lovewell "Oh, oh no my dear boys," he cried, "do not..." His heartfelt torment for the lads he had saved and treated as sister's children was roughly cut short by a tall pale pirate with a wild shock of carrot red hair whom I came to know as Thomas Quick. He slapped his hand with some force over Lovewell's mouth and dragged him backward by the hair, as a solid knot of his companions closed around and in front of our captain as I saw him struggling for air. Rackham cleared his throat and continued as if nothing had happened.

"Now then, here are three of your comrades who will feel the lash and the start no more. Three who will eat the fat of the rich, and strike fear into the strong. Is this then the limit of those among you with the ballast to carve their own way in the world?" No other man moved. "Then so be it and peace be unto you. Remember this day and Johnny Rackham when next you feel the bite of the cat." He turned then to myself, and Candy who stood beside me, and smiled in the friendliest of fashions.

"I am happy indeed to see that you two are already fast comrades, for I have need of you both, and your skills aboard the *Kestrel.* I fear I must prevail upon you both to remove your duffel to her decks with all haste. You must consider yourselves forced to our company.

I knew the meaning of forced, and my heart fell within my chest. I uttered not a word in response, but Candy spoke up quickly, and with great passion. "Jack, for the love of Christ do not do thus to me. Ye know right well that I've taken the Kings pardon, and that I am a man of my word. Ye must know also that I am content with my berth here, and that I seek only to pursue honest work in my old age — and the lad here. He is as honest, and gentle and hard working as can be found, don't blight his life in this way. You have three good men already from a crew of twelve. Jack, no one, including the captain of this vessel, will ever believe that I was forced to join ye. Did ye look up Jack, and see the albatross that had hovered over these barks all the long day? It cannot be a good omen for stealing men from their honest pursuits.

Rackham turned his attention away from us long enough to direct the last of his men to leave the *Rachel* and board their vessel, taking with them the three of our number who had cast their lot with the pirates; all they being as nervous as our own crew had been to cross the distance on the gangway. I knew it to be a solid, if not a steady pathway. Then with only Reede and the little bug eyed pirate Trinket standing with him, Rackham turned and spoke almost gently to Candy.

"Candy old comrade, beside Reede and Trinket here, I have only two other able ratings among my crew and I have need of at least two more. As to those who have gone aboard from this vessel, two I know to be boys, and waisters at best and still wet behind the ears, willing enough I'll wager but with no real skills to offer toward hard sailing. And we will be in for hard sailing. As for the other one? The boson? I have seen his back and it is a draughts board of cat scratches. A history of a little flogging makes for a sharper hand at this business, but a man who carries such a load of welts usually proves to be sullen, quick tempered and troublesome. I also take him to be one who is a little above himself in opinion, but still he is able rated — and claims to be gunner.

"I value every man who will join our commonwealth, but I am at the last the commander of a vessel at war and I must have — and will have — those tools I know to be most needed for success. We have aboard us foretop stays and jibs that I have not been able to use as yet — Reede cannot be in three places at once — and thus I have great need of a foretop captain with your skills old man." He turned then to regard me with a sly cat's smile.

"As for your young friend here, your high regard of him alone would be witness enough to his value were it not that we are in dire need of one skilled in carpentry, cooperage, and caulking. It would not do if I were to leave you both behind when our company has such need of you. Your once captain, and these men here, he said nodding to the remainder of the crew of the *Rachel*, are witnesses enough to your reluctance to cross over. Now I must insist that you both step lively and fetch your dunnage.

He sheathed his sword with a flourish, never once taking his eyes from us. "Reede, Trinket, see to it." he said softly, then he turned from us and crossed calmly over the swaying drawbridge to his vessel.

"Don't look so down in the mouth, Candy;" said the one called Trinket. "You know Rackham's a decent fellow and a fair commander, he'll turn you loose if you want when we find a good forward man to replace ye. And plus you've got old mates aboard to ease your mind, and to keep ye laughing. There's not just me and Reede here ye know, Pat Carty's still aboard, and Earl, and ye've seen McGinnis is still with us too. It'll be all right you'll see, she's a great vessel fast tight and snug. Magoon says the guns are first rate — rot his guts — and he knows such. Come along with ye then and I'll help ye remove your stuff."

As they went below to fetch Candy's duffel, Reede stepped over close to me. He smiled, and spoke in that calm and quiet way I learned of him, a way that calmed all those with whom he conversed.

"I've taken the liberty to having all your tools and personal effects transferred already, your cabin's clean of all your peck — though of course you're welcome to go below to look and make sure. You need have no fear that anything is missing. I took care of everything personally for you. I have moved your duffel and trunk and tools to the carpenter's berth aboard the *Kestrel.* I'm afraid it's not so large as the one you'll be used to. You'll need to hurry if you wish to inspect your old cabin, Master Carpenter, for Rackham's in a great froth to be away — as we've lingered here too long for his comfort."

I regarded the pirate before me carefully for the first time. I knew that he had saved my life earlier for I was sure that Magoon would have — as he had said — blown my brains across the deck as an object lesson to my shipmates. He seemed an odd sort to be about this business, he was remarkably fine boned for a rogue who enjoyed such respect from a man of Candy's wide experience. His face was broad, with high cheekbones and a strong prominent English nose. His mouth was generously wide and though he kept it thin and tightly controlled it still constantly seemed to me to be on the verge of a smile.

His eyes were gray green — like deep sea water — and squinted against the morning light that poured onto his face from over my shoulder. I could tell from his hands and face that he took great care of his person. This being remarkable enough in itself among those who follow the sea, whether pirate or no. I took him to be a man in his thirties; his face was lightly marked with character about the eyes and mouth. He was tall, standing only a handbreadth shorter than me. And frankly he was a very handsome man, with features and complexion so refined as to be almost fey.

"You saved my life today, sir," I said, "I think that I will trust you to have taken as good care of all my tools and personal things. I have no reason to doubt your truthfulness, or good intention to me." I paused in thought for a moment remembering the morning's toils. "It would seem that you knew early on that I would be forced to join your company."

"Aye. I knew early on and I will admit it is in part because I suggested such to the commander. We have, as Jack said, real need of someone with your skills to keep our little wooden world together and afloat. The *Kestrel* is a very fine vessel, very light and fast as I'm sure you know well enough by now, but she needs the attentions of a good ship's carpenter — as your papers indicate you to be. You will come to no harm while you are with us, you may have my personal oath upon it."

"How was it then that you came up just as your comrade was about to do for me? And how was it also that you knew I was speaking of the albatross?"

"I knew that Mike had taken an interest in you, and that you being the biggest and best turned out man aboard, Mike would look for some reason to have at you. Mike does not care at all for the tall and the handsome — there was a little snort of laughter — I know his ways. I knew about the albatross for I too saw it when I followed your gaze. I also knew of it for I had stood close enough to you so as to hear your voice as you talked to Candy." His eyes squinted very deep at this and his mouth became a hard line across his face. "Now come quickly, carpenter John, for it is time for us to be away."

I followed him across the gangway that I built, and stepped down onto the deck of the *Kestrel.* As ordered Jingles cut the he lines holding it in place and it fell away to fall with a thud against the hull of the pirate's vessel. The lines securing the two vessels were thrown clear by the *Rachel*'s crew and drawn back aboard, and so with some helpful pushing using the *Rachel*'s stolen spars we stood clear.

My first thought upon stepping onto the deck of the *Kestrel* was a muttered oath as I tripped on one or another of the bits and pieces of the *Rachel*'s looted stores scattered about her deck and between her guns.

The guns themselves however were obviously well maintained and housed. There were familiar cries from the quarterdeck to hoist or trim or clew up. The voice was sonorous and carried the length of the vessel effortlessly. Even this crew of rogues and cutpurses fell to in good order to its unquestionable authority.

I pressed myself tight against the bulwark to be out of the way of rushing men. I heard the familiar and somehow comforting slap and patter of bare feet on wood as the crew of the *Kestrel* hurried to obey that voice. There was also much crashing and thrashing and cursing as they tripped and fell over the jumble of looted goods on the deck.

I remember that moment as we pulled away, it being cast in my mind like bronze. I remember Captain Lovewell's bitter anguish to see his young charges destroy themselves. God help me I remember the feral smell of Mike Magoon as he pressed me helpless to the deck. I remember Reede's calm soft voice — "Belay that, Mike."

I remember also the white faces of the *Rachel's* crew gathered at her rail, looking at me and following my face as the *Kestrel's* main sail boomed and filled and we hove away.

Chapter 5
Aboard the *Kestrel*

For all of his desire to see a hanging when aboard the *Rachel*, Trinket proved to be a friendly and helpful sort of fellow as he brought Candy and me through the fore hatchway below to the lower or berth deck, avoiding on our way the groups of men still about the business of sorting and handling the sacks and piles of stolen goods that littered the deck. As soon as we had descended Candy was quickly surrounded by several of the pirates, and caught up in a friendly exchange of greetings, so Trinket then led me further down through the hatch to the orlop deck.

"Ye'll find all your gear right forward, to the starboard there." he said as we reached the foot of the hatchway. "There's stowage for lumber and such and a bit of a workroom — ye may bunk there if you've a mind. I wouldn't worry none about your tools and personal things and all; Reede took particular care in the moving of it."

He stopped me then just as we came to the workroom and looked up at me with a smile. "I know that you've been forced and all lad, but still I would not hold myself aloof from the rest of the crew if I were you. There are men here to be sure who will try you sore with either their smell or their meanness but there are also some good mates to be had and it's good to have friends wherever ye find yerself, y'know. I'll tell ye plain out that any friend of Candy Jones may be a friend of mine for the asking."

I took the moment now to more closely study the little man before me, the one who had called so hard for a hanging and who now appeared to be the gentlest soul one could meet. He stood only a little over five feet tall, with the hunched shoulders and the slightly sunken chest so common to England's poor. His eyes were a brilliant dark brown — very sharp, like a birds — and they seemed very large for his face due to their bulging slightly from the sockets — disconcerting at first but one became used to it.

His face showed the pox marks so common of his class as to be expected, and his jaw was large and strong looking for one so small in other respects. His eyes held me; they were very steady on mine

— not unkindly — and a strange sense of reserved power lurked deep in them. A line from a play that I had once heard, *"He is small, but he is fierce."* came to my mind. His hair was light brown and carefully braided into a long queue that hung nearly to his waist in the best man o' war's man fashion. He commonly wore a small round skullcap, much as might be seen on any street in Cairo or Acre, and unlike most of his shipmates he carried no weapon on him except a Scot's dirk tucked into the dark blue sash that girdled his very small waist. His common dress was a petticoat kilt of leather under a long one-piece shift — which in fact was the dress shirt of a much larger man — its sleeves cut off and hemmed just below the elbow. He wore a faded yellow kerchief around his neck — it was much later that I saw the scars it covered.

"I appreciate your kindness, sir," I replied, being in no position to spurn any offer of friendship. "Your high regard of my friend Candy and his for you recommends the friendship that you offer, and gladly I accept it, and as gladly extend my own. I would be very grateful for any help that you can give to me as I adjust to these new circumstances."

"Then its settled mate, give me your flipper," he said and we shook hands on it, "First off you're to call me Trinket as my mates do, and as our mutual friend Mr. Reede is not about for it let me be the one to show ye about the vessel you'll be serving."

With that he led me down another flight to the hold of the vessel. It was a mad house of jumbled spoils. I think he saw the look of dismay in my eyes — the proper stowage of the hold being the carpenter's responsibility — for he said, "ye're sure to have the master's authority behind ye when it comes time to shift this mess lad." I had no way to know at the time the source… nor the great power of that authority.

As the vessel tapered significantly to the bow, so the hold seemed to open to us as we moved aft.

It was low beamed but quite broad amidships. We picked our way through the bewildering array of barrels, firkins, kegs, casks and sacks, ducking and working our way eventually to a stout magazine, or powder room, which was full aft and just below the sail lockers, by the aft hatch. With its presence and its manner of construction it was evident to me that the *Kestrel* had been built originally as a ship of war, and not a merchantman. Here at the very bottom of the vessel, one or two men would sit in a low cramped cabin surrounded by barrels of gunpowder. Their world only dimly illuminated by a single lamp in a small lamp room twice shielded by thick oak and thick glass from their room's deadly contents. They would fill prepared linen sacks with the proper weight of coarse grain 'corned' black powder required for the vessel's cannon and hand the sacks out through a well saturated felt fire blanket to the waiting powder monkey — man or boy.

As I observed closely the vessel that I was now to serve — however forced — it brought to mind the drawing that Captain Johnson had given me of the vessel he wished to build, and I began to think that I was already aboard her. There were still men working in the hold as we prepared to mount the stern hatchway to return to the orlop, if stuffing and tossing and cramming and cursing could be called work. The real work would begin I knew when I was sent to bring order out of the heaps and piles. The orlop deck was nearly as cluttered, although the clutter there was quickly being transferred down to the hold to further complicate the work that must soon be got at there in order to assure the proper trim of the craft.

There were storage lockers, shot lockers, and small cabins forward of the sail locker, then the cable tier and at last the boson's storage, bread room, armorer's and carpenter's cabins and storage. We stopped by the forward hatch and Trinket once again spoke to me in his quiet and intense way, his dark eyes boring into mine.

"I see that ye are a quiet and observant lad. Don't let too many others see you observing so carefully anything but the wood ye work, lest there be some take it amiss. Be careful also to whom ye speak, and of what. Ye may be sure of me, and Candy and Reede, that we will advise ye and help ye as true mates would. There are some others as ye will meet through us. Now Rackham is generally fair-minded about things but he is an excitable boy. The quartermaster Dirk Corner holds the weather deck from the bitnacle aft as the quarterdeck, and none but Rackham may go there except as called by him or the master to service. Corner is very fierce about the articles and it is only through them that he will deal with ye. The sailing master, Fetherston, he cares only for the *Kestrel*, if ye serve her faithfully and cheerfully you will rest in the shelter of his very considerable wings."

"Well next thing is mate that you and me needs return us to the deck above, for there's an auction about to happen. Ye can see even now the lads as going up from the hold, done with the stowing as they are," He put his hand on my shoulder, "Every man who sails in a wooden world loves a good carpenter John and this will be a good chance for ye to get acquainted with the rest of your new shipmates. Ye'll see them all and learn a little of our ways." He cautioned me then once more about not seeming to be overly observant nor to as he said, "Linger long on a single face."

We retraced our steps up to the lower or between decks, and there I was introduced to one of the peculiarities of those who sail the account. The spoils of our vessel's cabins and armory were spread in piles down the center and almost the length of the lower deck. Now this deck had been flushed as it's called, all of its bulkheads partitions and cabins had been removed — excepting the galley stove and its brick fire wall — so that the deck ran like an unbroken cabin from the stem to the sternpost.

The space thus opened up removed all social distinctions between officers and crew, and served as a clear and open living platform for all hands. The perimeters were taken up by the sea chests, hammocks or bunks, and stowage of the crew. The central area was open to clear passage fore and aft. The deck was lighted by a half dozen shielded oil lamps, and the open hatches fore and aft, and there in the midst, spread out in orderly piles by type, were all the items from the *Rachel*'s cabins. Coats were in all one pile, shirts, pants, guns, edged weapons and personal effects in others. The pirate crew had drawn themselves up around the piles of loot, and were busy pointing and discussing items of obvious interest to them. Reede was standing with Candy close to the pile of guns aft; he smiled as I came up to them.

A tall well-built man was going carefully through the pile of personal effects, and taking out certain items and placing them into a small leather trunk. This I learned was the quartermaster Richard Corner, called Dirk by the crew. When he had finished with this chore and straightened up I saw a tall and pleasant looking fellow, with just a wisp of very short thin reddish hair on the crown of his head, fading into white at the temples, his hair was cropped close, but enough was left in back to wear in a small braided queue. He had a few days growth of white stubble on a thin face, and wore a bright gold earring in his left ear. I took him to be a man in his forties, very fit and seaman like. He called those of us who either come, or taken, from the *Rachel* and gathered us together about amidships.

"My name is Richard Corner. I'm the quartermaster of this vessel. I've been freely elected by this commonwealth to watch over all the accounts, and to serve their interests in the division of shares, and in all matters of their general welfare. We are about to divide what you see here among us. We know that there will be items of yours here, and we encourage you now to look through to claim those things which are. One pistol and a cutlass has been set aside for you new men — with this he indicated those three who had freely come — you forced men now have some time to claim anything of personal value. Have a care not to or-reach yourselves."

I knew that there was nothing of mine there, and not wanting to offend Reede by the pretense of looking, I stood back as Candy and the others went through the piles. Candy reclaimed a few small things and quickly stood back. The others took some little more time but at last stood away. At this the quartermaster stood up from the chest he had been seated on and once again addressed the company.

"Now for the benefit of our new men I will explain our actions. It is our custom to allow a shift of clothing for each man according to his need. He who has no coat may take one according to his need, so too with shirt, or pants, or shoes. Any items as are hotly contested must be auctioned off against the share each holds of the common cargo — although payment in gold, silver or stone will not be discouraged. Basic weapons, as I said, will be provided for the new men once they have signed our articles, all other arms must be bid on, and purchased from the common."

Rackham now joined us on the lower deck; he was accompanied by two others. One was a small fair skinned fellow, more a boy really, with rich chestnut red hair braided back from under a long green silk bandanna. He was dressed in a loose blue shirt, with a sash and broad belt over baggy dark pantaloons, all too big for his sparse frame. The other was very tall, very strong and formidable looking, he was wearing a wide tricorn and a dark gray doublet and waistcoat, and he carried an astrolabe. He spoke briefly with Rackham, then called three grumbling men away with him and returned topside.

Candy came aft to sit with me and Trinket, who showed no interest in the proceedings, other than to laugh shrilly at the small squabbles that broke out over this or that bit of the larder being divided. Candy greeted me, then he turned to Trinket and said, "I know the wee one was Bonny, was the other Fetherston the sailing master?"

"Aye, and a damn fine one too, I've never seen a better navigator — as ye know navigation is not Jack's strong suit. He keeps us running sharp and as Bristol fashion as ye can squeeze out of this lot, even though he's overloaded with waisters and ordinary, there being only four of us on the crew that every held an able seaman's berth — six now with this fellow Stevens and you Candy.

"The little one, the one you called Bonny, is he a ship's boy I mean he seems very young and small to be ... I hesitated to choose my words carefully… about this business, I said, what is his place on the crew?

"Oh ... he works closely under the commander offered Trinket with a snigger."

He and Candy gave each other wide fish eyes at this, and then broke into a gleefully helpless laughter. When they had exhausted their load of glee at what I could only presume to be a veiled reference to an impropriety on the part of Rackham with his cabin boy, Candy turned to me with still tearing eyes and spoke in a hushed tone.

"Yon Bonny is a lass, laddie," he said. "Rackham thinks none know aught of it, but all, well ... almost all that is, know the truth of it. She's the little hellcat bastard daughter of a Carolina planter. She run off to sea with a worthless sailor boy. She married him she did to spite her father and they came down to New Providence, her husband in the end was a paltry chuff and a cony so then two years back she ran off to sea again, this time with a silver tongued pirate captain — being our Rackham. He of course at that time throwing the king's pardon back and taking to the account again, and me bearing my pardon back to England where the Thumper found me a good berth with Lovewell… I pray the old man is well."

"She's quite a nice bit of fluff though under all that pirate get up." Trinket said softly.

"She weren't much of a sailor as I remember," Candy continued, "but she is a right little piss cutter when it's time for a fight. She goes right in bold as brass for all that she's playing at pirate. She's built like a whippet and strong for her size, fearless as a badger and is a right fair hand with a blade. I think she likes excitement and fights. We as know the truth of her keep it to ourselves, as it's most uncommon on a vessel like this, most crews forbid it entirely as causing too much jealousy and rancor amongst the men. But everyone feels sorry for Rackham, he being such an ugly sod and all."

"That's all too true," said Trinket when his laughter stopped, "She damned near caused a fight between Rackham and Reede at one time. She took quite a shine to Reede when he first joined us, and she started making mooncalf eyes at him. — This might be something for ye to make note of, John. Rackham took notice a'right and got right damned hot over it. Then it seems she and Reede had a long talk together, and went to see Rackham. There was the beginning of very heated words among them — we were all ready for hell to break loose I can tell ye — then Bonny leans up and says something to Rackham that made him step back and bite his hand. You'll see him do that from time to time, it's something he does when things are either really bad, or good, or as in this case, funny, for he threw his head back, and laughed till I thought he'd puke. They've all been best mates since."

The division of the clothing was finished about this time. The quartermaster stood beside the piles of arms taken from the *Rachel's* armory and began to hold up weapon after weapon for the bidding. He seemed to be very familiar with weaponry, for he was able to describe each piece in some detail, with calibre if a fire lock, quality and condition whether blade or fusel before opening the bidding.

The bidding as it were went in this fashion; any man interested in the piece made an offer, if any other desired the item a counter bid was made and so on until one had claim to the blade or firearm. There was no prompting or reaction of any sort from the quartermaster, and the bidding reaching any heat only over particularly fine weapons. There were a number of such fine weapons that were once been bound for the officers and gentry of Jamaica, several hotly contested. If the buyer had coin on him to pay on the spot it was well and his coin was added to the common, if not the quartermaster noted in his log the amount owed, and by whom. The amount was tallied against the man's share of the common holding, and would be recouped when the accounts were cleared at the close of the voyage.

I found the pirates to be keen on their weapons overall, and indeed I was to learn that keeping their weapons in good repair was required by the articles under which this commonwealth sailed.

Each man kept as many pistols as possible — some as many as eight — and a cutlass, a dirk or dagger and a boarding axe or short pike in addition to a musketoon or musket. They carried their pistols into combat in a peculiar manner that I've already mentioned. In addition to any thrust into their belts or sashes they hung others by ribbons or leather straps over their shoulders, the weapons instantly available for firing one by one, and then dropped to hang once more un-lost in the melee and confusion of battle. In this manner a dozen men thus armed could lay down a withering fire as they came aboard the close confines of a vessel's deck, as I would behold firsthand soon enough.

When the auction finished, to the great and obvious enjoyment of all hands, Reede who acquired the handsome set of Scottish screw barrel pistols that Captain Lovewell hoped to sell in Port Royle came ambling over to where we were and sat down next to Trinket. He seemed a little shy almost as he greeted Candy and then turned to me with that half smile I had noticed on the *Rachel's* deck.

"Have you found your things to be complete and in order as I said they would be?" he asked

"I have not yet bothered to look. Your assurances were sufficient for my comfort."

Reede's face was mercurial and changeable. He seemed very pleased with my answer and I saw warmth spread around his eyes and the corners of his wide mouth. "I've found you in the best of possible company," he said after a moment, "You will do well to ask of these two all you may need, and do well also to listen carefully to all they say. I'm hopeful that you and I might be friends as well. I only suggested your joining us for the best interests of all my mates here, and Jack was of a mind for a carpenter for us and liked your papers and the way you worked well enough …well he was of that mind anyway, so I prey that you will hold no ill will toward me for your presence here."

I replied that I held no man in my ill will as regards the twists that fate may throw into my path.

I told him that I could not say that I was happy to be held against my will in this way, but that I was prepared to make the best of it and to perform my duties to the vessel cheerfully.

He leaned forward then, looked hard into my eyes, and continued in a cautionary manner. "You, as a forced man carpenter, will be expected to go about all the duties required of you. These duties will be those that are common to the sailing and repair of the vessel upon which all of our lives, yours included depend. You must however never, ever, pick up a weapon, or shot, or powder; nor must you ever aid in the handling or loading of a gun when we are about our business. You must never go aboard a vessel we are at work on, unless it is clear that you are doing so under constraint. There have been enough cowardly rogues that have slit a throat one day, and claimed they were forced men the next, so that to be believed ye must stay altogether clean of our doings. If you wish to remain free of the charge of piracy, you must heed my words."

"He's right lad," said Candy, "If any man, and I mean even of those here who now are soon to be your mates, can bear witness that you ever aided this crew willingly in the taking or plundering of even one vessel, you will be held as much a pirate as any other man here to an admiralty court."

"All the God's own truth, young John." said Trinket, before jumping to his feet and yelling loudly for music, rum, and his supper. The cry was taken up generally by all hands.

From behind us, from up in the very bow of the vessel, three men came down. They had been so quiet and withdrawn from all the loud commotion and shouting of the auction, that their sudden appearance behind us and the sharp snarl of a fiddle startled me and Candy into jumping. The fiddle player laughed as the three fair jumped past us to the center of the deck. The fiddler was a thin man with a large nose and an unruly crown and beard of graying hair who pretended to well worn satins and laces for his dress. — on the whole I have found musicians to be a shameless lot — he being wonderful skilled however.

One was a short broad red haired fellow wearing much in the way of blue ink and little else and carrying a Bodhran. I would see him later when we came into battle dance naked and blue atop the longboats beating a wild heart racing tattoo on the ancient drum, his hair flying and in a strange high voice singing the song of Brian Boru in the old tongue. The third was small and swarthy with tight curly black hair and dressed in the remnants of what were once fine clothes, he played the fife and was near the equal of the fiddler. They bounded up to amidships amid cheers from the pirates, and as several men prepared the galley and set to gathering the makings of a meal, they began to play a sprightly hornpipe.

“What of the pipes I heard earlier today?” I asked of my companions.

“That would be the master,” replied Trinket, “he’ll not leave the watch until we are well clear of the place where we took your vessel. I think the lads are making salmagundi tonight, by way of celebration of the fat prize today — no offence, John. You’ll find our food far better on the whole than that served upon even the best merchantmen — we have worldly tastes I fear from feeding on the fat of the rich. — Hey! You there! Cracker Joe!” he shouted. “Leave up on that damned keg will ye, ye damned great bed presser, there’s other thirsty men aboard.” With that he was away to join the group who broached a keg of Barbados rum.

The galley fires were lighted, and a sweet woody smell filled the berth deck of the *Kestrel.*

Chapter 6
Salmagundi

The pirates, in celebration of their new prize, started up a general frolic, which lasted till midnight as best I can guess, without the regulation of a ship's bell my sense of time was lost. Some measure must have been kept however, for at a point in the evening Fetherston and a group of men came below. He went straightway to Rackham who after some discussion led Bonny and three others on deck, presumably to maintain the watch. Fetherston then broke out the pipes that I heard when the *Rachel* was stopped, and fired the little band up into a roaring version of *"Bob's Your Uncle."* The musicians took little in the way of a break throughout the evening, although their efforts were well lubricated with the contents of the several kegs of rum that were emptied that night.

The salmagundi that Trinket spoke so highly of was served out to all who could make it as far as the galley, the time taken in its preparation having been spent in spirited drinking. It was an unusual, but very tasty, combination of meat, fish and vegetables; being a sort of a stew — though not all cooked together like a stew and in a wine sauce not a gravy — with cuts of spiced meats, smoked fish, and tropical vegetables and fruits all mixed together. I saw too that the fine Spanish olives from the *Rachel's* cargo had found a savory home in the salmagundi.

Reede sat near me through much of the time, explaining the various unfamiliar ingredients of the dish, pointing out to me such native vegetables as plantain and palm hearts, and fruits like mango and coconut. He also explained the spiced meats — some of which were fiery hot — as being preserved in the manner that the natives of these islands used. The meats being smoke cooked, after being rubbed with various spices and herbs native to the area. All in all it was as Trinket had said, better food than was ever served on any merchantman I knew of. Even on the *Rachel* it was only bully beef, peas and ship's bread.

One by one through the evening tired drunken men dropped off to sleep, and at the point where my exhaustion finally took control of me, I took a candle lamp below to the orlop to find rest in the carpenter's crib. I found there all my tools and gear neatly stowed and all in order; more remarkably, I saw my hammock strung between two beams, and my bedroll laid upon it. I gave only a passing thought to the kindness of the one who took such liberties, as I extinguished my light before dropping into a deep stunned sleep.

I was aroused from what seemed mere minutes of slumber by the ship's bell, ringing at last. It was not the measured ring that announces the turning of the glass as on other vessels, but a loud very rapid clarion, like an alarm. I heard a scuffling and thumping, and terrible blasphemous oaths from the deck above, and then the familiar voice of Candy bellowing down the hatchway. "Get up and lay topside, John, the sun's topped the main yard and we're all called to assemble at the waist. There'll be a reading and signing of the articles. With Rackham there's bound to be a show worth the trip for ye." He belched and groaned. "Oh God, I feel like something with dirty feet crawled down to my gut and died last night."

I stopped to take a drink, and freshen my face, at one of several scuttlebutt set about the vessel. A man of war or a merchantman would have had only one and that out where the officers could observe its usage. The between deck of the vessel was the worse for the frolic of the night before, but I could still see much. While there seemed to be a general orderliness about the craft — a business like sort of order — there was no doubt however that the crew did little in the way of sailor's drudge work. This impression was supported by the condition of the main deck as I came up. Any, Captain, I knew would have had all hands on holystones and swabs for a week.

My first surprise as I came to the waist was that Rackham sat upon a chest by the starboard rail.

He was not the center of the coming activities. Bonny, Reede and two others sat about him. It was the quartermaster, Corner, who commanded the proceedings.

It is another of the peculiarities of the freebooters, that the captain of a pirate vessel has nothing of the power of that title, as the rest of the maritime understands it. He is more properly called simply commander. He is the elected official of a partnership, and is answerable to it. He leads by success alone, and receives a double share of the common. His command during times of pursuit, or combat is absolute, and at those times he may strike, cut or shoot without censure, any man who disobeys his orders or shirks at his duties. At all other times he is a respected senior voice in the meetings of the partnership, but no more. Any influence he gains beyond that is gained by shear force of character, and above all — and trumping any other consideration — success.

The business of the sailing of the vessel is under the direct command of the sailing master. All hands are expected to follow his orders in this regard, and to take their turn to come on watch as he directs. He, as all the officers, is elected; however, his is the position requiring the most specific knowledge, an incompetent master is quickly apparent, thus the position is most critical to the actions of the pirates. Any man may be lucky, or bold but not every man may be a master mariner. Fetherston was all of that.

All matters as to the account and the management of the partnership's interests come under the direction of the quartermaster. He is accounted second to the commander when the vessel is in action, and will take command if the former should fall. As his title may imply he serves as the "master" of the quarterdeck. On a naval vessel his would be a warrant officer's position under the watch lieutenant, here he represents the commonwealth that in fact commands the vessel. These two, the master and the quartermaster, each receive a share and a half of the common. It is in this wise that it was the quartermaster of the *Kestrel* who officiated at the addition of men to its crew, and who would read the articles under which it sailed, and under which they would live.

"Gather up lads, and pay attention now," Corner cried out, and thumped an oar upon the deck.

"We have new men aboard as you all know, and they must hear the reading of the articles before they are signed, and joined as members of our commonwealth. Gather up now ye gentleman of fortune."

My next surprise came as I observed in its entirety the company to which I was now attached, and saw their relaxed reaction to the call for all hands to assemble. There was no sense of regimentation about the way my new shipmates deported themselves, there were no measured ranks of jack tars standing to attention by division at the waist of a man of war, no quietly attentive and standing seamen, as on a merchantman. Groups of men sat where they willed, some brought boxes, or empty kegs on deck, and some sat on their haunches, as only sailors and Indiamen can do.

Others leaned casually against the rail or a mast, or sat atop the two longboats stowed side by side on gallows at the waist. There was the hubbub of a dozen conversations, bursts of laughter, little groans and complaints of the night before, little scenes of mock combat, and play-acting. The band of rogues seemed more like a convention of country drovers, or the meeting of a bowling society, than the crew of a vessel of thieves at war against all flags.

My third surprise put the two previous ones to shame, and it was only by my interested examination of each group of men that it came to my attention. There by the larboard rail, seated on an empty rum keg, was Mike Magoon. He was no longer the feral beast that rushed aboard the *Rachel.* He was dressed in a dark red brocade doublet, with a fine buff waistcoat and matching knee breeches. The waistcoat was open and he wore what appeared to be clean new linen.

His hair was now parted neatly and plaited into three hanging braids, in the best Bristol fashion, one to either side of the head, one larger behind, all tied with red ribbon; his beard done much the same in three, and with both head and beard glistening with the application of some oil. He was smiling, and surrounded by a group of about a dozen men, including now Parker Stevens, and the two boys from Liverpool.

Stevens looked much the same, although more scruffy and well hung over, but young Harwood and Peters had changed completely in the time since coming on board. They each wore the loose open shirt, baggy pants bloused at the ankles, and sash about their middle of the corsair — each also had been pierced for the silver earrings they now affected. Each proudly carried a dirk tucked into their sash. They were no longer the thin tattered ragamuffins who signed aboard the *Rachel* — at the bounty of Andrew Lovewell — rather than starve on the streets. They each carried themselves with the attitude of one who knows that he is about to cross a line. From this day henceforward, they would no longer be street litter, nor toothless beggars nor yet ship's boys, but accounted as men among men.

Candy and Trinket were gathered about the main mast, along with three of four others, and seemed to be in close and friendly conversation. Candy took note of me, and waved at me.

"Come over and join us John," he called out, "We've some old and true mates here for ye to meet."

As I walked across the deck to join them, I became conscious for the first time that Reede had hardly taken his eyes from me since I'd come topside, and seemed somehow solicitous that I notice him. Not wanting to offend one whom I knew would be a strong ally; I turned slightly and sent a broad smile and a wave in his direction. He then did a very odd thing indeed; he seemed to blush.

"Welcome up, and lay to lad." Candy greeted me in a warm and hearty manner. "Come and meet some old shipmates of mine that have managed to beat the gibbet all these two years gone. He introduced me then to some of the very men that Trinket mentioned as being still aboard when Candy and I were forced. Patrick Carty from Liverpool, a small and bright eyed man, I recognized as one of the judges of their 'court of free men," Alexander McGinnis thick set dark and fiercely loyal, he once served as a boson in the king's navy and thus the boson's pipe he played so expertly as to tweet along with the musicians when in his cups. I met as well Thomas Earl and Ben Talmer, both from Bristol like myself but unknown to me until that day. There was a feeling of genuine friendship and good will among these six, and I was glad to be welcomed in a warm manner to their company.

Corner then ordered the ship's bell rung again, and after thumping his oar once more upon the deck he began to read aloud the articles of the commonwealth from a large portfolio set before him atop the bitnacle, held in place against the wind by pistols laid on its corners. The first two articles provided for the free election, as well as the duties, authorities, and responsibilities of the offices that he and Rackham, and Fetherston held. These officers being freely elected at the beginning of the voyage, and their being subject to the remonstrance or censure of the court of free men and brethren of the coast, as well as to recall and replacement at the pleasure of, and by vote of the crew. As unusual as this organization and its election of its leaders was to my previous experience there were to follow even more unusual and interesting particulars of this commonwealth of thieves to which I was forced.

Each man who signed the articles under which we sailed was the equal of any other, and each had an equal vote in all of the affairs of their commonwealth. Each man had claim to an equal share in the common holdings of the company except, as I have mentioned, for the premiums allotted to the elected officers. Each man was there sworn to obey the necessary directions of the officers elected over them, and to uphold their civil authority in the management of the common affairs. No gambling was allowed among them, no fights or disorders were allowed them.

Any dispute, which arose, would be settled by the court of free men. Any dispute which came to blows would be settled with cutlass and pistol at the first opportunity ashore; no man, officer or otherwise, having the right to lay violent hands upon another. Any man might bring business before the company. Any man, who was found stealing from the common, or from another, would be marooned. This punishment of being cast out of the company and set ashore with just a loaded pistol and a flask of water being the harshest allowed, except for cases of desertion, 'mutiny' or outright murder of a mate, where the punishment was death.

There was even a system of payments set up for those who might suffer loss of limb, or sense, in the performance of their duties, or in combat. All such things being unheard of in the society which I had been part of only the day before — or any other that I knew of. There followed a sensibly long list of rules governing the use of fires, pipes, lamps, candles & etc., as well as rules concerning the care of their weapons, and rules even for the kind of frolic that transpired the night before. I was transfixed by the scene, and by what I heard. I knew I was witnessing a society of men unique in all the world. The culminating article of the compact between these equals was that their company could only be disbanded when each share of the common account was valued at a thousand pounds sterling.

The conversations which surrounded me fell little by little, as Corner read their articles, so that midway through his reading there was complete silence on the deck, but for the wind and the sea. Then he looked up from the document, regarded the assembled company, and called out.

"Let every man who has yet to sign these articles step forward and be accounted."

John Tanner, which is myself, Agamemnon Jones, Parker Stevens, Jonathan Peters and Noah Harwood all stepped forward as he directed. Four others beside lay up athwart us, the three musicians and a tall gangling Swede with lank barley colored hair named Jan Hanson.

"Is any man of you ready at this time to sign the articles I have just read? Ye become over two hundred pounds the better catch thanks to the articles ye may sign," continued the quartermaster.

Harwood and Peters might have tripped on one another in their enthusiasm. Stevens hung back a little I thought, and then stepped forward. There was a general cheer from the pirate crew, and then the young Swede Hanson also stepped forward. His action brought a renewed cheering, and good-hearted calls of 'there's the Swede up to take his medicine,' and 'there's another damn share shot to hell.' He was one of the other able seamen aboard, and very popular with the crew. He was forced several months earlier for his skills, and he bore on his back the stripes of having once been flogged. The 'little history of flogging' that Rackham thought so highly of.

A cry arose from Thomas Quick who as usual was standing with Magoon. "Candy Jones," he cried. "Why stand ye there like an old stump? Lay to and sign aboard, there's a hemp choker out there waiting for your neck anyway you damned old piss goat. Have you lost yer nerve as well as yer hair?"

Candy flushed at this tone and gathered his fists together; before he could act his friend McGinnis was quick to answer for it. "Belay that blather, and shut yer damned pie-hole ye know naught of it, and ye blow as usual through ye'r arse. Candy's taken the king's pardon, and all men here as know him know him to be a man of his word. He's not a man to give it loosely — what good would his word be to us anyway, if he'd lie to a king?" McGinnis, once part of Vane's crew, never took the offered pardon but had sailed away from Nassau with that famous captain two years before.

There were howls and murmurs, and shouts of harsh laughter among the gathered company, for more than a few among them — Rackham included — once took brief advantage of the same pardon, only to spurn it and return to 'the sweet trade' — as they called it. Each man who thus foresworn himself knew he would swing out of hand if taken in piracy. It is part of the perverted bravado of these rogue's world to scorn at hanging as 'just a sour look' to pay the piper for a 'brief but merry life." The man McGinnis, a pugnacious sort, turned and looked narrowly all about him in challenge to anyone who would take it up. There was a moment when I thought the red faced Quick would step up, but he thought the better of it and stood down with a snort and much the sour look he would wear some short months hence.

Corner stepped into the breach, and brought us all up close to the bitnacle, where those who made their decision were ready to sign. I had there the opportunity to see the articles as they were presented. I took the opportunity to study them in some detail, as though perhaps reconsidering my decision. They were as neatly written as any articles could be, in a strong clear hand, and took the whole of the one side of the folio. The other side of the folio contained the spaces into which Peters, Harwood, Stevens and the Swede would add their names. The pirates signatures, or mostly their marks, were affixed in a very peculiar way, there being no top nor bottom, no first nor last. Rather they were arranged in a circle, something like the spokes of a wheel. When the four new names were added in the spaces pointed out by Corner, the wheel was nearly complete. There being at that point a total of perhaps forty names as I remember. It looked as though perhaps another few might be added to make a filled circle of fifty or so names, thereby creating a wheel of destiny which then like the Oroboros would swallow its own tail.

One of the marks that I have stood out to me; it was of a stick figure of a hanged man. Several others were dreadfully lewd.

"Who now will take these new men," — here he indicated the three men from the *Rachel* but not the Swede — "Under his care, to make them familiar with our ways, and to arrange them such training at sail or arms as they may require?" asked Corner in a loud voice.

"I and my mess will do so," answered Magoon, to a chorus of approval from a half dozen or so men, including the man Quick. They were some of the roughest men aboard, all were hard and grim fellows who had been first to push or shove the *Rachel*'s crew I remember. All jolly and full of themselves now but a heartbeat away from violence at any moment — I've seen their like before, and since. Rot them.

Now the messes aboard a vessel about such business as this was upon are not so structured as they are in the naval services, and consist rather of groups of men who choose to eat, work and fight together. From force of habit, or some inner sense of proper human proportions, most messes will settle into six to eight men anyway. On the *Kestrel* there was much fluidity among the messes but each seemed to center upon a personality. The order of such personalities aboard the *Kestrel* was being made clear to me with every passing hour of my captivity.

Corner then turned and addressed Candy and myself in a preemptory manner.

"You men will be held for the service of this vessel, until such time as you shall of your own will come forward to sign our articles, or until your required services may be supplied by another who will. You are equally bound by our articles, and I may say equally protected by its provisions. You have, of course, no voice nor vote in our proceedings — though you do well to attend to them — but beyond that, if you acquit yourselves honorably with us and tend toward the services required of your berth, you will be safe and well provided for.

"I caution you however, that if you hamper our operations in any way, or cause any dissension or conflicts among us, or mutiny or desert, you will be shot and cast over the side. And if your actions should cause death or grave injury to any one of us — you will simply be cast over the side."

Corner turned again to address the assembled crew, "Who will step forward now to stand to for these forced men, to instruct them in our ways, and to be held accountable for them and for their actions while they are among us as guests?"

I only just contained the derisive hoot of laugher that fairly wished to burst from me. Candy gave me a wide-eyed and frantically warning look.

Trinket stepped forward, and to my astonishment Reede did also. "Trinket and I have discussed this matter," said Reede, "He will gladly accept the responsibility for our mutual friend able seaman Agamemnon Jones, and I will take responsibility for the conduct of the carpenter."

"This is as you agreed Trinket?" Corner asked.

"Aye it is yer worship, and Jones will be much the better man for it if it please yer honor."

Corner shot a sharp glance at Trinket — who smiled in return — and then addressed himself to me and Candy once more. "You men are to understand that these two brethren have the power where you are concerned, and that no friendship which they may bear or gain for you will protect you if you should betray this company. They are your guarantors of honorable treatment under our articles, and to the company of your loyal and honest service to it."

Addressing the assembly again Corner said, "Then this reading and witnessing, and signing of the articles is complete. Is there now any man who has some further business to bring to the attention of the court, or to the assembled crew?"

Magoon stood up and stepped forward.

"I have business to bring before the assembled company."

Chapter 7
The Business At Hand

I was struck once again by the complete change of character and appearance that Magoon underwent since I first saw him. He was a very short man indeed, but what inches there were of him, were every inch the pirate. I saw also that he wore freshly tarred shoes with brass buckles, and although he appeared to be unarmed I learned later from Reede that he carried two small French screw barreled muff pistols in the large pockets of his doublet, and a long Italian dagger with its sheath sewed into the coat's lining — Magoon was always ready to kill.

"Comrades, mates, and partners," he said, "it's now some four months gone since we cut this little French schooner out of the yards in Port O'Prince. In that time we have taken but four prizes of any real worth — not counting the fishing vessels and coasters that we have interfered with for our supplies and amusement. This is thin return for hanging work I say. I doubt that if we settled the account today there'd be much over two hundred pounds a share — and more than half of that in goods, not in specie. I will tell you all that when I sailed with Teach, we took as many prizes in a week.

I watched Rackham at this point to catch his reaction to such an obvious cut at his leadership. He took note right enough, and on the outside seemed casual, but I have always indulged in the observation of others and I could tell that he waxed very warm. He held his piece, however, it being their custom to allow no interruption of one bringing business to the attention of the court or crew. Bonny however was having none of it and started bolt upright from her perch next to Rackham and sent a fierce sputtering squinty-eyed scowl at the speaker.

There was a mixed reaction across the deck. There were several nervous coughs, a few men leaned forward looking at Magoon with approbation and nodding their heads; others kept their silence — and a wary eye on Rackham. being — as I learned — well known for sudden and violent bursts of action when aroused. There was a palpable tension on deck. Reede, I noticed, had to all appearances found some loose thread in his jacket, which was in need of immediate attention, and had apparently missed both the barb and Bonny's reaction. I noted however that the offending thread lay close to the two pistols tucked into his red sash.

"I am not here to fault the commander, entirely; in this; we all share the blame for a poor harvest." Magoon backed away from what I could sense was an abyss. "Much of the fault lies in where we do our business. Had we not ventured outside of our normal haunts and into the main shipping lanes we would not have found our last prey, which I warrant did double our common at a stroke. Among other concerns, there's no less than half a dozen men o' war cruising between here and the leewards — no more than two of which I'd care to meet — and Woodes Rogers has commissioned at least that many privateers to hunt for such as we, including Ben Hornigold, and Johnny Barnett both who sailed on the account themselves and know every haunt and hole that we do. There's good reason why commanders like Condent, and Taylor, and Roberts have gone eastward, and left these seas to gulls what pick the lee shore.

I thought Rackham would crawl out of his skin at this, one of the men with him stepped in front of Bonny, for it looked as though she would go right at Magoon. Reede now found something of great interest in the yards and stepped over in front of Bonny as well, as if to get a better look. I heard distinctly the muffled, sputtered words 'squat smelly little barrel of cheese."

Magoon appeared unruffled as he continued in a more conciliatory tone. "We have a fine fast French vessel here, and she could carry as many as fourteen twelve pounders with no loss of speed."

Magoon for any faults he had was a very good gunner, and his assessment of the *Kestrel*'s carrying capacity was essentially accurate. However, I knew that it is one thing for the vessel to be able to accommodate the additional weight topside — fourteen twelves would almost double the current weight of the vessels cannon — but that it is quite another thing to work the guns, and for the vessel 's structure to safely absorb the greater shocks of the recoil. This is to say nothing of the dramatic change in the vessel's sailing characteristics such a rearming would occasion. I thought it ill advised at the time, but none asked my opinion so I gave none.

"We have a good crew," he continued, "not lacking in guts or experience to man her. But we have very little cargo space, and that space should be taken up with jewels and gold from the great mogul's treasure fleets, not woolens, and linens, and olives like a damned Thames Bumboat. There are others here who agree with me, that we should make ourselves ready and sail eastward across the Atlantic and into the oceans of India. We can sell the goods we have at Cuba, refit with heavier guns, and go on to make our fortunes like Tew, and Avery off of the heathen, and the East India Company." He bowed and sat down.

There were voices among the gathered crew, which rose in agreement to this line of thinking.

'Oh Aye,' one said, 'Madagascar is all controlled by those of our trade, I hear they each have their own little kingdoms cut out — and room to spare.' Another voice offered, 'I heard that Avery's crew shared out at over two thousand pounds a man from one prize alone,' and another shouted, 'Teache took a whole damned city by God.' As they spoke I realized that from my dealings with Captain Johnson and his interests in such things that I in fact knew more of these matters than any there, but I kept my silence.

Rackham jumped to his feet and started in with great heat. "Christ's wounds! Teach, Teache, Teache; I've had me a belly full of Teache," "I'll tell you all you need to know of Black Beard Teache by God. He never once in all his days ever paid his crew off square, he'd send most of them ashore to fill water barrels, or some other such contrivance, and then abandon them there to sail off with his little group of favorites — and thus make twenty shares out of a hundred. By God's teeth, didn't he cripple poor Israel Hands, as fair a hand on a cannon as ever sailed, with a shot to the knee — on a twisted whim by God. There are men here who can warrant what I say. Teach me no more Teaches, if that's the sort of commander you admire Mike, you'll find none such here. Nor men foolish enough to follow after one like him who would lead them by fear and in the end betray them — or turn them into ship's cooks." He alluded to the one trade that a lamed man like Israel Hands could continue to serve on board a vessel.

Rackham made a great effort to compose himself as he strode to the bitnacle and looked out on his crew, and continued his reply to Magoon's proposal with less heat, tense and now controlled.

"Roberts, and Condent, and Taylor command ships by God, not schooners nor sloops. Their ships mount thirty, forty guns and they carry crews of a hundred and fifty or more men. Roberts commands a whole damned squadron for Christ's pity. We are but one small fast and sea worthy barky. As for Madagascar? I've heard some different tales of Madagascar mates. I've heard tales of squalor and dreadful rotting diseases, tales of murder in the night, tales of constant war with the natives — some of which I've heard are cannibals, and have developed a taste for the long white pig.

"Tew and Avery? They struck the mogul's fleets early days, long before the East India Company sold the heathen bastards good Sheffield cannon, and trained them in their use — they are easy prizes for a bold crew like this no longer. And the company's ships? They are all heavily armed, little less than men of war really, and they sail in convoy most of the time. Even were she overloaded with fourteen twelve pounders as Mike says, the *Kestrel* would still be only just a match for one of them; and they all sail under strict command to make a dead man's fight out of any attempt to take them.

"No, no mates; we are seekers after profit my men, like the *Kestrel* hawk herself we seek prey not combat. We want a meal not a fight. And as for the men of war who seek for us? There are no less of them in the Indian oceans whose purpose it is to suppress such as we. And finally mates, we have no friends in those far and foreign oceans, there are none there who speak the languages we know, there are no known and friendly smugglers to take our goods, and there is no great multitude of coves, and islands and cays such as God has scattered across the face of these seas as if placed directly for our very use and succor." He bowed deeply as much of the crew thumped and hooted in their odd manner and so returned to an adoring Bonny, and sat down.

Magoon sat calmly with his mates while Rackham spoke but I could see that he and several of the men with him carefully watched the reactions of the crew. It was clear that an undercurrent of division existed in the pirate crew; and while Magoon's party seemed much in the minority at present it held some of the roughest and seemingly most dangerous of the men aboard.

Perceiving that Rackham was finished the quartermaster thumped his oar and asked if there was any other man who had aught to add to the debate… "And I mean something to add besides the wind in his sails." This stopped the mouths of several men who started into a deep breath.

"Good then, well I have something to say on this matter, both as your quartermaster and as a man who's made the middle passage twice before. I agree with Mike in much that he says, as we have had only fair — just fair — fortune since we set out. Mike's estimate of the condition of the common is very close to the truth. I did some books yesterday as we set the last prize into the tally, and if we shared out this moment each share would come to a few odd shillings over two hundred pounds — about 90 pounds in specie, the bulk in goods."

"The goods we carry, particularly after our last prize, are all top quality and should bring a premium. We are fortunate to have recourse to one of the great smuggling houses on Jamaica. We should away to that island immediately to make contact with it — in my opinion anyway. As for Black Teache? Well it will be two years come November since Teache died in battle like a man, and I will speak no ill of him. He was a right dread pirate, and many fat merchants sleep the easier for his death. — Yet what the captain said is true enough, he did many good men out of their fair share of the account. What the commander said about the oceans beyond Africa is also true, but it is the journey there, which is even more to be considered. It is a long, long sail across to the African coast. When you get there, it's a very uninviting coast, either swamp or desert, and barren of any place to refit.

"Re-watering is a quite difficult undertaking, when it is at all possible. The coast is regularly patrolled by fast Frigates, from the cape north, to protect the slave trade. We would find no haven there. To even consider the crossing we would need at least one hundred days of water and victuals per man — and this we do not have. We must however set upon some course that will fatten up the common in specie, for we do not have space in the hold to add much more in the way of cargo. As your quartermaster I feel it is time to set out for Jamaica and there have our mate Trinket find us some turtle hunters so as to cash out our goods and make some hold space for whatever plan the commander will come up with."

A small ripple of good-natured laughter ran through the assembled crew.

"I followed all that he said till he came to the turtle hunters." I said to Candy.

"Its their way of speaking of smugglers," he said, "It used to be that if a smuggler was found out on the waters at night — prior to his making his contact of course — and any questions was asked, they'd maintain that they were just out hunting turtles — use to be. I doubt the line would stand these days, good for the laugh though."

"Let's hear the master!" Came a loud cry from the bow, "Aye Fetherston, lay fore'd and give us the master's voice," answered the helmsman. There followed a general swell of agreement across the deck seeking for Fetherston's opinion, for he was held in the highest regard by all members of the vessel's crew.

In answer to the growing chorus calling him, Fetherston stepped up past the helm and walked forward of the Bitnacle. He was an unusually large man, topping my six feet by a span. He had a huge powerful looking set of jaws on him, and a nose hooked like an Arab. He dressed every bit the master, and had a stony look about him. His head proved to be trimmed to the skull when he took off his cocked hat. He wiped the inner band with a kerchief and looked up to speak.

"I've made the passage before men, and have no reason to disagree with the quartermaster, except that I'd recommend a hundred and fifty days provision — and rationed from the start. I have in addition to the French charts aboard, some copied charts, slavers charts they are, for the Guinea coast down as far as Wydah. I have nothing south of there, and nothing for the Indies beyond. Them sorts of papers may be had of course from the first vessel we take.

"Before undertaking such a voyage however we'd need to scrape her bottom, and re-caulk her. And we'd need to lay up some spars, and timber fit for a mast or a boom before I'd venture that sail. There are fierce storms that brew in the bight of Africa and sweep across starting up in this time of the year, it is not a voyage to be undertaken lightly I will tell ye. Now as to the question can we make the trip if we have a mind to? This bonnie barky will carry us whither we wish her to, there is no doubt of it.

"The only doubt to be found is in the quality of the men who will serve her. And damn the lot of ye for the lazy pack of good for naught shiftless shit foundries that ye are, with some real sailors and some proper care taken of her, the *Kestrel* will sail in any sea, and show her heels to any dammed ship that swims, God be praised." This was answered by a great spontaneous roar of howling and stomping by the crew.

"Is there a call to make a vote?" Called Corner out of the tumult that greeted the master as he stepped back to the helm with out having once changed his expression.

There was no such call for an immediate vote on the matter, but there did arise a call for refreshment from several quarters. Refreshment meant rum I soon found. So rum, ships bread and one of the Wensleydale cheeses from the *Rachel* were brought to the main deck and all hands lay to.

I was carried along with Candy and his friends and listened to their discussion of the matters at hand — their thoughts seemed echoed by other bits of conversation I overheard. The gist of it being little support for such a risky venture at this time, but general concern over the taking of a good haul and getting profitably rid of the cargo they carried. There was another whose thoughts I was very interested to hear and I turned to look for Reede.

I found him not two steps behind me. He was in conversation with one of the two men who stood with him by Rackham and the little pirate lass Bonny, who looked directly at me. Her look was warm, a little too warm I thought and it brought to mind the warnings I'd received regarding her attentions.

Reede was turned slightly toward me and noticed my movement; he gave me a bright wide grin and said, "You look like a man who's had a very eventful past day young John the carpenter."

"You seem none the worse yourself for keeping such rowdy company."

"God has blessed me with no taste, nor stomach for rum. It gets me all befuddled and giddy early on, and then surly and short tempered later, and then I sleep hard and I wake up most unpleasant, no for my part I stay with good ale — or stout if need be — and I preserve myself sober and with my wits about me for the business at hand."

"What business is that then, Mr. Reede?"

He smiled at me, only I could see the warmth of it. His face was so changeable; it was as though two faces shared the same features. One face was not unpleasant, indeed most handsome, but firm and resolute of cast, the other somehow different in a way that eluded me.

"You have no need to ever call me mister, just call me Reede as my friends and my comrades do. I wish us to be friends and comrades." His gaze was full into mine and most friendly.

"The business at hand is the closing of the account as quickly as possible. It's no secret to any aboard that I wish to make this venture my last, and then take my brass somewhere away from the sea — somewhere where there are green hills, and rivers full of fat trout that belong to them as can catch them and meadows — somewhere I may sit upon my porch of an evening, and smoke cigaros."

He laughed at his own picture, and his laughter took the character lines from his face and for the instant he showed a very young face, very fair to see. "When I were a child," he continued, "we lived in the country for a time," his eyes drifted away to some place only he could see, "it was by a little river and there was a man once who gave me two small trout, just so as would fit in my pockets. He bade me take them right home to mama and to tell no one of them. I remember my mother was very affected by them. We ate them that very night, they were so sweet and good I asked if there were more. My mother cried I remember."

His eyes returned to mine, they were soft at first but then they seemed to turn to flint. "Then I came to know that my friend was called a 'poacher' and that he had risked a great deal to give a poor child a treat, and that all the trout belonged to the lord who owned the waters and all that swam in them, and that they were not for such as we but for his pleasure and his table only."

After a pause, he finally said, "Yes, I want to live where the water is shallow and clear and fresh and cold, and where I can smoke cigaros and where I may eat trout any time I like."

There was a cry from Corner for assembly, a thumping of oars, and the ship's bell was rung again. We reassembled at the waist facing aft; the watch was relieved at this point. One feature of the schooner rig, which endears it to a crew, is its simplicity of operation. We were running on main and fore sails, and the fore staysails. Six men could handle the vessel with ease without going aloft, and so hear and respond to the general points of the meeting.

The condition of our sailing may be judged by the posture of the master. Fetherston was leaned against the stern taffrail with his arms folded across his wide chest enjoying the ride, and watching the sea.

During the time spent in fortifying the crew, the elected officers sat apart in conversation at the bitnacle. The only crewman who spent time there with them was Trinket, who first brought a tray of food, and then stayed, obviously conferred with at several points in their discussions.

Corner brought the meeting back to order with the thumping of the oar, and when he had the attention of all hands he spoke. “The commander and I, and the master have discussed the concerns voiced here today. The worshipful commander will have a plan of action prepared for us tomorrow.

“We will reassemble here at noon tomorrow to hear his plan and pass judgment on it. God preserve the court of free men, the brotherhood of the coast, and this company. May it please you to be dismissed, to whatsoever may entertain such gentleman of fortune.”

Chapter 8

In the House Of Lords

"God preserve us, John, did I promise ye a show or did I not?" Candy's voice broke in brightly upon my thoughts. "Fit for any stage in England say I."

"You are justly known as a man of your word, Candy," I said, for so he was, "and I'll readily admit, that I have never experienced anything like these meetings before. To see a company of such men, strictly ruled by laws of their own device, and where every man signed aboard has an equal say, and an equal vote in all matters; and fashioned so that any member may bring any matter to the consideration of the company, quite remarkable, fascinating really."

He snorted. "Oh, you'll get your fill of such meetings my lad, of that you may be sure. It's the long days of no binding discipline as does it, and then of course ye cannot swing yer fid aboard such a vessel as this without you strike a sea lawyer blind. So then, it follows that every jaw party about the scuttled-butt turns into a meeting of some sort; and every such meeting then stirs the broth for the next one, and so on.

"I've heard tell of crews that wandered about in circles for a month, or more, trying to get a final vote on what sort of flag to have. Still, it can be the opportunity for a strong commander to shine, as I see it, by giving the crew a sense of mission, and stirring the company to follow an agreed plan. Now that Johnny seems to have surrounded himself with a proper house of lords, I think he'll rise to the occasion, and we'll see some real action soon enough."

"House of lords? What do you mean by house of lords?"

"Well, now, every man as signs the articles certainly has an equal voice, and vote, and share of course as ye say, John, but this is a society of men, and hard men, men who are no strangers to battle, and who are hungry for prey. Each one of them will fancy himself the better of any commander who cannot deliver the brass. Now, any commander, who wants to continue as such, will work to surround himself with steady heads, and solid hands, experienced men, men such as will give sound council, and firm support when needed. They are the ones that Johnny's reaching out to now for support and sound council; they become his 'house of lords' d'ye see?"

"His 'party' then you might say?"

"Well as might, but men such as Reede, and Trinket, and McGinnis are not such as will follow any man blindly. A house of lords will also rise out of them as are the real sea-dogs aboard too, them ye'll see as taking the most active part in the management of the vessel — men like Fetherston. And what can ye make of Fetherston? Aye, now there is one as is a real source of power behind Rackham. He is one, as has the dread-respect of every man aboard. He seems as he could be commander at the snap of his fingers, but his mind and heart are in the wind, and in the sky, and the stars, in the art of the sea. He stands firm with Rackham, for now, and it were an awful man indeed who would go up against him. Even Magoon stands clear."

He continued after a moment of thought, "In the end though, John, such as is pirate 'captains' remain so only so long as they provide prey for the account. And Johnny needs to make moves now to fill the coffers, or Magoon will sway the men in the middle enough to be a real challenge to him. These are 'gentlemen of fortune' after all, as they call themselves with only a small smile; and howsoever much they may prattle on about their republics, and all, when all is said and done, it is a society of knaves, and thieves. And a society of knaves, and thieves, must be watched, and guided carefully at all times, lest they fall out amongst themselves, and then into troubles."

"You sailed 'the account' yourself my friend," I said, "and I know that you are no-wise a knave, and cannot think of you as a thief. How did you come to it?"

"Natural enough I guess, like many others I were mustered out after Ryswick, I had twenty-two pounds to me name, and no skills past those of a man-o-war's man.

I had made a reputation for my fists though, being the fleet champion and all, and I thought to make my way as a pugilist. So for two years or so, I made the rounds from Portsmouth, to Bristol and Liverpool, knocking about drovers, porters and stevedores, along with the odd 'ships' champion. Then, thinking of myself as something to behold, I went to Scarborough fair to set up me own booth. It were there then that I met the 'thumper." He cocked his head to look at me, “do ye know why he is called ‘thumper,’ lad?”

“I suppose because he has given so many men a thumping.”

“Nah, though ‘tis true enough, and a fit answer on the face of it. No, ‘tis rather for the sound it makes when you hit him. ‘Tis as if ye hit a barrel of ale, or a swinging carcass of beeve. Just a sort of thump is all ye hear. I were fool enough to come up to scratch for the seventh time. Then he blew out the lamp for me. He is kindness itself, as ye know, bless his heart, and I woke up much later, in his own tent don’t ye know. He cared for me for two days, till I could walk again without wobbling. I worked with him throughout the rest of the year, and went to Bartholomew fair with him, as a sparing partner, and someone to watch the wagers.

We were in Bristol in 1703, just starting to gather students for the very school ye yerself attended when a press gang tapped me on the shoulder, polite as ye please, being as the Lieutenant knew me from the last war. Called me a right ‘cracker jack,” and said I were ‘alone worth the trouble of coming ashore,” treated me decent he did.” His eyes drifted out to the sea, and there was a pause. Candy had never talked to me in quite this manner before.

“Killed later he was, a fine lad, and a fine officer.” His eyes returned to mine. “I were mustered out again in 1713, at the end of the ‘Queen’s War.” I went from there back to sea on a merchant vessel,” here he spit, and his face twisted “and then I were freed from service on them hell ships onto the deck of the good captain Howell Davis, when we were taken by him, and I were called to my first meeting of the brethren.

“Speaking as we have of meetings,” he said with a start, “we’ve both of us got time coming with the commander. I’m past due now, along with Reede, Magoon, Trinket, and the Swede too I think. Anyroad, Rackham sends word to inquire if ye’d be so kind, as to be at his convenience in half an hour or so.” Then he gave me a very serious face, “Rackham will have questions for ye, John, be careful with ye’r answers. Jack’s very cunning with words, he is, so watch also for what’s unsaid.”

Leaving this caution with me, he descended the companionway to the great cabin, and I went below to my berth. Once there I took some time with a basin and soap, so as to present myself as well as I could in the coming interview. It was a discipline drilled into me by both of my parents, and the thumper. ‘Always look your best,’ I was taught, ‘shipshape and Bristol fashion, whether swabbing the heads, splicing the main brace, or fixing the captain's coffee.'

I took the fore hatchway up to the berth-deck a little later, the better to have a look at my new home. The between deck looked for all the world like some Arab camp. Sailcloth and linen and duck of many vintages was hung and tied about, so as to offer some privacy to the bunks, for there were few hammocks. The posts, knees and beams of the vessel were hung about with a variety of weapons and foodstuffs. There were muskets, pistols and swords, and nets full of limes, lemons, oranges and such fruits, and still others that I did not recognize. It was like walking through some strange orchard, and I found my head bobbing from side to side in order to avoid hitting one thing or another as I moved aft.

As I passed the main mast, I came to the area where, on any other vessel, a wooden bulkhead would have separated off the officer's quarters, wardroom and the captain's great cabin. On the *Kestrel* however there was only a screen of duck. As I passed by it to ascend the after hatchway, I heard Reede's voice. He had a very distinctive voice, and it followed me faintly as I went up and onto the weather deck.

I took my time walking along the weather rail; I was rested now, and calmer inside. I began to fully apprehend, and admire the *Kestrel*, whom I would now serve. Rackham had named her well I thought, for she was built indeed very like a lean, fast predatory bird. I wondered, to myself, of her original purpose. There was no doubt she was French built, and quite new, both newly built, and new in design.

I paced off her weather deck at one hundred and twenty feet from spar to sternposts, and marked her beam amidships at twenty-two feet. She had a broad transom stern, with small quarter galleys, and a marked tumblehome from her stern foreward to amidships; this gave her a beam at the water line of twenty-six feet. Beginning amidships, the tumblehome diminished smoothly as you went foreward, until it swept cleanly down into a sharp bow. I estimated her at something like 150 tonne. Her hull design was without precedent for me, and I made note.

She carried the very tall, slender, and sharply raked masts that the French love. One hundred and five feet to the main truck they were, and ninety-five to the fore truck. She was built to show prodigious sail at her topmasts; they were not twigs, but rather they raised up nearly the length of the main masts beneath. As the watch aboard the *Rachel* had noted when we were taken, she also raised topgallant masts on both her main and fore. Withal, she could carry, by far, the most sail I've ever seen on a schooner; and I made note at that time, for the vessel I planned to build for Captain Johnson, when the time came. The *Kestrel* was a splendid vessel.

And she carried a bone in her teeth, as we sailed west by south on a fine quartering wind.

There was no quarterdeck break whatsoever. Her spar-deck was a clear, level, fighting surface fore and aft, broken only by the hatchways and masts. The gunwale was topped, and the deck surrounded, by an unbroken bulwark four feet high, with gun ports that slid open sideways on the port sills, and opened quite wide, in order to allow maximum traverse for the guns. This being rather than the ports being hinged on the upper sill, to swing upward out of the way, as is customary; it was a another curious, and unusual feature. There were heavy bronze locks in place, next her guns, for six sweeps a side, the sweeps themselves were stowed, with the two launches, and several spars, on the gallows amidships between the masts.

Now it is a sailing characteristic of the sloops and schooners, being fore and aft rigged, as they are, that their best sailing is done against the wind. They can sail closer to the wind, by several degrees, then any square-rigged vessel. They can be at some disadvantage when the wind is large abaft, unless they have sea room enough to gybe, and take long reaches before the face of the wind. The top-hamper that the *Kestrel* carried would have her be unusually fast before the wind, more than a match for most square rigged vessels. She was rigged to show either gaff tops or square, depending on the winds. Against the *Rachel* she had to have been making all of twelve knots, close hauled on the bowline, in order to come up so quickly with us. I marveled at the vessel I was forced to serve, and I made note.

"Ahoy, John," came Reede's already familiar voice from behind me, "the commander would be pleased to see you now, but before we go to see him, I want a moment with you."

I drew back from my observations, and prepared my mind for the upcoming interview with Rackham. "Take what time of mine you require, Reede."

"Remember what I said about keeping yourself clear of the charge of piracy, John. Be careful when you speak with Rackham, not just of his questions, but more so of his assumptions."

"Why do you caution me so? What would his purpose be? To lead me into what?"

"He will seek to draw you into our world, to make you part of the crew by association, so that you will more easily fall into the position the Swede came to."

"What do you mean, what position?"

"Hanson entered freely, and naturally into our concerns, he made friends, and his friends brought him into helpful actions during a boarding, actions which would have hung him anyway, having signed the articles or not. I know that you do not want this, and I do not want it for you."

I thought his personalizing the matter to himself was odd at the time, but I put it off to a lingering feeling of responsibility on his part, for having had a role in my abduction. "Reede, you have yourself just now warned me again against making friends among this crew, for fear they would lead me to unlawful actions. You have been very helpful, and kindly, to me and I deeply appreciate it, but I wonder why it is that you have taken such an interest, enough so as to caution me thus, and against your own captain."

He flushed at my words, but I thought less of anger than of some embarrassment. He turned his face away from me for a moment. When he returned his gaze to me, his face was changed yet again. His eyes, and his voice, seemed somehow far away, as if looking upon some other scene entirely.

"You remind me of someone who was once dear to me, John, one who is now gone," His face tightened again, to that countenance he wore in the presence of hard men. I came, later, to think of that look as the 'lion's face. "Come ye now, we must lay below and speak with Rackham. Heed what I've said though. I like you, carpenter, you speak your mind. Rackham also likes those who are well spoken, so long as they do not crowd him. He has a skin far thinner than it may at first seem; if he feels slighted, he is capable of rash bursts of vile temper."

Reede led the way below, and when we arrived at the great cabin he parted the sailcloth screen and we stepped through into the heart of the *Kestrel.* I was immediately struck by the fact that a half dozen or more of the pirates lounging about the cabin space paying varied degrees of attention to the conferences of their commanders, indeed, at least one of the rogues looked to be asleep.

“Welcome, Mr. Tanner, thank you for being prompt,” came Rackham’s high clear voice from under the transom lights. “You can see a joint of cold harness, cheese, and fruit on the trestle, please help yourself as we speak, there is a demijohn of a choice Madeira as well, courtesy of your late employment.” He smiled broadly, and directed me to the foot of the table, “Please, pull up a seat and sit ye down, sir.”

There were a number of kegs and sea chests about, so I picked one as suggested, drew it to the foot of the trestle and sat down. Reede seated himself about midway down the table on my left, next to Trinket and Ben Talmer. McGinnis, Thomas Earl and Patrick Carty sat directly across from them.

Rackham was seated on a chest at the aft end of the table; there was another smaller trestle next to him on his left covered with charts, and I could see several London papers from Captain Lovewell’s duffel were present as well. Corner was seated at the far side of that table with a mulatto helmsman named Holly, who was Fetherston’s favorite and his ears at such meetings. Bonny, was seated on Rackham’s right hand. I took some wine and fruit and waited upon the captain. Four or more of the pirate crew came in behind me and took seats, or flopped to the deck, about the cabin. I took a glass of the Madeira, a biscuit, and a slice of the cold bully beef; it was from the *Rachel’s* stores and best quality. The Wensleydale was safe.

“As the captain of this vessel, Mr. Tanner,” he said, “you can see that I do not have the enforced, lofty and sacred privacy that I’m sure you are used to with other captains, on other vessels. Here every man is free to enter, as he will, with some regard for decorum and civil order of course. Our meetings are always open to any who would observe the actions of their elected officers. I have here before me, your papers, Mr. Tanner. I am suitably impressed with what I’ve read. You have gained broad, and varied experience in a few short years. Your journey-ship and master’s papers, I have noticed, were sponsored under patronage by a ‘Captain’ Charles Johnson, is this the same ‘Captain’ Charles Johnson that the brethren all know of as a prissy little, hunched-back, warty, weasel-faced, black-eyed gallows chaser?”

This was so outrageous, and poetical, an appellation for the captain, that rather than raising my anger, it brought me first to a blinking incredulity, and then into a helpless burst of laughter. I would have embarrassed myself I fear, or choked to death, had I been in mid-bite or swallow at that moment. "If he were present to hear such flattery, Captain, I'm sure he would give this room full of rogues, some useful employment in pulling him from your throat." This was very well received by the room, which echoed with hoots and guffaws.

Rackham's face wrinkled up and he gave a little bleat of high-pitched nasal laughter, he then bit at his hand, still snorting in an honestly gleeful way.

"Yes," he said with a final snigger, "I've heard as much of him myself. I'm right glad to see a fearlessly loyal man, and I can see in you some of the qualities that he praises in your papers. I see also in your papers, a commendation, stating," here his voice rose in pitch and volume so as to carry, "that during a 'late combat with Tunisian corsairs in the middle sea, you proved yourself to be 'uncommonly steady and effective throughout the fight," and that your conduct were 'a cheerfully manly, and hearty encouragement to your comrades.

"These proven qualities of courage and loyalty, combined with steadiness and good humor, are such as any other man may admire. I commend you, sir, and I have mentioned this part of your papers aloud so that the men of the *Kestrel* — with this he bobbed his head toward the pirates present — may know that you have 'stood to it' like a man, and showed sufficient stones, to have gained the attention of your officers."

He glanced up at me from the papers, "If you sign the articles today, I'll make you a corporal of marines right off." I joined wholeheartedly in the gales of laughter that filled the cabin. "Some as told me that Johnson writes a book about our sweet trade," he began again, "a history, as it were, of our business. Is that so Mr. Tanner?"

"Yes. I have been privileged to see some of his notes, and I've heard him relate several of the histories he's followed. One of a pirate named Gow, and the one called Blackbeard for instance, so I know it to be true."

"Are we in it?" He asked it blunt and outright.

"Not to my knowledge. I saw, and heard, no more of the content of his writings than I have said — but I am sure that if your story is not yet included, it soon shall be."

"Gentlemen, whom I trust, have spoken well of ye in all things.

They have assured me, that although you have declined, at present, to sign our articles, ye bear no ill will festering beneath your smile. That you seem to be taking your present position in a cool and manly manner, and that you may be trusted to faithfully serve the vessel, which is our home. Still, sir, the weight of my office requires that I have a personal assurance that such is indeed the case."

"I will personally assure you, that I will serve this barky, if not the company she keeps, faithfully. I am fully aware that my life, like any other aboard her, is dependent upon keeping the vessel secure and seaworthy. I am most jealous of the preservation of my life. In that regard, I do assure you, Captain, of my most cheerful best in attention to her needs."

"I understand, from some, that you have already begun a professional inspection of the vessel." He said with a sort of purr in his voice. I admitted as much.

He leaned forward then, and fixed me with flat, expressionless eyes, and a small smile played about his face. "So then, Mr. Tanner, what think you of re-arming the *Kestrel* with 12 pounders as has been suggested?" The question brought a complete silence to the cabin.

I caught Reede's wide eyes before I answered. "I am no gunner, Captain, and I will have no willing part in the arming of this vessel, but as you have put my life in harm's way by forcing my services, I will comment, only, upon the matter's effect upon the vessel's, and thus my own safety."

I cleared my throat. "I believe the *Kestrel* was built all of a piece, Captain, and that her armament was very carefully, and most particularly, included in the builder's calculations of her trim, and her sailing properties. Roughly calculated, she carries now about seventy-eight hundredweight in cannon on each broadside. Such a re-arming as suggested would bring that to well over twelve hundred weight a side, and so add over ten thousand pounds above the waterline. As the vessel's carpenter, I cannot recommend such a re-arming."

"What think ye then of fewer 12 pounders, say, five per side?" He asked me.

"I am not a gunner, Captain, thus I could not advise you on the relative value of one set of cannon against the other. As I have said, the structure and sea-worthiness of the vessel is my only concern. I will not be drawn thus, in to advise you, Captain, in what armament to use in your thievery."

He first looked like a man about pitch a fit, then sat back and sighed. "Reede warned me that you would take an obstinate, obdurate stand regarding your position as a forced man." He shook his head ruefully, and leaned forward to fix me with a jaundiced eye.

"I will humor you in this, for now, sir, because you are young and bold, a man as seems to have no knots in his keel. I like you carpenter, and I take ye truly for a stout fellow, but do not mistake me, sir, I do caution you, I have the power to bring you to heel if needs be, or to cast you over the side, if you so truly wish to win at a battle of wills, that you would prefer to swim ashore."

He came smoothly about to a new tack, ""Now then, the master has said that the vessel sails somewhat crank, and he insists that if we do not shift the cargo, and stow it proper, there is a real danger of our broaching in a blow. Moreover, he is insisting that now as we have a proper carpenter aboard, a thorough inspection of the vessel is long required. So then, carpenter, for the safety of the vessel, I order you to remove cargo as required from the hold, in order that you may inspect all of the interior of the vessel's hull. Mr. Fetherston wishes that you will start in the foreward compartments.

"Further, I order you to do, and to supervise others in doing, such repair and caulking as you may deem necessary; and then to re-stow the cargo in such a manner as to secure it from any water damage, or any shifting that may effect the trim of the craft.

"Mr. Corner will further advise ye on what goods as will require to be unloaded in a hurry; he and master Fetherston will have the final decision at all times. Reede will work with you, and help with the crew. Mr. Fetherston will consult with you regarding the desired trim. You will have such aid as is required to shift the cargo, and produce the oakum you need for caulking. Do you understand me, sir?

"Aye, Captain."

"Mr. Fetherston is quite hot about this, and you'll soon learn that when Mr. Fetherston gets hot about something, the crew gets more sailor like. You'll get all the help you need to do the job smartly, and I mean smartly. Inquire of Mr. Corner as you find need for further hands."

With this he stood up, spread his arms with a sweeping gesture and sang out in a great hearty voice, “I see we already have a stout looking group of the brethren present, who have volunteered by coming in to join our discussion. Excellent, let’s see now,” he made a great show of the counting, “six, seven, eight, Snowden I see you there, yes, thank you Dowd and Percy. I think that might be a good number to set you to work with. Will that number be sufficient for your present needs, do you think, sir?” He asked. I nodded.

“Excellent then, Reede, take these ‘gentlemen of fortune,’ ” he indicated the eight who did not slip out quickly enough when the talk turned to labor, “and follow after the carpenter.” The laughter of the House of Lords followed us as we parted the duck and stepped through to return to the berth-deck.

Reede turned back to me. “We may as well lay topside by way to the forward hold, and enjoy a little more of this fine day before we are in the dark,” he rounded on the grumbling gang we led, “don’t you swabs go wandering off as we travel the deck, I know who you are, damn ye. I’d as soon set Fetherston after ye as spit.”

He led the way up and onto the spar deck, we passed down the starboard rail, it was the lee side in a lovely fair quartering wind. Aloft, I could see the Swede directing men in the rigging, and others tarring the main shrouds. As we passed the waist I saw Magoon, with Stevens, Quick and some others, inspecting the mountings of the larboard guns; he looked up to see us pass and never so much as nodded, though Reede bowed the head a bit, and touched his finger to his brow.

We started down the forward hatchway. Reede stopped at the orlop, and gathered the, now seven men, with us together.

“Where’s Snowden, the slippery sod?” He said, almost sweetly.

Chapter 9

La Bahia de Manteca

We were three days under sail before we reached the coast of Cuba, and sighted the Sierra Maestras, which loomed some three leagues off of our starboard quarter. And then as a bloated violet sun sank upon its face in the western sea, we sailed goose wing on a strong following wind into the Windward Passage. Our course thus set us upon the first step of Captain Rackham's plan.

Upon the day following my interview with the captain and the general meeting of the company, as planned, the company was once more brought together at the waist directly after the master took the noon sightings. The company was brought to attention by the insistence of the quartermaster and his bell, and to the thumping of his oar upon the deck. The man McGinnis also added the call to quarters on his boatswains pipe.

"Gather up ye gentlemen of fortune," Corner cried out, "gather up, give ear and pay attention to the business of the company. The commander as he promised has prepared a plan to bring more specie to the account. In this plan he has conferred with myself, Mr. Fetherston and others of the court of free men. We are all in agreement that it is a sound plan and we bring it forward to you for your approval, amendment or rejection."

Captain Rackham, who had been circulating amongst the company greeting shaking hands smiling spending time with Magoon and Quick and Percy, prominently spending time with Fetherston and Trinket, stepped out into the center of the main deck and was thus surrounded by a ring of excited and eager faces, thus comprised of his company.

"Gentlemen, brothers and mates, no captain ever looked out upon a better or more jolly crew," he said taking time for a broad sweep of the faces surrounding him. "We have skilled men aboard, men skilled at war, fierce and fearless men, men who are hungry for riches and ready to take back what is rightfully theirs from the society that has spurned them and used them and robbed them of their youth and freedom." Here he alluded to those men who were pressed into service against their will, “I myself am no less hungry then thee brothers; and, now that we have sufficient of able seaman aboard to keep us sharp, and a master carpenter aboard to care for our barky, I am prepared to share with the company a plan which I have thought of many times and am now prepared put to the company for action.”

There was the thumping and the roaring and the hoots and shouts and cheers that I had come to expect. The bodhran rattled and rumbled, the fiddle scratched discordantly and the piper piped. Rackham smiled benignly, and lifted his hands to still the raucous display.

“I propose that we set sail immediately for Manteca, and once there that we send Trinket with a party ashore to make contact with the House of Vasquez and that arrangements be made with that fine house for the selling of our cargo in toto, saving only that which is needed for the sustenance of the men and the security of the barky — excepting those arms and pieces that we may trade to the Maroons for food — we may then water at Davis Cove while treating with them. I propose then, that once we are watered and victualed we sail south to The main and harry the daygos for their silver.”

The company fairly erupted in approval; pistols were drawn and fired into the air; the bodhran, pipe and fiddle played wild and unmusical. It was a display of the deep visceral hatred for the Spanish inculcated into these men by years of war, I think any plan which would bring them into conflict with this decade’s old foe, and perennial source of stolen riches, would have been so greeted.

Candy came up alongside me, even as the tumult turned into men dancing the jigs and reels common to the sea. ”Ye see there, John, the work of the House of Lords, our Rackham is indeed a master at bringing order out of such a crew, and then filling them with wild dreams of fat Spanish silver ships for the taking, it being the proper season for a treasure ship or two to gather in Maracaibo prior to sailing to Portobello to form convoy for Spain and all.”

”These will be armed ships then, ready to defend themselves,” I said, “not fat slow merchantmen crewed by tired, ill fed, ill paid, ill treated men with no reason on God’s earth to risk their lives in defense another man’s riches.”

”No Spaniard will give in to us without a fight you may be assured.”

Reede came alongside just then, "You may indeed be sure of it, John," he said. "I've fought them on land in Flanders and I've fought them on the sea. The Spanish are fierce and proud. There will be blood."

Fetherston's brass voice cut through above the noise, "Avast ye damned monkeys," he roared," belay yer prancing and get back to your proper places, ye who are on watch return to your stations, ye who are below to serve with the carpenter in trimming the vessel gather up with Reede there by the hatch. Mr. Corner will join ye below shortly to make a manifest of those items to be sold at Manteca."

As I was learning, when Fetherston spoke men jumped.

Two days of our sailing found me in the dark hold of the *Kestrel* cramped, sweaty, dusty, constantly moving cargo weaponry and stores all to satisfy Fetherston's demands. In the beginning of our labors the vessel seemed to ride hard on the sea, bucking and jumping like an overloaded carriage on a bumpy road. At the end of our trials the singing of the sea along the hull of the *Kestrel* was testimony to our efforts and Fetherston's skills.

The hardest labor we came under was in the shifting of two 3-pound field pieces broken down to all their limber and carriage. We were unable to lift them safely so we needed to slide them along the keelson, once they were settled in place, one on either side of the keelson just forward the beam, Fetherston was at last happy with the trim of the vessel.

Magoon came below several times, as armorer and gunner for the vessel his interest was in the storage of the shot lockers, swivels, powder and langrage, his dark presence only made the work more unpleasant. He seemed always to be glaring at Reede and me in a particularly baleful and threatening manner; Reede for his part stayed close to me through these times.

As I think of it now, Reede always seemed to be close to me.

Apart from sweating and cursing I spent time observing the men that I worked with. I was struck by the ordinariness in the men that I saw. Some like Quick were recognizably dockside thugs, men as I was used to seeing along the Quay sides of Bristol, Marseille or Acre; others like Dowd and Snowden seemed as normal as cobbler's apprentices or farm boys; these having been press ganged into the Kings service. They were tie-mates, men of war's man, messmates devoted to one another in a manly way.

During breaks in our labor, while topside, I had occasion to speak with Reede in regard to both Fetherston and Magoon. It was obvious that Magoon was a much-feared man; yet, in the presence of Fetherston he seemed meek as a lamb.

The respect in which Reede, and indeed the company in general, held the master was evident at all times and when I asked about him Reede was only too happy to relate his story.

"Ah, Fetherston, now there is a story to break one's heart, John, a story somewhat like my own."

"His family were penniless ex cottagers living in Edinburgh's undergrounds, his father taking any menial work that was available to feed his wife and son. A two schilling debt sent his father to die in debtor's prison, and later he saw his mother hanged for stealing bread to feed her child. There is no Mercy for the poor in Scotland but plenty who will crow their Christian twaddle.

"As to the man and the master born out of that cauldron, I've come upon none better in my travels. He ran away from the workhouse he was assigned to at 10 years old, and on the docks at Edinburgh found his way onto a merchantman as a cabin boy. He later fell in with the famous privateer Jean Bart who took him under his wing and from that association learned the skill of navigation — at which he has few peers. He seems to live and breathe the sea, and the wind.

"It is rumored that he bears a Viking crystal which allows him find the sun even on a cloudy day. He is as fierce as he looks and yet gentle at heart a stout friend and true. He has taken a shine to you, John, and that is a very good thing indeed."

"I'm right glad to hear that as I have noticed that even Magoon steps aside for him; and speaking of Magoon, I can understand the dreadfulness which he brought on board the *Rachel* as being part of cowing the crew into submission but I do not understand why I have so obviously attracted his ire, nor do I understand the obvious tension between you and he."

Reede laughed. "And, John, it was just such a laugh that purchased Magoon's untiring anger toward me.

"Magoon is a strange man, very patriotic in his own way, he stood up freely and took the King's schilling right enough — and the King never had a more loyal servant. He learned the gunners trade from the best the Royal Navy had to offer and no vessel could ask for a better armorer. His fault lay in his stars. Magoon is a famous sodomite, John, and sodomy is a hanging offense in the Royal Navy.

"He came under suspicion, and found that he must needs dessert the life he loved or dance on the air. Freed from the disciplined life that made a man of him, he became the feral dog as ye see him now. He is a truly dangerous man and you would do well to stay clear of him."

"Laughing in the face of such a dangerous man seems ill advised."

"The truth is that I was not laughing at him. Rather my laugh was drawn from me as a result of the interview I just finished moments before with Rackham and Bonny. Shortly after I had to come aboard and signed the articles some question had arisen in the captain's mind as to the relationship between Bonny and me — the question was answered to Rackham's satisfaction. It were the circumstances of that meeting which still amused me as I came on deck.

"Truth be known, Magoon was most solicitous of me prior to our meeting on deck that night. He came up to me like a puppy; he touched my arm and asked if I would share a tankard with him. His meaning was clear enough to me and considering the interview I just came from, I could not contain my laughter. He wished death to me with his eyes and never taking his eyes from my face he backed away into the darkness, from that moment till now he has hated me as much as he once desired me."

"I've heard of such things, Reede, but they are foreign to my nature and I have no direct knowledge of them, and I fail to see why Magoon has settled on me as an object for his anger."

"It was hard enough on poor Magoon when he imagined either Rackham or Bonny as the source of his discomfiture, they of course being untouchable to him and his rage; however, you who seem to be the center of my attention — which you are as I am responsible for your actions while you are forced to our company — are an easily available target for his frustration and anger. He imagines that you have become my nanny boy."

Here Reede laughed as if he would burst, a bright ringing laughter.

The course which Fetherston followed was a circuitous one keeping well to the north of the most traveled sea lanes in order to avoid being brought to the attention of naval patrol vessels. Thus I had a week's time for careful inspection of the *Kestrel* stem to stern, the bilge to the main truck. She was a solid tight seaworthy vessel built for speed and under full sail I believed she could show her heels to any vessel afloat.

I also had opportunity to observe the functioning of the crew in regard to the handling of the vessel. The bulk of the crew was indeed made of lubbers and waisters; these being such a men as are capable of hauling on a sheet and following the directions given to them by the real sailors aboard. These being such as carried able or ordinary ratings from either the Royal Navy or the merchant service, Trinket and Dowd, the Swede, Candy, McGinnis and of course Reede carried able ratings, while Snowden, Carty, Dobbins McKay and several others carried papers as ordinary seamen.

Fetherston was careful in calling the watches, so that each watch consisted of one or two of the able rates, one in the tops and one forward. There was no regimented calling of the watches as there might have been on a naval or merchant vessel, rather after an appropriate number of turnings of the glass Fetherston would call out the names he wished on watch and so it was done without dispute.

I was also able during this time to observe Reede in his natural element high in the top hamper, his being as graceful active and as at home as a squirrel in the trimming and setting of the main top and gaffe sails. He seemed to delight in the pitch and roll of the vessel, riding at seemingly ease the topmast spar, I sometimes could faintly hear him singing to himself while aloft.

There was some grumbling amongst the crew regarding in the idea of taking a prize or two while we were on the way. This came to a head on the second occasion that sail were sighted on the horizon and the *Kestrel* under orders of the commander backed away from pursuit. Many a pirate commander was removed from his office due to such reticence in closing on potential prey. Several like Magoon, Quick and Percy became disruptive over this caution and thus again the company was brought to meeting by the quartermaster. Being called to account in this matter Rackham appeared before the crew with Fetherston and Corner and Trinket at his side. Rackham appeared wrathy and ill disposed for the meeting, he carried a brace of pistols in his sash. He had once been quartermaster under Charles Vane, and voted captain of that crew when Vane was disposed as commander having been accused of cowardice due to a reluctance to close with a vessel he appreciated as a man-of-war. This circumstance was on Rackham's mind and he was prepared to challenge to the death any man who accused him of cowardice.

"Does any man here accuse me of cowardice or dereliction?," Rackham asked with a treacly tone in his voice, notwithstanding the audible click as he cocked one of the pistols in his sash.

"God's breath no man could accuse you of such, Captain," cried a voice from the pack of men, "but what harm in taking a prize or two as we sail about in circles?

"What harm? What harm indeed? Gentlemen we are about the business of slipping quietly into Butter Bay a few days hence with no alarm having been made as to our presence, nor the business which we are upon, so that we may meet quietly with the house of Vasquez in order to offload stolen goods and make arrangements to meet and trade with the rebels and the Maroons that so sorely vex his majesty's government of the island — which government of course frowns upon these activities.

"We carry a belly full of dunnage dammit. We carry cheese, we carry bolts of cloth, we carry furnishings; we will be damn lucky to get a third of their value from Vasquez. Should we risk an alert to our presence in order to plunder a fishing boat, or another small merchant man carrying a cargo of cheese and bolts of cloth and furnishings, when there is Spanish silver to pursue?

"Now I and your officers have provided you with a plan to fill our account with Spanish silver and unless we can slip unnoticed into and out of Butter Bay that plan will be brought to naught, stealth and secrecy is what is needed now. Mister Fetherston has assured me that he can put us into Manteca two nights hence with none but us the wiser.

"Upon our arrival there we will lower away a boat with Trinket and some turtle hunters aboard, they will make such assignations as are necessary to pursue the next step in our plan. Now stand to your duties, such as they are, and dream such dreams of wealth as ye may."

He turned away, and then turned back. "Ye are a free company, A company as may decide for itself to either work the plan to which it had agreed, or to repudiate its officers and make its own damn plan — do as thou wilt."

I had by now come to realize that the rogues looked on these meetings as entertainment, as theatre — as well as business — and that they honestly looked forward to Rackham's declamations. They knew that Rackham once sailed with Vane, and England and Davis, and that he was an experienced and proven commander. The greater part of the crew, I believe, looked on Magoon and his cadre as a goad, useful in keeping their officers, howsoever trustworthy, on their toes.

There was indeed a coarse honesty to their humor as they roared and thumped hooted and rattled their weapons in applause.

There was a boisterous and rowdy celebration that evening, a keg of rum was scuttled as well as a great deal of ale, the company was to say the least exuberant. The talk were all flushed hot with the desire to get at the daygos and their silver. In the midst of it Corner called out loudly for Candy and me.

"Avast there, Master Carpenter, and ye good Agamemnon. I hear ye both are celebrated masters of the pugilism, what's say ye to a demonstration of the art?"

Candy and I looked at each other, then to Rackham who smiled and nodded.

With great amusement and merriment the crew set apart a circle for us, some 12 feet in circumference with a scratch line in the center. Candy and I striped down, stretched and squatted and went about putting on a show of our preparation to box.

"Gar! Look at the great hairy ape that poor man must grapple with…terrible." Came one call." God help the poor old Weezer he's split his drawers on that last squat." Came another, "I seen a fight oncet at Scarborough fair that'd fair freeze yer blood, follow came out looking as he'd been kicked several times by a horse, fair fainted away on it I did."

As I squared with Candy, once again I came to respect him as a man and a boxer. He was squat and powerful and as I've said I would not be happy to square off with him except for sparring. We bobbed and weaved and boxed and explained and taught as we did so and a great goodtime was had by all involved. All lingering tensions across the deck faded away in good fellowship.

When darkness fell Fetherston called the watch and most of the crew stumbled below deck while the few stayed topside — several simply unable to navigate the hatchway — and some approached Candy and me for individual instruction in the art; these included young Harwood and Peters, the refuse of the Bristol docks to whom Captain Lovewell gave a new life.

Both of these young men were eager to establish themselves in the eyes of the crew as truly man among men. Young Harwood showed real promise; he was wiry and quick with his hands. I was also pleased that he had taken up with Fetherston and was learning navigation from the master. Young Peters unfortunately fell in with Magoon and was learning the gunners trade, although I was afraid he might be learning other less wholesome things from black Mike.

The bright morning sun found our course due south under reefed main and fore with the top hamper bare, save for the presence of a man on each top spar with a glass scanning the horizon. Running thus gave the company a slight advantage in seeing before being seen; it was in this condition that the *Kestrel* was first been by the watch on the *Rachel*.

Rackham called the company together, and after Fetherston had called the new watch, called for quiet. "The master has assured me that we will raise the coast of Jamaica in the late afternoon this very day." This announcement was met with cheers from the assembled company. "Mr. Corner, and Mr. Fetherston will be assigning work crews to those tasks which needs be accomplished ere we set the turtle hunters off this night."

A gang of men under the direction of Trinket were worked at constructing several long bumpers made of rolled sailcloth; McGinnis and another man muffled the oarlocks on one of the two launches. A casting net and a long pike with a hook like a crozier were brought up from storage and placed on a long pad of sailcloth in the longboat.

"All the correct gear for proper turtle hunters," said Reede who came up close to my larboard quarter, "there is no better cover of course then having a turtle in the boat with ye, and so Trinket will keep a sharp watch for one as he guides them along the coast to the proper spot, with luck they may even bring one back for the pot."

"Proper spot?"

"Aye John, the house of Vasquez keeps several spots — families really — along the coast where such as we may safely put ashore and make contact with friendly people who will send notice of our arrival ahead."

Six bells of the afternoon watch brought a cry from the main top, "land ho two points off the larboard bow." And by the end of the first dogwatch the green coast of Jamaica lay a league off our larboard beam. Rackham called all hands below and as the setting sun touched upon the horizon Rackham addressed the assembled company.

"We have now entered into enemy waters. We will be lowering a boat within the hour and I command ye to complete silence upon this vessel. Only the watch as called by Fetherston and those men going ashore as well as those assigned to their launching will be on the spar deck, all the rest of ye shall remain here below. After the launch is well away we shall work our way upwind till we are once again in open waters, at that time ye may come up from below, but by God's teeth ye shall content ye with quiet talk."

With Reede at my side I witnessed activities on the weather deck, Candy was part of the group of men assigned to lower the longboat into the sea. The longboat carried a black lamp, and a series of signals were agreed to by the away party. Each man going ashore was allowed a pistol and a dagger, no more.

All five were dressed in veritable rags so as to appear as the poorest specimens possible — notwithstanding the fact that the longboat was highest quality. Assigned into Trinket's hands was a parcel, which Reede told me contained a manifest of those goods, which the company wished to sell, along with those items, which the company might seek, in simple trade.

As the blackness of night engulfed the *Kestrel*, and a scattering of pinpoints of light appeared off of our larboard bow, the sailcloth bumpers were lowered into the water then drawn back up and secured. With much quiet cursing and grunting but with no thumps or crashes the longboat was lowered over the bumpers into the sea.

As the longboat pulled silently away Trinket tossed a jaunty salute to the quarterdeck.

Rackham returned it.

Chapter 10
The Maroons

Upon the second night following, about the end of the first watch we received the agreed signal from those who went ashore. Receipt was acknowledged and aboard preparations were made to rendezvous with the launch. The able rated men, most of them Jack tar, men as knew the drills needed for the sailing of an armed ship, had this process smoothly in hand — teaching as they worked.

The agreed series of blinking codes from the black lamps brought the launch alongside the *Kestrel* during the middle watch. The canvas bumpers were lowered dipped thus drenched and hauled up and made secure.

The tide was running that night and the sea was choppy so the retrieval of the longboat went not as smoothly as its launching. The efforts of rowing against a rising tide and an unsettled sea were evident in the exhaustion of the crew of the launch, thus they were instantly fortified with rum and brought below deck for comfort.

Trinket, looking nonetheless for his nights work as coxswain, hurried below in the company of Rackham and Corner. On deck the same crew which lowered and launched the mission stowed and secured the longboat, while the watch under the direction of Fetherston hoist full the main and fore courses, and on a strong land breeze set sail nor' west from the island.

There was little sleep that night among the crew, the four men who did the prodigious rowing were plied by all for news of their venture; these men, Cole, Howard, Fenis and Eton had little to offer, having been sequestered at the fishing cabin of one of the Vasquez employees for the entire time the group had was ashore, and only Trinket going into the town proper to meet with the family Vasquez.

For their part they had no complaint save for the constant smell associated with the rendering of lard, from whence the town and the bay takes its name. They were treated with every kindness and well fed while kept out of sight, as well as the longboat being covered with fishing nets and duck, the time.

Sometime after the calling of the morning watch Trinket at last came out from the great cabin, a rosy smile upon his face. Good morrow, Mates," he cheerfully greeted those assembled and waiting for him. "All is in good order for us to proceed upon the next step of the captain's plan. Ye would do well to get ye to rest as tomorrow there will be hard sailing to be done and Rackham will call the company together at the noon sighting for to make the results of our venture ashore known to all."

As was his constant practice Reede escorted me to the carpenter's berth on the orlop, and bid me a good night before ascending up the forward hatch to his own berth.

I wondered once more as I drifted off to sleep of Reede's constant solicitation.

The sea remained choppy and the wind veered and backed fitfully through the forenoon watch, delivering several brief rainsqualls throughout. Difficult sailing to be sure.

At the turn of the afternoon watch Fetherston with Young Harwood in attendance took the noon sightings, and Fetherston again called a watch made up of the most experienced men aboard. Due to the unsettled conditions on the weather deck Rackham called the company together below deck. There was a great shuffling and expectation as Corner called the company to order.

"Give list gentlemen of fortune and yer full attention to the business at hand. We have in hand a more generous offer for our cargo then I anticipated."

It would appear that the luxuries that we shipped the board from the *Rachel* are greatly desired by the landed gentry of the island, fine quality linens, woolens, wines and cheeses from the homeland being much desired; so that I am pleased to report that the account has been pleasingly fattened by the offer made by Vasquez. We have now only to deliver the goods to Vasquez at Bloody Bay five days hence."

And what of the shares Corner?" cried a man from the back.

"When our business with Vasquez is completed, each share will stand at a few bob over 300 pounds I am pleased to report."

This was received with great approbation by all hands, and then Rackham stepped forward with an agitated and brusque manner about him.

"It is well that ye are all pleased with these as yet unlaid eggs mates. As we will now enter into a period of hard work — ye remember hard work do ye not — and it promises to be hard work done in dangerous water for such as we.

"South of Lucia, there is a sheltered cove, known to Howell Davis and through him to me, and into which flows a fine clearwater river. Two days hence we are to meet there with certain of the Maroons in order to refresh our water butts and take on jerked beef and plantain for our endeavor. We will deliver to the Maroons two-dozen firelocks, forty good flints and a keg of powder for their troubles. They will provide such security as may be needed on the land and will assist us in filling the butts and loading them upon our longboats.

"You there, Mr. Carpenter, when we are finished here, take such men as ye will to help ye and reassemble a half dozen barrels and some additional butts from the staves and hoops available in stowage forward."

Rackham went on to explain a timetable of arrival at a place called Bloody Bay at the north end of Negril in order to rendezvous with the smugglers. The actual transfer of cargo to the smugglers would take place in the broad bay of Negril, as there we would find sufficient open water in case our activities were apprehended by any patrol vessel. He then dismissed the company and I turned to descend the aft hatchway to see to the cooperage required of me.

Reede immediately stepped forward, along with McGinnis, Dowd and Snowden to offer their assistance in the needed cooperage. Over the next two days of sail I was once again in the hold, sweating as we reconstructed the half dozen barrels with lids for dry storage, and the same number of 10 gallon butts for additional water.

At noon on the second day following we came upon the narrow mouth of a deep Cove near the extreme northwest of the island, and a bright red pendant was run up the main, twice dipped then run up again.

Rackham now was agitated; he was no longer commander he was now captain and his orders were to be meticulously obeyed. He ordered that the sweeps be brought topside, and that larboard and starboard have a murderer in place on a swivel. He commanded that we be friendly, but that we be alert and watchful.

We were a cable off of the mouth of the cove when several black men appeared from the forest and waved a blue pendant in a manner I took to be prearranged. Fetherston brought the vessel into the cove and maneuvered about until the bow of the *Kestrel* faced its mouth; main and fore flaked and an anchor dropped. We were a pistol shot from the shore.

Smartly limbered, the longboats were lowered one on each side of the vessel, and manned. Trinket took the tiller of the lead boat, and McGinnis the other. They pulled briskly away, each going to a separate side of the mouth of the river.

As the longboats drew up at the mouth of the river and tied off in waist deep water, they were each greeted by about a dozen black people, both men and women it appeared.

The crews, with the help of the Maroons, quickly unloaded the empty ten gallon butts and moved upstream afoot, each man rolling a butt before him to where the Maroons indicated the water would be fresh and not brackish. Upon their filling, the butts were rolled back in the same manner to be loaded into the waiting longboats.

As the longboats tied off to begin their work several long canoes pulled away from the shore laden with tightly woven sacks of jerked and dried meat as well as plantain and various root vegetables as are common to the island.

"Akee, Jicama and Papa — and several bags of rice I'll warrant," said Reede who had come up behind me," all will need to be stowed in the dry barrels that we made else the rats will make short work of it for us."

"Any which them as escapes the stew pot." said Trinket, who came up with Reede. His comment was greeted with laughter by all who heard it, and a scowl from Hollis who served as cook for the company.

Rackham was not as sanguine, and paced the deck in an agitated manner." We will be the rats here if even a small patrol vessel sights us in this cull," he said." It's not like the old days when these coasts were friendly to us and a vessel might come into a cove like this to careen and scrape the hull without worry."

The canoes pulled up alongside the *Kestrel* and the foodstuffs were hauled aboard and shifted below to storage in the waiting barrels. The muskets were passed down and each one was inspected, its lock dry snapped and the ramrod inserted down the barrel. The bag of flints was opened and each flint carefully inspected, one shook a little of the powder from the keg into the palm of his hand and then tasted it. They remained with us — no words having been exchanged — until the loaded longboats pulled out from shore.

The canoes then pulled swiftly away from us and returned to the shore, where they and their crews and the rest of the Maroons disappeared into the forest from whence they first appeared.

The transfer of the water butts aboard and down to storage in the hold took some little time as each full 10 gallon butt weighed in at about 10 stone. When the water and foodstuffs were properly stowed preparations were made to work the *Kestrel* out of her vulnerable position in the cove.

The anchor was raised and the sweeps were deployed and with much the same grunting and cursing with which the pirates greeted any physical exertion; the vessel began to gain way. At the mouth of the cove Fetherston ordered the main and fore courses raised. Once we were well clear of the cove he ordered hands aloft to set the topsails, and as the night engulfed us we caught the land breeze and sailed away into the dark open sea.

Later that night, as we rode the swells three leagues off of Negril I inquired of Trinket in regard to the Maroons.

They are the descendants of escaped slaves," he told me," and other slaves released to the wild by the Spanish — as a gift of generosity to the new masters of Jamaica — when Penn took the island for the crown. They are fierce and independent and a major vexation to the government, their insistence upon their freedom and independence and all, and there is as ye might say a constant state of war against them — to one degree or another. There is already talk of mounting a major campaign against them.

"There is a loose confederacy among all of the villages, war on one and you war on all. Their great strength is in the Blue Mountains North of Kingston; their current main chief is called Cudjoe, a formidable piece of work. Later we are agreed to deliver those three pounders below to him for gold, to this smaller western group today we delivered muskets and powder. If their women had caught sight of the calicos in our hold there'd have been hell to pay. They'll later pay dear to Vasquez for the same cloth."

The following two days we spent coasting the island. There was much work to be done in the hold to ensure the efficient removal of those items to be unloaded to Vasquez. I knew that once so much was removed there would be another bit of work to be done to trim the vessel. Reede as always at my side in any task and two other men, waisters Bodie and Syms

Above us we could hear the rumble of the gun carriages as Magoon drilled his gun captains and their gun crews in the speedy recovery and loading of the nine pounders. I could hear Magoon's harsh voice and bellowing curses.

Since coming aboard, I had no contact with Magoon to speak of except in passing and his one-day in and out of the hold previously. He had never ceased to glare at me even then. The majority of the crew was civil to me — indeed there was a cadre centered on Trinket and Reede who are quite friendly to me — it being the cadre that followed after Magoon who were openly hostile to me. The man Quick indeed was as good as his name for insulting comments and bodily noises for my consideration.

So it was that I was not prepared for Magoon's sally on me that day. I came up the forward hatch and made my way aft seeking the quartermaster to report and receive instruction regarding the stowage which I believe was finished, being most scrupulous in avoiding the guns and their crews. I would never have taken such a course had the vessel been in action; nonetheless Magoon's active assault on me was unwarranted.

"You bloody bastard," I heard him yell as he shoved me bodily so that I stumbled and nearly fell down the aft hatch. "Ye've fouled me gun crews about their work ye damned nanny boy," adding a kick for emphasis. There was as close to a dead silence as possible across the deck. Magoon's hand fell to the hilt of the long Italian dagger in his belt. "Ye have naught to say you piss whelp?"

Quick, and another of Magoon's men fell in at his side; both of them had the look of mastiffs eager to be loosed.

I saw Dowd and Snowden, who serviced the number one gun, give a start and come to full attention, several others as well. As one may imagine I was loath to take such treatment from any man, but at the last I realized that I was a prisoner amongst such dangerous and unpredictable man that any action on my part would result in a quick thrust of a dagger and a quick heave over the side.

I'm ashamed to say that my retort was to scurry down the aft hatch to the music of curses and laughter.

Later after an inspection of the hold by both Corner and the master, Reede confronted me. "Why did ye no tell me of Magoon's outrage of you earlier?"

"Why in God's name would I bring such a matter to your attention? I am a prisoner here; am I to be seen running to you for protection when it is your quarrel with Magoon that brought me his attention, and with such a man as Magoon afoot I am in as much danger when I close my eyes to sleep. Am I indeed your nanny boy?"

I was taken aback by Reede's reaction. I saw in a flash both his faces, the one hard and set, the other look exposed something else, only now, looking back have I come to understand.

"I meant no such offense. God's truth, John, but you are my charge as a forced man and I am responsible for not only your conduct but for your safety as well, and I do not wish you to be outraged or abused by any member of the crew. So long as your duties are faithfully observed both Rackham and the master are in agreement on this matter. You are correct that the matter between myself and Magoon has complicated matters, but remember ye that Magoon attacked ye first on the deck of the *Rachel*."

"That's true, and I remain grateful for your stepping into that situation, but I will not run to you for protection, neither will I take any action that sets me at odds with any group aboard this vessel. I am grateful for the friendliness that you and Trinket have shown me, but my life hangs in the balance here. I will do what is necessary to my survival, and act in a manner that will not inflame the situation."

Later that day, at the end of the second dogwatch Candy broached the situation with Magoon.

"Ye do well to avoid Magoon in every instance," Candy said to me. "His attack on you today is the talk across the deck. His men, of course, accuse you of cowardice and deliberate interference in the drilling of the gun crews. Those who know such things, Dowd, Snowden and some others who are sympathetic to your situation know better. If you had gone against Magoon today he and his men would have stuck you a few times and heaved you overboard. Oh yes, there would have been a fuss over his actions but in the end ye'd have been as dead."

"I don't understand Reede in all of this," I said. "I understand that he is responsible for me, at least for my actions, but I do not understand his solicitousness for my well-being. Is he truly responsible for my safety?"

"I've spoken of this with both Trinket and Bonny. They both seemed oddly amused by the situation. I will admit I was sum taken aback by their attitude — I thought Anne Bonny would split a side laughing. Rackham as well seems amused by Reede's attachment to ye."

We sat in silence for a bit worrying down some of the jerked meat and after a few moments he added. "Did ye make note that Magoon's attack on you came at the only time that ye were alone on deck without the presence of Reede or Trinket or another of the officers? As I've said, there are many aboard who are sympathetic to your situation. You have acquitted yourself well and done your duty by the barky, they understand the importance of having a master carpenter aboard this vessel once we attack a truly armed prey, they will do their best to see you safe, for their own safety later if for no other reason."

I slept no better that night for this assurance.

I was awakened early in the morning watch by a sudden increase in activity on the deck above and the harsh cries of: "Sail ho, sail ho! Off the starboard beam, well-off hull down and making signal."

Chapter 11
The House of Vasquez

The great Bay of Negril lay on the extreme west, or leeward, of the island of Jamaica. It stretches some three leagues down the coast, with Bloody Bay taken as a bite out of its northern most limit. It is framed by a great savannah that stretches its entire length and is at least a league in-depth before meeting higher ground and the forest beyond. It is a wild and forlorn coast well away from the shipping lanes, and with the open sea readily available for maneuver and escape it made a perfect rendezvous for such business as of the *Kestrel* was about.

At the start of the forenoon watch a blue pennant was run up on the main and a red pennant on the fore, and then Rackham called the company to attention at the waist.

"Look ye sharp today lads, I want men aloft with glasses throughout our business, keeping close watch north and south for any patrol. Mr. Magoon I wish the guns loaded with grape and primed as well as swivels readily to hand. We will meet several boats today in the employ of the House of Vasquez, and though I have no reason for suspicion still it is a risky bit of business that we are upon and all cautions must be taken.

"Mr. Fetherston, choose ye carefully your watch, as we must be ready to come to full sail in a trice as the situation may require. I wish you to bring up the sweeps laid readily to hand so as they may be needed for in close maneuver.

"Mr. Corner, gather up the waisters and lubbers for the purpose of shifting cargo, that they may indeed do something of value to justify their shares." This sally was met by good-natured catcalls by that portion of the company so referred to.

The officers and crew of the *Kestrel* set about making good on the captain's orders. Dowd and the Swede climbed to the top spars and set themselves as watch. Magoon and his men brought up cartridges and grape from the magazine and with the gun ports closed so that their activity would go unnoticed loaded the vessel's cannon as ordered. Fetherston called to the deck watch the best hands aboard to trim the sheets as we sailed in for the mouth of Bloody Bay.

Corner, in regard to his instructions, set me to re-assembling the gangway which had been used to transfer cargo from the *Rachel* and then disappeared down the forward hatch with Reede and several other men to begin shifting cargo. He set Trinket along with Candy and a few others to rigging block and tackle on the foremast boom along with a sturdy cargo net for lifting plunder to the deck by way of the forward hatch.

The pennants on the *Kestrel*'s fore and main were dipped and raised several times by way of signal, and answered in-kind by those on a Bermuda sloop, which lay to in wait for us a mile or so outside of the headlands of Bloody Bay. Two additional sloops of the same character came into view in the long bay further south; they too ran up corresponding pennants in answer to our signals.

An hour of maneuver brought us to hailing distance of the first sloop, which for all intents and purpose looked more like a fishing vessel than the flag ship of a smuggler's fleet. The sloop looked in poor repair, in need of paint, and prominently displayed along its beam were fishing nets, its sails looked worn and tired and patched and its crew visible on the deck were poorly clad in the manner one would expect of the crew of a fishing boat.

"Don't let the appearance fool ye," said Trinket as we stood together at the gunwale. "Nor yet the smell of fish as we get close, those sails are as stout and handy as our own and only stained and patched as cover. That sloop and that crew are as good as any afloat and she can climb up the wind as ready as a squirrel up a tree. She is called the *Queen* and is captained by no less then young Jorge Vasquez the first son of the elder Vasquez; he is a sunny and friendly sort of fellow, but bold as brass and not to be trifled with."

A figure appeared on the rail of the sloop and raised a speaking trumpet. *"Buenos días señor capitán* Rackham," came a bright clear voice across the water. *Tengo su permiso para subir a bordo?*

Rackham turned to Trinket. "Tell him that we are pleased to have him come aboard.

Trinket took up the speaking trumpet. "Capitán Rackham *dijo días que más le dan la bienvenida a bordo de nuestro buque,"* he called out in reply.

"Ah, *El Baratija! tan bueno verte de nuevo espero que nuestras discusiones."*

"Speaks perfect English so he does," said Trinket as he turned around, "it's just their way, the island was Spanish for a long time and they are a proud people. You will find them warm and gracious so long as you treat them with proper respect and do not cross them."

Within a few minutes a boat was lowered into the water, five men including the one I took to be the young Vasquez, all dressed in the same shabby manner, climbed down the fishing net into the boat. One of the four men who manned the oars was a large and powerful looking black man. They pulled smartly away.

"Mr. McGinnis stand to and prepare to pipe our visitor aboard," said Rackham.

The boat dispatched from the *Queen* bumped against the hull of the *Kestrel* and the boarding ladder was secured and rolled down to meet it. As the young Vasquez mounted to the deck he was greeted by the bright twittering of McGinnis's boatswain pipe. He smiled a sunny smile and offered a brief salute to Rackham, it was returned and the two men shook hands. Vasquez was a very handsome man of middle height, well built with bright intelligent brown eyes that twinkled in amusement at the circumstances of his greeting.

I smiled to myself as I witnessed again the conceits practiced by these rogues. They consider themselves a republic of freemen at war against all flags and think nothing of mimicking the ceremonies commonly practiced among the navies of the world that they had spurned. It brought to mind the trial, which was held aboard the *Rachel*. There seemed to be great curiosity among the men regarding the Spaniard who had been so welcomed aboard.

I reminded myself that most of this crew had spent long years of enforced service to his Majesty's navy in conflict with just such Spaniards, and that they were indeed creatures of habit to the practices they had learned. Some of them indeed evidenced looks of distrust but under Rackham's sharp glance kept a civil continence.

The four companions of Vasquez mounted to the deck of the *Kestrel* just as the last notes of the pipe faded away. They looked a poor group of rascals all in all, save for the black man. He was quite large and powerful looking and dressed all the more colorfully then the others, he wore a long flowing garment belted at the waist and although faded showed bright colors in an interesting and unfamiliar weave.

After Corner and Fetherston were introduced to Vasquez, he turned to regard Trinket with a broad warm smile upon his face.

"Dear old friend of my family," he said in perfect English, "my father sends his affectionate greeting to you, and reminds you that the house of Vasquez is your home as well as mine." They embraced warmly.

I will admit that I was thunderstruck by the obviously filial affection between them. Its circumstance explained a great deal to me in regard to Trinket's position in the crew of the *Kestrel*, and in his having been sent alone to meet with the family Vasquez. I was beginning to learn how much more there was to this little man than met the eye.

After a brief meeting on the quarterdeck, Rackham, Corner and Vasquez returned to the waist and signals were given by Vasquez to his crew on the *Queen;* and with both using sweeps the vessels were drawn closer together. I was given orders to make the prepared gangplank ready for use. Corner and Reede descended into the forward hatch. Candy and I and several others were stationed at the boom in order to drop the cargo net down into the hold.

The bumpers of rolled sailcloth were once again deployed as the *Queen* came close alongside and the two vessels were secured together fore and aft. The gangway was secured in place and with block and tackle the first load was brought topside from the hold. Vasquez and his men carefully inspected the contents of the cargo net as it's settled on the deck, comparing the contents to the cargo manifest and the agreed properties being transferred. Working together the crews of the two vessels began transferring cargo to the *Queen*, and Candy and I again lowered the cargo net down into the hold.

This process was repeated until Vasquez called a halt. The gangway was retrieved to the deck of the *Kestrel*, and the lines let go from the *Queen.* On signals from Vasquez the *Queen* pulled away, then raised sail and made for open water. A keg of rum was broached for refreshment as the second sloop drew close alongside and was made fast in the same manner as the first. Reede and Anne Bonny came topside at that time and two men were sent down to the hold to take their place.

Vasquez greeted Anne Bonny with all the graciousness of a Spanish Don, sweeping his tattered hat off and bowing deeply at the waist. "You are as beautiful as the stories say, and I am happy to at last meet you," he said with a broad smile, "I hope in future that you and your gallant captain may be my guests at the house of Vasquez."

"You're very kind indeed, Capitan Vasquez, and I too hope that future circumstances will allow such a visit. Please allow me to introduce my friend Mark Reede."

Vasquez' reaction to this introduction was very odd. He stared sharply at Reede, looked back to Anne questioningly and seemed to blink in some confusion before returning his attention to Reede. He looked as if he were ready to bow again then thought better of it and extended his hand to shake Reede's hand, regarding him very closely all the while. As I remember it now from that moment on I caught Vasquez several times looking thoughtfully at Reede.

Throughout the introductions and the transfer of cargo to the first of the sloops Magoon and his men stood well apart by the cannons, offering no help or commentary. Magoon indeed looked particularly surly even for him, and I noticed quiet talk and private amusement among them. They seemed to take particular interest in the huge black man who came aboard, who worked diligently with the others and evidenced great strength in moving the heavier parts of the cargo.

It was about noon when we begin the process of loading the second sloop and being now the month of July in the tropical latitudes it was indeed hot work. The dead air in which we worked made our labors on the deck oppressive, the circumstance worked to our advantage however, in that the likelihood of a patrol vessel being at sail was slim. Two men had hoisted up from the hold passed out from conditions there. The men working on deck found great hilarity in tying a rope around their waists and tossing them overboard, then hauling them back aboard and watching them flop back into consciousness.

After the second man passed out, Corner brought the rest of the crew up from the hold. He and they were drenched in sweat, gaunt and pie eyed with exhaustion. Rackham cast a glance around the deck and seeing Magoon and his men being the freshest hands, having as yet taken no part in the labors, ordered them down into the hold. There was a tense moment when I believed that they might protest his orders; glaring and murmuring among themselves they reluctantly descended to what I knew to be the stifling conditions below. Magoon on his part took the opportunity to shove me roughly as he went by. Corner, exhausted or no, descended with them.

Rackham ordered the watch aloft to be relieved, and after a few minutes the loaded cargo net was hoisted up in the process of filling the second sloop began. It being now the hottest part of the day it was not long before a third man was hoisted up unconscious from below and roughly revived in the water.

It was about six bells of the afternoon watch when transfer to the second sloop was completed and it cast off and began to move away. The third and final smaller sloop now came alongside, and the process of tying off and positioning the gangway commenced. Everyone at this point was exhausted and moving slowly. Rackham called a break as it was clear that the great bulk of the work was finished. The men were brought up from the hold and a rough dinner of cold bully beef, peas and ships bread from the stores taken from the *Rachel* was served out.

"Ye have only to the end of the watch and then we must set to finish our work ere night falls near midway in the Second dogwatch," said Rackham. "We must be ready to away on the land breeze when it rises."

Having said this he, Corner, Vasquez, Trinket and oddly enough the large black man who boarded with Vazquez retreated aft to the fantail bringing wine and cheese with them and began a quiet though sometimes animated conversation.

The first two sloops now held many very heavy crates of fine porcelain and pewter dishware, dozens of kegs of Oporto, Madeira and Sherry, a dozen each of great 10 stone wheels of Cheddar, Caerphilly, Stilton and Wensleydale cheeses. Great care was taken in an inspection of the plunder. Random kegs broached and sampled and as careful attention taken to Corner's manifest, the manifest of The *Rachel* and the seals and shipping marks, as would any freight broker on the Bristol docks.

Trinket later explained to me that Vasquez wisely broke the illicit cargo into three separate vessels in the event that if one vessel were interdicted there would not be a complete loss for them. Also of course a lighter burden on each vessel allowed faster sailing and easier maneuvering, all of these being important considerations for their business. He also explained that the vessels were not been loaded willy-nilly, but rather each vessel's cargo was for unloading at a specific destination.

The heaviest burden of the work in this transshipment was by those who had sweated and bellowed below as they lifted and heaved in order to fill the cargo net, those who worried the weighty items across the gangway as the two vessels rolled and bobbed, and those who had carefully stowed the plunder into the smaller vessels.

Candy and I, and the men who helped us in hoist of the block and tackle, and the swinging of the boom had perhaps the easier task in lifting the loads up from the hold, although the aching in my arms and back and shoulders belied the apparent relative ease of the task. My friend Candy was beginning to show his age, so happily what remained now to be loaded into the smaller of the Vasquez sloops were the large bolts of linen, cotton and woolen cloth sewn into large protective duck bales of a uniform five stone weight.

Fetherston, who had hitherto patrolled the deck of the vessel, fore and aft, with his glass scanning constantly both land and sea, now called the watch to order and relieved those men aloft. Corner, with a twinkle in his eyes, called together Magoon and his men once more to the hold. I thought Magoon would go into a rage and that Quick's face would burst what's the blood that rushed to it.

Vasquez came to the rail and called down orders to the pilot of the little sloop who then quickly disappeared below deck and came top side again in a few moments with two burly fellows carrying a small heavy chest between them, this action elicited murmurs of approval across the deck of the *Kestrel.*

Leaving the captain of the bull sloop on deck to inspect the final merchandise, Vasquez, Rackham and Corner along with a black man who was now burdened with the chest that was brought aboard descended to the berth deck presumably to finalize acceptance of, and payment for the plundered merchandise. The cargo net was lowered to the hold and work began again for completion of the transfer.

I must accept some responsibility for the clash with Magoon that took place on deck in the final minutes in which Vasquez and his crew were aboard the *Kestrel.* Had I been more diligent and attentive to the swinging of the boom as we brought the last bales topside Magoon would have been spared the ignominy and the bruises that befell him, not that I cared a fig.

The final unloading proceeded quickly, the burden of the net and the hoisting thereof very much lighter and easier then all of the work that had gone before. The captain of the small sloop, whom Vasquez had left in charge of this final part of the transfer, opened one or two bales at random to inspect that the cloth contained therein matched the manifest and the shipping marks. It was all very perfunctory at this point and a transfer to the sloop made very smoothly. A lightness of heart settled on the deck as the men understood that the labor was soon to be completed and it all aspects of the transshipment went smoothly.

Magoon, Quick and Percy returned to the deck just as the last load was hoisted topside. They had the misfortune to stand in the wrong place, and too close to the rail as Candy and I swung the boom over so that the net could be lowered to the deck. Lines had of course been set so that the boom would swing only so far and no further, unfortunately Magoon, with his back to me, stood within the arc of that swing. I could have shouted warning, but I did not.

Magoon turned at the last moment and caught my eye just as the cargo net slammed into him and knocked him overboard. This was of course met with great hilarity by the men on deck, though not so much by Quick and Percy who with fiery glances in my direction quickly threw a rope to the foundering Magoon and hauled him back aboard.

Rackham, Corner and their guests returned to the main deck to be greeted by the howling laughter of the crew, and the howling rage of Magoon as he rushed across the deck, pushing several laughing men aside and lashing out to send me sprawling. Cursing wildly he wrenched a pistol from Quick's belt, cocked it and would have killed me on the spot if it had not been for a sudden arm that swept his arm and the pistol upward so that it fired harmlessly into the air. Reede pushed Magoon backward so that he stumbled against Quick, laughter ceased immediately and hands fell to pistols all across the deck.

"What the bloody hell?" yelled Rackham, "Magoon you bastard, what do you mean by firing a weapon on this vessel without my orders?"

"Mr. Magoon and I were demonstrating the quick disarming of a leveled pistol and the discharge was accidental, no harm has been done, Captain." Reede said with a smile.

Magoon for his part stood silent and glaring. Rackham seemed less than happy with this explanation but was ready for a quick end to the situation.

A little later as Vasquez swung over the side to descend to the sloop, he turned to me with a curious look and said softly, *"Usted es un hombre muy afortunado mi amigo, que es muy bonito y muy feroz y ella te ama. Vía con dios."*

At the end of the second dogwatch Fetherston ordered all sail set with the rising of the land breeze and the *Kestrel* was away to open water.

Chapter 12
Santa Maria Oloroso

The night was overcast and black, and far off to our larboard, on the very edge of the horizon a few tiny pinpoints of light marked the location of Port Royal. Fetherston took his final bearings from this known landfall. He then called young Harwood, who was now his constant companion, to his side.

Reede and I along with Trinket were aft at the fantail with him and thus privy to the instructions Fetherston gave to the young man, slowly and patiently teaching Harwood the skills that he had learned through a lifetime at sea.

We will now bear off due south from here," he said, "and when we reach the 11th degree of latitude, which is the latitude of Barranquilla on the coast of Columbia, we will then turn due east until we bring that coast into sight, marking well that we have indeed raised the city of Barranquilla.

"We'll then follow the coast northeast seeking the great bay that leads to Maracaibo at 12 ½°. The captain's plan is then to cruise off of Aruba seeking what prey may come to our ken. There is a great potential there, but also great danger as no Spanish ship will be ours save by force of arms. Ye will find your fill of pirating there I do assure you young Noah.

"We have up until now filled our sails in familiar waters and never far from sight of land. We will henceforth be long days out upon the open water far from the sight of land and so we must keep close watch at the bitnacale marking well every deviation from true south as may arise in the course of our working with the wind. We will throw the log at the change of every watch, marking well our speed and the compass position. All compensation possible must be made to bring us back on our true heading; the casting of the log shall your responsibility. We will take the noon sightings together."

With that Fetherston called the first watch, and to a blustery following wind the *Kestrel* was brought about to its southerly heading and Harwood went forward in the dark to cast the log. After a short interval there came a cry from the bow: "8 knots and a half if you please sir!"

"I'm pleased to see that Fetherston has it last found himself an apprentice.," said Reede. "He seems quite taken with Harwood, and considers him an apt pupil. For his part the lad would be hard pressed to find a better instructor."

"I believe I saw the man smile yesterday, though it may have been air on his stomach," added Trinket.

I related to them the story of our good Captain Lovewell and his having saved Harwood and Peters from a pitiful existence on the docks of Bristol, bringing them aboard the *Rachel* feeding and clothing them and starting the beginning of a new life for them.

"Aye we all knew he was a decent sort from the beginning," said Trinket.

"You and the court were prepared to hang the poor man," I said.

"Nah, had he indeed been a proper brutal bastard to his crew we may have, but it is mostly for show and to put the crew in the proper state of mind. There have been times, John, when all of the crew of a merchant vessel has come over to sail the account — if the captain were a cruel enough dog. Them as we got from the *Rachel* were two young boys eager for adventure, and a proven malcontent with the sign of the cat on his back, a good gunner though says Magoon. We impressed of course the service of two fine man, such as yourself and Candy, as we needed."

Over the next two days of sailing the overcast grew darker, the wind waxed and waned, veered and backed so that the constant maintenance of the sails was required. Fetherston prowled the quarterdeck watching the sea and sniffing the air like a hound.

On the second day the sun was so obscured that it was impossible to get a clear sighting. Fetherston brought up on the deck an odd crystal stone little bigger than a man's thumb, placing it to his eye he swept the sky with it until at last he found what he was searching for and then he and Harwood took a sighting on a part of the overcast sky that looked no different to me then any other part of its lowering expanse.

Upon the third day the sky was low and black with threat and the sea was agitated about us. There was apprehension among the crew when Rackham and Corner called all hands altogether on the berth deck.

"Mr. Fetherston has reason to address all of us, you will needs give him your full attention," said Rackham.

The atmosphere was charged as before a battle, and it was quiet as it is possible to be upon a vessel at sail. The only sounds were the shuffling of feet, an occasional soft cough, the sighing of wind and water upon the vessel and the creaking of the hull.

Fetherston was perhaps the most stoic man that I have ever known. His presence brought an expectant calm normally, so to see him tense was most unusual. His all too apparent gravity settled onto the crew, who hung on his every word.

"I would caution you mates; we are coming in for a blow, and I believe it will be a big one. We have a few hours in which to ready ourselves and there is no time to be lost. We will need to bring the top hamper down completely and as soon as possible." Here he turned and addressed Reede, "take Dowd, McGinnis and the Swede with ye, and such others as you may choose and get ye aloft as quickly as ever ye may."

Reede quickly gathered his men about him and with the selected crew went topside immediately to begin the work of bringing down the topmasts, topgallant masts, and spars as well as the trucks and the masthead housings. All to be lowered to storage in the hold, several hours of dangerous work in all but a calm sea.

Turning to Trinket, "I wish that ye and Candy, Dobbins and Snowden take the deck to man the hoists; bring with ye both Peters and Harwood. It's time that they saw real sailors about their work, and learned of them as they may."

With this he turned and addressed the company in general, "Everything loose aboard must be secured. The hatches must be battened down securely, everything loose on deck brought below and made secure. Carpenter, take such men as ye need and go to the hold and make sure that all there is secure so that there be nothing that might shift and effect the trim of the vessel."

"Mister Magoon, I know I need not tell you how important it is but that the cannon be properly secured for a storm.

"Now mates we have a fine stout tight and seaworthy barky. We have among us experienced proper Jack Tars and thus naught to fear from the impending storm. It will come upon us sometime in the middle watch; it will blow down on us from the northeast with a following sea. Only such men as I shall call to the watch will be allowed on the weather deck, the rest of ye shall remain below unless I call ye topside."

At eight bells of the middle watch the storm was upon us just as Fetherston warned. Under his guidance all proper precautions had been taken and except for those men who Fetherston called to the morning watch the entire company was gathered together on the berth deck. Men were gathered together, close to the hull, on both sides of the deck so as to distribute weight evenly. Groups of friends naturally gathered together to ride out the storm. I was seated toward the bow on the starboard side with Candy when Reede came up and set down close beside me. We were joined by Trinket with McGinnis, Dobbins, Carty and both Young Harwood and Peters.

Trinket brought with him a keg of best Barbados rum, and a bag of ship's bread left over from the *Rachel.* It was quickly apparent that this crew, who had served the hoists while the top hamper was brought below, had grown close with both of the young Bristol boys and the conversation turned quickly to a subject of great interest to the new young pirates — that being Trinket himself.

"Mr. Trinket," says young Harwood, "you promised to share your story with us when time allowed.

Aye," young Peters said, "the story of how you came to know the Maroons and the Vasquez family."

"And how are your eyes came to pop out," added Harwood to the amusement of all present.

"Aye, I promised this much to ye and we'll have the time now until Fetherston calls us to the watch. Precious little to watch as we are running on a fathom only of sail main and fore and a single storm jib.

And so it was that as the *Kestrel* rode the stormy sea and the waves throughout the day, Trinket told his story to those who had gathered around him. His sharp high-pitched voice carried easily the length of the berth deck so that many others were witness to the compelling tale he told.

His story explained much to me regarding his apparently familiar and filial relationship with the house of Vasquez, and the Maroons, and indeed his intimate knowledge of their workings, and this north sea, with it's islands, peoples and secret hidden places.

My story is simplicity itself. I come from the city of Ely in Essexshire, my father was a fuller and I his slave, after I'd thought that I'd carried enough buckets of piss I ran off to Portsmouth, took the King's schilling and made my mark. It was my misfortune to be assigned to an old converted Dutch butter box, HMS Whately she was, a tub really, and that being assigned to take soundings and chart the west coast of Jamaica for the Admiralty records. The captain of the vessel was a fat drunken grey haired lieutenant named Quigsley who knew that he would never make post.

"This sweaty whore's son was abetted both in his drunkenness and in his disregard for the men under his command by as vile a purser as ever left a trail of snot across a deck." Here he tapped the keg. "Though as I think of it now they may have done me a good turn in that I'm here with jolly mates and true, on my way to riches and wetting my tale with fine Barbados rum the while."

After a long appreciative visit to his mug Trinket continued his story. "As some of ye may know the purser of one of his majesty's vessels has many profitable opportunities to short Jack Tar of his due, if he has a mind to — this sod was one who had such a mind. A proper captain of course can keep a crooked purser straight, but this captain was in League with the purser so to share in the profits to be made in their abuse of office.

"And so it was that although our vessel worked slowly along the coast of God's own rich garden of fresh food available, their having taken ration weight in flour and ships bread while the purser charged off peas and cheese in his accounts — he and the captain to fatten their purses with the difference — the first signs of scurvy appeared among a few of the men, no need for it, none at all.

"My mess and I took the lead and drew straws in the forecastle, I having drawn the short straw was sent to speak to the officers. The first and second mates were both midshipmen, long in the tooth, both having failed their lieutenant's papers long years before. They, after a second and yet a third approach, brought the matter to the captain's attention; it came to nothing save for a black mark against my name, a call to quarters and a dressing down of the crew as regards the articles and their position as servants of the King." Here he snorted derisively. "Did I mention the reduction to six to one grog?"

This brought curses and groans from those who had served aboard any of his majesty's vessels for they knew that this too would turn to the profit of their abusers.

"Some fortnight later we were taking's soundings a cables length offshore from a small settlement from which several canoes had approached the vessel to barter with fresh vegetables and fruit.

Such fruit and vegetable as came aboard went to the captain's table and to the wardroom, no thought given to Jack."

After another visit to Barbados, so to speak, he continued. "So it was that very night that a subscription was taken amongst the crew, some coppers, a few shillings, some knives and such brought together for barter. Since the earlier drawing all hands looked to me as representing them further and to the procurement of such fresh fruit and greens as might be had.

That same night, and silently as one could swim I slipped into the water, untied the little dinghy that served through the day to take the inshore soundings and brought it about to below the heads so that I might slip into it and row ashore to make contact with the village and bring back such fruit as I was able.

"Although the oarlocks were properly muffled I had gone only a little distance when a shout came up from the officer of the watch… deserter! And then there were the clear sounds of a boat being lowered and the thump and the clatter of men manning the oars.

"There was nothing for me but to make for shore, it was a near run thing. I could've spit to the shore when my pursuers caught up; they rammed and overturned my dinghy, and someone nearly split my skull with an oar. I was returned to the Whately, placed in irons and thrown bodily into the brig like a trussed hog.

"The next morning, the captain, after he drank his breakfast, had me carried to his cabin where I stood before him, the first mate and the purser. 'Seaman Sackett," he said to me, 'in the presence of these, his Majesty's servants and officers you are found and discovered guilty of desertion, theft of his majesty's property and mutiny. You are to be taken hence to be stripped, flogged and hanged in the presence of the ships company, may God have mercy on your wretched soul.' I should have been delivered in irons to fort Charles at Port Royale; my fate would have in the end been the same be that as it may.

"Not two bells further into the watch divisions were called on board, and I was brought out on the waist. The articles of war were read, and then the charges against me. I was stripped, I was lashed to a hatch cover set upright against the mizzen and the boatswain gave me two-dozen well laid on. I was taken down, my hands and feet bound and a duck sack placed over my head, a rough thick new rope placed on my shoulders and around my neck and snugged in;

and with the soft squeal of a pulley above my head I was hoisted into the air to die. The rope tightened down upon me, I felt great pressure and a roaring in my head — but then after a few moments I felt nothing.

"I awoke several times swinging in the air there and realized that I was not dead. It was that thick new rope what spared my life — let that be a lesson to ye to use old supple rope if you're ever in the hanging business — I passed out one last time as I heard voices below me, and again the squeal of the pulley.

"The next time I awoke I first realized that the rope was no longer about my neck and that I had been wrapped in a shroud of tired and dirty old sail cloth. I could feel that I had been laid down on God's good Earth and that I was no longer on board a vessel. I sat upright with a start and a cough. I heard loud panicky shrieks and the scurrying of feet.

'The captain hired some of the villagers, who came out to the vessel to trade, to take my body ashore and bury this 'Trinket' — as he called me — in an unhallowed and unmarked grave. My sudden resurrection just as they were about to lay me down resulted in the shrieks and in the running away that greeted my revival.

"Now these Maroons are as superstitious as sailors, and from the moment that I was unwrapped from my grave shroud and the blood wiped from my neck and these popped eyes were seen, I was treated with the greatest possible deference and superstitious awe by the entire village. They gave me a small hut at the edge of the village, the best food and every comfort available to the simple people. Many came from the surrounding forest on a daily basis to see the man who had come back from the dead

"After several days I received a very important visitor and thus I met Ashanti, the father of Cudjoe, who was then the premier chief among the Maroon villages. He understood completely the circumstances that brought this great juju to his people and quickly adopted me into his village high in the blue mountains, and into the life of his people.

"I was three months among the Maroons there in the hills. They would go down to the coastal village from time to time to trade with the smugglers and it was thus that I met Vasquez — not that young Vasquez as ye've met, but his father. So bidding a very grateful farewell to Ashanti I signed on with Vasquez, and served the house of Vasquez for near 10 years both on the sea and on the land. They smuggle and trade from the Cayman Islands, Jamaica and Hispaniola all the way to Puerto Rico. It was through them that I came to know the North Sea, and through them that I came to meet the great Charles Vane and first signed onto the account as a guide under his command."

At this the wicket on the aft hatchway was opened and Fetherston's face and shoulders, followed by great gouts of water and wind, appeared and called for Trinket and his watch to take the deck.

The watch being relieved stumbled and slid down the hatchway, drenched to the bone.

As they staggered about to find dried meat, biscuit and ale they sloshed water all over their mates as they settled in. 'Arr! Damn ye! Lay off it then and get over by yerself ye great sodden bugger' — or suchlike was heard from several quarters.

The storm raged about us that day and into the night, on the following morning the sun arose amongst scudding clouds, and the sea settled in to long shallow swells. Routine returned to the vessel and the crew settled into mend and repair, and to careful attention to their weapons.

Five days after the storm Fetherston and Harwood took the noon sighting and agreed in their figures that the proper latitude had been reached, and so the *Kestrel* was brought about to an easterly bearing and all sail was laid on.

A spirit of barely contained excitement set into the crew and daily exercise with sword and buckler, pistol, musket, boarding pike and axe took place. Reede and Anne Bonny took Harwood and Peters aside and began to teach them the use of cutlass and pike.

Reede, having served in the infantry, also began instruction in the efficient use of firelocks. I wondered to myself what Captain Lovewell would have thought about the transition that these two young men were about to make, for it was generally agreed that the vessel was here to take prey and that any prey worth the bother would be armed and would not be taken without the spilling of blood.

On the evening of the third day of our easterly course lights were seen on the horizon off of our starboard beam. Fetherston, being satisfied that we had raised Barranquilla, ordered all the top sails brought down and furled, so that the *Kestrel* would cruise once more on fore and main courses alone, ready to pile on topsails in a trice when needed.

Our course was now roughly northeast, standing out about a league from the shoreline.

The unspoken hope being that a rich galleon would be found driven ashore by the storm.

Men were now constantly set and relieved at watch high in the top rigging, and others would climb the shrouds to watch the sea as each man knew that the first to sight the prey would earn a 10 pound bonus and have first choice of captured weapons.

The coastline we saw had indeed been ravaged by the storm. There were many downed trees, and much flotsam tossed up on the shore including several smaller boats which were still being pounded by an active surf. Fetherston worked the vessel in closer to shore so that these boats could be carefully examined, none were deemed worthy for us to lie to and send a launch to search them.

"We are not here to scavenge the shoreline by God!" Rackham yelled at the first suggestion that we do so.

It was just after dawn on the third day following that the cry came up from the lookout high on the mainmast. "Sale ho! Sail ho! Two points off the starboard bow." Rackham was quick to unlimber the long glass and after a few moments of observation turned to Fetherston.

It's a galleon by God, an old one by the look of her, and sailing crank, looks like she lists to starboard. Make all sail to intercept her. I smell Spanish silver.

At Fetherston's commands the deck became a fury of activity. Reede and his crew went quickly aloft to set every bit of canvas in the top hamper; 'helm a' lee' came a shout from the quarterdeck and with the now familiar groaning the great booms of the main and foresails swing across the deck to bring us on to the starboard tack.

Reede and the top men unfurled and raised the topsails fore and main in a time the equal or better of any seamen serving in his majesties navy, or anywhere. I still remember seeing Reede, in his element, high on the topgallant spar, his slim figure catching the wind at his back and the little tassel on the red cap he favored blowing out in front of him, he seemed as content as a cat on a pillow.

As we closed on the Galleon it became obvious that the vessel was sailing in a distressed manner. There was indeed something like a 10-degree list to starboard. The vessel had obviously made us for what we were about and put every scrap of canvas on her masts; it was at no avail however as even so she was slow and lubberly, down at the head and making no more then four knots at best.

We crossed her stern the first time about a cable length behind her and then keeping that distance we passed between her and the shore. As we passed her bow Magoon let fly a warning shot from number two gun that cut the water not fifty feet in front of her. She returned a ragged broadside that fell short and did no damage.

We backed topsails and dropped off, coming back around to pass her stern again.

This time one by one as of the starboard guns came to bear Magoon let loose on her.

Each shot was well placed to burst through the vulnerable stern and spread destruction and death the length of the vessel.

As we came about to pass her stern once more Rackham called out to Trinket and asked if he had made her name. "She is the *Santa Maria Oloroso*," he called back.

Chapter 13
A Column Of Smoke By Day

I believe Rackham would have much preferred to drive the *Santa Maria* into the shore and run her aground. There to pound and worry her with grape and ball while sending the longboats to storm her by the stern. The uninviting shore was half a league or more to starboard and as it was her captain had already clewed up all her main courses and cleared for action. There was no question of a surrender; it would be a fight to the finish.

The wind was moderate and steady from the south-southwest, ideal for the captain of the crippled ship limping northeast to reach the shelter of Maracaibo, but also ideal for the sailing properties of a speedy and agile schooner such as the *Kestrel.*

With all sails set we pulled steadily away from and before the *Santa Maria* until we were a mile or better in front. This time was spent in loading and charging the cannons and in dividing and assigning the crew into two assaulting divisions. One to be under the command of Reede, and the other under the command of Rackham himself. Magoon would of course be in command of the guns.

Corner was in general command of the deck as quartermaster, but it was Fetherston's masterly sailing skills that commanded the field. Very demanding, close, tight and skillful maneuvering would be required over the next hour. Candy and I, as forced men, were set to the starboard sheets along with several other good hands, Trinket, Dowd on the larboard; Reede and Hanson of course to the tops.

I saw Rackham near the fantail with Fetherston and Corner, it was obvious by the way that he moved his hands that he was giving it very specific direction regarding the movement of the *Kestrel* in relationship to the prey. There was a deep discussion among the three of them, much nodding, and shaking of heads and always the moving of hands regarding the movement of both vessels. After a few minutes there was an apparent agreement, Corner took the helm, Rackham came to the waist and Fetherston took command of the sails.

I have on many occasions made mention of the waisters and lubbers who made up a good half of the crew, I myself must be classed as a waister as I have no particular sailing skills. These men were all decent hands, being freemen bound together for a single-purpose, ready and willing to apply themselves to any task assigned and all having complete confidence in the master of the vessel.

So then these waisters and lubbers while not skilled sailors were all skilled in the use of firelocks and prodigious skilled in the wreaking of mayhem. Dozens of muskets and musketoons were brought up on deck, along with boarding pikes, boarding axes and grappling hooks. Trinket himself brought to the deck a wooden box in which a dozen short fused grenadeos set cushioned in deep oakum.

There was much activity on the deck, muskets and pistols being freshly charged and primed last-minute preparation of cutlass, dagger and buckler, grappling hooks placed a-top their flemished lines and loaded muskets passed up to sharpshooters stationed high in the shrouds. All activity came to an abrupt halt when Rackham stepped back to the quarterdeck and raised his speaking trumpet.

"Gentlemen, we have brought a Spanish vessel to heel, we have asked politely for them to heave-to for our inspection, and they have fired upon us in reply. I do not know if they carry silver, nor what the cargo that they are willing to fight for may be. As for myself, I am inclined to wish to inspect that cargo regardless of their resistance." Here he shrugged and made a depreciating gesture with both hands. "However, I will lead no man into deadly combat who does not wish to be there, and so I leave it to you, the company, do you wish to see what these daygos are holding back and take their vessel by force of arms, or should we rather back away and find some fishing boats to plunder?"

With a roar, the crew as one voice answered him: "TAKE THEM!"

"So be it then, prepare thyselves for a fight," Rackham shouted. More moderately he said, "Mr. Magoon has informed me he believes they are armed with eight pounders, 10 pieces per side. They fired on us from their starboard side, that being the list side, and with no adjustment made for that list their shot fell short. I'm sure they will chock their muzzles for elevation, and that their next fire may be more accurate.

"I intend to come across their stern another time and send our shot through and down the length of their gun deck. Then reload with grape and langrage to sweep their deck, and then close in, muzzle to muzzle, grapple them and storm aboard. Reede and a dozen men at the forecastle, I and a dozen others at the aftcastle. The rest of you will keep your stations at the waist and in the shrouds with muskets and continue to cover us with your fire, ready always to storm aboard when called."

Shortly afterward Fetherston brought the *Kestrel* about, any sailor will know the difficulty of doing so without going into irons, and we bore down on the *Santa Maria* on the larboard tack.

The captain of the *Santa Maria* had no choice really but to fight it out; at her best the *Santa Maria* was no match in speed or maneuverability for the *Kestrel.* His vessel was down at the bow and listing, lumbering northward at the speed of a man out on a country walk. What he did have was his Spanish honor, his courage and cannon.

When we closed the distance between us by half, Fetherston put us on the starboard tack and we sped past her to seaward at a great clip. Her larboard guns had been depressed to the gunwale itself in order to compensate for the vessel's list, and as we swept past her we could see the flash of her guns and the gouts of dark smoke.

In that second that it took for the thump of the guns to reach us, I heard Rackham yell, "Get down boy!" to young Peters, who in his excitement of the moment stood up, exposed over the bulwark, the wind blowing through his hair. In that instant his fair head disappeared in a puff of pink and his body collapsed to the deck.

Magoon and one of his men quickly picked up the still twitching body and tossed it over the side.

"God be merciful to the poor lad," said Candy beside me, "at least he died as a man among men and in the glory of the moment, not stinking of Geneva, toothless, penniless, ragged and poxy in some Bristol gutter."

When we had come down past the *Santa Maria* Fetherston brought us across the wind so that we passed once more across her stern, and as each gun came to bear Magoon and Stevens delivered six well-placed shots into her soft belly.

All of the topsails were dumped as we came before the wind to her starboard. Our speed was now checked to match hers as Magoon, Stevens and their gun crews were furiously active reloading our larboard guns with grape and langrage prior to a final closing.

The results of our two previous salvos through her stern were evident in that only five of her cannon fired on us, the others presumably dismounted or otherwise disabled by our shots roaring down the length of the vessel. Two shots went through our mainsail, the others passed harmlessly overhead.

"Now, get in under her guns, Fetherston," Rackham shouted.

The helm was then laid over and we drove in sharply coming up parallel to her, a musket shot away. We could see a small company of men on her deck, being the more vulnerable to our fire due to her listing.

"Those are Spanish soldiers," cried Reede, "they are not there to guard furniture.

"Watch them carefully; they are trained to fire by volley only, when you see their signal to fire drop down, they will reload by the numbers, we may rush them then."

This was greeted by hoarse cheers, and the marksmen in the shrouds began to fire at will. A great gout of fire and smoke interrupted from the number two gun, and one by one the *Kestrel*'s cannon spewed iron across the deck of the *Santa Maria.* All was enveloped by thick powder smoke as the two vessels thudded against one another and a half dozen grappling hooks sailed onto *Santa Maria,* followed by a half dozen more. They were quickly pulled taught and secured, the vessels now grinding together in the swells.

A great roar went up from the pirates as fore and aft they surged up side of the vessel to fetch the fight directly to the deck of the *Santa Maria.* Reede caught my eye, in the lead of his division; he made a prominent target in his short blue Jacket, red sash and jaunty tasseled cap. He jumped boldly to the top of the bulwark and clinging to the shrouds urged his men up and over. I found myself strangely worried for his safety.

Candy and I, no longer needed to man the sheets, ducked down into the forward hatchway, and shielded by its combing we watched the fight unfold before us.

Magoon and Stevens and the gunners raced from one to another of the *Santa Maria*'s gun ports firing buck and ball into the very faces of anyone foolish enough to try to service them.

There were loud shouts in Spanish from her deck, and then the sound of a ragged volley. Immediately afterward I saw the sparkling trails of the fuses of the grenadeos being tossed onto her deck, their sharp pops followed by screams and then the incessant patter of pistol shots as the pirates advanced across the deck, Rackham and his men from aft and Reede and his from the forecastle, emptying pistol after pistol. It sounded for all the world like a team of horses being driven across a wooden bridge.

The pace of firing slowed, to be replaced by the sound of clashing steel and screaming.

Rackham appeared on her shrouds and shouted down to those of the pirates still aboard the *Kestrel.* "Come on ye lazy bed pressers. Come up aboard and join the fun."

Magoon, the gunners and the last dozen or so of the crew swarmed up the side of the *Santa Maria* with great shouts. There was a renewed spattering of gunfire and then the roaring and clashing and screaming of hand-to-hand combat punctuated now and again by a pistol or musket shot.

I saw Quick and Percy scramble down again onto the deck of the *Kestrel* and make directly to the hatch combing where Candy and I were sheltered.

"Carpenter," Quick said with a snarl, "Rackham wants you immediately to the deck of the *Santa Maria.* If you resist I am to kill you here on the spot for mutiny, so step lively."

When I arrived on the deck of the *Santa Maria* there was still the sound of some continued struggle on the lower decks, and the last holdouts of her crew and officers had retreated into the after castle, closing and barring its heavy door behind them.

I reported to Rackham, who was covered with blood and black smears of powder residue. His face flushed with excitement and victory.

"As soon as Trinket comes top side to tell us that all is secure below," he shouted, "I order you to this vessel's hold in order to inspect and give reason for it's list and being down by the head. I saw no fothering at the bow as we came aboard, but I need to know if the vessel is sinking. I have no time or patience with you, do not resist me or you will feed the fish. Do you understand me?"

I nodded and then looked about the deck to dozens of bodies scattered about, some still moving and moaning. The smell of death hung over the waist of the *Santa Maria,* and the acrid smell of powder. I saw several bodies that I knew to be pirates and was much relieved that I did not see Reede among them, though the depth of that relief was alien to me at that time.

Moments later Trinket appeared on deck; Snowden was with him as was Dowd, who was wounded, and several others of the pirates. They brought with them a half dozen obviously terrified and shivering ship's boys and stewards, none appeared older than 10 or 12 years, save for one emaciated looking old black man who stood straight and unafraid, with the younger children gathered in clinging to his legs.

"We found these slaves," Trinket said, "huddled in the sail locker. They surrendered to us on promise of quarter, of which I have assured them." He looked intently about him, from face-to-face; there was clear challenge in his bearing.

"The little ones are like mice in a cupboard and they know where everything of value is hidden aboard this vessel. They have promised me of their cooperation in return for their lives. We have two dead among the bodies below, including Percy who dropped in just in time to meet his doom. Below decks is secure for inspection."

In heed to Rackham's curt jerk of his head I started immediately down the hatchway into the bowels of the *Santa Maria*, and bowels they were, reeking of blood and death and with the cloud of powder smoke still hanging in the air. More bodies, a few torn in half by the shot we had sent coursing the length of the gun deck, more moaning, and more feeble movement. I hurried through this hell, down the gangway to the orlop.

Moving forward I startled Reede, who appeared to be secreting some large bundle among the shattered debris. He turned suddenly on me and again I saw the two faces, the first fierce and set and deadly, then his face turned to a softness and a release of tension.

"Thank God it is you, John," he said. "Here, help me save this boy."

He then turned back a portion of the torn and filthy duck to expose the face of a very young man, with very handsome and refined features, who wore a silver Gorget around his neck. He looked no more than 16 and yet he wore the insignia of an officer. He had a great gash and swelling in the middle of his forehead and evidence of several sword slashes to his upper body, none appeared deadly.

"He came at me bold as brass he did, a fine little swordsman as well.

I could not bear the thought of killing him. I wore a Gorget like that myself once.

He reminded me of myself. And after the slaughter on the deck I could not bear to take another life. We moved among them like a reaper's scythe, they were all young men. After their first volley passed over our heads we charged among them shooting them down and cutting them down with sword and axe."

There was a soft moan from the boy and his eyes fluttered open, there was fear in them.

"No tiene nada que temer de nosotros cuando nos hayamos ido usted debe ser muy tranquilo, así que ningún otro que descubrir," I heard Reede say to him in Spanish.

His actions here were one of many things that seemed out of place with Reede. I asked no questions as we hid the boy, nor later. It was enough to have seen the act of mercy, for there was little of it aboard the *Santa Maria* that day.

I was conscious of the fact that I was unarmed and that I might come upon another armed refugee from the carnage and be helpless. I asked Reede if he would accompany me, which he did most gladly, and we descended together into the dark of the hold.

The cause of the *Santa Maria's* distress was immediately evident to me. She must have gone through the thickest of the storm and been so violently battered by the waves that supports had given way and barrel after barrel of water and provision had rolled down and settled into the starboard bow. It was also evident that work had begun by her carpenter and a crew to correct the problem. Her bilge was deeper than I liked so I suspected that some seams may have sprung but there was no way of making a full inspection without the barrels having been removed from the bow.

With Reede beside me I headed back up to the weather deck in order to report my findings to Rackham. We passed Corner and Trinket with several other pirates on the orlop, they were accompanied by two of the younger of the prisoners who — still in tears — were pointing and leading them aft.

When I returned to the weather deck I saw that Magoon had set a charged cannon against the heavy barred door to the great cabin at the base of the after castle. Quick and Stevens behind him with a dozen armed men ready to storm this last refuge, all decks above and below now having been secured.

Rackham stood to one side and called out for a surrender, he was answered with what I believed to be rude Spanish and Magoon touched off the piece. There were a few shots fired when Magoon and his men stormed in, a few screams and curses, some clatter and clash of steel, then they came back out one man limping another cradling a badly slashed arm. Magoon, I remember, was covered with blood and black all over with powder residue; his eyes were wild with bloodlust.

It was several hours of hard work, particularly for men who were deeply fatigued from the great stress of the battle, to fully plunder the *Santa Maria.* Even the pockets of the dead were emptied before their bodies were tossed over the side. The mortally wounded were accorded the mercy of a slashed throat before they too were tossed overboard. The less gravely wounded, half a dozen or so, were simply shot and then thrown to the numerous sharks that were already surrounding the vessels in a hellish feeding frenzy.

Those prisoners, who surrendered to Trinket, were set to work helping the pirates to plunder their own vessel. Firearms and other weapons gathered up and transferred to the *Kestrel* along with powder, fuses and flints — the *Santa Maria*'s 8 pound shot, of all sorts, being useless in the *Kestrel*'s long nines.

I heard loud excited cheering breakout behind me and when I turned I saw that Corner and Trinket had returned to the main deck, broad smiles on both of their faces, and following shortly afterward the remainder of their group came onto the deck carrying two small but obviously heavy chests. His face alight Corner called for order.

"Gentlemen of the company, thanks to our young friends here," he pointed to the two children whom I had seen leading them below, "I believe we have found what our late friends were so ready to defend. They have brought us two cleverly hidden chests of Royal mint doubloons and pieces of eight bound for some Duke of something or another — by God! — in Maracaibo. The whole worth some 20,000 guineas or I am an addle pated cull, I'll be bound."

The hoarse and raucous cheering that swept the deck was cut short by Rackham firing a pistol into the air.

"Let's away then," he said, "we have carried off all the silverplate from the officers' quarters, enough muskets and powder to arm every Maroon in Jamaica — for the right price of course — rum, wine and victuals for the journey north. Take Trinket's prisoners and secure them in the forecastle, chop down the masts and let the vessel drift here until it is found by the Coasta Garda and they may be relieved, see to it."

Magoon raised a harsh voice in objection. "With all due respect, Captain, many of us see things differently. We think it ill advised to leave so many witnesses behind, let us toss them all overboard and scuttle the vessel."

"I gave my word to them," Trinket said softly, Reede stepped in beside him "they are children really, and slaves as I was once a slave. They have no part of this and they have honored their word, helping us in our work and leading us to the very chests that we have so heartily cheered. The man who makes despise of my sworn word does not live, Mike." His eyes grew cold.

"As ye wish then, damn ye sir." Magoon moved off grumbling to himself.

I will admit that I was nonplussed by Magoon's swift surrender over the point. Only later did I understand the depth of his willful cruelty.

"It is settled then," said Rackham, "Trinket, Reede see to the prisoners forward, secure them tightly in the forecastle. McGinnis take some men and chop through the masts."

He moved to the rail and called down to Fetherston to make ready.

Everything moved quickly now as the pirates clambered down from the *Santa Maria* onto the deck of the *Kestrel.* All remaining small items of plunder were tossed down and the grappling hooks retrieved. The sweeps were deployed and we made ready to pull away when it was noticed that Magoon was not on the deck.

Just at the last moment we saw him come out running from the after castle carrying a small bag. He jumped from the *Santa Maria* into the main mast shrouds at the last possible moment, and under sweeps we made away to gain sea room.

According to their laws and custom Magoon was seen to hand the bag to Corner, so that it was clear that he held nothing back from the common purse. The bag contained only a few small coins and personal items, papist rosaries and such, of no real value and so it seemed strange that he had returned to bring it away. Corner gave him an inquiring look after seeing the contents.

There was a spirit of uninhibited joy on the deck; every member of the crew knew that a goodly haul had been made. Rum and wine casks were broached and buckets of seawater were hoist aboard so that men might wash the blood and the powder blacking from them. An account of heads was taken, and including Peters and Percy seven of the company had been killed in the fight, and as many wounded, two grievously who perished within a day.

While some of the company might have mourned a lost mate, most of them realized that the value of their share had risen because of the casualties taken.

I was appalled by the brutality with which the defenders of the *Santa Maria* have been killed, murdered really, and disposed of, and so I sought out my friend Candy.

"They were Spanish. Brutal warfare with the Spanish is where they learned their trade. When they took the *Rachel* it was an English ship with Englishmen aboard, it made a difference — if they had met resistance in taking the *Rachel* it would've been bad indeed, but not so bad as this — there is peace now between Spain and England and we may expect no mercy from an admiralty court for this day's work."

We were well away and the *Santa Maria* sat on the horizon when notice was first taken of the column of smoke rising from her. It took me only a few moments thought to realize that Magoon himself had set fire to the vessel under the pretext of returning for some small bit of plunder not worth the effort.

I saw a wild look come over both Trinket and Reede, their rage clearly evident and I knew that they reached the same conclusion. A pawl of silence as inherently deadly as the black pawl over the *Santa Maria* settled upon the deck as men looked about them expecting a violent clash at any moment.

There are times when something needs to be said; it has been one of the burdens of my life that as often as not I am the one who in the end says it, regardless of how I work to curb my tongue.

It was clear to all now why Magoon had been so tardy in returning to the deck of the *Kestrel*, that indeed it was he who set the fire that was in the process of destroying the abandoned and helpless *Santa Maria*, along with the abandoned and helpless prisoners whom we had promised safety in their ravished, dismasted and drifting hulk.

A great rage engulfed me. I could see the look of shock and anger on Trinket's face. It was he who assured the brave little men who finally surrendered that quarter would be granted to them, it was he and Reede who had secured them in the forecastle to their now fiery doom. In that moment my rage put my tongue to work.

"Magoon," my voice carried, "you are a dirty murderous foul stench of a dog."

The quiet became a deathly silence for a moment, and then Magoon exploded and drawing his dagger charged across the deck at me, ramming his shoulder against Reede and so sending him violently against the mast.

"You damned piss whelp. I'm going to drop your guts on the deck and then deliver your whore pipe and nutmegs to your nanny — by this he clearly meant to Reede — before I toss you to the fish."

I waited calmly for him, I knew he would strike low and prepared to block the thrust.

As it was when I boxed, everything seemed to happen slowly and time itself to stand still.

I remember his mouth was flecked with spittle and his eyes were wide and crazed with rage as he reached to grab my neck and drew his right arm back to strike.

I swept the hand with the dagger aside with my left arm taking a nasty cut along my forearm — the scar of which I still bear — and unleashed on him all the fury and strength of my body in a right cross to his temple. Oh, did I indeed lean into it with all my power.

His eyes took on a look of surprise before glazing over, and his head wobbled from side to side as he collapsed like a sack of wheat to the deck, leaving go a great fart as he did so.

The dagger, meant for my bowels, dropped from his hand and stuck in the deck at my feet.

Everything seemed to stop for a moment, and the roaring in my head was matched by the roaring on the deck around me.

"Lord almighty carpenter," I heard a voice in the distance say, "if ye live long enough to do so, I'd like ye to show me how to do that."

"Oh John," Candy said.

Chapter 14

True to Their Code

Blinded by the power of the red rage that swept over me, I was at once conscious of the turmoil building around me, and yet separated from it by a terrible singleness of purpose and the roaring of blood in my ears. I had the same consciousness and heard the same roaring all those years later at Norridgewock, when the battle raged at close quarters and the screams of men and women filled the air.

There was a moment frozen in time when I gazed down upon the prostrate form of Magoon and moved to finish the work I'd begun. I dipped my knees slightly and reached for the hilt of the dagger that stood in the deck at my feet — the dagger he had meant for my bowels. My intention was to pin his black heart to the deck of the *Kestrel* with it before any of the bodies moving toward us could prevent the blow.

Strong hands at my back gathered my shirt together with my belt and jerked me backwards so quickly that I never touched the weapon, and had no reaction except to grunt slightly. I was conscious of two men stepping in front of me. Standing between me and the cursing men now quickly gathering around the twitching murderer on the deck. It was Dobbin and Snowden; Candy stood behind me, keeping me firmly in check.

"It is your death to touch a weapon," He yelled. "Stand quiet for me now."

There was a general tumult on the deck. Cries of "toss the bastard overboard," and thunderous oaths calling for my blood as a mutineer were heard. Chief among those calling loudest for my dispatch was Stevens, my shipmate on the *Rachel* not so many weeks before.

"Piss in yer pants ye snot filled bag of guts," Snowden cried in return and hands dropped to swords and pistols all across the deck.

Rackham leaped into the space between those attending to Magoon, who was just coming around, and those who stood between me and their growing wrath.

"God's blood! I will kill the first man who draws a weapon." He displayed his resolve to do so by pointing a cocked pistol at both Stevens and Snowden. His face was still smeared with a residue of blood from the battle, which set off the deathly pallor of his skin. His eyes were wild and hot.

For all of his carefree bonhomie, quick humor and generally lighthearted attitude toward the day to day running and discipline of the vessel, every man knew Rackham and knew that he would follow up on his threat without a second thought. And each man knew that the articles under which they sailed gave him full authority to do so; the *Kestrel* was still "in action" till they were clear of the black cloud aft.

Both Corner and Fetherston stepped into the breach in the next instant — neither was armed, although the sight of Fetherston's face was more than enough to cower any man he turned his fierce cold eyes upon.

"God's peace gentleman of fortune," said Corner with something like a purr in his voice, "let us return to some order and begin to make the arrangements necessary to have this matter settled according to the code we all are ascribed to."

"I will make sausage of your guts pretty boy, and fry your heart for my breakfast," came Magoon's sour and all too familiar voice. I saw his eyes were still clouded, and his head unsteady.

"Ye'll needs return from hell to do so," came a second, much thinner voice.

Trinket along with the Swede and several others of the topmen stood with Reede next to the main mast. I had never seen him thus. He was deathly pale, his face like the face of a shocked child. His eyes were saucer wide and they darted between Magoon and me. For the first time I saw real fear in his eyes; it was only later that I knew it for what it was.

"Stay AVAST, Reede," Magoon yelled with a quick glaze at him, "this be betwixt the pretty boy and me — the bastard struck me down. We have come to blows and it is the crabs and the gulls for him the next land we see — I'll bring ye back his cod to remember him by if ye'd like."

Reede started, and then flushed a deep scarlet indeed, and I saw him bite his lower lip. There was a tittering among some of the crew, and a few open howls of laughter.

"You struck me to the deck you damned sweaty little bed presser — you drew my blood and I will have yours in return," Reede shouted. He waved a bloodied rag over his head for all to see.

"Reede, the question really is between Mike and the carpenter," Rackham said, conciliation in his voice. "It was the heated press of the moment between himself and the carpenter that lead him to — without malice — push through to confront the man who had insulted him. I'm sure no harm was meant to you, for you to take such an… ill advised position."

He turned to Magoon with a drawn smile. "What say ye, Mike? No harm meant eh?

"Bugger that scrawny pie assed sod is what I says, if he wants to go meet his nanneyboy in hell after I've done him. So much the better says I — damn his eyes!"

"You will not dictate," shouted Reede, his voice high and shrill, "You will not dictate. I'm a member of this commonwealth and you will answer to me you nasty pig, both for my honor and for my blood — no man — nor yet half a man strikes me and lives to tell of it — none!"

During this heated exchange Fetherston bullied and pushed several of the steadier hands into keeping the *Kestrel* properly before the wind, and her sail trimmed. Rackham, with Bonny at his side now, kept loaded pistols leveled at Magoon and at Snowden.

Corner stepped into the breach, Earl and Carty both with freshly charged musketoons at his side. "This matter needs now be put to the court of freemen as it touches upon the code, and the articles under which we sail." His tone was confident and assured. "We must all hang together in this matter shipmates, for it is our doom if we allow this matter to come to blows, or angry parties amongst our number." He paused and then continued.

"We all signed the articles as free men, and each man swore to abide by the terms of our account — and to defend it with our lives. Without it lads we are lost, for every man's hand is turned against us who is not aboard our barky — and plenty now who would see us hang. Shipmates, as your quartermaster I call all men here to stand back from this matter, further, I call upon the court to assemble itself in the great cabin in an hour's time. And now I call upon the men in dispute to be removed from each other, and kept separate until such time as they are called upon to explain themselves to the court."

He turned to Snowden, and glanced at Candy who still held me with an iron grip on my belt. "Take the carpenter below to his berth — he has no voice in this and his fate will be decided by the court and in accordance with the articles." He looked at me, "you, sir are warned that if you move outside of your berth before ye are called, you will be shot and tossed over the side immediately. Am I clear in this, sir?"

I nodded.

"Now gentleman of fortune" Corner continued, "I call upon you all to stand easy, to go about what business you may have and to wait upon the time shortly hence when you will be called upon for your considered opinion in this matter."

"Lookouts aloft damn ye — ye great lazy monkeys — aloft wi' ye!" cried the master, as the sun sank into its face upon the sea.

His was the last voice I heard on deck as I was escorted below by Candy, Snowden and Dobbin and led to my berth. By arrangement Snowden remained at the door of the crib and Candy and Dobbin went to the weather deck to keep involved and informed.

I observed to my self that this was the second time that Snowden interjected himself into the situation between Magoon and me. My curiosity overcame me.

"Matt, it is now the second time that you have stepped up to my support, I'm most grateful for it, but why you would put yourself into Mike's bad graces on my account?" He was quiet for some little time so that I wondered if he would answer me at all.

"Ye worked and sweated beside me in the hold," he said quietly, "and any man who will work and sweat beside is my mate do you see? I will stand by a mate through thick and thin. Ye took no airs upon yerself as we worked together, ye lead us to the work as was needed and did not presume to order us about, ye joined in our laughter, and showed yerself a man as will laugh in the face of sweat and toil. You have proven your courage time and again, and that you cannot be cowed by bullies nor by being a stranger amongst us.

I know also of Reede's high regard for ye. Now I regard Reede as a prince among pirates, and Dowd as the blood of me heart. Their regard for ye alone is enough for me to stand beside thee…also I cannot abide the sight, sound or smell of Michael Magoon." He paused here a moment and looked me in the eye, "I assure thee mate, that if ye do not come off the beach, Magoon will be found on the next morning with his own dagger in his throat."

I believed that Snowden would do as he said, and that Magoon would survive me only by a matter of hours. It was cold comfort.

Dobbin and Candy returned a few minutes later and told us that Reede and Magoon broke apart from their escorts and that only Rackham's pistols kept them from finishing it on deck with daggers. They also told me that the matter was bringing all of the sea lawyers to life, and that it had taken on all the elements of a grand entertainment for a sizable portion of the crew.

The odds set of my surviving an encounter with Magoon were given as nil — or so to say in the realm of direct divine intervention. One rogue said he would give up his evil ways and return to the church if ever I walked off the beach. All hands however expressed real admiration for the "monstrous great thump" I'd given Magoon; many said they would be right sad to see me left as meat for the crabs…I was touched.

The matter between Magoon and Reede was another story indeed. It was a subject of considerable 'professional' interest and debate amongst the crew. Most gave the edge to Magoon if it came to blades, he being a noted strong arm with a cutlass — though there were some who saw it another way and stood by Reede's more polished use of the saber. Generally there was agreement that Reede was by far the better pistol shot and might end the matter within seconds. All agreed that they would not like to take the place of either man on the beach, and that the vessel would lose a valuable and hard to replace hand either way.

In the hour between Corner's clearing of the deck and the first call for assembly aft in and about the great cabin, both Candy and Dobbin came to me with these reports, and brought me also greetings from Reede. I was of two minds in his regard. While I admired him, and was deeply drawn to his person, company and friendship, it was the common perception of our relationship as fostered by Magoon, which led to the bitterness of the current divisions. And many of the crew blamed me for bringing the two to this dread pass. Reede also, once again, interjected himself into the ongoing enmity between Magoon and me, reinforcing the supposed relationship. Only by reminding myself of the first unwarranted attack on the deck of the *Rachel*, and Reede's interference could I explain Magoon's obsession to do him and me harm.

The thought struck me that Reede may have used me as a sort of boson's start in order to goad Magoon into just the kind of precipitous and raging attack as happened on deck, thus leading to a final and fatal clash between them. I rejected it after some bitter thought. It made no sense; Reede simply could not be that certain of the out come of a duel to the death with a man like Magoon. In my sober moments I knew that I indeed stood no chance at all in a contest of pistol and sword with him. I felt a chill of fear for my friend and protector.

At last Earl arrived with a party of four men to escort me to the assembly that was gathering on the berth deck. Earl informed me that I must consider myself under restraint and would be clubbed to the deck at the first sign of agitation, or of attempting to break out of their protection. Matt Snowden and Agamemnon Jones fell in with me as we ascended the hatchway.

The depleted and exhausted crew of the *Kestrel* — save a three man watch — was gathered aft on the berth deck. The wounded men as well were carried in. The duck curtain which separated the area known as the great cabin were drawn apart so that all hands could witness the execution of their code in its purist form. Haggard, dirty and bloody they were, but all quickened and excited by the drama about to unfold. No London stage ever enjoyed a more rapt attendance.

The *Kestrel*, on gaff tops and forestays alone, rode a gentle sea bearing west by west-northwest and some three leagues off the shore.

At a table athawartships full aft at the transom and facing forward sat the elected officers of the vessel with three other men, they being Trinket, Eaton and Cole. There was no harlequin of an admiralty court this time; save that a cut down oar held at the vertical was displayed in Corner's hand. The articles of their commonwealth lay open on the table before them, its pages weighted and made secure with pistols and daggers.

Magoon and Reede were seated near the front of the press of crew, and separated by the width of the deck. Magoon was accompanied by Stevens and Quick, and Reede by Davis and Howell. Magoon cast terrible mad dog looks toward Reede, who further enraged his mood by looking up and laughing in that odd tinkling way he sometimes laughed. He seemed to have not a care in the world.

The mumble and rumble of a dozen and more conversations rising and falling, giddy cackles and bear like grunts and barks faded quickly when Corner thumped the oar and called for quiet.

"Gentlemen of fortune come from the sea, belay all else and hearken to me," He called in a hard singsong voice. Silence apart from the creaks and groans of the vessel fell upon the scene. "We have had a long and deadly day shipmates, and now we must labor yet some little while so that justice and our articles might be properly served. It is never a pleasant duty to judge a dispute that has come to blows between two of our mates, still less so when the dispute is between two such fell and respected ones.

"Sadly it is beyond our power to dissuade either man from a meeting that will prove fatal to one, or perhaps both. It is only to give order to the matter that we are come together, for we are not animals to settle such matters by tooth and claw in the midst of our home. Redress must be made according to the code. We have also to consider a charge of mutiny brought against the carpenter, as against complaint of a blow struck —"

"And a damned smart whacking good blow it was too," hollered a voice, "Aye, and Mike had the good sense to get down and out of the way of a second," called another. The sally was greeted by a burst of general raucous laughter and some disgruntled hoots. Magoon grunted and started up in a rage, but Stevens quickly pulled him back as Rackham reached for one of the pistols on the table before him.

"...As against a blow stuck by him upon a member of our company on the deck of this vessel," yelled Corner as he thumped the oar for order. When the deck was silent again he began to intone in an officious manner.

"Your officers and the honorable members of the court of freemen have carefully questioned those witnesses to the incident, and have looked over the articles of our commonwealth as it pertains to these matters; and we are now ready to present the case to you for your consideration, and your approval or disapproval according to those articles."

With this Corner turned and addressed the members of the court.

"Ye three men have been freely elected to be the final arbiters on matters touching on the application of the articles to affairs of our league. Tell us how you see the matter so that an end may be made to the enmities that threaten our livelihood. "

Eaton rose and addressed the assembly.

"Gentleman, and brothers we have spoken to every man who was a direct witness to the unfortunate action on the deck of our wee briny home. The events seem clear enough to us and we have decided that the charge of mutiny against the carpenter is unfounded."

Magoon howled at this and started up again. Again Rackham reached for a pistol, and again Quick and Stevens pulled Magoon back into his place. Reede looked back and met my eyes, strangely warm and moist.

"Our reasoning is thus," Eaton said. "The ranks of carpenter and gunner being equal aboard a man o' war —

"He is NOT my equal on this tub." Magoon hollered as he jumped up again.

"Damn your eyes, sir," shouted Rackham as he in turn jumped up, this time the cocked pistol in his hand. "Stay in your seat as the court goes about its duty to us all."

"… The ranks being equal — as warrant officers — the matter may be considered as a dispute between men and not as an act of mutiny against the authority of an officer of this company. This dispute having come to blows and parties it may, and indeed must, be settled according to the code.

That being by cutlass and ball at the first opportunity ashore, the principles being kept apart of one another by restraint until such time as a proper landfall can be made. How says the crew?"

Apart from some token grousing from Magoon's party, there was general agreement that such in fact was the code, as they understood it. Too bad for the poor carpenter and all, but some order must be kept aboard the barky. Wondrous fine thump by the way, always to be remembered in their world. There was in fact a question put out as to whether there might be time for a pugilistic lesson or two before the fatal day. Magoon did not bear this well.

The matter settled by common assent Eaton sat down and Trinket stood up. He was held in some awe by the crew — sailors being a very superstitious lot — as a hanged man he was looked on as a sort of a "Hand of Glory," being somehow other worldly, never to be trifled with, a sort of walking dead, fearless and fearful. I came to know later how outrageously Trinket played to this. And how he used it to get his way in matters he saw important enough.

"Gentleman, shipmates and partners," he said in the queer squeaky voice that so rattled men like Quick. "We come now to the matter between our shipmates Mark Reede and Michael Magoon. It is no secret among us that there has been an uncomfortable strain between these two over a long period. This has lead to what we of the court and your officers see as a dangerous degree of partyism, which divides the crew, and threatens our account.

"Open violence between these two was avoided only by the intercession of your officers not an hour ago. Our witnesses agree that it was no mere shouldering in the heat of the moment that sent Reede slamming into the mainmast but a very deliberate action by Mike, made with every intention to insult and harm him physically. It is our decision therefore that Reede is justified in his challenge, and that as a signed party to the articles his challenge must take precedent over the issue between Mike and the carpenter. How say you brothers?"

Reede's eyes locked on mine in the most peculiar way, as if asking me something. They were warm and searching, making me uncomfortable really with their intensity.

I could only return a blank and uncomprehending stare. If I had known then what I came to know in a few days time I think it would have meant the death of me.

There was much discussion this time, not so much in disagreement with the decision but more so a curiosity regarding the exact wording of the articles as they bore upon the case at hand. I was struck again at the punctiliousness with which these thieves and rogues approached their articles, and how closely the articles under which they sailed echoed the very articles they sailed under in their past lives as man o' war's men.

The differences were that here they were the equal of any other man aboard, here there was no lofty and unapproachable hierarchy with the power of life and death over them, here there were no starts, no kiss of the cat. Here they were invested partners in a nation of their own making. Here it was one man, one vote, one share, and every man signed of his own free will. They made a true republic on a small wooden world.

I have never seen it's like anywhere else in all my considerable travels.

When the discussions were exhausted, and certain of the articles read aloud for clarity general agreement was that the officers and the members of the court reached the correct decisions and that all was understandable and correct. When this assent, Corner rose to his feet again to address the assembled company.

"Those men who are in attendance upon the several principles in this matter are hereby enjoined that they are fully responsible for the conduct of their charges until such time as a suitable landfall may be made to put an end to this dispute. The principles will be held apart from one another until that time and any outbreak of violence between them will be considered a breach of the court's authority, and thus mutiny, and the terms of the articles as regards mutiny will be rigorously applied." He paused and looked about him, gazing from face to face among the crew.

"For myself," he said, "I find it distressing that abroad as we are in a world where every hand is turned against us, and where we have only ourselves for comfort security and defense, that such circumstances should come to pass. In a few days hence we will certainly lose one, and perhaps all three, of these good mates — for the carpenter too, although he has not signed to our company, has acquitted himself honorably and rightly done his duty by the vessel, which is our world."

He turned to the master. "Mr. Fetherston you have witnessed the will of the commonwealth in this matter. By the authority of the court, and the assent of the members of the company here assembled, you are directed to lay a course, which will bring us to a place where there is accessible beach, which is wide and deep enough for us to land a party. Once there we will see to the execution of the articles, and to the settling of these accounts.

Fetherston nodded, rose from his seat and gathering several men around him climbed up the hatchway to the weather deck. His harsh voice could be dimly heard as he set the watch to putting the *Kestrel* under full sail.

Chapter 15
Of Cutlass and Ball

The *Kestrel* ran before the wind that night under all sail, the Swede as captain of the tops. The evening was warm, and as we sailed with the wind there was no sense of a breeze aboard to help cool the nerves or the tempers of the crew. What there was, was rum and the wines taken from the *Santa Maria.*

With sailors an excess of rum is bad enough, but wine does not settle well with them in particular. Men puking and falling asleep on the weather deck in a winey stupor were all that spared the vessel an outbreak of fist fights or worse as the day and our dire errand was discussed, if bellowing in the most blasphemous manner may pass as discussion. The musicians were kept at it the while, passing from lecherous drinking songs to maudlin ballads later in the night.

Where at first much of the crew were in agreement burning of the *Santa Maria Oloroso* removed all witnesses to their act of high violent piracy, upon drunken reflection many now realized that the plume of smoke was visible for many leagues of sea around.

Trinket was heard to remark that we "might as well as hung a shingle out saying pirates at work." Within a day, he promised, every Guarda Costa and man o' war in twenty leagues would be on high alert for us and in the matter of a few days every armed vessel within one hundred.

If the fire was set deliberately, there would indeed be a case to be made for mutinous conduct. But of course there was no way of knowing.

It was sometime after the thuds, and howls, and the retching and cursing died away that Reede came to my berth. My greeting to him was I fear rather formal.

"Mr. Reede."

I saw Trinket in the passage behind him talking with Snowden, who had not left the area before the carpenter's berth in some hours. Snowden knuckled his forehead to Trinket and headed for the fore hatchway.

"John," Reede said my name in a very soft way, then I saw his jaw tighten. His jaunty little tasseled stocking cap was drawn back high on his forehead, so that an arch of light hair framed a high clear, intelligent and determined brow. He was dressed on loose fitting clothes and carried a yard long roll of linen. "There is so much I wish to say to you — there was a small sigh — but there is not time nor place for it now. Fetherston has driven the vessel hard all this time despite the dangers and the roaring of the crew," he staid my comment with his hand. "There is little time. Let me speak as I must for the time for talking is short.

"The officers and the court along with the steadiest old hands of the crew are very worried and vexed about the deep factions this thing has exposed. Rackham fears that Magoon will try to replace him as commander. They all want it settled tomorrow — if it needs be done, on a mud flat. Most all realize now that the burning of the *Maria Oloroso* did them no favor, but will only bring on the king's dogs."

He turned aside from me slightly and reached inside his breast. He drew out one of the Pennsylvania rifled pistols and a small brass powder flask.

"I have loaded this piece very carefully for you." He looked up at me with strange eyes, "The primer in the flask is the finest French, the flint is new, and personally tested this very night." Again I was silenced. He then unrolled the linen to expose his naval officers' cutlass.

"I have also addressed the edge of this. It is a beauty to use, so beautifully balanced. The first span ye may shave with, the second slice beef, the third cleave bone and the last turn steel."

I have never in this life forgotten the look that came over his face as he spoke to me in this manner, very like the look of a mother, so tender it seemed. His face was of a sudden smooth and glowing, it took me aback. Then his face took on the darkness and the lowered brow of a man about serious business.

"Now hearken carefully to me, and I will prepare ye as well as I may in this short while. Trinket will add some later. How much real experience with weapons do ye have?"

"Little, and that with musket, bayonet and short pike — drills with cutlass and pistol of course, but no practical use of them."

"Good, then ye have few bad habits to overcome."

We spent an hour or more together there in the gloom of one small oil lamp. He stood close and showed me how to use the rifled pistol to best advantage, how to hold it, how the sights should line up at twenty paces and at forty. Where I was to aim on Magoon's body, and how when he was down I was to rush him, even through the smoke of the discharge, to finish with his head, either to split it or remove it. "It must be done so, John!" he said in answer to my shocked interjection. "He is too dangerous to take any chances with. I have seen men come out of a deathlike stupor on the field to down a man walking away from them. The animal vigor of a man like Magoon is not to be taken lightly — for your life. John swear ye'll follow all my instructions."

"Mark —"

"Never call me that. I hate the name…taken for the sake of a letter" he trailed off.

Being never wise to bandy words with a pirate I said, "Reede then."

"Call me thy friend John, just that please…just thy friend."

"Then friend, as I am yours, you speak and instruct me as if the contest with Magoon is already over, and it is all for me to avenge thy death."

"Never so, John, by my blood not so. We both know the fortunes of war; for all that, I would not stand in Magoon's place to face me tomorrow. However, if fortune favors the odorous —" We both burst into laughter at this and the mood of the moment lightened just so much. "And I must fall I would be no friend to you if I did not show you as much as I may."

From that moment on I made neither further comment nor question except to clarify that, which was being taught. It was surely another hour or better before we both heard the soft cough outside the little cabin. Some time had been spent on the use of the blade. The drills he taught were shortened and altered, economy of movement and staying close to my body with the movements, as well as several fencing moves as are used by the Flemish cavalry.

Reede's eyes and skin began to shine in the dim light of the lamp. His words coming softly and with deep sighs from time to time as he guided my arms and my hands, or moved my body this way or that, or prodded my legs into the proper positions with his legs. The scent of limes and coconuts filled my berth. Trinket's cough came just as I began to feel an odd sort of unease.

"First light is a glass away, Reede," Trinket said, 'the master has turned more southerly to raise the shoreline by dawn. The casting of the line through the night shows we come near twenty leagues since dark fall, prodigious sailor is Fetherston. Stepping over — or onto — drunken sacks of worm meal the whole time he was — kicked a few of the puke swimmers into the scuppers he did, God love the man."

Dobbin came with me to the weather deck just as the sun seemed to leap out of the eastern sea as if to not miss a moment of the coming drama. It flooded as clear and hot a morning as I have ever seen with a dry intensity that made the leeward side of my face seem cool.

A goodly sea breeze made skirting the shoreline easier, though we needed frequently to beat up wind in order to keep some water between us and a lee shore. We sailed thus for the hours till noon. Rackham pacing and chewing his hand the while. Magoon did not appear on deck but laughter and boastful talk could be heard through the hatches from the berth deck below. Candy and Snowden joined us after the glass turned and we gathered up by the larboard cathead forward of the windlass. We watched the shoreline as all aboard did. We spoke little, as there was little to say.

Reede came up through the forward hatch as the watch changed. He wore a long loose fitting linen kaftan with a short blue Moorish jacket and his favorite little tasseled nightcap. His Flemish saber was slung on a simple cord over his shoulder, and the other of the rifled pistols tucked into a wide red sash along with his Spanish dagger.

"Good morrow friends," he said and squinted into the sky, "it looks like hot work today."

The rest of our little group drew a little aside so that Reede and I might enjoy what time we had left. Reede reached over and took both my hands into his own. I was taken a little aback by the intimacy of the gesture, and again I was startled by the delicate structure of them; they were strong to be sure but built along a finer line than any other man's hand I had ever touched. He looked deeply at me.

"Ye remember all we practiced together last night, John? Ye will be sure will you not that if I fall you do not let anger overcome you to the point of rash actions. Ye must keep thy head clear if it comes to action. Magoon is not a thinker; it is your advantage of him."

"If I fall, John," he said it again much as I hated to hear the words, "it will soon enough that the truth will out and you will at last know something of the regard I have had for you since first we met. If such should befall ye must not let even that knowledge cloud your actions...swear to me John!" He said with great emotional force."

I swore as he requested, and he continued in a cryptic manner. "I swear in turn to thee John that if I return alive ye will know of all that I have set aside for thee alone ere the sun rises a second time from this moment."

A cry from the tops came. "I see beach, two points off the larboard bow...beach ahoy!"

The beach in question sat at the far end of a shallow bay with a small mangrove covered island at its head. Sight of it had been hidden from view until the moment we coasted about a promontory. Fetherston and the top men went into furious action to beat us into the first, and the broader, of the two channels of the bay. With his own hand on the wheel the master worried the *Kestrel* into the bay. The presence of other conditions prompted the more experienced seamen of our company to ascribe the presence of any sort of beach in this spot to have been a result of the recent storm, and that it would soon enough wash away again.

We dropped anchor in five fathoms about a half a cable or so from the shoreline, and hands began to unlimber one of the longboats. As the anchor splashed into the quiet murky water Magoon came up the aft hatch with a bound, and a blasphemous curse at the heat.

"Ah there" he said, "are the two sugar plums I will pluck this day," and then laughed.

It was generally agreed among officers and crew that no time must be lost and so I was to be already in the longboat ready for my turn if it came. The shelter of the promontory, and the island at its mouth, rendered the little bay nearly airless and Fetherston was concerned about our having to warp out past the point before we would be able to fill our sails. Thus it was that Reede; Eaton, Snowden and I sat together at the stern with Trinket as the coxswain. Rackham stood in front of us facing forward with his legs braced apart. Eight stout men at the oars sat between us and Magoon at the bow with Stevens and Quick.

As the longboat pulled away from the *Kestrel* the crew left aboard gathered at the rail and in the shrouds. As many glasses as could be had were present and squabbles were already breaking out over their use; the hair of the dog had also been broken out for all aboard.

Our passage to the beach was quick enough but during all that short time Magoon could not keep his mouth shut, a constant stream of badgering and taunting was hurled at Reede who sat quietly glancing at me time and again. I smiled in return, the wan tick of a very dry mouth really.

Magoon wore one of the wide brimmed plaited hats that give the wearer some portion of shade at least, a loose fitting shirt, once white now dun silk, it's sleeves cut off just below the elbows. It was tucked into a dark blue petticoat kilt and his broad thick leather belt. He carried an exceptionally long screw barreled pistol, a very heavy bladed cutlass and a long dagger.

The beach itself proved only a sand bar some few hundred feet from end to end and perhaps a hundred feet deep at its widest point. A few logs had been washed up onto it, along with mounds of seaweed and other flotsam. It was humped slightly toward its center, perhaps a fathom above the water at its greatest height and fell away sharply to the sea in several places.

Trinket brought the longboat gliding smoothly onto the island; Stevens and Quick vaulted over the side and steadied it as first Magoon and then Rackham stepped off. As Reede picked his way carefully the length of the boat Magoon continued his taunting banter.

"Come along then darling, I have a nice lunch of blood sausage waiting for me when I'm done with thee my pretty." He gave a suggestive snort.

Reede bounded lightly onto the sand. Turning to face me, his eyes flicked to Trinket then to Snowden, next to the *Kestrel*, then to the sky then to me again. He raised the saber, blade up in a cavalryman's salute then turned smartly and strode away to meet his fate, being all willow and coiled steel.

Rackham checked them close to mid island. "Ye have both read the articles as concerns this thing." His voice carried, as a commander's voice must. "Only one of ye will come back aboard. If ye have not come to blows in five minutes once we have tied onto the barky we will leave you both here. Neither shall either move toward the other until we do tie on…we will not be caught on a lee shore for the sake of ye'r personal affairs."

He then set them back to back and counted off fifty King's paces for them. When they came to the end of the count he said, "Now turn and look death in the face whilst we return to the vessel. Hark ye now, this thing must be done in the turning of a glass from this very moment" he waved his hat to the *Kestrel*, "…one or the other lads, one leaves or both stay."

As the longboat pulled away toward the *Kestrel* my eyes were fixed steadily on Reede.

He stood straight and still, his saber's point in the sand at his feet. He reminded me of the effigy of a knight I once saw in one of the Bristol cathedrals.

I never took my eyes off of the antagonists facing each other on the small sand island; the outcome of their combat was my own fate. If Reede fell I knew I would be facing Magoon as soon as the longboat made the short trip back to the fatal beach. As we bumped against the hull of the *Kestrel*, and the line was thrown to the hands aboard, Magoon and Reede began to approach each other with pistols raised.

Knowing Reede's reputation with his Pennsylvania pistols Magoon wisely chose to use a screw barrel pistol. As the shot in a screw barrel is introduced at the breech end, and not rammed down the barrel as in the ordinary pistol, the shot may be larger in relation to the bore then usual. Thus the shot fits tighter in the barrel and makes for increased power, giving the weapon greater range and accuracy. As the barrel must be screwed into the breech it is not a weapon that lends itself to a quick reload.

Against Reede Magoon was more concerned with the range and accuracy of his piece, as there would be no reloading to be done in the contest. I saw cradled in Steven's lap the pistol Magoon had chosen for use on me, a very ordinary piece indeed.

As if in a final lesson to me, Reede advanced as he instructed me to do.

His left hand cradled the pistol in its palm, his arm extended under it as if it were a musket. His right arm was up, the elbow raised level with his shoulder. The left side of his body advanced slightly toward the target as he took careful half steps forward, neither his eyes nor the barrel of his pistol ever leaving Magoon for an instant.

Magoon advanced in a manner more ordinary to his calling. Square on he came in full steps, the pistol held high in one hand. His arm was fully extended and rotated inward toward the body so that the lock of the pistol faced more up then to the side. His left hand grasped the hilt of his dagger. There was an uncanny hush that fell upon the crew of the *Kestrel*.

After advancing ten paces Magoon stopped and did a most extraordinary thing.

As I have said before in my story, whatever else Mike Magoon may have been, he was not a coward.

We could not hear clearly what he shouted to the silently advancing Reede, but his next action raised first a gasp, and then a cheer from all hands…save one or two.

Magoon lowered his still extended arm off to his side and then discharged his pistol into the sand. He shouted at Reede again then slapped his chest several times with his right hand before drawing both cutlass and dagger and advancing steadily on Reede, whose movements and demeanor changed not a wit.

"God's knees, to be alive to see this…Jesu! There'll be talk of this fight for years to come," came a hoarse whisper from the deck. Little did the speaker know.

"It was right enough a bold thing to do," Trinket spoke to me in a lowered voice, "but he knows well enough the one who he faces. He knows well too that me, or Rackham, or the master himself would just walk up, shoot him down and come back aboard for an ale. And then get the hell out of this close space we're in…I like it not here lad, not at all."

There was silence save for the creak of the rigging. Reede continued his advance as if nothing out of the ordinary had occurred. When the two were no more than twenty paces apart he stopped in his tracks. Magoon, as if caught for the moment in Reede's web stopped as well.

A breathless moment as Reede continued to hold Magoon square in his sights.

A gull cried.

There was a flash, and a sharp retort delayed to us by the hundred yards separating the vessel from the shore.

A lusty extended cheering rose from the crew as Magoon's wide hat flew from his head.

There was not a breath of air in the little bay, a cove really, created by the storm surge of the few days prior and sure to be no more with a few weeks time. Not enough air to move the *Kestrel* at anchor, nor to move Reede's caftan, nor yet to clear the billow of smoke from his shot.

I saw him continue his lessons to me as he charged through the cloud of smoke, casting aside the sheath as he drew the weapon and took a savage stroke at Magoon's head all in one furious movement.

Magoon showed his surprise by the flailing parry that saved his life; he was quick to respond with a low darting stab with the long Italian dagger he carried in his left hand. Reede in turn showed his skill with a smooth hard parry in two that struck the dagger from Magoon' s hand and sent it flashing into a pile of flotsam some yards away.

This dramatic flash of action drew howls and cheers and a great thumping of weapons by the crew. In spite of the articles' prohibition of gambling among the crew I knew that quiet but intense bets were being wagered.

From that moment however there was a marked change in the nature of the combat. Magoon seized the initiative and began a bull-like advance behind a shower of powerful swinging blows. His attack seemed very like a windmill, although Trinket told me that there was nothing uncontrolled about it. It was, he said, exactly what it appeared to be; a concentrated attack of sheer power intended to batter Reede and his sword arm down to a helpless position.

Reede appeared barely able to contain the assault and his steadily less frequent attempts to repost or counterattack seemed weak and unsure, easily undone by Magoon's seemingly overweening power. Blow after ringing blow fell on the bright ribbon of steel that stood between my friend and a bloody death on an unknown beach. Fathom by fathom he was driven back as though by some terrible wind. A cold dread started to settle on me.

The once boisterous crew was now mostly silent except I had the sense that bets were changing in the whispers I heard above me. The men on the *Kestrel*, the crew of the longboat, Rackham, every mans' eyes were fixed on the now seemingly unequal contest save for two.

Snowden and Trinket sat quietly in the stern of the longboat braiding a long Sennett between them and whistling and old song called 'The Three Butchers." One or the other glancing up from time to time to report to the other 'not yet."

Reede turned away from the *Kestrel* now and backed down from the height of the little island with his back to the shore. He seemed to me to be making his position even more vulnerable and dangerous. Magoon must have seen it in the same light as he now began to rain even more furious blows down at his faltering foe. The pace of his blows slowed however and each seemed more deliberate. The clash of their blades sounded truly like that of a blacksmith's shop heard from the same distance, so steady and ringing it was in the oppressive heat.

Reede appeared to lose his footing at one point as he retreated backwards towards us.

A gasp came up from the crew. When he regained his footing we all saw that he had discarded the sash, which fell, away from his waist. As he stood up straight we saw that his and Magoon's heads were on the same level for the first time in their struggle. Reede's blade arm hung down at his side, his left hand was hidden from our view.

He shouted something at Magoon and then jerked his caftan away from with his left hand; his body hidden from our view was exposed to Magoon in an obvious invitation to the next and fatal blow. My head fell to my chest when I heard Trinket say to Snowden, "I think now mate."

There was a heartbeat when Magoon faltered in his strokes, seeming to freeze.

In that moment Reede dropped into a deep crouch, his upper body shot forward in this odd position and delivered a clean strong upward thrust deep into Magoon's mid torso. Magoon's terrible sweeping slash tore the little red tasseled cap from Reede's head — for a heart stopping instant I thought he had taken the top of my friend's head with it.

Magoon jerked erect and rigid, thrust to the heart, his body still answered the call to combat and his right arm began to rise for another impossible blow. Reede sprang up and with both hands on the hilt of his saber swung it as if to poleax a beeve.

Magoon's body collapsed to his left from the force of the blow, his severed head, rolled and bounced down the right side of his body and away onto the sand. There was a veritable curtain of blood sprayed into the thick tropical air. An ungodly roar went up from the assembled crew.

"Great God Jehovah!" came a singular transported voice, "a scene of such terrible truth and beauty, and a battle worthy of broadsides and ballads till the end of time." It was Fetherston.

Reede fell onto his knees in the sand and rearranged his clothing before rising and turning to acknowledge the cheers that rose from the *Kestrel.* Behind him the right arm of the headless corpse still twitched as Magoon's terrible animal energy finally ebbed away.

As he clambered onboard the longboat, covered with blood and sweat, Reede flashed me a smile of exhausted triumph, his eyes were preternaturally bright and had a look almost like longing. blood covered or no, I clasped him to me and thumped him on the back both in heartfelt congratulation and as a release for my own tensions, which had reached crisis in the moments before his masterful stroke ended the battle. He yielded to my embrace then pulled away.

"Do ye want aught of these weapons of Magoon's we've gathered?" Rackham asked.

"Could ye have not rinsed off in the water before climbing aboard? Ye'r slopping blood all over the floor of the boat Reede…damn ye welcome back."

"I have all of Michael Magoon I'll ever want covering me at the moment, and Magoon had as such plans for thee, Jack, a month or so hence, if it were he now slopping my blood on this wood. The bastard did for my favorite little bonnet mores the pity."

Snowden glanced up as we pulled toward the vessel, and called for Rackham's attention.

"There is a very storm of activity aboard the barky," He reported. And so there was, with men running to the windlass and others to the anchor cable or into the tops. Still others at the rail waved frantically to us and shouting and motioning us to greater effort.

"Sail ho!" cried Trinket from his position at the tiller of the longboat, "there is what has set the bees amongst them Damn me! There is a Guarda coastal cutter wearing in toward the mouth of the channel, and lifting signals as fast as ever she can."

"Shit!," was Rackham's retort.

Chapter 16
Men of War

Rackham was loath to abandon the longboat and so it was tied off the sternpost, as there was no time to hoist it aboard. He was already shouting orders to the vessel before we bumped alongside and all hands scrambled up and over onto the spar deck. His orders had been anticipated, the anchor cable was already cut, and the sweeps were already appearing on the deck.

"We MUST clear the headland before the cutter blocks our way, Johnny!" came the cry of the master.

"Sail ho Sail ho!" from the top. "Another cutter — no a sloop! Half a league beyond."

"All hands to the sweeps." yelled Rackham. He meant all hands indeed and the musicians and Candy and I along with Rackham himself and even Fetherston put our hands to the dozen sweeps. The three wounded able to walk were put to use as well. Fetherston put Dowd, whose pass through wound in his right buttock cheek was painful but not debilitating, to the helm after a very brief set of instructions given with much pointing. He sent the other two, Barre and Beall, forward with the lead. Again there was careful albeit brief instruction from Fetherston.

Reede, still covered with Magoon's blood, hitched the long hem of his caftan up between his legs and tucked it into his sash. Although exhausted from the ordeal on the beach his spirits were high as he joined Snowden and me at a sweep. The crew of the *Kestrel* now numbered thirty-one sound men plus the three musicians and Candy and myself, three men on each of six sweeps starboard and larboard sides. The 'eyes' of the vessel were two wounded men, and the helmsman. Well, it would be some time yet before he sat down comfortably again.

"Heave hearty lads," cried Rackham, "Heave as our safety is in peril, heave ye bloody bastards. Come about now crisply lads heave and pull, heave and pull," he cried out as the Starboard sweeps backed and the larboard pulled for all they were worth to bring the *Kestrel*'s bow around. It was the hardest work of the rowing we did that day and seemed to take forever, though I was told later that no one aboard could remember ever having seen a dead turn done more smartly, nor in a more constricted place.

When the bow was pointed at the mouth of the little bay the full thrust of the sweeps gave over to gathering way. It was eight full backbreaking strokes before Dowd yelled out.

"She answers!"

"Full away now lads," called out Corner — as if we were not already at such. And the grunts and groans of striving men filled the tropic air as the sweeps dug hard into the water.

"Drummer! Piper! Belay and fall to and give us a tune to heave by," Rackham said. "Even out the hands lads" he called and men changed stations to free the two musicians. Within moments the bodhran and the fife picked up a sprightly Hornpipe, the drummer striking a sharp patter ta patter ta pat pat at each stroke of the sweeps.

It is worthy of note how this accompaniment brought all the straining hands into harmony and in a dozen strokes we could hear the sound of water hissing on the hull-always a comfort to those who sail the seas.

"I see a third sail" called Dowd from the helm. "Another cutter by the look of her, just come to sight beyond the headland."

"Full fathom three by the mark" came the cry of the linesmen at the bow.

"Starboard ye'r helm two points" shouted Fetherston over his shoulder to Dowd.

Now the *Kestrel* was a complete overmatch for either of the two Guarda costa cutters even in her present undermanned condition. Though the cutters were indeed fast little vessels, their armament of half a dozen four or six pounders would be no match for the *Kestrel*'s complement of nines. However, if the first of them made the narrow mouth of the bay before we came far enough out to catch the wind, and took a broadside position there, we would have no choice but to row straight into her for boarding, while being swept by her guns from stem to stern with grape.

However brief the fight to board and take her might be it would be too long and in that, and the time needed in clearing of her to gain the open sea, the other cutter and the sloop beyond would have closed to cannon range. The safety and freedom of the *Kestrel* depended on making the open waters before the three vessels could attack in concert.

"Full fathom five" came a cry from the leads men forward.

"The first of the cutters is up past the headland," shouted Dowd. There was an audible groan from many men for it seemed our race was lost.

"She will lose her wind," cried Trinket.

And so in fact she did, as Dowd jubilantly reported moments later. The captain of the cutter in his urgency to cut us off came too close into the lee of the small promontory and in a moment the wind that had been his, was his no more.

"Two men to a sweep," said Rackham "I want men aloft with glasses."

So it was that Reede and I shared our sweep alone together as Snowden laid aloft at the main and Carty at the fore. Reede was a dreadful sight to see, his caftan tucked up between his legs and it and his person head to toe covered with the now brown blood of Mike Magoon in great smeared sweaty blotches. His face was literally gray with the tension and exertion of the day, and his arms trembled a little with each deep powerful stroke. There was evidence in the hair of the top of his head as to just how close indeed had come Magoon's final grim slash.

"Will ye now affect the mullet with your hair Reede?" I said, "seeing as such a good beginning has been made for ye."

"Bugger thyself John," he said just as Carty shouted down from the foremast.

"The sloop is flying English colors, she carries ten guns and has every sail filled!"

"I smell the wind!" cried Trinket a moment later and as if he had again conjured the lay of the winds a cry went up from Snowden that the gaffs and stays were at last drawing. There was a slight surge by the *Kestrel* that backed our sweeps in our hands. The fore and foretop stays popped loudly and as they filled the master sprinted back to the helm just as Dowd fainted away.

"Belay the sweeps and secure," Rackham shouted, "top men way aloft wi' ye, make ready for top courses when the wind is abaft the starboard beam. Main and fore courses ho! Unfrapp them and make ready for all sail." As the master took charge of the men working the sails of the *Kestrel*, so Rackham bound off and gathered such of the gun captains and best gunners he could lay hand on and set about clearing the deck and readying the cannon for action.

The main and fore courses were raised. And the booms let go so that the great sails of the vessel could fill with the wind that was now coming strongly from about three points off the starboard bow, as they filled I once again felt the powerful sea legs of the *Kestrel* take hold.

The becalmed cutter had broken out sweeps and with much disjointed flailing was bringing herself about so as to have her broadside on us. A puff of gray smoke erupted from her.

The first ranging shot from the cutter splashed harmlessly into the water half a full cable length short, although well on target. "Damned little pop gun," someone said. "A four pounder by God, the arrogant little bastard is just trying to irritate us.."

As the *Kestrel* gathered way it was obvious that the cutter was no longer any real threat to us by way of blocking our exit from the cove. I looked behind us just before we rounded the mangrove-covered island at the bay's mouth. I saw the beginning of a great flock of gulls descending on the sand bar.

The efforts of the crew of the cutter now brought her far enough clear of the headland so that her sails began to fill and her bow came about. Her captain, too bold for his vessel, was trying one more run to cut across our bow and hold us in action long enough for the English sloop to come within cannon range. This first cutter was a quarter mile or less to our starboard.

The English sloop was a mile perhaps out, and the second cutter a mile or more beyond her.

"Make ready the starboard guns and prepare to give this fellow a taste of our iron."

Rackham shouted. Men ran to the guns. Corner began lighting the linstocks. Spontoons were pulled and the pieces laid level for close work.

The overwhelming majority of the crew of the *Kestrel* were experienced hands in a fight like this. They having been "men of war's men" or privateers through most or all of their seafaring lives. They required no instruction in the readying of the guns for the work soon at hand. In a very few minutes every gun was cleared for action; the gun captains standing by their pieces with smoldering linstocks, each turned and attentive to Rackham who stood at the edge of the quarterdeck.

Shortness of manpower put each gun crew at an acceptable minimum of four men rather than the six as was customary on a man of war. Considering the skill and experience of the crews it would be no disadvantage in the coming action.

Fetherston brought the bow of the *Kestrel* a bit to larboard; the movement brought the starboard freeboard up a strake and so improved the angle of fire for her guns. At a range of now well less than a quarter mile the captain of the cutter found himself about to be raked.

"Open the ports," came Rackham's commanding voice, "make ready to fire as they bear."

The scrape and hiss of the ports being slid open was quickly drowned out by the rumble of the guns as the crews heaved on the running stock and the muzzles cleared. A few last second adjustments to the lay of the guns with some scrapes and grunts and curses and the deck fell silent again save for the hiss of water and the creak of a vessel under sail.

"Steady lads…steady," Rackham's calm voice, "Quarter gunners fire as they bear."

Stevens and Quick were the quarter gunners, Stevens of the forward guns, Quick of the aft battery. Rackham nodded to them and they ran to their posts to oversee the gun captains firing.

Stevens leaned over and sighted along the number one gun, he stepped aside with a word and the gun captain bowed in over the piece and touched the linstock to the touchhole.

There was nothing that the captain of the cutter could do. One at a time in intervals of about five seconds the guns of the *Kestrel* gave out a great thud and a billow of white smoke. Round after well aimed round slammed into the cutter. She shivered and shock under the impacts and on the fourth round her mast was sprung and fell away to her leeward, greeted by a great hoarse cheer from the pirate crew. By the last echo of the *Kestrel*'s guns the cutter was dismasted and down by her bow.

The second cutter still well out was seen to bear away to the west, less anxious now to close with such a much stronger vessel. The English sloop however continued to bore in hard toward us, not slacking an instant, eager for the fight.

Fetherston brought the bow of the *Kestrel* back to his original heading, which was the shortest way for open waters, where the speed of the *Kestrel* was her safety. On deck the gun crews were busy reloading the starboard guns. There would be no flinching in the exchange, which would soon take place between the *Kestrel* and the sloop of war now closing rapidly.

The guns were double shotted and four loaded muskets were brought to each station.

Rackham walked the length of the deck calmly giving instruction. “This will be a very close action lads, methinks a cables length or less. You gunners, on the first round aim low for wind and water toward their bow under the cathead, as soon as ye’ve fired reload with chain or bar shot, then run out and fire for their stays as soon as ye’r reloaded. If they try to close with us load with grape and langrage to sweep their decks. There is no profit for us to close and board, our aim is to bloody them up good and then to get the hell out of here.” He then ordered the black flag raised on the main.

A furious lifting of signals from the sloop brought the cutter to heel, and she began to work her way slowly in again toward an eventual rendezvous — though she seemed in no hurry. The sloop however was closing at all possible speed. A little over a mile separated her and the *Kestrel.*

The wounded men were once again brought below deck, Dowd having bled profusely for his efforts on the helm. Candy and I were sent below to see to them. On the main deck the three musicians struck up a bright tune I did not know. “Those are English tars we are coming up against,” said Dowd through clenched teeth. “They will prove far stouter foes then what we have had to do with till now, your freedom may be a hour away carpenter.”

“I wish no harm to any man aboard this vessel, Daniel” I answered him, “I have found friends here and am torn between wishing to see them escape and wishing for my own deliverance from these circumstances.”

Trinket’s head appeared at the aft hatch. “Rackham’s run out the guns, John, ye may watch the action in some safety from the hatch combing. There are few on the account who would trade blows with an English man of war as we are about to, it’ll be a story to tell around the fire in a publick house later.” And so it has been.

When Candy and I topped the combing, the English sloop was half a mile or less off of our starboard beam and she and the *Kestrel* were running neck and neck so to speak. The musicians, save for the fife, were sent below and he a — broad shouldered little Welshman — seemed unconcerned as he played a simple and bright little round. The vessels continued to close the distance between them, each captain loath to fire until close enough that there would be no misses.

"It's a fair match this" Candy said, " the sloop is fast, and she'll carry five eight or nine pounders in her broadside. Her commander has his chance here to make a name for himself. Few enough chances to do so in a peacetime navy — pirates being the only game in such times. Our advantage in the exchange will lay in the quality of the gunnery."

"Is it their advantage then?" I asked. "Their being however small, an English man of war."

He laughed softly. "Not really lad, they're drilled better than the Spanish crews we've bested but they are allowed precious little powder for gunnery practice so their drills though constant are dry. I'd wager — were I a gambling man — that this crew has had far more experience at real gunnery and may outshoot them two to one, and hit them with every shot at the present range. Which range I believe to be a quarter mile or less. No, John, this sloop will try to close and board us."

At the next instant I heard Rackham call out. "Let's give'm what they come for lads. Forward the cathead steady on. One and three reload with chain for their forestays if you please."

Of the instant the number one gun gave a belch of bright fire and the *Kestrel* shuddered.

From our vantage point low to the deck and seeing the sloop clearly through the number nine gun port Candy and I saw the shot hit at the waterline just forward the cathead. At that moment the number three gun flashed and roared, its shot striking further aft and under the cathead and a little above the waterline.

The hoots and jeers of the number one crew were drowned out by the number five gun's concussion. Then the larboard guns of the sloop erupted with flashes and billows. Candy's strong hands jerked me down as the *Kestrel* shuddered with impacts and the immediate deafening crash of number seven. Numbers nine and eleven followed almost as one terrible roar just over our heads. In the relative peace that followed I heard the cries and curses of wounded men mixed with whoops and cheers from the aft battery.

The English captain fired a true broadside; his cannon all discharged simultaneously.

The combined force of the discharges had rolled his vessel a full strake. The quick reaction of the crews of numbers nine and eleven in firing on his vessel's roll had placed shots below the waterline of the sloop.

A ball from the sloop tore a section of the railing atop the breastwork off; the splinters had badly wounded several men on the number seven gun. Two shots struck just below the gunwale forward and two punched holes through the main course. The wounded were dragged aside and Reede and another stepped in to man the gun.

"Aft battery arm with grape if you please," shouted Rackham.

"Forward battery ready," Stevens called out "all bar and chain, Captain."

The sloop brought her helm over and was now making a run at the *Kestrel.* Her captain was intent to close and board as Candy had surmised. It was not to be.

Fetherston, who it appeared had been waiting for the moment the Englishman would turn into the wind, brought the *Kestrel* across the wind, she heeled sharply enough that some men lost their footing and slid into the larboard scuppers. The range to the sloop was sharply reduced and we came across her bows at a hundred yards or less.

The forward battery fired in salvo and all hands saw all of the sloop's fore staysails and jib go all aflutter as the chain and bar shot took away both standing and running gear. She yawed and her speed dropped sharply off. A steady hand on the helm, and good jack-tar were all that saved her from broaching.

To be fair, I will say that the captain of the other cutter made a respectable effort to close into the action after his first, quite understandable, hesitation; he was however some half mile off and of no present concern to the pirates. The sloop came about and brought her head into the wind; she lowered her main sail and we could plainly see men already at work forward.

"Even with a full crew of right cracker jacks she'll be some hours getting right," Candy said.

With the wind abaft the beam the *Kestrel* had a bone in her teeth and was making over ten knots as we drew away toward the safety of the open sea. Even our leeway served to put more water between us and a frantically working English crew. As we watched we saw the cutter come up within hailing distance of the sloop and then turn aside.

“He’s waved her on to pursuit of us,” came a call from main tops.

The crew of the *Kestrel* was alive with battle excitement at this point, their blood was up and there were many cries for us to come about, and to reengage, and to finish the fight to sink the sloop, or better yet to take her by boarding and bring her into consort with us. Even the normally sanguine Corner was shouting for the final clash of arms.

“Think the better of it lads,” cried Rackham, “those are stout English hearts with whom we would have to do, and they have already bloodied us in the exchange. At best we would gain a battered and hulled hulk for our trouble, and at what cost ye may imagine. There be no profit for us here mates, we have bested them gun for gun and we are best to be away.”

“Draw your shot and swab yer guns if you please.” Rackham’s voice cut through the general whooping and thumping that greeted him. He flushed with suppressed pride, bit his hand and gave a great toothy grin.

He commanded a pirate vessel that bested an English man of war; he had reason enough to be proud.

He had reason to dread as well, for England did not forget such things, nor would she forgive.

Chapter 17
Our Mutual Friend

As fast a swimmer as the *Kestrel* could be with such a fine wind off her quarter, it was late in the afternoon, a turn of the glass before sunset, as the top of the cutter's mast dropped below the horizon. She had dogged us the time, losing ground to us by the minute but a speedy little craft non-the less and handled very well. There was of course no further thought of turning on her. The enterprising English captain who had waved her on to continued pursuit of us would have liked nothing better then for us to sail back toward him.

The crew had fought three sharp actions in as many days and as the high nervous energy they had been forced to wore off, men literally fell asleep where they were, only to be jostled awake by Fetherston and sent below to their bunks. Reede retreated to the berth deck shortly after the action with the English sloop. When next I saw Reede the world turned upside down.

Corner and Bonny came up from the magazine where they had returned the unused cartridges to the powder room. They reported that 'quite a bit of powder had been burned' one hundred and fifty pounds had been used over the three days. All of the best French corn gotten from Vazquez was gone.

We had remaining a hundred and twenty pounds of good common grade and forty of the fine primer. Enough for forty-one rounds from the main batteries. There were available forty rounds of ball, ten of grape, six each of bar and chain. The three hundred pounds of Spanish powder taken from the *Oloroso* was considered inferior and would go with the captured arms to Cudjoe and his Maroons. With that report to Rackham they too stumbled down to their berths and the deck of the *Kestrel* seemed deserted and quiet for the first time in several days.

Deserted save for Rackham, Fetherston, Trinket, Candy and I and three very groggy pirates left topside to handle the sheets as needed. And so it was that I was privy to a detailed exchange between Rackham and the master.

The long and short of which was that the bottom of the vessel needed scraping. That we should have been able to get clear of the following cutter in two hours or less, and that if we had not stymied that fast sloop with our cannonade she would not only have kept up but would have kept our stern under fire the while. That a more experienced captain on the sloop would have kept us at extreme range until the cutter came up forcing us into a life or death fight, for the *Kestrel*'s one weakness was that she had no provision made for stern chasers.

Speed was the vessel's greatest asset and that speed was now markedly reduced by the build up of growth on her hull. Fetherston's final advice was that we make all good time back to Jamaica and unload the weight of the armaments meant for the Maroons. Then find a safe place to careen the barky, and scrape her hull before any further serious cruising.

"Make your course north by northeast then George," said Rackham. "I will have Dirk call the crew together tomorrow so that they may be included in our plans, and a future course of action be discussed openly. Carpenter, ye can see to the shot damage tomorrow, I bid ye all a goodnight." And so he descended by the aft hatch to his comforts.

Before stumbling exhausted to our berths Candy and I joined Trinket and the watch crew in trimming the sails to a new course as Fetherston brought us around to north by northeast.

"It is a very dangerous proposition for pirates, careening the vessel," said Trinket as we descended to our berths, "A week or more in a helpless state, not to mention the considerable labor of unloading and then reloading the vessel, for such men as these is not to their liking. That's why most captains would simply take the first likely looking outbound vessel as a replacement — but Rackham would never entertain giving up the *Kestrel*."

"I cannot say that I blame him," Candy said. "I cannot remember ever seeing or sailing on a more likely vessel; a fast sailer, quick in her stays, sailing two points and better closer to the wind than any other and with real teeth — the perfect vessel for such business as ye are on."

"Well said and truly brother, a perfect vessel for such as we," Trinket said as we separated to our berths. The smooth roll and gentle pitch of the *Kestrel* rocked me to sleep.

I awoke to music, and from a confusing dream wherein I was seated on a rough hewn porch overlooking an unfamiliar river and smoking a cigaro, there was someone strangely familiar, whom I could not see clearly, seated beside and slightly behind me. It was the first of many aching dreams that have troubled my slumbers…and my waking these many years.

The boys of the band were playing "Drops O Brandy" on the main deck, and the call for assembly was being piped. Waking thus a man might have thought in his first seconds awake that he were aboard an English man of war. But there were no long roll of the drums and no rushing patter of feet responding. There were instead cursing and groanings. Instead of hot oatmeal and cheese and butter, there was cold jerked pork and ship's bread for breakfast as the crew came once again to life.

As I had no voice in the deliberations about to take place on the deck, I was ordered below to examine the damage from the two rounds that had struck high and amidships on the *Kestrel.*

The damage was slight and posed no danger to the vessel. One round had struck the gunwale itself, bruising and splitting the heavy timber but ultimately falling away into the sea. The other round had struck a little lower and had pierced the hull, coming finally to be half buried in a knee, where I left it. It was while I was involved with this minor duty that Anne Bonny came up behind me and spoke. Her approach had been so silent that I started and bumped my head on a deck beam in turning to her.

"I wish to have private words with you after our meeting on deck is over, carpenter," she said, with a little smile for my having knocked my head. She had a most peculiar look in her eyes, and regarded me with a slightly cocked head. "I will seek you out so that we may find a quiet corner." Having said this she mounted to the weather deck. In a short while I followed after.

As I examined the damage to the starboard bulwark to begin the repair I came to hear some of the subject matter under discussion. There was apparently some heated disagreement regarding the contemplated careening and scraping of the hull. Stevens spoke on behalf of a goodly portion of the crew. Their opinion, as he expressed it, went in this wise.

Since the crew had been seriously depleted by the preceding actions — there being now only twenty-nine sound men left from the original complement — the burden of labor would be too great. The time needed to complete such an undertaking too long considering the conditions at sea, by this he meant the number of vessels searching for pirates. They proved themselves, he said, beyond any question over the last few days and it was neither cowardice nor lack of zeal that prompted their misgivings.

Their joint considered opinion was that it was perhaps time to cash out and disband the company while their luck held good. There being by their rough estimate nearly twenty thousand pounds in specie or goods in the common. A vote of apology and thanks was taken for the carpenter while I was below deck — with this he turned and indicated which carpenter — for all saw how I cared for their wounded with motherly kindness, and had did all my duties toward the vessel with all honor.

I bowed to the crew in appreciation of this recognition, and went back to my measuring and listening.

The quartermaster Corner being called to make an account of the commons answered.

"Gentleman of fortune and shipmates, first I agree with all my heart that this crew has shown itself the equal of any crew of like size that has ever sailed the account. Your estimate of the value of our commons is quite accurate. Once the arms are safely delivered to the Maroons as promised, and the other goods delivered to Vazquez, the commons should stand at a few hundreds over twenty-two thousand pounds…in every manner of coin known to man of course.

"A very few good hauls from this point could easily put the account at the thousand pounds per man as noted in the articles for disbanding their company. However as it now stood, and once the needs of the wounded men had been met, a closing payout something in excess of six hundred pounds per man could be expected." This figure representing about two years pay for a post captain in his majesty's navy. There was murmuring and discussion across the deck as all hands digested this and began to debate the future of their common enterprise.

It was at this time I first noticed that Reede was nowhere to be seen. He was however the subject of many conversations — interspersed with the business at hand. Most centered around the deadly combat they witnessed on the sand the day before. "Most terrible and inspiring fight I've ever seen," one said. There were murmurs of agreement.

Another said however, "I seen him take a whole damned fire bucket of fresh water into his berth earlier; damn him and his washing all the time." "Well ye should go below then and confront him about his wasteful ways," came one voice. "I'd pay good brass to watch ye do it." came another. "I prefer to keep my head where it's stowed — damn ye" the first replied. "Which be up yer arse." rang out, to raucous delighted laughter all around.

"When ye have gone below, I will come to see ye, carpenter." Bonny said as she walked by me laughing.

I was just beginning to cut a replacement top rail for the bulwark from the little oak we had left for repairs when Bonny appeared as she said she would. "I have words for you from Reede," she said, "and I wish us to sit together for a while and speak." I saw Trinket outside. "We will not be interrupted or overheard." Bonny said having seen my glance.

When we were seated across my small worktable she drew from her belt Reede's Spanish dagger unsheathed it and placed it on the table between us. "This is my token for ye that I speak with the full knowledge of our mutual friend.

"Our shipmates will be much involved over the rest of the day with the decisions which needs be made regarding our future plans. Their ultimate decisions affect me little, as I will stick with Jack whatever betides. Their concentrated attention on these matters allows a very convenient time to attend to the errand and matter which concerns you and our mutual friend.

"There is a closely kept secret aboard the *Kestrel*, John" the first time ever she used my Christian name. "It is known to a very few indeed. Jack, of course knows, and I and Trinket and Snowden." Here she sniggered. "Snowden came to the knowledge in an abrupt and painful way." Again she laughed. "And the master of course," she added.

I took this time to closely observe the little masquerade Anne Bonny. All previous contacts between us had been brief — though friendly enough — now with the talk of secrets, and of some arcane knowledge known only to an obviously select part of the crew...Snowden? I thought. I will admit that my interest was engaged so I studied Bonny as she spoke.

She was built on a small scale perhaps five feet and a few inches. She seemed lightly boned, though fit and strong as her actions and reputation attested. Her hair was truly a beautiful color, like much copper mixed with chestnut. Her eyes, bright and brown and slightly almond shaped, seemed to dance about my face as she spoke.

Her nose had once been more prominent than presently I surmised, as in one or another of the combats she had taken part in her nose had been broken — smashed really — As strange as this might at first seem it only added to her charm, and yes to her beauty. She was as Trinket once said ‘a nice bit of fluff under all the pirate getup.”

The wound had healed very well with only one thin scar, and it was not a disfigurement to her, but rather it gave great character to her lively face. It added a wonderful vulnerability to this dashing and dangerous little figure of a woman.

“Can you keep a secret, John?”

“As long as it does not touch on mutiny or murder…or some cruelty.”

“It is none of those things.” She smiled at me. “But it is a purely personal secret that Reede has hidden away from the world for some time, and now wishes to share with ye.”

She stopped abruptly and gave me a look like a man who is having a sudden attack of the gas. She then exploded into an uncontrolled fit of merry laughter. For the life of me I could not imagine why. I heard Trinket’s odd twittering chuckles outside in the passageway. As she stopped gasping for breath she looked up at me through tears of laughter. “It’s all good, John.”

When the storm of laughter blew over she became very serious again.

“There is a manner in which you must swear regarding this secret John, once you have been made privy to the secret ye may do with it what you will — I swear that her mouth twitched again at this — except that ye cannot tell another soul of it. This ye must most solemnly swear.”

“I swear most solemnly that I will keep any personal secret entrusted to me by Reede as sacred to my honor and will not divulge it to any other.”

“That is all very well, but there is a prescribed method for ye to make the vow.” With this she picked up the dagger and handed it to me. “Ye must prick your finger and draw blood with this, then smear the blood the length of the blade while ye say the very words as before.” Her eyes were now very serious, there seemed to be a fire behind them. It was as if I were caught up in a spell, one from which I have never escaped, not to this very hour.

I picked up the dagger and turned its point to my left thumb pad. I looked back into her heated eyes and I pushed it sharply up under the pad next to the joint, an eighth inch no more. As the blood came I ran my thumb down the length of the blade to the choil.

"I swear most solemnly that I will keep any personal secret entrusted to me by Reede as being sacred to my honor, and so will I not divulge it to any other by word or action."

Bonny picked up the knife and blew lightly on the smear of my blood to dry it. She looked up at me with a warm smile and what could be called a twinkle in her eyes. "When the middle watch is on deck and the vessel is quiet I will come for ye, John, for Reede insists that it must be a very private occasion between the two of you only." Her pixie face broke into a broad smile at this then she bid me a good day and left me to my work.

Now I cannot say that my curiosity was not sharply aroused by this odd turn of events, but sailors are a strange lot in many ways, inhabiting as they do their own closed and dangerous world for so much of their lives. And pirates, having removed themselves another step farther from the world most men know, take on an even more pronounced oddity of superstitions and rituals. So I took the matter lightly in my heart and went about completing my duties to repair of the vessel. By the noon sightings the rail was patched and painted.

Progress of a sort was made in the matters before the company.

Fortified with wine and the dwindling supply of rum, discussion took taken place on the sun-swept deck of the *Kestrel* as she rode the gentle swells of the North Sea, as the Caribbean was still called by some of the older hands.

There had been surprising little rancor amongst the men; the crew being split nearly evenly between those who thought the voyage ill omened and those who thought the original term of the articles should be maintained regardless. The former pointing out that seventeen men of the original crew, over a third of it, were either dead or wounded. The latter being divided into two thoughts on that subject.

One group in favor of continuing the account, lead by Quick, thought it simply a matter of 'more then for them that survive' and a second group, lead by Howell and Eaton, who had a superstitious scruple about breaking the agreed bond of the articles.

All hands however were in agreement that their adventures over the last three days would be spoken of wherever the sweet trade was practiced.

The officers of course were all in favor of living up to the original and agreed terms.

Rackham, to his great credit, did not make the decision making process a personal matter.

All hands knew that his leadership during the crises was above reproach. He gained them treasure, he led them to victories over three armed vessels, he fought, sweat, strove and rowed beside them. 'We have declared war on all the world' he reminded them 'and casualties are the fortunes of war.

"This is the finest deck I have ever trod. This is the finest vessel of her burden that sails on any sea, she has proved herself to — and for — all of us time and again. I would not trade her for the best Bermuda — still less for some hermaphrodite tub that falls prey to her."

The quartermaster stood and called for the crew's attendance.

"This is all so much spin drift," Corner said, "And until we deliver the muskets and cannon to Cudjoe's followers, and make a rendezvous with Vazquez to sell our recent plunder we are all bound together. Once we have accomplished these two goals, then we can decide upon the termination of our compact. We will have some weeks in which to calmly consider our final decision. In the meanwhile shipmates we are low in all supplies, the *Oloroso* being at the end of her voyage added nothing but some little sour beef and musty rice to our larder. Our cheese is fit for use as shot, and our peas for grape…and our shipsbread? We are receiving complaints daily, even from the millers," — this being a sailor's reference to the rats aboard.

At this there were healthy waves of laughter across the deck. "And far more dire and importantly I regret to inform you that we must agree to limit rum to a pint per man per day." This ended the laughter.

When the weeping and the gnashing of teeth subsided Trinket stood up. "What of the great pirate among us, George Fetherston?" He cried out in his high thin voice, "Master of the vessel, give us your council on these matters. Have we not sailed close to mutiny in speaking of paying down early, are these men who broach the matter perfidious dogs?"

There were several appreciative grunts of recognition regarding this fine point.

"Nah!" Fetherston's rumble stilled the crew. He gave the helm to Corner and stood to. "Mutiny is clear enough when it rises lads. It is either an armed assault upon the very authority of the articles in the person of its freely elected officers, or the refusal or disobedience of their lawful orders in time of peril or pursuit. We are all freemen here mates, free by our own hands, and we may speak freely of all things.

"Now the control of free men may be accomplished by force, or by custom or by consent. If it were by force — it be raw tyranny, if it be by custom it is a civil agreement based on the sound habits of the generations prior, but if by direct consent then it is a contract between those who are to be governed.

"We here have all agreed to abide by a compact amongst equals. This compact gives all authority to the majority; we officers serve as the visible expression of that majority, and serve at its pleasure."

"Now I tell ye all that I do not consider this voyage ill omened. I do not think it ill omened to have attacked a larger and strongly guarded vessel and come away having both taken and plundered it. That is what pirates do.

"Nay do I think it ill omened," he continued with a rolling boom that seemed to vibrate through the deck. " to have seen two of our number live out the spirit of our articles as regards private disputes to their deadly peril — and in full sight of us all. Nay! To me it were a thing of beauty and truth. God knows I were no fond of Michael Magoon, but jayzuz what a doughty and ferocious pirate he were. Nor yet do I think it ill omened to have come away from the fowler's trap, having boxed the fowler's ears in the getting."

"Now as to the matter of the vessel and the articles," He continued, "I will stay with the vessel and with the original terms of our partnership but I will hold no man to either by means of force. As both your quartermaster and commander have commented we are bound together by custom now until such time as we may exchange the weapons and goods that we carry for the gold we have all come for.

"As for me? When the required deliveries have been made any man who wishes to be paid off and leave our company is free to do so. Every man here has proved his courage and worth, I count each of you as a brother. So says I."

Having said all this he returned to the helm of the *Kestrel.*

The galley fire was lit for the first time in four days and a stew of rice and pork and peas was made, seasoned with the spices of the islands and thickened with shipsbread.

Talk of Reede began again, many commenting on his absence and questioning if he had sustained a serious wound in the combat. Assurances from Bonny and Rackham that he would be up and about on the morrow satisfied that curiosity and other matters engaged the crew until late in the watch as a quiet fell upon the vessel.

It was nearly midnight when Bonny came to my cabin as she promised. She walked boldly in, put her fists upon her hips akimbo tossed her head back and asked simply.

"Are you ready, John Tanner?"

I admit that I was indeed ready. As the evening progressed my thoughts wandered more and more frequently to this mysterious secret, which had Reede enlisting the aid of two shipmates to act as go betweens. I thought, why did Reede not just come to my berth and say, 'Ho! John me mate! I've a great and terrible personal secret to tell ye — IF ye will hear it, and also that ye swear on yer mother not to tell it to another soul.'

It was mystery upon mystery with Reede, Reede the reluctant pirate, Reede the pirate with the manners of a gentleman, Reede the merciful, Reede accounted by the crew as a right fearsome pirate indeed, and now Reede the pirate with a great personal secret.

It struck me again as to the company I was being admitted to. Two of the officers of the vessel as well as several of the leading pirates in the company — the thought of Snowden made me pause again, what had Bonny said about his admission to this select group? Painful and abrupt was it?

All thoughts of the danger Reede once warned me of in becoming too close with members of the crew — closeness that would compromise my standing as a 'forced man' if the vessel was taken were pushed aside in my great curiosity.

"I am fresh and preened and bushy tailed Ma'am, fit and ready for anything," I answered. I remembered Bonny's laughter at this later on.

Bonny led me a-stern to the very most aft part of the orlop deck, past the aft hatchway to the *Kestrel*'s sail locker. I remember stooping slightly and pushing aside the duck draped from the beam to the deck. I remember Bonny slipping quietly away behind me.

I remember the smell of limes, and the smell of must from the sails. I remember the dim golden glow of the whale oil corner lamp.

I remembered Vazquez, that day weeks before, when we were unloading in Negril bay '…very beautiful very fierce…' he said.

She sat before me on a couch made of sails, her face was lowered slightly her eyes bore deeply into mine, her mouth was pursed. Her unbound hair seemed to absorb the lamplight.

Her loose caftan was open so that I could plainly see her slender form, and the wonderfully soft whiteness of her breasts.

She was indeed very beautiful…in a fierce sort of a way.

Chapter 18
Mary

I don't believe that I could have been more dumbfounded in that first moment if I had ducked under the tarp to find an elephant in the sail locker, but I am a Bristol boy and not some sheep drover's lad. So ignoring my confusion and the hot flush of blood that swept over me, and quickly gaining my wits about me I said, "So Reede, what is this great secret for which you have summoned me abroad — at an hour when all honest men are abed?"

Her eyes went wide with surprise and then her head rocked back as she burst into a deep and throaty laugh. The shaking of her body did nothing to calm my rushing and confused heart.

She rocked forward and stopped, looking at me with her face still creased with lines of mirth and her eyes sparkling "John Tanner, I have loved thee since the moment I saw thee, and the knowing of thee has only strengthened my regard."

She just up and said it to me, just like that, there was never any hesitation or yawing with her. "Don't ask me to explain, John for I cannot." She sighed deeply. "We are about a dangerous business here John, and our friendship could be ended on any day by the fortunes of war. I could not contain my longing to tell you of it any longer.

"I swore to myself when I went ashore with Magoon that if I survived I would make myself known to you as soon as possible. I knew that if Magoon had killed me you would have soon enough known the truth of me, and I hoped think of our friendship in that light."

"Reede, I —"

"My name is Mary," She said, her spine going very straight.

She quickly continued, as she gathered her clothing more closely about her and looked toward the deck. "I feel like some Whitechapel trull casting her wares at you. I don't want to be that to you John — I WILL not be that to you sir, Damn-me I will not…no matter how much my heart yearns for you."

"Mary, I —"

“I offer ye freely the love that I have for ye, John, true and faithful it is. I have not known a man since my husband died…” Her eyes seemed to implore me. “I can understand that ye cannot take all this in…this change and all, in what you thought you knew of me”

She laughed a forced and rueful little laugh. “Think about it for a bit if ye like.” She said, facing away from me for the first time. “I understand, really I do, it is too sudden…I should have known you’d be shocked — and then there is the matter of some years between us as well. I’d been blind to that till just now; I’m being so foolish to think that ...” Her shoulders fell, and her voice trailed off.

“Mary …” I began once more.

“You have given your bond regarding this secret of mine,” She straightened and looked into my eyes again. “And I know that you are a man of honor. I am only hopeful that you will still consider us to be friends, regardless. I know that this is quite a shock and I understand — but I could not contain myself any further for this love of you.”

I cannot adequately describe the manner is which my heart was twisting inside of me, watching this strong, proud and beautiful woman open herself to me so completely. Watching her face work itself through laughter and hope, then to despair and self-doubt.

In my mind — I think my soul really — the transition from Mark Reede the bold, friendly and mysterious pirate I thought I knew, to Mary Reede the bold, friendly and mysterious woman in front of me, was taking place.

It came upon me as the feel of the deck of a vessel as it shifts and rolls and pitches under your feet as the helm goes a-lee, and then the deep groaning and vibrations that are made by the great booms of the *Kestrel* as they swing ponderously across the deck, the sails luff, and are then snapped by the wind onto the new tack. The vessel seems to leap into the wind.

I had always sensed something amiss with Reede, something at the corner of my mind, something in the air, so to speak. The fine facial structure, a softness in the eyes. The much-commented bouts of privacy, the cleanliness, the smell of limes.

Now finally it all became clear to me. The slight discomforts when we were too long alone together. The slight edge to some things that were spoken of between us. Her mouth and her eyes smiling at me, her hands, touching me so often…and her solicitous seeking of my companionship.

Vazquez as he first passed me that day at Negril, *"Que Mujer"* he said, 'what a woman." He called me a 'lucky rogue.' " I'd thought he called me a woman And lucky Magoon did not kill me on the deck. But he knew — knew about Mary, and her love for me. It was clear to him and completely lost on me. The crew was justified in their curiosity regarding the nature of our relationship.

I smiled at these rushing thoughts and laughed a little snorting laugh. She completely misunderstood my laugh, and her face took on that look of flint I knew so swell, her mouth set tight; however, I thought I also saw the wet eyes a woman gets when she is close to tears.

In that moment the great boom came to rest, the sails drew, and the deck settled.

I looked at the courage and honesty and beauty of the woman…the bold and singular person before me. As she opened her mouth to speak again I stepped closer and I knelt down in front of her — she who would be the great and only love of my life.

"It's all right Mary." It was at once the first thing I ever really said to her, and the first full sentence I'd gotten in since I'd lifted the tarp.

"I can return your love Mary, fully and without reserve. I will never tire of your face."

I took up her hands; they were dry and chaffed from the life of a sailor. They were at first stiff in my hands.

"My hands have been so cold tonight," she said looking at them cradled in mine and then her gaze crept up wonderingly into my eyes.

"I have warmth enough for two."

We looked at each other for a frozen moment, her eyes were soft now, moist, brimming, they the deep gray-green of the northern seas. Her face slowly relaxed and it seemed to brighten and expand once more in the soft glow about us.

"Will you…I mean can you," she asked it so softly, "I mean will you kiss me."

"God help the man who tries to stop me." I leaned toward her. Our lips more bumped then kissed in our shared nervous laughter. Then her hand came to my cheek, and my hand found her face and our eyes melted to one another and our lips met again — and my world changed forever.

I'm not sure how long we spent thus, touching each other's face and hands, touching ears and noses and brows, brushing hair and cheeks. Looking deeply into each other's eyes, both of us honestly trembling under the other's touch.

Kissing at first tenderly and tentatively, then more deeply, each holding the other's face — breathing into the other's mouth as the *Kestrel* rolled and gently pitched beneath us.

The kisses became at last a deep and surrendered kiss that has never ended. I remember as if it were this very morning, the first roaring rush of passion that swept us away. Its fires were never slaked, and have never died. It roared the last time, as it did the first. The sweet smoke of its burning still stings my eyes to this very hour. I will speak no more of it.

What I will speak of is my Mary.

Her face was a smooth as a young girl's, looking up at me from the crook of my arm.

I saw her, as she must have looked at nineteen. She might have been a milkmaid from some sonnet by Johnson. Her breath was soft against my chest as she slumbered there in contentment.

My heart has never been my own since that night.

This was the first of many times that we were able to enjoy each other through an entire night, and sleep in each other's arms. There was so much I wished to ask her. I was then — and now — in awe of her and I wondered how to begin without offending or angering her with my curiosity.

She stirred and stretched herself against me her eyes opened and for a moment she looked up at me with some concern. "Is there something amiss, John? She asked. I knew she meant to ask if I were sorry.

"I wonder how you could have kept this masquerade. Vazquez saw through it in an instant. How could I, who spent so much time in you company, not see you as the beautiful, unique woman that you are?"

"How did you see me then? How did you think?"

"My admiration and respect for you knew no bounds. It still is the same, more so really as the stories of your past are all the more remarkable. But now that I see you as you really are, I simply cannot fathom how so many could be mislead, on board a vessel or in the army."

"I mean my appearance, what manner of man did you take me for?"

"I thought you a very handsome and...well genteel man, particularly for a pirate. I thought you a little fine boned and delicately made for so rough and ready a life. Very mysterious as well. I was drawn to you, and frankly the warmth that I felt toward you confused me a little. I thought at one time that you might be the scion of some aristocratic family — the black sheep — you seemed so fastidious and particular in all that you did. So much in control of yourself."

"And all about me; that has always been the secret of it, careful control of myself and my surroundings, my relationships with men. I have had an advantage over any other woman — save Anne for whom it is only a game — any other that would take on the masquerade of a man, in that from the first I was raised as a boy."

My surprised look brought her story out in a rush.

"My mother, for whom I am named, was a woman who was, well 'airy' in her relationships with men. She married her husband — not my father — in a fleet marriage. They were happy enough when together as she told it to me. She became pregnant with my brother Mark, and was content for some months. Mark was a sickly child and shortly after his birth her husband went back to sea, he never returned.

Mark was only a few months old when she met a very handsome Scot who was bound for these same waters within the week of their meeting. She told me he reminded her of her husband, being so tall and blond and handsome...I think the gin helped a little."

She gave the little tinkling chuckle of a laugh I noticed once before, all the little things began to make some sense to me now.

"In any event she discovered to her dismay that she was once again to give birth, that being to this woman who loves you now. Her husband, good man that he was, left her sufficient resources so that she should live carefully, but comfortably, till his expected return. She lived in a respectable section of London, and her shame would be soon found out and reported to her husband's surviving mother in Portsmouth without doubt.

"She was nearly beside herself as she told it to me. She decided at last to quit London for the countryside, for Mark's health as she put it to acquaintances — little did she know. Once settled at Fotheringhay she passed herself as the widow of a sailor lost at sea — again little did she know."

I longed to draw her to me again, but her eyes remained in the past, and she continued in a soft voice as the *Kestrel* creaked and groaned about us.

"It was only a matter of months till Mark's health did fail and he succumbed to the colic, God rest his little soul. My mother's natural grief was comforted by the life inside her — mine — she also at once realized that now with a little forethought and cunning my birth might be masked by Mark's death.

"She wrote to her husband's family that Mark was still very sickly, so much so that she was worried that his development might suffer of it and that she would not travel back to London with him until the clean country airs had worked their healing properties."

She sighed and stretched in my arms, then turned her glowing face to my kisses.

"Imagine her surprise when she was delivered of a right plump and frisky girl child"

She snorted with laughter at the thought before continuing her story. "Mother thought she was now lost entirely when her husband returned, having left a boy behind. He might be deceived for a time, but at some time he would know, and then what? 'Oh dearest the midwife was mistaken did you not receive my letter telling you the droll tale…so silly really ha ha ha.' " Her body shook with suppressed laughter against mine. I stifled her laughter with my kisses.

"John, my darling, how am I to continue my story for you with all these interruptions?" She laughed into my face and grasped me to her once more with great strength.

"A year or more of this tension ended when a letter from her husband's family told her that his vessel never made its appointed landfall. The guilt of her relief at that news haunted my mother all her life; it ate away at her till at last it destroyed her. She was a thinker was my mother, and she began to think."

There came the thumps and pattering of the changing of the watch, and the voice of the master at the foot of the stern hatch. "Up ye go lads, ye can slumber on the deck, the wind is off the starboard quarter and the sea is a mill pond, there is naught to do but to enjoy the night."

"Within a few weeks we moved further into the country to a little village in Surrey and my mother began to dress and present me as a boy, as my brother Mark so I ceased to exist. So it went for the space of nearly four years. I was very early on bold, active and a little aggressive even as a small child so the role suited me more than it might have someone of a less spirited nature. So I was freed from the constraints placed upon women very early, and accustomed to the role that I play from first I walked.

"As the money her husband had left her dwindled, my mother began to write to my Grandmother how that dear Mark was beginning to strengthen and although slight and thin for his age, remember I am the full year younger, that he now appeared the picture of health, and the image of his father. She received letters in return desiring that she bring the precious grandson to London to meet his family. She demurred for another year so that I might grow and strengthen more before my presentation. I obliged her by shooting up like a weed and getting some nice scraped elbows and knees to show."

"As my mother told me the story, my Grandmother was so smitten with me that she wanted instantly to adopt me into her home. She made quite a case for it to my mother. How she was still a young and attractive woman who might easily find another good husband if not encumbered with a child's daily care. My mother, who blanched at the thought, quickly and tearfully told how I was the only part of her adored husband left to her and that though she had very little to sustain us, she would be parted with her child only by the cold hand of death.

My grandmother then contributed a crown a week to our maintenance and we lived frugally together my mother and I, as mother and son, all the years of my childhood. "

"I went to common school with the boys; I wrestled and fought with the boys. I learned to make up with subtleties and well practiced skills, and fierce aggressive action, for whatever I may have lacked in brute strength."

I lay enthralled with the story and enraptured by the woman. Her hand came up to touch my cheek in a gentle caress, and then she continued.

"When I was in my fourteenth year my grandmother died and the support from her ended. My mother then found me service in the stables of a lady of consequence she was acquainted with.

A decent enough woman and a decent enough position for a 'lad' of my station in life. And one in which, as is my habit, I sought to learn all I could of horses — the knowledge served me well a few years later. It was as well for my mother was already given to a little too much Geneva, and I believe she wanted the best she could do for me, while she could still do something.

The day before I left to take my cot above the stables my mother sat me down and advised me in the strongest possible terms to continue living my role as a man. She reminded me that there would be no outlet for my active spirit living as a woman, and that the poor must make the most of every opportunity that is presented to them. She warned me of things as regards my 'womanliness' that I should be fearfully certain of his quality before, as she said, 'discovering myself to a man.' She was most adamant as to the power you would have over me John."

"I do not seek any power over you."

"If you'd sought it, it would not now be yours. I love you so that I feel as if I may burst out of my skin; that is the greatest power any man may have over a woman. How I longed to kiss your face each time we were together, and now I both may and I must."

She slid up in my arms grabbed me by the ears and fairly covered my face with kisses.

We smothered our laughter in each other's shoulders.

"Once I'd learned about horses, and the grooming, feeding, farriering and shoveling thereof. I found the world of the working poor to be too constraining for what I'll admit is a restless and adventuresome nature. I found myself wondering down to the docks as often as possible and detouring any errand so as to pass by the quays.

There one fine day I saw a real man of war the *Ajax*, a beautiful fourth rate of fifty-two guns, shiny and new, sails white as milk. By the next morning I'd made up my mind, and by that night I'd signed aboard her as a lubber. It being a year and some days since I'd been taken in service."

"Yes, I remember you telling me something of you life from that point early on. Your story would be incredible to me were it not that I have known you these months, and seen first hand your prowess with weapons. And now I hold you in my arms and I feel my bond to you grow by the moment. Who would believe this story was it ever told? When I saw you go ashore with Magoon I worried with the worry of a friend, but now, now my blood runs cold at the thought of it. You've saved my life, Mary, three times is it?"

Then as that thought sank home another sprang from my lips. "Mary! Why in God's name did you not finish Magoon with your shot? Why did you put yourself in such peril? If I had known I would have shot Magoon dead in the longboat rather than —"

"That is exactly why you never knew. Things between Mike and me had to come to a head at some point — forgive me for saying it, as I never thought of you in this way, but you were the final stroke between us. He knew from the first that I was deeply smitten with you and it drove him furious — the great wheezing sodomite that he was. He remembered my laughing in his face, it burned him fierce.

He shouted it at me there on the beach. He loved me — in his own twisted way. He shouted that if he could not have me, then no other man would — and that he would delivery you to me in hell within the hour. But this does not answer your question beloved. The answer is simple enough, I missed."

I have never believed that.

"Then tell me of the combat that I saw then, and now see so differently. Your crewmates have all waxed poetic about it. They and I hung on every blow, I with increasing dread. And of the crew? It is impossible to overstate how excited and agitated they became."

"These are men that live a violent life; their joys are simple ones really, rum, danger and violence being chief among them. I cannot say that I was conscious of anything save the ferocious little man who sought so hard to kill me. I always knew that Mike was a terrible strong man but little did I know until I felt the power of his blows. Each one shook me to the ground, and he was much faster than I thought as well."

"I nearly despaired for you at one point. You seemed about to be simply overwhelmed by his attack — and then that slip at the last, my heart was in my throat. It trembles within me now as I remember those moments."

"It was indeed a nearer thing. Mike was no trained swordsman to be sure but his power and speed were formidable. His parries were very workmanlike, and his recoveries, very quick. He had learned his skills, such as they were, on the decks of his prey and by beating down the weapons of terrified men-of which I was not one."

She laughed her little chuckle at this and continued. "His lack of height made things very difficult for me. His blows came in high, and it kept me from trapping his blade for a thrust. After taking the full power of his blows for a time I realized that he indeed would wear me and slow me down unless I took back control of the contest."

She sat up now in a state of excitement as she relived the great drama she survived.

"Mike's great weakness lay in the fact that no one had ever attacked him on the low line-from below his waistline. I knew from our play that he had no skills in that quarter. He had never met a man shorter than he, but for me to take that line I would have needed to open myself to a deathblow. I needed to make my way backwards to the shore line where it fell away and thus arrange that he stood above me — I needed his eyes to be on a level with mine at least. The 'slip' as you recall it gained me a yard of space and time for me to draw my trump card."

"What in the world are you talking about?"

"I knew that my life — and the life of the man I loved — hinged on the next few moments.

I knew that I had strength enough for one powerful and sudden action in me, and that it must not fail. So I cast away my sash and opened my clothing so that he might see my breasts, I shouted at him 'think on these in hell you poxy little squid.' Lord, the rage in his face turned to shock and then to a foaming wildness.

The break in the beat of his attack gave me my opening. I dropped — as you saw — into the crouch of a mounted cavalryman and thrust up into him from below. It was an ultimate blow for me my love, all my strength was in it, if I had failed in it —"

"I thought for an instant that he took a part of your head with the blow that swept your little cap away," I said. "There was a great gasp that went up from the crew as well."

"Yes." She laughed. "My little bonnet, I suppose that I owed him a hat but it was such my favorite — it was indeed very close. I felt the kiss of his blade across the top of my head. It took all my strength to pierce his bodkin; it was like thrusting into wood.

"He'd have fought another two or three blows had I not finished him as I did…his eyes never left mine, I can see them still."

She was deathly quiet for a few heartbeats and then turned once more into my arms.

"Now that is enough of talk of fighting and death my beautiful John, hold me to you while we may my love, tell me that you love me, show me that you love me, let me swim in your face."

"I love you, Mary."

"Later as she drifted into slumber in my arms I whispered to her again "I love you, Mary."

"I love you too, John." She answered in an already dreaming voice.

Chapter 19
Hispaniola

I awoke that first morning together to find the pirate Reede standing over me with a wry smile upon his face. He was in the process of adjusting a wide red sash about his waist, and tucking a pistol and his Spanish dagger into it. I saw that what I had taken for a gown in the dim light was nothing more than one of Lovewell's voluminous nightshirts put to far better use on the slim handsome figure before me.

"It is good, Mr. Carpenter," he said, "that we serve upon the vessel where every man takes upon themselves the hours of an idler. All hands are called together for a meeting upon the weather deck, however much you may wish to lay about."

"And for pity's sake clothe thyself." It was Anne Bonny's voice — and laughter — from just outside the sail locker.

Out of Reede's stern face Mary's soft eyes regarded me searchingly as she asked in a quiet voice. "Do you wake to regrets then, John?"

"I have no regrets except for where we are. I am yours.

"And I am thine," she said before turning to join Bonny and mount to the deck.

In a brief meeting that morning it was determined that we should sail northeast through the Mona passage, and then back toward Jamaica through the Windward Passage, so as to come upon Jamaica from the north, rather than the south.

It being generally understood among the company that the English captain of the sloop of war, which we had so bested, would be fairly foaming at the bit to get at us again. He certainly knew who we were, and that we would be bound north for Jamaica. He would make every effort to intercept us, and would not underestimate us again. He had a fast vessel and was much our match in broadside iron. As his honor was involved, it was a bad prospect for the company.

It was also clearly understood by all hands that in firing upon one of his majesty's warships a line had been crossed. No case more clear could be made for piracy.

We were ten days at sail to cover the 500 nautical miles from the latitude of Barranquilla to the southern mouth of the Mona passage on the southeast coast of Hispaniola, foul weather and contrary winds having dogged us the while. We were now short of all provisions and Trinket suggested that we risk contact with the Boucanieros in order to procure meat and fresh water.

Resupply of the vessel was always a problem as no port was safe for us. And regardless of our needs we had deliberately avoided any contact with other vessels on our journey north so as to leave no trace of our passage for any patrolling English warship.

We came to anchor about a half mile off of the southeastern most coast of Hispaniola, lying between the large island of Saona and the mainland. It was the new moon and later when the sun set we were to be enveloped in a palpable blackness.

Under Trinket's instructions we signaled by gunfire for the attention of the Boucanieros who still inhabited the wilds of the flat green featureless peninsula that stretched away to either side as far as the eye could see.

"The old Boucanieros are in their way the fathers of us all," Trinket said, as he and Candy and Mary and I sat together in the shade offered by the longboats, "they go back over a hundred years and some on Hispaniola; there are a few enough of them now but years ago they were the terrors of these seas, and a prime source of willing hands for Henry Morgan when he brought fire and sword to Panama."

"They started out as wild hunters in the forests of Hispaniola, French mostly, tho' there were also Dutch and English among them, all of them an unwelcome challenge to Spanish authority on the island. The name comes from their method of smoke drying meat that they learned from the Arawak — which is what we are here to get for provision."

"A really untrustworthy and unpredictable brood of rapacious thieves," was Rackham's assessment in passing, which I found amusing considering his trade, "happily, we will be able to smell them before we see them."

Rackham was nervous as a cat since our arrival, particularly as night fell and an unrelieved pall of darkness enveloped the *Kestrel.* He ordered the boarding nets deployed, no lights, except for black lamps at the ready fore and aft, and a dozen armed men positioned around the deck at all times.

"The Spanyards have been working to root them out for many years," Trinket said. "They drove most of them north and eventually off Hispaniola to the island of Tortuga. No herds of wild cattle and swine on Tortuga for them manage and hunt so they turned their full attention to taking Spanish vessels — Lord the Boucanieros hate the daygos right fierce — as I said, a prime source of men for Morgan."

"Tell of their methods, Trinket," Candy said.

"From the beginning they would come out at night in their long canoes, guided by the stern lantern on vessels laid to for the night, and silently slip up to the stern of the vessel and jam the rudder so that the vessel could not be steered — then if the circumstance allowed simply board and murder the crew. If it came to a fight — their being hunters — they are deadly shots and their favorite being very long muskets with which they may standoff and kill anyone who came to the deck."

"The ones we will deal with however are not their grandfathers equals. There are less of the old hunters each year, and more what's in the way of being escaped slaves and others fleeing imprisonment or the Spanish courts. The old ones had more of a sense Commonwealth, as we have, today it is not so. They will trade, Vasquez deals with them, and I have done so for him, but as Jack said they are generally untrustworthy.

"These days they will as circumstance presents itself go out to take a vessel now and again, their canoes are fast and maneuverable and mount a lateen sail; they are no longer mariners however and will not leave the sight of land. It is good that we are strong, for such as we are outcasts and outlaws; there're none who would miss us. Were we not in such need of provision I would not recommend dealing with them at all."

"Are you sure they will come," I said. "They've not yet answered our signals."

"They will tonight, directly the sun sets."

The tide was up and the sea was calm that night. Trinket was on deck, and Rackham ordered an utter silence upon the vessel. Two men each were stationed at both the fantail and the heads, equipped with loaded musketoons, a black lamp, round shot to drop-down through the hull of any canoe that came under them, and with several grenadeos to hand as well.

At the turning of the glass to start the middle watch a faint sound came out of the dark silence surrounding the *Kestrel.* It might have been a fish breaking the surface.

Every man on deck strained to hear the darkness about us. "Who are ya?" Came a harsh and surly voice out of the darkness from the mainland side, our larboard, well off, beyond the range of the black lamps glow, faint but clear.

"We are Gentlemen of fortune," Fetherston's deep rolling voice answered the darkness.

"Where ye from?" said another voice from the darkness, on the island side, our starboard.

"We are from the sea," Rackham said from the bow.

"What flag? Faintly asked the darkness off of our stern.

"Our own, damn yeah," answered Fetherston.

"Black as the night it is, and bearing the Jolly Roger," said Trinket's from amidships.

This was greeted with laughter from several sources in the darkness surrounding the *Kestrel.*

"Where are ye bound then, ye gentlemen of fortune?" Asked the darkness off our bow.

"TO HELL!" Came the answering cry from all of the men on deck, punctuated by thumping and roaring, and the rumbling of the carriages as the cannon were run out through the gun ports.

There were several long moments of silence, except for the creaking of the vessel and the lapping of the water on her sides.

"What d'ye seek then?" From the first voice.

"We seek 500 weight of yer meat buccan, and fresh water," Trinket answered into the darkness.

What d'ye have for us?"

"We have powder and lead, flints and good Spanish wine."

A quiet pause again.

"Have ye silver?"

"Aye damn ye!... and we have black murderous hearts! — And we have grapeshot aplenty! — And we have cold steel as well for ye if you wish!" Fetherston roared into the black night.

A longer pause, the lapping of water was the only sound now.

"I am called Etienne — you will deal with me — so then bring yer powder and such to Boca De Yuma two days hence," this coming again from the first voice we had heard, "ask for me of any as may greet you," then a pause, and then a parting — "*Obwa Anglaz!*"

Then a stirring in the water, and then no more.

Then there was a complete silence from the waters and the darkness, strain as we might to hear the stirring of a paddle. There was no rest that night for any man aboard. Even most of those who were relieved sought such rest as they might get on the deck under the shelter of the longboats with their weapons close to hand.

At the turn of the morning watch we rode the tide down the channel between the mainland, and the island on our starboard, keeping the sweeps busy to give us way. We caught a bit of a land breeze when we came out from the shelter of the island but soon enough found ourselves working against a rising sea breeze.

The men were tired, the constant tension and watchfulness over the last two days took its toll, but Rackham and Fetherston were insistent upon working the *Kestrel* reach after reach upon reach until we had cleared sight of land.

Only then did we come about onto a long easy starboard reach, belay the sheets, and drop exhausted to the deck.

Exhaustion or not, an immediate meeting was called on the weather deck. No pomp or ritual this time, just a meeting of tired men.

"Gather up, mates," Rackham called out, "there will be rest enough in the grave. We need to consider our actions when next we meet our hosts. We will meet with the devil two days hence. I wish to repeat a knowledge to ye all, so that each man has heard it, and each may ponder it as he lays his head to a well-deserved slumber:

"We are the perfect prey for these rogues; we are not needful to them as Vasquez. No one would miss us, every man's hand is set against us, and perhaps our heads would even bring a bounty for them in Kingston or in Port-au-Prince.

"Like feral dogs they are, bold and cunning, they understand only strength, so we must show it to them, for like feral dogs — they seek a ready meal not a fight.

"Mr. Corner, as ye made know, keeps wonderful and particular records of all such things as may touch upon our account. He has informed me that at best we have provision sufficient for only ten days to a fortnight, so it is needful then that we do our dance with the devil… let us be ready then to play old Ned a merry tune if needs be.

"Now were I you I'd get such rest as ye may, for tomorrow will be spent on preparation. Carpenter, I wish to speak with you below."

I received instructions from the captain that as soon as I had taken a few hours of rest to begin work on the mounting of two of our swivel guns aft-most on the fantail so that they might be depressed sufficient that their fire sweep the area about the rudder. I acknowledged his order and straightaway sought my berth for some rest.

As I hoped, just as I was drifting into sleep Mary joined me and we settled into each other's arms.

Mary and I, the while trying not to expose the new relationship between us, spent as much time together as our duties allowed. My favorite time together, other than these times when she was able to slip unseen into my bunk, was after what was — at least for me — a stomach churning climb up to the main top cross tree, there to ride the wind as Mary loved to do. Mary of course was like a squirrel in the rigging. It was there that we first spoke of the future; it was there that we were able to hold hands.

"John," she said after a fond kiss, "I know that Rackham, and the crew, will demand that both ye and Candy take up arms when next we meet these 'buccaneers." I believe that we are far too strong, and that they will not make any attempt on us, and will simply trade; however, they are dangerous and unpredictable, and thus it is only prudent to visibly arm all hands."

I replied that I expected as much, and that frankly the idea that we had been so easily, quickly and silently surrounded by their canoes the black night prior unnerved me.

We were shocked from our sleep only moments later it seemed, by the insistent ringing of the ship's bell and Fetherston's loud call for all hands.

With the help of Mary, Snowden and Earle the stanchions and hardware for the mounting of two breach loading murderers on the fantail bulwark was complete when Fetherston took the noon sighting. They were set, as Rackham desired so that they might be depressed to sweep the area around the rudder. There were now two such mounted here at the stern, two more athwart the quarter deck just forward the bitnacale, a brace each side amidships, and two at the heads.

All hands indeed worked throughout the day in preparation for our attempt at resupply. Loaded pots were prepared for the murderers; the deck appeared awash with loaded muskets and freshly honed steel. Everything cleared for action.

At the turn of the first dogwatch the bow of the *Kestrel* was turned landward once again.

Rackham came on deck with Corner and Fetherston, Anne Bonny and Trinket. And the company was called together.

As soon as Corner had called things to order, I stood up. "If it please the company, I am the slave of the company, having been brought aboard against my will; however, I am led to believe that this company is in danger of being attacked and that my life is no less at risk then any man of the company's. Therefore I wish the company to arm me so that I might protect my life. I warrant to return all weapons when the danger has passed, and to make no attempt at escape."

I had no illusions as to my fate with the Boucanieros if taken alive, slavery perhaps, held for ransom a certainty…also I would not be separated from Mary.

"I too wish to be armed Jack," Candy called as he stood forth, "that night, we being surrounded in the blackness, made me very uneasy. These are not men to trifle with.

This was all greeted by loud exclamations of approval across the deck. Rackham wore a rueful smile, as he nodded to the company and raised his hand to enjoin quiet upon it.

"It is so noted then, pistols and swords will be issued to ye and ye shall both be assigned to that fresh brace of murderers on the taffrail.

"Pay attention now all of ye, the Bahia de Yuma is a league broad and deep, there is a playa and a small settlement on the bluff where the Yuma flows into the bay. We will ride the tide and the sea breeze into the bay tomorrow, and then drop anchor a cable off that settlement, broadside on starboard, so that we might blow it to hell if we have to."

"Trinket says he has dealt before with this Etienne back when he worked for Vasquez. Trinket thinks that if Etienne meant to attack us he would've done so back there in the blackness, and that any attack is unlikely. Etienne knows that we are a heavily armed vessel and manned by dangerous men. We will be on our best behavior but we will remain ready and alert at all times."

We were early, the day following, coming into the bay of Boca de Yuma with the tide at the turn of the afternoon watch. It was Rackham's nature to be early.

The bay itself was quite beautiful, broad and deep as Rackham said, with deep, dark blue water. It was ringed by low to moderate height limestone bluffs and had several good anchorages in or close to the little harbor of Boca de Yuma.

The village itself sat atop a headland that jutted out into a small natural harbor formed by the highest rocky arms in the bay; they seemed to embrace its numerous fishing boats and large canoes. The port had once been known as Higuey, the site from which Ponce de Leon set forth on his adventures of discovery.

It appeared now as a sleepy backwater of a foundering Spanish Empire, surrounded on all sides by the vast expanse of a savannah of low-lying brush and trees, made lush and green by good water and abundant sun regardless of the poor soil.

A small Spanish fortification overlooked he port on the southern arm, un-flagged and un-garrisoned, much to the relief of all aboard — save me, for I thought if I could swim ashore I might find relief from my captivity in sanctuary with forces of the now friendly nation of Spain. Then I thought of Mary.

Showing his usual good caution, Rackham ordered us brought in close to the southern cliff and thus anchored under any guns on the Spanish fort. He ordered the sweeps brought up and ready to hand if we needed to gain sea room quickly.

We were not long at anchor when a fishing skiff with five men aboard made out from the base of the cliff below the town. As it drew near — under the watchful eyes of the *Kestrel*'s crew — a tall slender man with eyebrows, eyes and closely trimmed pointed beard of a coal black, stood up in the bow. He wore a very broad brimmed low crowned plaited hat, a long bright red kerchief about his neck, a loose white shirt that billowed about his lean figure, and leather knee britches belted about his slender waist. He carried only a dagger thrust into his waistband.

"Ahoy Le Bateau," he cried out, *"bienvenu* a' Boca de Yuma, I am Etienne "

Trinket and Rackham stepped forward to the rail…Trinket's appearance elicited a great 'whoop' and a swooping gesture of greeting with both arms by the figure at the bow, who then turned and shouted with obvious merriment to his four companions. *Voici amis! Il est la petit yeux de grenouille, le bibelot."*

He then turned back and addressed Trinket with a wagging finger. "Be advised that LeBaiseur's fat sister is still looking for you Ami." This was greeted by a raucous laughter from both his companions and the crew of the kestrel. Trinket blushed.

Etienne turned his attention to Rackham and addressed him in a great booming voice. *"Bon Jour Mssr. Le Capitan.* I am finding you in good company. My name is Etienne LaBeouf, my gran-pere's name was Etienne Roland LaBeouf who marched with Morgan — and was defrauded and robbed of his share by Morgan, may God scour his black English heart — no offence." He made a dismissive gesture with his hands.

"My father was Henri LaBeouf who died in honorable combat with the grandees at Sabana Real. My name is Etienne LaBeouf, and I answer to no man but Jesu. We thought to take you that night, Captain, but we could see that you prepared for us, we could see the black lanterns and armed men — hard men — at every quarter. There were thirty of us but we knew that to take you, men would die, and my men…well, they do not care to die so much… so we decided to talk, and to trade.

"I have for you Mssr. Le Capitan, 500 English pounds of good jerked buccan — if you keep it dry it will stand till Jesu returns. I have as well six butts, filled this very day, of fresh water from the Yuma — I will require an equal number of empty butts in exchange of course. I can also supply you with plantain, mangos, beans and limes. What do ye have for us in return?"

Trinket said, "We offer in return 25 pounds each of powder and lead bar, 2 barrels of red Spanish wine and fifty new flints."

"Do you wish rum?"

Rackham said, "I will inquire amongst the crew"

"Regrettably *mes amies* rum is for silver only."

The haggling began.

Mary came aft to speak with Candy and me and I lost all interest in the waving arms and bickering that went into the final arrangement. She brought orders that we were to be friendly and wave but in no wise to relax our vigilance.

Within the hour canoes and small boats began rounding close about the headland and coming up under our lee. Etienne, and his boat with Corner aboard, served as an 'accounting house' as food and water were delivered according to the agreed terms.

The boarding of the heavy water butts was accomplished by securing two stout lines on deck, then a loop — or bight — of each was sent over the side, with stout hands ready to haul on the running end. The barrels were encompassed within the bights of the lines and by hauling on the running ends the barrels were rolled up the side of the vessel. They were then lowered, by the pulley and cargo net attached to the main boom to the hold. Each was tested, and the waters were indeed sweet.

It was of course impossible to accurately weigh the dried jerked meat that came up rack after rack onto the deck, Corner's inspection and approval was sufficient; I noted that in fact several racks were not accepted after he felt and smelled them. The dried meat that came aboard gave off a wonderful smoky scent that made my mouth water.

The very last to be shipped aboard were four barrels of rum — strict orders were circulated from all of the officers to the crew. No one was to broach them prior to our gaining the sea. The order cautioned of marooning for any man who disobeyed.

Rackham, Trinket, Corner and Etienne toasted one another with the Spanish wine, which Etienne and his men carefully inspected, along with the powder, lead, flints and agreed silver payment. Our final salutes with the Boucanieros were full of good spirits and bon home. Despite this, Rackham ordered the sweeps and we moved out into the center of the bay. Every vigilance in place, every man armed, and every gun charged.

We stood out from Bahia de Yuma with the evening tide, and were soon upon a fine and fragrant following land breeze. At the turn of the middle watch all hands were stood down except for six very tired men who took the normal watch. Candy and I surrendered our weapons as agreed, and I stumbled off to my berth.

Mary and I slept together that night like stunned sheep, wrapped in each other's arms.

At dawn we passed Punta Borrachon and left the Mona Passage behind us.

Chapter 20
McNast

The noon mess on the *Kestrel* that day included the last of the cheese aboard. It was deliberately the last cheese to be used, as it was a hard cheese from Suffolk. The cheese preferred by the Royal Navy's Victualing Board, as it stored well for long periods of time — much like a wheel of Oak might.

> "Them as made ye were not civil
> They made ye harder than the devil
> Iron won't cut, nor fire light thee
> Dog's may bark but kenn'no bite ye!"

Trinket cackled at this rhyme aimed at the Suffolk cheese commonly served on board his majesty's vessels. It was a fine day, a bright sun, a fair breeze off the starboard quarter, the singing of the water on our hull was accompanied by spritely little aires and jigs from the musicians.

We sailed as was normal for such conditions, on main and fore courses alone with the top hamper bare and a watch at both tops.

Our 'mess' as usual consisted of myself, Mary, Candy, Trinket, Snowden and either Dowd or McGinnis or both. It would be both today as we saw Dowd carefully making his way along the rail to join us.

Dowd settled in with us, it was difficult for him, as he had lost all feeling in his left leg due to his buttocks wound. He fell away from the tiller, the day of the duel and the escape from the English war dog, because his leg went numb. I made him as good and as light and comfortable a crutch as possible. 'None better ever made' was Snowden's appraisal when we presented it to Dowd.

Dowd's condition was the cause of much consternation and regret for Snowden, he knew that he must soon lose his old tie and mess mate, as Dowd's condition would have him paid down and set ashore at the first opportunity. Two other of the wounded, Bodie and Syms, would be paid down as well as a result of their wounds incapacitating them for work aboard a vessel.

The company discussed the matter of where these men might be safely evacuated in some depth. The court of free men allotted 500 pounds for each of them, little enough really but far more then they'd have received from any other source. A final decision awaited an opportunity, and as it sometimes happens opportunity would present itself that very day.

"Sail ho!" Came a cry from the tops, "hull down off the starboard beam."

There was the usual flurry of activity on the deck whenever such a cry went up.

A shout went down the hatchway for Rackham's immediate presence, Corner took the helm and Fetherston called hands aloft, including Mary, to set the topsails. All hands stood to the sheets awaiting orders. In a few moments Rackham gained the quarterdeck.

"It's a damnet butter box," came a cry from the maintop.

"How do you make her," Rackham shouted up to the maintop watch.

"She's an old fluyt, heavy laden by the look and flying Dutch colors."

Rackham turned to Fetherston with a questioning look.

"Slow steady sailer," Fetherston replied to the unspoken, "an older pattern Dutch cargo vessel, wide of beam and boxlike, lightly armed with a few four pounders at best."

"Make us a course to intercept her, George," said Rackham.

I wondered at this decision, as to my understanding we were looking to slip into Jamaica unheralded from the north, taking any additional prizes seemed contrary to that goal.

But dogs will be dogs, and pirates will be pirates.

Over the next hour we worked ever closer to the Dutch vessel, on her part there was absolutely no indication that they saw us at all. There was no deviation from her course, no actions aloft, no sign of any alarm at all…nothing.

At musket range we pulled slightly ahead and a shot was sent across her bow.

There was no discernible reaction, so a second round was fired.

Flustered, Rackham ordered us into pistol range and set himself into the shrouds with the speaking trumpet in his hand,

"Heave to ye bastard, come about and back yer sails." Rackham shouted through the speaking trumpet.

"Bugger thyself. Ye randy little piss sack," came an answering hail from a large man who appeared on the narrow high stern of the fluyt. He wore a bright yellow and red tartan kilt, an unbuttoned dark green Dublet over a common linen shirt, and a tricorn.

"My God it's old McNast," cried McGinnis.

"Lord preserve us," said Fetherston.

"Damn ye sir! howled Rackham, "heave to for I have a will to inspect your cargo."

"Inspect yer arse ye wee stoat,' McNast's replied. "I'm carrying no'but Palo De Tinto Jack'o, ye kenn'no eat it — nor drink it — nor yet bugger it. So what use then is it to pirates? Ma 'crew is ma own sons, and I will scuttle the tub b'fore dipp'n m'flag to ye

…so piss off."

Rackham heaved a great deep sigh, the sort of sigh a man may heave when he knows he's beat going in.

"Would he do such a thing?" I asked of McGinnis.

"Sure as you're standing there," McGinnis said, "She'd be salvage then, useless to us."

By this time much of the crew had gathered around, they being both amused by Rackham's fusticated reaction, and curious about the unexpected nature of the vessel, and its obviously unimpressed and mouthy captain.

"Log wood," one said, "that be a rich prize." "Aye," said another, "but what to do with it if we took it, during the wars there were opportunity with such a prize, but not now."

"We're only two leagues or so off the coast here," McGinnis continued, "she's carrying a load of wood, he could waterlog her and use a sea anchor …any other but us could board her and claim salvage rights."

"Who is this terrible old man who stops pirates in their tracks?" I asked of McGinnis.

"He's an interesting and colorful old bastard to be sure. He'd be in his 70s now and wracked by the rheumatisms, but he was the very devil when he marched with Morgan to Panama back in '71, he was maybe 20 then, a Scot through and through. He couldn't stand the English, and only marched with Morgan as Morgan was Welsh… and of course for the gold… of which he was defrauded… typical Morgan.

"Sailed as a privateer only, never went on the account. His ship *Lady Grace* wrecked in a gale off St. Martin's, he were rescued by a Dutch captain, sailed with him for some years, married his daughter, last I heard they raised a hell of a brood of right hellions."

"Fetherston and I were serving together, privateering with Ben Hornigold, on the *Mary Anne* when we come upon McNast on the main one day, about a year before the Treaty of Rastat. He was holding letters of marque and reprisal from the Dutch and the French at the time, had two of his sons aboard, and rough looking boys they was too.

His legs was pretty bad already, gimped up left arm too, cool as can be in a press, ferocious hot temper, always thinking deeper than ye thought he was, and oh lord the mouth on him… as ye've seen."

Rackham, Corner and Fetherston were in a deep conversation at this point. When they apparently come to some conclusion, Fetherston stepped up into the shrouds.

"Squire Thomas," he cried out' "Tis me George Fetherston, and Alexander McGinnis is aboard as well, we have a proposition we would like to make to ye."

"Ah! George me lad, I thought I recognized that great noble beak of yours — and McGuiness too? Lovely. What sort of proposition do ye have in mind, laddie?"

"We have wounded aboard and would like to arrange passage to the American colonies."

"I've no sick bay, George, and passage for honest men may be booked in any port."

There was laughter from both vessels.

"They are not sick, but they are incapacitated for any further work at sea; they have been good mates and true, and we wish to assure them a safe landfall. Alexander and I both attest to their good nature. May I suggest that we visit one another here to reacquaint, and to discuss the matter — and of course the fees. What say ye, will ye heave to here and tarry with us long enough?"

"Do ye have yer warpipes aboard then, laddie?"

"I do indeed."

"Ach, it's been s'long since I've heard the sweet sound of the He 'lands — yer a silver tongued devil ye are George. Ken'ye still the Ballad of 'Seathan' darling boy?"

"Aye Thomas, and we have the Bodhran, Fiddle and wee pipe to hand."

"Ahh, make ready then, I'll come a'boot and tarry a bit w'ye."

Fetherston gave the orders needed, and the *Kestrel* came about into the wind. The fluyt was well handled, but being broad of beam and heavy-laden she took some time coming to about 100 yards off our larboard.

The orders from Corner to the crew were simple enough, it was an old friend of Fetherston's come to visit no more no less. Such as we had of rum and wine and victuals were brought up and the musicians made ready as Fetherston disappeared down the aft hatchway.

I watched as the launch that had been tied off to the stern of the fluyt was brought forward and the process of manning it began. Four men, two of them obviously young boys, came down first, and then the man McNast was carefully helped down the ladder into the launch, his difficulty was plain to see.

In the years that have passed since I have seen many others of those who made their lives upon the sea crippled up in the same manner by injury, and wound, by constant dampness and hard work and cold.

As the launch bumped against our side Fetherston returned to the deck carrying his bagpipes. Our ladder was unrolled down the side. The crew of the launch were most solicitous in their aid to the old man as he painfully mounted to the deck of the *Kestrel*.

The old man was infirm on his feet and supported by his two young grandsons. He had short steel grey hair, a grizzled handsome and intelligent face, fierce grey blue eyes, with a ready and engaging smile, which blossomed brightly when he first saw Fetherston and McGinnis waiting for him.

From the curiously frayed edge of his tricorn a tiny green head appeared, took a few cursory chews on it, and then swooped off to make Snowden and two others duck before landing on McGinnis' head and becoming abusively vocal — to the delight and laughter of all who witnessed the little rogues' storming of the vessel.

"Ach now laddies, Ma sweetie's no'but a wee hen Parrotlet, weigh'n n'more then a good fart. Now if she were two or three stone that might be another thing entirely, but for now she be naught of a threat to such brave burley pirates as ye are…and of course I'll kill the man who harms her." he said with a broad smile.

"Here are ma' two eldest sons, Hamish and Resin, and ma' gran'bairns Colton and Oengus," and so he introduced his companions as the little bird returned to its roost in his hat — still complaining and hectoring all about.

McNast and his two sons — both sturdy hard looking men — settled in on kegs brought up from below as rum and such were made available. I noted that the two grandsons never strayed far from the old man's side and were quick to accommodate any need.

After some small talk and reminiscing of the past war, Fetherston took up his warpipes and after the blowing, wheezing and bleating that is common to getting bagpipes ready to assault the senses he was joined by the *Kestrel*'s musicians in playing a long and mournful ballade to which the old man sang in Gaelic with a fine tenor voice, he was joined on the repeating choruses by McGinnis and several other hands who were familiar with the tune.

Dowd, Bodie and Syms, sitting near the center of the assembled crew, joined also on the choruses. Dowd turned to Mary and I as we sat together, as we always did now.

"Seathan is the name of a son of the king of Ireland," he told us, "it is a tragic love song, very old it is, a waulking song, usually sung by women pounding new tweed to soften it but also popular in the old days with sailors hauling on the sheets — a fine voice on the old man is it not?"

As the song wove its spell over us, Mary and I turned to each other, our eyes locked and we gazed into each other, and a deep understanding seemed to pass between us.

When the last sad notes of the Seathan died away the Bodhran player beat a long rattling tattoo and all broke into a wild series of warlike marches starting with the familiar strains of the march of Brian Boru. Men danced on the deck and muskets and pistols were fired into the air both on the *Kestrel* and on the deck of the fluyt nearby, and the rum flowed freely. There was a thumping and a roaring.

I noticed that the old man drank sparingly and seemed always to observe all about him, his placid gaze fell on Dowd, Bodie and Syms and lingered on them in no obvious manner. After a time Rackham broached the subject of passage for our wounded and Dowd, Bodie and Syms were brought forward.

The old man addressed them.

"Two stout men and true, who are like the blood o'ma heart to me, have recommended ye to me," he said, "and for that I take ye aboard ma barky for passage to the American colonies, and for their sake alone I am willing to do so. Only sa'lang as ye understand and faithfully obey ma rules. Ye may bring yer duffel aboard and yer dirk only, no other weapon may be found upon ye and if any be later found ye'll all be tossed overboard together, and so also if ye cause any disruptions to ma crew. Ye shall be well treated and fed, and will confine thyselves to the foc'sle and the heads only."

"Nay'sight of ye must be seen by any vessel or person till we release ye in Charles-Town. We will deliver ye safely ashore with yer duffel on the Charles-Town docks. Ye shall pay me one hundred Guilders each for yer passage and board. Thy mates who recommended ye to me, can attest that I will do all what I say or perish in the attempt. Now let's have some of that Barbados while ye and yer captain determine whose purse shall be the lighter."

"It is accepted as proposed, and the account will pay their passage," Corner said.

As arrangements to transfer Dowd, Bodie and Syms to the fluyt were being made — the farewell between Dowd and Snowden was a pitiful sight and Snowden disappeared into a great melancholy for some days afterward — Rackham — well in his cups — drew me aside.

"I am no fool, John," the first ever he used my Christian name, "I know that you and Reede have become…close." He chuckled. "Most of the crew have noticed as well, though they do not know the full of it. Reede is committed to stand to with the company until we have scraped the hull in the Caymans. "She," the first ever that he admitted Mary's true nature, "wants the full bounty of a thousand pounds — and who may blame her, eh?"

"Fetherston, Corner and I have discussed the matter and if you will give the company your bond, that you will make no attempt to escape or to subvert the company, and will remain with us — freely — to supervise the scraping and caulking of the hull, then you shall have all the freedom of a signed member, and when that necessary work is completed we will set you and her safely ashore at Kingston… and you shall have 100 gold guineas in your purse, what say ye?"

He had me, and he knew he had me, and upon reflection I could only give one answer, as I would not be separated from Mary. "It shall be as you say, Captain; however, I will not accept your stolen guineas. I wish only to be released from this captivity and allowed to pursue my life with the woman I love."

“So then it is. I knew ye’d strike a hard bargain,” he said, laughing as he walked away.

The first benefit of this agreement was made available to me when I was allowed to accompany Mary, Trinket, Fetherston and McGuiness to go aboard the fluyt with Dowd and the other wounded.

McNast and his sons were already back upon the fluyt as the *Kestrel*’s longboat pulled away for the short row to the other vessel. We bumped along side where the ladder had been left hung prepared for us.

The old man met us at the top of the ladder himself as we came aboard, the affectionate friendship between Fetherston, McGinnis and him apparent for all of his crew to see. The crew consisted, in addition to those who had come aboard the *Kestrel*, of two other sons, two older grandsons, two sons in law, a brother in law and two nephews in addition to a daughter in law named Pym who served as cook for the voyage.

He and his crew were justly proud of a trim and shipshape old vessel, the lines all Flemish, the brass all shining and the deck clean and open. I remember the clean perfume of the logwood filling the air above and below deck. The vessel was indeed heavy laden with the rich fragrant dyewood from which the nation of Brazil gets its name, and from which the vibrant red dye used in cotton and woolens is made.

The foc’sle was clean and tidy, well aired and wholesome and our wounded were given good bunks. Once we had settled them comfortably in and hearty farewells had been given all around, McNast invited our party to his cabin for a farewell tot of Dutch GraanJenever.

As we entered McNast’s cabin we were greeted by a harsh strident demanding voice “Damn ye deliver yer purse!”

“That would be Lord Squakington,” said McNast, indicating a cage in the corner of his cabin where-in sat a large green parrot with its feathers all puffed out at the sight of so many strangers, “Pieter Squakington if you like,” he continued, “if ye have a finger ye have no further need of be sure to poke it into his cage.”

Once we were comfortable and McNast’s ‘wee hen Parrotlet’ was returned — complaining and scolding — to her cage next to Lord Squakington’s the liqueur was poured out into good Dutch glassware and a farewell toast was made, then a second glass was filled and Fetherston turned to McNast.

"Thomas," he asked out of the air, "are ye still a deacon of the Wee Church O'The Heather as well as captain of this vessel?"

"I am both indeed laddie, why would ye ask such a question?"

"Because I would like ye to marry these two." Fetherston said indicating Mary and me.

I thought McGinnis would choke on his glass as he blew some of the liqueur out through his nose, Trinket cackled with his odd laughter. Mary and I were both thunderstruck by Fetherston's blunt address. We looked at each other questioningly and indicated clearly to each other no prior knowledge of such a thing. Our eyes locked again in the way they did so often, and the die was cast for us.

"Ach no laddie, not even for thee, I care not personally how you…any man…but marriage be made for man and woman alone. As a Deacon o' the wee Church of the Heather I kenn'no do such a thing, and as captain I will not.

"I am a woman." Mary said.

McGinnis choked and spewed again.

"Now laddie —" McNast began

"Are ye deaf old man?"

McNast gave her a long hard look. "Aye I ken now that you are, and a right proper gnarly one at that…are ye sure ye know what yer about with this one laddie?" he asked me.

Mary and I laughed together. The laughter spread around the room till the cabin rang with it and the birds began to chirp, and the one Pieter began to bob his head

"All right then gather up here I've log wood to deliver," McNast said, "who will give the bride?

"I will," said Fetherston.

"Do ye have a best man, and a ring"? McNast asked me.

"I'll stand with him," Trinket said, "and he has no ring save the iron one about his ankle."

"As soon as he can breath proper again I'm certain that Mr. McGinnis will be happy to witness the marriage" He continued.

"What are yer full names then?" asked McNast.

"John Tanner."

"Mary Reede."

“Gather up close here together w’me then John and Mary and take each others hands.

“Will ye then, John Tanner, take this Mary Reede as your wife, to love, honor, serve and protect her all the days of her life, to be faithful and true in all things, to bear her council and treat her as you would your own flesh. Do ye so swear before God, and by yer honor?”

“I so faithfully swear,” I said

“Will ye, Mary Reede, take this John as your husband to love, honor, serve and protect him all the days of his life, to be faithful and true in all things, to bear his council and treat him as you would your own flesh. Do ye so swear before God, and by yer honor?”

“I do so swear,” she said

“Then by my authority as captain of this vessel, and as a deacon of the wee Kirk o’ the Heather I declare ye as married, making ye as one flesh before the great God Jehovah, and may no man presume to put asunder that which God has joined.”

Mary and I embraced…and McGinnis began to cry.

Chapter 21
Queen Nanny

I was in an odd dream. I was once again in a shipyard, not the Albion, much smaller.

All of the familiar sights, smells and sounds surrounded me. The sweet smell of fresh cut wood, the scent of tar, the thud of mallets and the singing rasp of saws. I came up behind an older man seated on a workbench and writing something on a stern-plate.

I looked over his shoulder…in a fine sweeping hand he was writing, 'Mary'…

Then I awoke to see her face beside me in the gloom of the orlop, peaceful, beautiful.

The creaking of the vessel, and then sleep enveloped me again

Two additional vessels were taken in our journey back to Jamaica, for what purpose I could not imagine. Both prizes were small trading sloops with cargoes of perhaps two hundred pounds in value, additional food and rum of course but still. I felt that we were simply Announcing our presence and wondered at the wisdom of doing so. In neither case was there a captain's trial, or any attempt at recruitment, just a businesslike plundering.

One such taking in particular resulted in Mary's unmasking to the crew. On board the sloop was a woman who made notice of Anne and Mary's true sex. Anne's was of course an open secret among the men, but Mary's remained unknown to almost all the crew — the exceptions being those I have before mentioned.

This woman verbally, and loudly, assaulted both Anne and Mary as being, "wanton, drunken, poxy sluts and unkempt whores," and as the "rum soaked, villainous, and hell bound spawn of Satan." Anne and Mary, by way of return, spent some time in a loud discussion as to the best method of killing the woman. Other members of our crew aboard the prize witnessed all this with their mouths agape.

As I have said before, sailors are among the most superstitious men in the world.

They have a peculiar superstition that women on board a vessel bring bad luck.

Bonny's presence on board never set well with many among the crew, some grumbled in the beginning, but made no major protest.

The disclosure thus of an unknown and secreted woman aboard nearly lead to a mutiny.

The subject of an ill omened voyage was spoken first in whispers and then aloud. It was of no consequence, to some in the crew, that the account was full or that we had bested all comers. "The voyage h'aint or' yet…is it?" was put forward in answer.

"Don't forget that albatross that we seen when we took the carpenter aboard," Quick said, "I told ye all then that them birds is not a good omen when ye see them circle ye like that."

I will admit that I had some fear of violence breaking out between Quick and his party, the remnant of Magoon's faction, and the bulk of the company, who for their part seemed as much amused as anything by the surprise development, and entertained in remembering the scene between Mary, and Anne and the woman aboard the prize.

Rackham was of no use in this, he and Bonny being looked at askance in the matter, and Corner just seemed dumbfounded by the situation. In the end Fetherston and Trinket resolved the issue both held in an almost religious awe by the crew.

Fetherston made clear his opinion that such superstitions were unworthy of men, and belonged on vessels manned by sheep. He reminded them as to who led them aboard the *Oloroso*, whose prowess was unquestionable, who struck down a most fearsome man who wronged her. He reminded them of the articles, and wondered if any would care to go ashore with Reede to settle the matter.

Neither Quick nor any of his group ever mentioned the matter again.

When Fetherston brought us in sight of the headland to the north of Port Maria on the northeast coast of the island, the *Kestrel* turned south along the coast keeping about two leagues off. On the third day, just at sunset, Trinket spied the bay that he sought. We lay to for the night.

The bay and the village lay two leagues or so northwest of the little harbor of Port Antonio. The village lay at the bottom of a broad shallow bay a mile of so from the mouth of the Rio Grande. We came in to anchor at dawn about an half-mile west of the river and a quarter mile off shore. Rackham was never at ease in this sort of circumstance and as usual paced the deck anxiously as a boat was lowered away so that Trinket could make contact.

Preparations were begun on board to deliver the two little three-pounder field pieces promised to the Maroons, along with a last dozen of muskets as well as powder taken from the *Oloroso.*

Shortly after noon our boat returned. Trinket made contact and runners were sent to the main Maroon village high up in the forest, called Nanny Town. Trinket brought word that men and transport would meet us on the beach at high tide the next morning. Shortly after Trinket's return canoes came out from the village carrying fresh produce and provisions for us. It was evident in Trinket's dealing with them that the high regard in which they held this little man who returned from the dead was not diminished.

We lay at anchor, and on full alert, throughout remainder of the day. On three occasions sail was seen on the horizon, in each instance Rackham and the crew where sent into a flurry of tense indecision. The quandary of the pirate struck them, were the sail those of a man-of-war that we must flee? Or were they were rich prizes that we might miss through inactivity? The night brought relief from that tension, but the vessel remained on high alert.

Prior to turning in for the night, Rackham called myself, Mary, Trinket, Snowden and McGinnis to a meeting with him, Corner and Fetherston. We were informed that we were to land with the cannon and proceed to the Maroon village in order to assemble the guns and instruct the Maroons in their use. Once the landing was made, the *Kestrel* would proceed out to sea, and return for us in a week.

At dawn the next day, and at the high tide, as promised a large company of armed black men with mules and simple carts appeared on the beach, and both of the longboats were lowered away to receive the guns and their carriages, and their loading begun.

The guns were light field pieces designed for direct use in line of battle — sometimes referred to as 'grasshoppers' by the infantry that used them. The barrels were brass and clearly marked at 2.1.3 or 255 pounds apiece, great care was taken in lowering them into the boats. All of the various pieces of the carriages were accounted for, cheeks, transoms, trunnion plates, wheels and axletree bodies, as well as the required linchpins washers and bolts plus the rammer, ladle, sponge and hand spikes. Total weight of each gun and assembly about 500 pounds.

Those of us assigned to accompany the guns to Nanny Town arrived with the first boat, and the man who first greeted us as we waded ashore was the same imposing black man that I saw as we dealt with Vasquez at Negril. Trinket introduced him as Cudjoe, chief captain and brother of one he called Queen Nanny. He was tall and powerfully built, with coal black skin and closely trimmed hair and chin whiskers of pure white; he carried himself with unquestioned authority among this company of about 50 strong and smiling black men.

Landing the cannon barrels proved to be the most difficult part of the operation. The longboats were beached, and after the carriage parts, muskets and powder were removed to several low narrow carts waiting at the water's edge, the barrels were secured by strong ropes and strong men over one gunwale, then the longboat was careened on the off side so that the barrel might be gently coaxed over and out onto a waiting sledge. A mule then pulled the sledge off the beach and up toward the forest.

Corner met briefly with Cudjoe and accepted a heavy leather bag from him, containing as Trinket told me, not only silver pieces of eight, but weighed pigs of silver melted down from sliver services taken from several raided plantations. Corner gave his hand to each of us in turn, reminded us of our duties and of the return of the *Kestrel* in a weeks time.

When the longboats returned to the *Kestrel*, she wore away out to sea.

The climb to Nanny Town was only a ten-mile or a little better journey, but one that took us two full days laden as we were, and traveling uphill through very rugged country. The path was narrow and wove through the thick forest in such a manner as to give numerous opportunities for ambuscade. Throughout the journey at intervals we could hear the sound of horns from the forest.

The town was finally reached at the top of a ridge, a very defensible location. The trail broadened slightly and ran straight for a hundred yards, giving a clear line of fire on anyone ascending to the village. Nanny Town was bordered on the south by a fast flowing rocky river, and there was already the beginning of a stone redoubt at the north end of the town where we came up.

We were met by general rejoicing as we entered the village — wonderful singing and dancing as our exhausted column came onto the center of the town. The 'houses," rough hewn huts really, were built solely from the materials at hand in the forest; they were solid and dry and surprisingly well 'appointed' inside with the results of plantation raids.

Including the fifty or so men who had labored the guns up the trail and into the town, I estimated the village to contain perhaps 500 people in all.

There was a sudden and sharp increase in the volume and activity of the celebration surrounding us and the addition of a high-pitched ululation as a diminutive figure stepped out from one of the larger huts in the center of the village.

Nanny was very slight of stature. She had a regal flowing walk, and her brightly patterned caftan, which reached to the ground, made it seem that she floated. She wore a white turban instead of the more colorful ones worn by the other women. Three imposing black men belted and armed with muskets and cane knives accompanied her. These I learned were her other captain 'brothers," Accompong, Johnny and Quao. It is impossible for me to overstate the 'presence' this handsome little woman radiated, or the obvious affectionate awe that she inspired from all about her.

She approached Trinket first and great radiant smiles illuminated both her face, and his.

'Wui Enyan' she called him. Trinket told me later it was something like 'the dead awake' in the Akan language of the Ashanti people, referring to his sudden reanimation when cast ashore after his 'hanging' by Captain Quigsley. They embraced warmly and Trinket proceeded with introductions, the intensity and regal authority she carried without effort affected every man in our company in the same way. Mary in particular appeared transfixed by her.

Trinket saved my and Mary's introduction for last. The little queen stopped short in the middle of Trinket's introduction and stared first at me and then at Mary, and then her gaze moved between us and a little above our heads and into the forest beyond; her face lost all animation, it became as still as death. She reached out and drew Mary's hand into her own then, with no conscious direction of mine, my hand was drawn and came to rest on top of Mary's; then Nanny placed her hand palm down on top of our joined hands and after humming for a moment said in a soft voice: "so brave…so true…so good …so bye an' bye children… yea, bye an' bye you be together…bye an' bye…oh my yes…bye an' bye."

The remainder of that first day was spent recuperating from the exhausting Journey up through the forest to the town. For those of us who lived until recently in the confines of a small wooden world the expansive of forest about us, and the presence of abundant cold, clear, sweet running water…well it was as if we have entered another Eden. Joyfully we leapt with abandon into the flowing stream. We were joined by all of the men who labored to bring the guns to their people, and eventually it seemed by every child in the village.

That night there was the first of nightly meetings about a central fire with the captains, and others of the chief warriors of the town. The discussions involved the placement of the guns, the training of crews to man the guns, and the general defense of their position.

McGinnis, that first night, pointed out a ridge that overlooked the town as being of hazard to it if an attacker brought guns up onto the height. It was determined that the redoubt at the head of the trail leading into the village was indeed the perfect position for one of the guns, and that the other gun should be mounted along the river at the west end of the town so that it might sweep any attackers advancing north along the river.

Trinket, Snowden and McGinnis were given a large hut close by that of Queen Nanny's. Mary and I received a smaller hut near the center of the Village. We collapsed in exhaustion late that evening as the sounds of the village died away and all that might be heard was the whispers of the forest. We were awakened the next morning by the competitive crowing of at least a dozen enthusiastic roosters.

Work on assembling and mounting the guns began in earnest just after dawn. Half a dozen of the senior warriors joined Mary, Snowden and I in the assembly of the gun carriages. Mary's field experience from the past war was helpful, and while there were some issues in communicating with the Maroons, they were serious men who knew they were about serious business. They were quick to learn, and the second carriage came together much more readily than the first. By the middle of the afternoon we were ready to mount the guns.

Throughout the day it seemed that the entire village, including the children, were involved in bringing more rocks up from the river to strengthen the existing redoubt and to build a much smaller one in a location chosen by McGinnis at the west end of the village, overlooking the river.

I was struck by the position of women in this society, and by its children. The women worked beside the men and obviously gave no particular deference to them; and the children were expected to add their hands, however small, to whatever work was necessary. The older women, the 'grannies' — of which Nanny was most beloved — clearly exercised the underlying authority of the village; all deference was shown to them.

Late that afternoon, an hour or so before sunset, and with the entire village crowded about us there to witness, the cannon were lifted into place on their carriages and the trunnion plates bolted down. The hand spikes, sponger, rammer and ladle stacked against them in proper order, the sponge buckets properly placed, and so the guns stood ready for training their crews come the morrow. The guns, and in particular their shiny and glowing brass barrels, were source of wonderment to the entire village, and the children found a great delight in their faces reflected in the barrels.

That night as with every other night during our time there, there were long friendly meetings with the captains discussing the defense of the village; there was also talk of the people. Their history and their future plans to free more slaves and make more settlements; there was much talk of a general slave rebellion. Quao and Johnny were particularly hot to lead a general uprising, while Cudjoe and Accompong seemed more inclined to take strong defensive positions, and find accommodation with the government for their independence. In any event their common commitment to maintain, defend and expand their independence and freedom was unquestionable.

At dawn of the fourth day the process of choosing and training — however briefly — the gun crews began. In this instance as well, the influence of the 'grannies' was evident. The best and most active young warriors of the village would not be tied down to the guns, rather the six older warriors who helped in assembling the carriages would make up the gun crews. They decided on this course long before the guns arrived.

A young and beautiful black woman was assigned to improve our communication with these older warriors. She once served as a tutor and nanny to a plantation family and spoke fluent Ashanti and English, as well as the patois of the as. I thought that Snowden would faint when he first saw her.

An equal number of mature women were attached to the gun crews, as well as several of the older children. One of the women I noticed paid rapt attention to McGinnis throughout the lessons; she was quite handsome and light skinned, more native Arawak than black. I also made note that Snowden paid equally rapt attention to the young lady as she used an incomprehensible — at least to him — language to communicate more clearly to the older men. She was delightful in mimicking McGinnis and his bombastic and enthusiastic manner as she translated what he was saying.

In the meantime Mary gathered about her a dozen or more of the younger warriors and started to instruct them in the efficient use of their muskets. It was instructive of this society that there was nothing unusual about a woman teaching men about weapons. Who better to give the instruction? Mary was free here and ceased binding her breasts.

There was nothing for me to do really except to sit in admiration of this woman whom I loved, and still love. There was nothing feigned about her; she was a veteran of bloody combat; she marched with Marlborough; she stood and fought in the line of battle; she later rode in the cavalry and was twice commended for bravery under fire. I found her beautiful beyond words.

She looked up once while showing one of the young warriors how to freshen a flint and smiled at me. She no longer wore a cap and the sunlight caught in her hair.

The exertions of the march to Nanny Town and the work required to assemble the guns left us both exhausted at night, and it was only now on the fourth night that we had an opportunity to talk of things other then the business at hand. It was also only now that we were married, and had worked together, and had unbroken time together that I felt free to speak with her in more depth about her past, and question her about her commitment to Rackham and her choice of turning to piracy.

"I was tired John, tired of wearing my brother's skin. I am tired of playing the man. I was happy once as a woman, married to a good man — how I do not wish to hurt you by mentioning it, but I must, for you asked and it is a part of the whole. You are the first man, the only man, since then to reawaken the woman in me."

"Michael, my late husband, was a very good man, honest, gentle, full of courage and goodwill. His death forced me to once again pick up my brothers skin, and live as a man, in order to survive — in order to make some future for myself other than scullery or worse. To escape the trap I found myself in, I foolishly reenlisted, and it brought back only sad memories and no real hope. The great wars were finished and garrison life in the army was not for me John, so I shipped out again, this time on a merchant ship. I was once again a slave, with no future, no dream, everything was dust to me."

"The vessel I served upon was taken by Rackham, not far from where we took the *Rachel* actually. He had our captain and first mate tried and flogged and then he gave his speech; in it, I saw a final opportunity for me to free myself, shed my brothers skin, and give myself an independent life.

"A thousand pounds, John! A thousand pounds! Enough money to free myself, to buy myself a little cottage, to make a quiet life for myself, to have a garden. It was the only chance I could see of making myself a future."

"I signed onboard, and I then made for myself a dream, a dream where Mark Reede, with his heavy duffel, takes a final room in a clean and decent Inn. He orders a bath brought to his room. Later that same day a well and modestly dressed woman, with a heavy shoulder bag, leaves the hotel and flags down a hansom."

"A little later, in another part of the city, this same well and modestly dressed woman of independent means takes residence in a clean and decent boarding house for ladies while she plans her future."

"The next morning, when the Inn's owner and staff come to roust the guest, all that will be found is a man's clothing laying upon the un-slept bed, spread out, as Christ upon his cross, with a silver piece of eight laid upon the jacket where the heart would be."

"You have brought a great change to my dream John; now in my dream, this well and modestly dressed woman of independent means keeps a rendezvous with you, her beloved, and we find a world for ourselves, and we live in a cottage by a river, where we may sit on a porch and smoke cigaros of an evening, and we have children, and our home is filled with love, and I am at last free of my brother's skin. Oh, how this time together here in freedom has made me hunger for you and that place and that time."

Oh John! Oh John, do you love me dearest, as I love thee? I am fair sick with this love of thee, my hope, my dream, my future."

"I love you, Mary, with all of my heart. There shall be no other heart laying so close against my heart, until mine beats no more."

And so it has been all these years.

She turned to me then and met me with an urgent passion that my heart cannot bear to dwell upon.

On the last night, and after the last meal that we would all together share with our kind and gracious hosts, we sat in the honored inner circle. Snowden sitting close to the girl Efua, and McGuiness fairly pressed against the Arawak woman Hadali, Mary and I together of course and Trinket seated on the right hand of Queen Nanny. To either side were her captains, and around and behind her the grannies. There were conversations to all sides of course. And on the edge of the gathering there was singing and dancing when Nanny began to hum, and then to rock side to side.

She did so alone for only a few moments before the grannies around and behind her began to hum and rock, then her captains, and then from the edge of the forest we heard the Abeng horn, and then a great silence fell over the village broken only by the deep humming of the simple song. There was the rustle of movement as mothers brought their children through the crowd so that they could clearly hear the elders and leaders of their people. When that rustle died away there was only the song.

After a few moments Nanny stopped, and then the captains and the grannies stopped.

Nanny's face in the firelight took on the same nature as it had when she had spoken to Mary and me on the first day. She continued to gently rock from side to side, her eyes were closed and she began to speak in a high thin voice that nonetheless enveloped and commanded the air.

The story that she told to her people remains vivid to me to this very hour.

"Oh my, my yes, my children listen to me. When day muslimens come day burn ever-ting, all mans who fight are killed, all young womans taken and raped, all young mans taken, some have their

man parts cut off, all old womans and mans killed, all lil'babies killed, all de animals killed, ever-ting killed. We go to sleep as free peoples, we wake up to slaves, we howl, and we cry out but no-one to hear"

"Day take us into de forest, where we find many udders, some our tribe, some udder Ashanti, peoples, some Akwamu, some Ewe peoples, some, not our tribe, all in chains, we be chained to dem' and marched away, some north, some to the coast, many of the cut young mans bleed to det' on de way, day bodies lef' fo de animals, we fed thin gruel, lil bit, ever'night more rape."

"Dese muslimens, day prey all de time, ever'day day bump day heads on the de-groun' and day wail away in day prayin," I wonder to me, what sort o'god day prayin' to?"

"We come to de coast, we be crowded into stone houses no windows no light, many of us, womans in one house, mans in de udder one, like goats, like cattle — only not so good, gruel to eat, little waters, no wash, no clean, some die, day bodies just burned."

"Den we be brought one morn'in out into de sun and a Spanish man look us up and down, he feel us up and down an he look at in our mouth, he take some aside and hurry de udders — include me — into a pen outside, udders den brought out an' he do the same w'it dem, we all day in dat pen in de hot sun, no water, we cry out but no one to hear."

"Den de Spanish man count us an' we be taken down to a boat. We never seen a boat like dat, or the great water b'fore an' we are very fearing, we be prodded, and cursed, and whipped to go onto the boat, like animals — only not so good."

"On the boat we be chain one to a'nudder, made to lay on our side so more can be chained t'gedder, 'nudder floor right close over us, mo' laid in chain dare, packed so tight, no air, no light, we lay in our own dirt. Once a day we led up on de deck, thin watery sour gruel, sour water, shuffle round de deck, day throw buckets of water from de sea on us and den back on down an de next group go up, goes on till dark, den some are raped right on de deck, still in day chain."

"One time, strong man chain next to woman be'n raped have enough and he strike de rape'n man down, day beat him bad in his chain, oh my yes, den day un-chain him and day tro' him over de side. Den day lash all de people on dat chain and put dem below, no

food, no water fo' dem that time, some die. De dead always over the side next day."

"We come to dis island and be brought out into a'nudder pen near the dock, mans come and prod us, an' poke us, and feel of us, and look inside our mouth, an' buy us like we be animals. Me and my brudders here — she indicated the four captains who surrounded her — *we work fo' de same plantation, me I clean up aroun' de white mans, my brudders work de cane fields, two maybe tree' years in dese fields, den even strong mans die from de work. Day bodies toss' in a hole like dogs."*

"Dese white mans too, day prey all de time one day, day prey an' day sing, an' prey some more an' den next days day whip us, and curse us, and watch us die, we wonder what kine o'god day pray'n to."

"Den one night while I am sleeping de forest spirit come to me and he say, 'Sistah why do you stay here? Only death for you here, come to me, bring your brudders, coming be free again, I will hide you, I will protect you, come I will feed you, you be my chillin.'"

"I say to him, Oh Spirit, I am ready to come, give me a sign."

"Den tree days his sign come, oh my yes, big storm, biggest storm ever blow in to de island, cane blow down, trees blow down, masta'house blow down, ever'ting blow down, me an' ma brudders hear the call fo de forest spirit and we run follo'in de call fo de forest spirit. De forest welcome us, we meet udders who have hear de call, and udders of de forest spirits children, de ol' peoples of the island, here be'fo de white man, be'fo us, day welcomes us, day helps us."

"Now we be a free people agin," oh my yes, we live free, an' we be ready to die free, never no mo' slave for us agin. Never!"

Her voice lifted, became shrill and eerie, and seemed to ring through the forest in that last phrase: 'never, no more slavery for us again, never!'

A great shouting and a high-pitched ululation rose up from her people, muskets were fired into the air, the Abeng sounded from several sources around the village. Then the very ground seemed to tremble as the village began a rhythmic stamping of feet and a wonderful call and response song lifted around us from an hundred voices, I felt the hair on my neck rise

I was reminded of the great noisy roaring that would break out among the company on the deck of the *Kestrel* from time to time;

however, the tumult in the village that night was different, it had an air of sanctity about it that I have never forgotten. What indeed may be said of a people who had suffered as much these people, and who took their freedom for themselves, owing no man thanks for it, and who were prepared to defend their liberty to the death?

Later that night, as Mary lay asleep beside me, I thought to myself, why do you not slip away into the forest and make your own bid for freedom? You are the only slave here.

I arose quietly and stepped outside of the hut, it would take very little preparation, a jug of water, one of the loaded pistols from Mary's side, one of the cane knives… I looked at the blackness of the forest and thought more…

I was in the middle of an unknown place, deep in an unknown forest. Should I strike off north in the forest? South in the forest? Should I strike off down river? Up river?…and bound for where exactly?

I knew also that Trinket would not shirk his duty to the company, and that despite himself, and the thoughts of the others, a party would be sent to recapture me.

I would not have the protection of the forest spirit, I would be helpless there, and once I was recaptured I would be held in chains as Rackham promised.

I returned to the hut, I looked at the beautiful face of my sleeping wife, and I lay down.

We left for the coast at dawn the next morning. We were accompanied by many of the people. They sang and laughed as we traveled through the forest. Cudjoe and Johnny with armed warriors went before us, and the women and children followed after and with us — Efua and Hadali among them.

Snowden and McGinnis walked closely with the women. Snowden held Efua's hand, and Hadali's arm was entwined with that of McGinnis.

It was just after noon, we were still some two miles or so up in the hills when we caught sight of the sea, and although in the brief distant view that we had, no details could be discerned, it was clear that there were two vessels in the bay.

Chapter 22
Barnett

How shall I approach the telling of the final days of the *Kestrel*?

Our party was spotted as we came down from the hills, and the sound of the Abeng rang in the forest. Johnny and a dozen warriors went ahead to secure the beach, and there was a longboat drawn up on the sand waiting for us. Candy was the first man I saw, and he rushed forward smiling to greet me.

"Ah Johnny!," he cried out to me, "so glad to see ye I am, the old place is not the same without ye."

We embraced and slapped each other's back, I was right glad to see the old man.

"What is to do with that little sloop next to the *Kestrel*," I asked him right off.

"Oh that," he said, "well we're a damn right flotilla now. We have a consort vessel by God, I think next thing Jack will be running up the blue pennant of a damn Commodore."

There were farewells, and expressions of gratitude all about, the children in particular seemed sad to see us go. We and our doings having been a great source of entertainment and diversion for them. They too had seemed most taken by Mary. I noticed also the warmth of the embraces exchanged between my two shipmates and the two women who had come to the beach with them.

As the longboat cast off and we rowed for the *Kestrel*, Candy and I talked mostly about the time spent in the hills, and the village, and the placement of the guns. The water was choppy that day and our conversation was punctuated by the familiar grunts, groans and curses commonly attached to pirates forced to endure physical effort, to no obvious reward. Looking back toward the beach I noticed a small group stayed behind and gathered up in a relaxed manner at the edge of the forest.

As we first came back aboard the *Kestrel* I felt a curious mix of reactions. There was some small sense of a return to 'comfortable' surroundings — coming aboard a fine vessel again; and yet I was whelmed by a certain unnamed dread. Mary's and my time in the forest with the Maroons was a sort of idyll for us, we had roamed and talked at will, we had slept each night in each other's arms. It's ending filled me with foreboding.

A week of freedom in the forest affected all of us, and particularly Mary. She gave up all pretext to a portrait of manliness now, her breasts were no longer bound, but rather the red sash that she fancied was drawn up a little higher, and perhaps a little tighter so that her beautiful slim figure was enhanced. She no longer wore 'the face," she no longer wore the cap, and the wind was allowed to play in her hair. Stevens went positively slack-jawed when first he saw her.

The reunion of Mary and Anne was clearly a joyful one; there was a true sisterly affection between the two. And even the normally grim Fetherston face was alight with a happy smile to see us. There was a general sense of welcome reunion among all the crewmembers; only Trinket seemed to be ill at ease and somehow withdrawn.

Shortly after coming aboard McGinnis and Snowden took Rackham aside. I surmised the purpose of the conference when I saw Rackham, in a most agitated manner; call for Corner's attention; after a few moments they went below.

Within the hour I was bidding a fond farewell to McGinnis and Snowden, who had, as I suspected they might, chosen to be paid down and return to remain with the Maroons. Both men, contrary to the popular report of sailors, became deeply attached to the loving women they so recently met. Both were ready to utterly change their lives as a consequence; something that I could certainly understand. …Although most of the crew, and particularly Rackham, were thunderstruck by the development.

I knew that McGinnis would be a great asset to the Maroons, as he was knowledgeable in all matters regarding discipline, armaments and tactics. Snowden, faithful Snowden, what might I say about him? Apart from his sunny nature, he was a steady hand and very skilled in the use and maintenance of muskets, and other equipment needed for serious mayhem. It is after all one thing to have the will to fight, and quite another to have the training, equipment and skills to do so in an efficient and deadly earnest.

Saddened as I was to lose the company of these two men who befriended and protected me in my captivity, nonetheless I was happy to see them go, and to put their skills and energy and courage into a far more worthy and noble calling.

After the launch that brought Snowden and McGinnis ashore returned and stowed aboard, we lay to, both vessels, at anchor throughout that day waiting for the evening tide. I could see the little *Bermuda* rode the swells beautifully. Her 'crew' was aboard the *Kestrel* at the time, and only returned to her after sunset.

In the days that followed there were things said regarding the Maroon women, particularly by Quick and his crew — for so it was as he had been given 'command' of the little Bermuda that was now consort to the *Kestrel* — that had either Snowden or McGinnis overheard, would have been paid for in blood.

In addition to the new consort vessel, other matters as well changed aboard the *Kestrel*. In subtle ways over the course of our sojourn with the Maroons the 'feeling' aboard the vessel became noticeably more tense.

Trinket took me aside as soon as possible after he reunited with members of the crew, and shared what appeared to be a heated interchange with Rackham. I had never seen Trinket in such an agitated state.

"I don't understand what Jack is thinking. We've taken another three vessels over the week — and stolen that little Bermuda practically off the beach at Ocho Rios — not one of the prizes worth the effort really, some rum and some food and a few bob at best. On top of that he's forced a couple of Frenchman aboard as well.

"My understanding was that we were to sail north around Hispaniola, so where as to finish our business in Jamaica quietly and go off to scrape the barky, all of this activity around the north of the island is working against us. Cudjoe told me of reports he received of much increased activity by the militia, and coastal patrols.

"I have something to share with you John. I've questioned Rackham about this flurry of activity, and given him caution based upon my last meeting with Queen Nanny, not in detail, but enough of a warning from her to make him hot in his collar by God!"

"It was on our last night in Nanny Town, and late that night Queen Nanny sent for me. When I entered her hut she sang out to me. *Akoaba! Nua-banyan kakra dofo* — 'Beloved little brother.' There were two very old grannies with her and a small fire burning. The grannies would drop leaves and such into it so that her lodge was filled with a fragrant smoke. She seemed to be already in a deep trance, and just sat there humming and rocking side to side, then she spoke to me in that high pitched sing song way.

"She told me that you and me are spirit brothers, wove together sort of and that we would be separated but would come together again in a distant and cold land far to the north."

"Then she sort of jerked upright, and stopped humming and rocking side to side. She closed her eyes and began to shake her head a little, kind o' twitchy side to side, like as she was saying no to something. Then the two old grannies began to humming and singing softy back and forth to each other, in that sing and respond way that they have.

"Then Nanny began to speak in a hissing voice. I tell ye, my hair stood up.

"She told me to beware of the nighttime. She told me of a dark cloud, and that she heard shouting, fighting, cries for help; she warned of ropes and chains, a great sadness, and that she saw a black man, hanging in a cage on a tree next to the big water."

"Have ye ever seen a man on the gibbet tree John?" I admitted that I had not. "These days they save it special for Highwayman and pirates, covered with tar ye are, then they truss ye up with iron bands so's yer held erect, then they hang ye in your cage on a post at the high water mark — or off a tree at yer favorite cross roads were ye a highwayman… Oh there were no doubt in me as to what she seen… damn me none!"

"What did Rackham have to say to all this?"

"Oh he puffed on about the jungle savages and their queer superstitions, and preferred not to hear of their black magic 'twaddle." He pointed out that nighttime and battle and all such as she mentioned were the common doings of our business, and that no part of her ramblings were of interest to him. It was useless to try to explain to him the richness of the Ashanti culture and religion, and the importance given to the visions of a great Obeah like Nanny. He would have none of it. In the end all I could do was to push him to finish what we need to do in order to get clear of Jamaican waters."

"My feeling," he continued after a moment, "is that we have drawn far to much attention to ourselves here. I'm sure that we have marked ourselves for the Admiralty's attention and if we are to continue on the account we will need to make a change in our hunting grounds…however, he was insistent upon connecting with Vasquez once more before leaving the island."

Candy had joined us by this time, and we had a moment now to continue our reunion. He of course knew nothing of Nanny's vision, and heard only the last little bit that Trinket said. I asked him about the changes on the vessel.

"Nothing seems right upon the vessel these last days. We cruised about the first day after landing you, avoiding contact with other vessels. After the noon sighting on the second day, a call went up from Quick, who spied sail, Rackham ordered us about to avoid contact but then Quick, Eton, Cole and several others raised a stink about not taking the prizes available to us. It came to a shouting match on deck, the crew about equally split. Jack read the signals and rather than risk a vote on the deck he agreed to close on such vessels as were sighted. Not one prize worth a damn.

"Quick is smarter than Magoon was, and he began the work of removing Rackham as commander. He wanted his own vessel, and Jack was damned if he did and damned if he didn't — nothing was mentioned about the women, but you could sense that there were still some suspicions there as part of the mix. Corner and Fetherston held solid with Jack, but there has been deep division within the crew"

"How did you come about getting that sweet little sloop?"

"Two days ago, as we returned for the rendezvous with ye. We stood in close to Ocho Rios, beautiful little port, looking to see as there was any merchants looking as they was outbound, weren't none. The little Bermuda was anchored close to shore right in the middle of the half moon of the harbor, she caught Fetherston's eye right off. He was sure that she was fresh scraped, and that she had the look of a right fast little swimmer — made her for 30 tonne or so.

"A little later on Rackham up and says to Quick, "Ye you know, Thomas, it's best for a man to steal his first command, and that little vessel would be perfect to sail the account in consort with us, what think ye?"

"Well right off Quick, he gets together with Eton and Cole and they talk with the rest of the faction that was giving Rackham the most irritation. They come back to Rackham a bit later and says as they'd like to cut the little darling out.

“So late that night we sent a boat in with Quick in command. They slipped aboard her and took her quiet as cats. The only people aboard at the time are the two frogs that’s been forced along — Quick, figuring they’d be of use as being familiar with the vessel; problem is neither one speaks English, and nobody here speaks more than some, ‘get me food, wine and a woman’ tavern French — but Rackham, sly dog that he is, he let Quick get his vessel all right…just not this one.”

“She’s unarmed. They’ll be looking to you and Stevens — now what McGinnis shipped out and all, for as to mount some of the murderers on her. She’ll need to be stocked up as well, seeing as she was fresh scraped and had not yet taken on any supplies.”

Our conversation was cut short by the familiar thumping of an oar and ringing of the ship’s bell as Corner called the company together at the waist.

“Gather up now men,” he cried, “we will be putting out with the evening tide and every man should be informed as to our sailing plan over the next week. We shall henceforth be sailing in consort with Captain Quick” — I thought Quick’s buttons would pop is he heard himself so mentioned — “and the *Vengeance,* for so she’s been re-named by common agreement.”

Rackham came forward then. He stepped down from the quarterdeck into the waist in order to be surrounded by his crew, *‘primer inter pares,’* the first among equals. He was brisk and matter of fact in his manner.

“Gentlemen of the company, we have now satisfied our commitment with these Maroons. Apart from the profit we have made for the sale of the two 3 Pounders, we have also established a useful relationship with them, and may depend upon friendly contact with them when needed. Any member of this crew, for instance, may by use of the *Kestrel* name, secure succor and safe passage by them to any port on the island. In my estimation however the loss of two such hands as McGinnis and Snowden — I wish them well — is a high price to pay for the profit we’ve made.

“We sail on the tide tonight, bound for Manteca in order to make contact with Vasquez again to lay in supplies of, water, food, shot and tar. We will then make for the Caymans, to a particular small island that Fetherston is familiar with. There is a sheltered bay on the south face of the island, with a lovely little white sand playa, which will serve our purposes admirably; and a very small fishing settlement from whence we may hire hands to help with the work.

"There is, however, absolutely no natural source of water on the island, save for one small well and what is saved in cisterns from the rainfall, nor yet so on any of the Caymans for that matter. Hence we shall be shipping aboard as much water as we, and Captain Quick may carry, and may indeed use some portion of that water as currency when dealing with the natives."

"The *Vengeance,* Mr. Fetherston assures me, has been freshly scraped and promises to be a right fast little swimmer. She will serve not only as our tender while we are about the tedious business of scraping the barky's hull, but she shall also be our eyes and ears — and if need be a decoy. After we have tended to the needs of the *Kestrel,* Captain Quick and I are determined to leave Jamaican waters, and to cruise the main and the Leeward Islands in concert search of prey.

"Sailing aboard the *Vengeance* will be Thomas Quick, commander, John Eaton, quartermaster, Edward Warne and John Cole, as masters mates, and a crew consisting of Thomas Baker, Benjamin Palmer, Walter Rouse, John Hanson and John Howard."

Here he turned back toward the quarterdeck.

"Mr. Fetherston, please make us ready to hoist sail at the turn of the tide, gentleman of the company enjoy your ease. Captain Quick, Mr. Eaton, join Mr. Corner and me below deck to work out such signals as may be needed for us to communicate while under sail, and also to determine how the two vessels would best work in concert, one with the other, for the common profit.

"Mr. Carpenter," he turned to me, "I will needs speak with you when we are through."

The careening and scraping of the hull of a vessel is a major undertaking, made necessary, particularly in warm southern waters, by the growth of plants and animals on it, like the barnacle. These growths can dramatically reduce the speed of a vessel, and the *Kestrel*'s greatest asset was her speed. In the course of the work the hull would also be re-caulked as needed, and then re-tarred. The tarring of the hull not only discourages these marine growths, but is also protection against the dread Teredo worm. All of this work is customarily supervised, overseen and inspected by the carpenter. During the process the vessel and its crew would be helpless if found and attacked.

My interview with Rackham and Fetherston, was brief, and limited to the upcoming cleaning of the hull. He repeated his promise to me that upon the completion of the work I would be released from my captivity. Mary and I, together, would be given over to the custody of the Maroons and delivered by them safely to the port of Kingston, richer by a thousand pounds.

Fetherston looked at me, he took my eye very pointedly for a few moments, long enough for him to nod his head gravely several times; assuring me that this would be so.

Rackham then inquired as for the amount of tar needed for the work, and instructed me to put some of the crew to good use in preparing sufficient oakum, from the plundered cordage stowed in the sail locker, to see to the re-caulking of seams.

I returned to the weather deck accompanied by Fetherston; he stepped up upon the quarterdeck, rang the ship's bell, and yelled out for all hands.

"The carpenter will call out such men as he may need to produce oakum, and he wishes all men who have experience in scraping the hull of a vessel to make themselves known to him. Five such men came forward.

That first night aboard, as Mary and I lay together in the familiar confines of my berth, she lay on her back next me, she was strangely quiet for awhile, and then reached over and placed her hand on my thigh.

"Dear husband, I know that on the last night in Nanny Town, that you arose from our bed and went out into the night. I came to the door and watched you in the darkness. I saw you look at the forest, and I'm sure I know what you were thinking. That you were truly the only slave in a village of freeman. I thought to myself, if my husband flees his bondage, then I must follow him in order to 'love, honor, serve and protect him' as I have sworn to do."

I was stunned into silence.

"I'm glad you did not decide to flee. It would not have ended in freedom. Remember that in perhaps as little as a few weeks hence we shall be free of this life, and we may pursue that sweet life, that dream that we share: A little cottage by the water, with a garden and"… she paused here, and gazed at me with a particular and searching softness and then continued…"a house filled with love…and children — and good cigaros on the porch of an evening," she added laughing."

She rolled over to me then, brushed my cheeks with her hands, and lowered her mouth to mine, silencing me with her lips.

Three days later we lay off Manteca, and as before a boat was lowered away and Trinket was sent ashore to make contact with Vasquez. He carried with him a manifest of those items taken from the *Oloroso* for trade, and our list of needs. Only Trinket was to be left ashore, with instructions to rendezvous with the *Kestrel* by canoa the next evening at the start of the middle watch. The longboat returned and was shipped aboard that very night.

We spent the following day at sea, three leagues or so off the coast, staying well away from any sail, and with men aloft at watch throughout. The next evening as arranged a canoa gave signal by black lantern at the appointed hour. The canoa was a large one and rigged with a lateen sail, it carried four men in addition to Trinket. Everything was done in careful silence as it drew up to the *Kestrel.*

The canoa was tied off and Trinket climbed aboard alone.

He brought word from Vasquez, and a warning, that both John Barnett and Ben Hornigold had been commissioned personally by Gov. Lawes to fly the swallowtail burgee and clear Jamaican waters of pirates. Essentially it was a royal commission, Rackham's name at the top of their list. Every man aboard seemed to know of them as being experienced and deadly privateers, very dangerous men indeed. Vasquez was understandably nervous under these circumstances.

Vasquez agreed to meet us in three days off Negril point, but only if Trinket returned to Manteca and personally supervised gathering of the needed supplies. Trinket would sail as super cargo on a sloop chosen by Vasquez, and return to us with the materials three nights hence. We would then rendezvous, about the middle of the first watch, a cable length off the south point of Bloody Bay, between Booby Cay and the point.

Vasquez also sent along a gift to the crew, that being a firkin of the best Barbados Rum from Mount Gay, Trinket's favorite.

The three days were spent well out to sea, 10 leagues or more south west of the island.

The opportunity was taken to test the sea legs of the *Vengeance*," and perfect the series of signals by which she in the *Kestrel* would communicate. The *Vengeance* proved to be indeed very speedy and maneuverable. Even Fetherston agreed that she was well handled by her crew. All hands on both vessels were excited by the prospect of the two vessels working together for the common profit.

We approached the rendezvous point at one bell of the first dogwatch and anchored as directed, 200 yards offshore, in the lee of Booby Cay and just south of the point. We were thus sheltered from the sight by any vessel except those coming due north along the coast. Our bow was brought about so that we were in a position to quickly set sail to the south and west. The *Vengeance* took her anchorage in the same attitude, a pistol shot away on our larboard.

The crew of the *Vengeance* came aboard shortly after dark. The firkin of Barbados was tapped. It was as Rackham said, the last opportunity for such celebration before we would all be bound in the serious hard work due to start within the next three days on the Caymans.

Mary, Anne and Stevens were given the first watch, and I settled into my berth.

I was jarred awake by the sharp bang of a swivel gun, followed by a thunderous volley of fire.

There was a great crash upon the deck — later I saw the foremast boom shot away and fallen onto the longboats. There was a thumping and grinding sound as a vessel bumped and scraped along our starboard beam. There were shouts and curses, the sound of many feet, and loud calls for assistance from the watch on deck. I distinctly remember Mary's voice, from directly over my head it seemed, crying out for men.

I shook myself from my slumber as the tumult on deck increased, and I headed for the aft hatchway grabbing the first musket I came upon, I'm not even sure that it was loaded, and started up the hatch for the deck.

When I was nearly at the top, I looked up to see Mary standing in the hatchway with a musket in her hands.

"No! Damn ye John! NO!" I remember her shouting at me.

Then I saw the brass butt-plate of her Musket loom up between my eyes. There was a painful flash of white light…and then a feeling of falling…and then a great booming and roaring…

… And I was seated in the grass by a river… and I saw Mary on the other side ... she was dressed as she had been when I first saw her…barefoot…duck slops and a white linen shirt…she wore her blue cavalry jacket with its shiny brass buttons…she had a broad scarlet sash about her waist with the hilt of her Spanish dagger showing…on her head was the little red stocking cap with its tassel… I remember her calling out to me.

"John my love, ye must abide for a while, I will come for thee anon, wait for me."

And so I have.

I woke to pain, rough treatment, harsh cursing and iron shackles.

Chapter 23
The Silver Oar

Once the weather deck of any vessel is secured, any resistance from those isolated below deck is generally futile, it is equally so onboard a man-of-war or on a pirate schooner. The result is a sort of stalemate, in that passage up — or down the hatchways is a risky and deadly business. Grenadeos could of course clear the way down the hatchways, but there was the attendant danger of a fire or explosion below deck. The disciplined crews, and the marines, of a man-o-war have on occasion stormed up the hatchways and retaken the deck, always with heavy loss. The crew of the *Kestrel* knew of the man with whom they had to deal, and that if they stormed up a hatchway it would be into the mouth of a cannon. The fight, such as it was, was over when Stevens was killed, and Mary and Anne were overwhelmed.

Barnett's dire reputation amongst our crew was found to be justified. He and his crew cleared her deck and stormed aboard the *Kestrel* in a trice. He knew who we were and what we were, and was prepared for an immediate direct and overwhelming assault.

Stevens answered a hail from a sloop looming up out of the darkness, without giving the agreed 'sign," and even more foolishly had answered — before he could be silenced by either Mary or Anne — with 'Rackham of Cuba' to the shouted question 'who are ye and where are ye from?'

To his credit, it was Stevens who discharged the swivel gun, once he was aware of the true nature of the danger bearing down on the *Kestrel.* And in so doing, of course, committed an additional act of piracy, for Barnett sailed under an Admiralty burgee.

A tremendous salvo of musketry and swivel guns was immediately directed at the flash of the gun. He was killed instantly, and the foremast boom was severed and fell upon the longboats with a crash. The concentration of fire onto his position spared Mary and Anne from injury as they dashed to the gangways calling for aid.

Barnett then rammed his sloop against the side of the *Kestrel,* and two-dozen men stormed onto her deck, as Mary and Anne cried out at the hatchways for assistance. They were quickly overcome and surrounded by hard man and muskets and boarding pikes. I believe these men recognized them as women, and extended a quarter to them that they might not otherwise have granted to armed men on the deck.

Barnett's first call for surrender was answered by shouts of defiance from below deck.

A volley of musketry was sent down each gangway. In a few moments a cry for quarter came up from below in Rackham's familiar voice.

The hatch cover for the foreward hatchway was seated, secured and guarded. The crew of the *Kestrel* was instructed to come up the aft hatchway, one man at a time and unarmed. Each man who came up was searched, his name taken by Barnett himself, and then immediately put into shackles and forcibly seated at the rail. I'm told that it was Candy and Dobbin who carried my yet unconscious form up onto the deck.

Finally Rackham, Corner and Fetherston came topside. They were greeted in a courteous manner by Barnett, separated from the crew and personally shackled by him.

It appeared that Rackham had made good use of the time, and the good sense to toss all of the *Kestrel*'s papers out of the transom window. The destruction of the papers and the signed articles of course did no service for Candy, or me whose names did not appear as signatories to the company. This would lead to problems for us both later, as several men, including Dobbins, claimed to being forced as well.

The common belief was that Rackham and Corner had also jettisoned overboard the two small chests that held the common. It mattered not, for everything, including both vessels, was seized by Barnett for the crown; and no man of the crew had any hope of return; their only future hope lay in an experienced and skilled hangman.

Quick, and the crew of the *Vengeance* made an immediate claim as to being simple turtle hunters who had stumbled upon the vessel in question at anchor, and had been invited to board for refreshment. Barnett turned his back and walked away shaking his head and chuckling.

The two Frenchman began right in, even as they mounted the hatchway, to slapping their chest lightly in a submissive gesture and singing out *"Je suis un prisonnier! Je suis un prisonnier! Un homme force.!* Barnett ignored all of it, but made note.

The darkness was illuminated only by the lamps that were held by members of Barnett's crew at the top of the hatchway. They cast but a feeble glow over a part of the deck and as I came to my senses I looked about for Mary there in the gloom. She and Anne were shackled and seated together separately. When at last I found her I could see that she had been staring intently in my direction the whole time. Our eyes found each other. We continued to gaze at each other in this way, oblivious to all else around us, until Barnett gave orders to bring the prisoners below.

A Prize crew took command of the *Kestrel*, and its erstwhile crew was put in chains on what had once been their own berth deck. Heavily armed guards placed over us. Mary and Anne were chained separately in the sail locker, and well guarded. No conversation was permitted between the prisoners, enforced — at least on the berth deck — by several kicks well placed into the ribs, or a musket butt to the head.

We were two days in this condition aboard the *Kestrel*, until we arrived at the same Davis Cove where we had only short months before met with the Maroons for water and supplies. On this occasion however we were rowed to shore and given over to the custody of a company of royal Jamaican militia under the command of a Major Richard James. We were chained together in groups of six and loaded into three large cane wagons. A fourth smaller wagon was used for the transport of such supplies of and water as needed for the journey, Mary and Anne were chained together in that cart.

The journey to Santiago De La Vega prison took a full four days. Word had gone out before us and our route was frequently lined with the curious. From some quarters we were pelted with fruit and rocks, our guards made a halfhearted effort at keeping the abuse under control.

Now and again a plantation owner, mounted and bearing with him two or three of his bully hands would storm up to the wagons offering as it were to save the crown and the colony the cost of a trial by simply hanging us on the spot. Major James would have none of that, and drew up our militia guard to dissuade any attempt at seizing us by force.

The prison at Spanish Town was a raw and dirty place. The food was sour bully beef and weevily ship's bread; the floors were hard packed dirt and stones. Quick and his men were kept in one common cell. Rackham, Fetherston and Corner were kept in another separately, as were the women. The remainder of the crew and I were held in another common cell. Our bedding was straw and thin blankets, our water warm and murky, our privy a bucket in the corner of the cell.

It was the morning of Tuesday, November 5 of 1720 when my captivity at last came to an end. A sergeant of the prison guard came to the cell with two armed guards and called out my and Candy's names.

"Tanner and Jones," he yelled, "you are to come with me immediately to see the Provost Marshal. Stand to at the door, the rest of ye stand away at yer peril."

I expected us to be shackled, to my surprise we were not. The sergeant led us down the hall past the other cells. I remember much murmuring among the prisoners but the memory that is burned into my heart is Mary's face looking out through the bars of her cell. Her face was drawn, and pale, her hair was matted and filthy but her eyes were bright with love, I could do no more then return it with a wan smile.

We ascended a flight of stairs into the administrative section of the prison, and down the hall to the office of the Provost Marshal. The sergeant then opened the door for me, and motioned Candy to a bench outside the door.

There were three men in the Provost Marshals office. Alexander Forbes, the Marshal himself, I recognized, short and squat, rumpled and sweaty. A very elegantly dressed man was seated with the Provost Marshal behind a long table in the center of the room; a second well-dressed gentleman was seated in the corner. The details of the room itself are lost to me; the details of the interview are is clear to me today as they were then.

"Come in and take a seat at your ease, Mr. Tanner," said the elegantly dressed man seated next to the rumpled figure of the prisons Provost Marshal. He addressed me in the friendliest possible manner — I cannot express my amazement at being referred to as Mr. Tanner under these circumstances.

"My name is Leslie Unwin. I am the personal secretary to his Excellency Sir Nicholas Lawes, Royal Governor of the island of

Jamaica. This gentleman," he then referred to the other well-dressed gentleman seated in the corner, "is Mr. Matthew Pettigrew, he is a solicitor for the Merchant Venturers Company of Bristol here in Jamaica.

"Mr. Pettigrew has recently brought to the attention of his excellency the Governor, a letter, specifically dealing with yourself, and one Mr. Agamemnon Jones, in regard to your position as forced men aboard the pirate vessel recently taken at Negril by Captain Barnett. Mr. Pettigrew has been holding this letter since July according to instruction, that it should come immediately to the Governor's attention in circumstances such as these.

"I'm sure you can understand, Mr. Tanner, that many man arrested in these circumstances will claim to have been forced to their lot. A difficult prospect to prove at best."

He then laid several documents on the table before him, and looked up at me. "It is not very often," he said with a smile, "that his excellency the Governor receives a letter concerning such a claim, and more to the point one counter signed by a Knight of the Garter.

"The letter, the document in question," Unwin continued' "gives full details of the taking and the plundering of the brig '*Rachel*' on 23 June of this year, by the pirate John 'Calico Jack' Rackham and his crew. It is very specific as regards yourself, and Seaman Jones having been taken by force — and under strong protest — into the service of the pirate company commanded by the self-styled Captain Rackham, and documents an occasion of extreme violence against you in being so taken.

"The letter was written by the captain of said brig '*Rachel*,'' Mr. Andrew Lovewell, by way of a report to the Merchant Venturers Company of Bristol, and specifically to his direct employer Captain Sir Charles Johnson KG M.P. in regard to the loss of the said vessel and it's cargo."

That blue ribbon! Of course! I thought to myself. No wonder that doors swung open for Captain Johnson. There, in our humble lives and home, there laughing with my father, there eating my mother's food, and casting his wings over me, a Knight of The Garter, and a member of the Parliament. No one ever the wiser for his boisterous yet humble presence. I could feel my heart melt within me, and a chill of gratitude for the great bounty of grace given to me.

"The letter is further annotated and countersigned by Sir Charles personally, with particular attention to you as a trusted member of his personal staff, and the wish that both you and Mr. Jones be released immediately.

"His Excellency Sir Nicholas is only too happy to accede to the wishes of the right honorable Member of Parliament and Knight of the Garter, Sir Charles Johnson. Therefore, by direct order of his excellency the Governor: Yourself, and Mr. Jones are herewith immediately released without prejudice from confinement in his majesty's prison at Santiago de La Vega, and into the care and attention of Mr. Pettigrew."

An Half-hour later, Mr. Pettigrew escorted Candy and me from the prison confines; he kept a scented pomander handkerchief pressed to his nose the while. Later on the street he kept a safe distance from us as well; I could not blame him, and took no offense for we were both indeed rank, fairly reeking.

"I have," Pettigrew said, "the responsibility to see that you gentlemen have clean and decent accommodations, you'll need… a bath… and of course fresh linens, footwear and clothing. I have as well as a purse of 100 pounds at your disposal. I'm also instructed to inform you that passage to Bristol can be arranged for you on any vessel belonging to the Merchant Venturers Company of Bristol, or to Sir Charles. A vessel of the honorable company is due in Kingston in mid November.

"Able Seaman Jones, upon your return to Bristol you are to report to the offices of the Merchant Venturers Company to pick up arrears for your time in captivity, and for reassignment. Captain Lovewell spoke very highly of your skills as a seaman, and would be most pleased if you could be signed back aboard the newly outfitted '*Rachel*'."

"Mr. Tanner," he turned to me, "Sir Charles as requested that you wait here for his arrival. He has an interest in all matters pertaining to pirates and their trials, as you know. He will want to gain access to them, and wants to hear your story as soon as possible. I have a week past sent word to him in Charles Town by packet, as the *Elizabeth* is due there on or about November 10th."

The accommodations that Mr. Pettigrew made for us were indeed decent and clean. How can I describe the luxury of a hot bath after so long a time, and the feel of crisp new linens? Fresh clothing, hose and shoes. A day spent rebuilding ourselves, and ending with a most delicious supper, fresh warm bread, good wine and a surprisingly jovial Pettigrew, when in his cups.

When we had supped, and Mr. Pettigrew left, Candy and I had an opportunity to speak freely.

"Do you think Vasquez betrayed Rackham?" said Candy.

"It is entirely possible. I found it curious his insistence that Trinket should remain behind, and certainly the increase in patrol activity around the coast due to the *Kestrel*'s predations served to endanger his operations. Smuggling is piracy after all, and Barnett and Hornigold would have swept the coast clean in their search for Rackham."

"What of Mary?" He asked me next.

That question tormented my spirit and my slumbers in all of the days that followed.

I slept and lived in comfort whilst she whom I loved lived in misery… and fear.

I determined in my heart to do all that I could.

I met with Pettigrew the next day and enjoined him to help me bring some comfort and succor to the two women pirates. He looked askance at me and with some suspicion, but I worked my words well in my mind, and answered quickly enough that they had shown me great kindness and had on at least one occasion saved me from some of the more brutal elements aboard the pirate vessel. I sought only to return the favor.

With Pettigrew's help, and a few bob to several guards, it was arranged for Mary and Anne to receive soap, combs, fresh clothing and decent blankets, and further to receive fresh fruit every several days. I chose all these items, and the fruit myself; there was nothing further that I could do.

On Saturday November 16 a vice admiralty court was called into session by the Governor Sir Nicholas Lawes, for the trial of John Rackham, George Fetherston, Richard Corner, John Davies, John Howell, Patrick Carty, Thomas Earl, James Dobbin and Noah Harwood for high piracy.

A Vice admiralty court is constituted to hear cases of piracy in a colonial setting; it is essentially a drumhead court-martial. The court is called by, and seated under the authority of the colonial Governor as representing the crown, Governor Lawes being under direct royal commission for the suppression of piracy.

The court consists of the royal Governor, and other high officials of the colonial government. The court must by law include one or more post captains of the Royal Navy. There is no jury, and the crown is thus spared the expense and inconvenience of transferring prisoners and witnesses to England for trial.

A single witnessed act of piracy is sufficient for a finding of guilty, and the recompense for piracy is hanging. Small mercies are sometimes shown, but not often.

The symbol of the authority of the Admiralty is a silver oar. It is either suspended over, or mounted upon, the dais. The authority of the Admiralty is absolute in maritime matters; its authority is exercised upon any navigable water, and its jurisdiction is limited only by the high water mark.

The formalities of the court were, as Pettigrew cautioned me, long, and tiresome.

Beginning promptly at 9:00 a.m., all those acts of King and Parliament specifically relating to piracies, felonies and robberies committed in or on the seas, or on any navigable waters under the jurisdiction of the Admiralty were read in all their detail. The jurisdictions and the authorities of his Majesty's Royal colonial Governors were carefully listed, and in particular those directly relevant to the commission for suppression of piracy. The constituted make up of a vice admiralty court and its authority clearly explained. Those offices, and officers qualified to serve, and who have been formally taken under oath for service to the court.

Throughout the week prior to the convening of the court, notice was made in all public places calling on those who might serve as witnesses regarding the actions of the men on trial to step forward; and on the day of the trial three separate public announcements were made calling on witnesses to make themselves known to the court.

Like all trials, but specifically those for piracy, great public interest was aroused and the court and the area all about the building was packed with curious onlookers. Vendors of food and refreshments were present, and broadsides had already appeared regarding piracy in general, and the deprivations of which Rackham and crew were accused in particular. One might even say that there was a festive atmosphere gathering, for the trials were indeed entertainment and diversion for the multitude.

Candy and I stayed well to the rear of the court so as not to draw any attention to us by any of our erstwhile companions. As I looked upon the thirteen robed and be-wigged members of the court, and their generally solemn demeanor, I was drawn back in memory for the trial that it been held upon the deck of the *Rachel* now five months past… and could not suppress a faint chuckle.

Rackham and that part of his crew to be tried that day were brought forward, they were ragged, and pale and obviously filthy but they bore themselves well considering the gravity of their position. Each man was individually named and formally charged with the crime of piracy. Each specific charge was laid out in detail. 'Severally and in collusion with — upon such and such day — upon this vessel — did feloniously and violently — plunder and put in fear etc. etc.'

Almost every instance of piracy being charged happened within the last fortnight along the coast of Jamaica, just as Trinket, and others, feared. The charges levied included the theft of a certain sloop named the 'Mary' belonging to one Thomas Dillon of Ocho Rios — here was the re-named *Vengeance* — each man at the dock was individually charged and each man individually pleaded not guilty to the charges.

Witnesses were then brought forth for deposition, as the Bible says 'a great cloud of witnesses.' The accused were then asked if any of them had questions for cross-examination of any witness by the court, or if any could bring forward any defense or any witnesses on their behalf. None could. The end of it was a foregone conclusion.

The court was cleared, the prisoners returned to confinement, and the doors of the court closed for the period of about an hour. The courthouse doors were re-opened, the galleries once again filled, and the prisoners brought forward to stand before the bar. They were informed that the court had unanimously found them all guilty of the piracies robberies and felonies charged against them. They were asked if any of them had anything further to offer in their defense, or any reason why sentence of death should not be passed upon them. There was nothing of substance to be offered.

Then, as the president of the court, his Excellency the right honorable Sir Nicholas Lawes his majesty's Royal Governor of the colony and island of Jamaica pronounced sentence upon them:

"You, John Rackham, George Fetherston, Richard Corner, John Davies, John Howell, Patrick Carty, Thomas Earl, James Dobbin and Noah Harwood are to go hence to the place from whence you came, and from thence to the place of execution; where you shall severally be hanged by the neck, 'till you are severally dead. And God of his infinite mercy be merciful to every one of your souls."

The hangings began with Rackham, Fetherston and Corner on Monday 18 November at gallows point Port Royal. They were tarred and set in gibbets on three separate Cays off of Fort Charles at the entrance to Kingston Harbor; by the Monday next all of the condemned had been hanged. Two additional trials were scheduled, the first, for Mary and Anne, set for Thursday 28 November and for Quick and the remainder of the crew on Tuesday 24 January 1721.

Candy had an opportunity to ship out for Bristol on a vessel sailing for the Merchant Venturers Company, but knowing of my devotion to Mary, and my emotional state regarding the upcoming trial he elected to stay with me and offer such solace and comfort as a friend may give under the circumstances.

I spoke at length with Mr. Pettigrew and tendered to him 10 pounds, thus engaging him as my solicitor so that therefore our conversations might be protected by a client privilege. I spoke to him at some length about my relationship with Mary, our marriage and my devotion to her. He was not as surprised as I thought he might be, but had little comfort to offer me. It is a trial for piracy he reminded me, there was no hope for her, and if my relationship to her was made known to the court it would in all likelihood strip me of any protection as a forced man regardless of the intercession of Sir Charles.

He helped me to do what I could to ensure that both Mary, and Anne, were as comfortable as possible under the circumstances, supplied with such items as needed, fresh fruit, clean water, soap and such, and of course fresh garments. He also arranged that I might send an unsigned note to Mary — it cost a piece of eight for the delivery.

The note itself was simple. '*I love you Mary. I will do all that I can for you, and I shall love you for as long as my heart beats."*

And so I have, as yet it beats.

On November 28 promptly at 9:00 in the morning the trial that I had dreaded began with the same long tedious and tiresome readings of the laws, and the warrants, and the proclamations, and the royal commissions as before.

I was there when the doors were opened, and I took my seat, this time in the front of the room so that Mary might see me there, for whatever comfort that might give her. This trial, being unusual in that two women stood trial for piracy brought an overflow crowding of the room and of the building, all of Santiago de la Vega seemed to be in attendance. Pettigrew told me that it was the largest such crowd ever seen for any trial. I spent the intervening ten days preparing myself to witness the trial of the woman that I loved, knowing full well its outcome before hand.

Just at the end of the readings and just before the prisoners were brought to the dock, officers of the court came and with some much ado cleared room on the benches directly behind where Candy and I were seated. This apparently was done for the special seating of important enough visitors to warrant such attention. I was too distracted and distressed to take much note.

The trial proceeded in the same manner as the one I had witnessed some days before, the reading of the charges, both Mary and Anne pleading not guilty. Then the witnesses were called and the depositions began. The most telling witness against them was a Mrs. Thomas, the very woman who revealed their sex, and despoiled them verbally and whom — as she said — was 'put in mortal danger of her life' by reference to several vile methods of murder openly discussed by the prisoners at the bar. The humor of which methods was of course lost on the court.

At noon, all evidence having been taken, the court recessed as before and reconvened an hour later; whereupon as expected the finding of guilty was brought and once again the president of the court addressed the prisoners at the dock, and in a monotone listed off the charges to which they have been found guilty.

As the guilty verdict was read in detail Mary's eyes met mine and all the world except her face disappeared about me. She actually smiled a little smile and I saw her mouth the words 'I love you, John." How can I describe the trembling tension of my emotions?

I wanted to scream as the next the dreadful words were spoken.

"You Mary Reede and Anne Bonny — alias Bonn — are to go hence to the place from whence you came, and from thence to the place of execution, where you will be severally hanged by the neck

'till you are severally dead, and God of his infinite mercy be merciful to both your souls."

Then as the president of the court finished the last sentence, the voice of Anne Bonny rose like the ringing of a bell in the room.

"We are both pregnant m'lord, and we claim our bellies for stay of execution according to the laws protecting the innocent lives within us."

Amidst the great tumult that shook the room at this disclosure, my heart jumped within me, my Mary! My child! And I was no longer able to contain myself and my emotions. I started up from the bench with Mary's name climbing to shout from my lungs.

I felt then a powerful hand close up on the back of my neck, as a man might grasp a chicken, and then a second, rough and calloused, hand clamped down upon my nose and my mouth utterly stifling both breath and sound. And then my full weight was taken up bodily and I was sat down again most forcefully — all breath and strength taken from my body.

In the uproar about me I saw Candy looking past me, over my shoulder, first in a rage, and then with the light of a great smile upon his face.

Chapter 24
William Cormac

Later that night, as requested, Candy and I arrived at the *Elizabeth* promptly at two bells of the last dogwatch. She was dockside in Kingston Harbor and quite the most handsome vessel there, the very model of shipshape and Bristol fashion. We had been instructed to fetch our kits and to take berth on her for the duration of Captain Johnson's visit to the island; we were to accompany the captain as his staff throughout his visit.

I can hardly express the relief I felt knowing that Captain Johnson had arrived, the remaining ache in my neck and jaw from Thumper's ministrations in the courtroom that morning notwithstanding.

Captain Lovewell's letter, and particularly the appendix of 'The Right Honourable Sir Charles Johnson KG MP," saved Candy and me from well… a questionable future.

I can only say that to prove oneself to be a forced man was very difficult at best. Barnett and Major James had only coughed and sniffed at the mention, while the guards laughed out loud. I had feared greatly for Candy, to say the least, for he once took the King's pardon, so his prospects were grim indeed. I worried only a little less for myself, and particularly should the 'intimacies' of my relations with the crew come out in open court. And of course any mention of the one instance of our having stood on deck under arms would have pooped my defense, as well as his.

The musicians were as was customary released with the notation that they were 'just musicians." cooks too were generally released, because most, like our man Hollis, had lost a limb and to be a cook was all what they could do. Any 'cook' who was not so un-abled stood a good chance of hanging as a pirate.

As I was leaving the Provost Marshal's office Candy was being ushered in. I looked at him and smiled, and said to him "It's a right fair following wind in there mate." I was pleased to see him square his big shoulders, and for the glow of life to return to his face.

Candy and I had been invited or better directed to a private dinner with Captain Johnson that evening. As we ascended the gangway to the deck we were greeted warmly by the crew, with special attention to Candy who was well known and well liked among them. I made happy re-acquaintance with many men whom I had fought beside that day in the Mediterranean, when we sank the Tunisian galley. We were attended by the captain of the vessel, Mr. Russell, and led down and aft to Captain Johnson's private suite.

It was one of the great strengths of Captain Johnson that no differentiation was made between 'classes' of men. He surrounded himself with men of strength, honor and integrity whatever their background. The table that evening consisted of myself and Candy, Captain Johnson, Frank Woodley, Mr. Pettigrew and a striking other gentleman.

He was a large beefy, hard looking man with a florid complexion, and close cropped curly hair the color of scraped carrots. He had a large forehead, which was accented by a receded hairline. His eyes were intelligent, and vigilant, sharp and green, and seemed to bore into mine as we were introduced. His hand was firm and strong, and carried the roughness of a hand that works. He was William Cormac, Anne's father.

"Mr. Cormac and I are acquainted through business," Captain Johnson explained. "He received word of Anne's arrest on the same day that I received word of Rackham's apprehension, and your and Candy's 'indisposition.' As the Elizabeth was by far the swiftest vessel available, and ready to sail, I suggested that William allow me to offer him passage hence."

With this, both men raised a glass to each other in salute, and Captain Johnson rang for service. The familiar face of Jackson, his steward, was positively wreathed with smiles for Candy and me, and the two cabin boys that assisted him seemed awestruck by the company they served that night. They moved cautiously and apprehensively about the Thumper, who seemed to take pleasure in glowering at them, only to break into good-natured laughter when they jumped and scurried… they were delightful nippers in full dress blues as befit the occasion.

A haunch of roast mutton was presented along with roasted potatoes, fresh baked bread and sweet butter, and peas. A delightful Madeira was served with dinner, followed by a sweet Oporto with Stilton and fresh fruit from the island for dessert. The clink of glasses toasts to the King, and to the cook, and spirited table conversation, indeed all the things that an Englishman holds dear; I could have wept thinking of Mary.

When the table was cleared Captain Johnson drew Candy aside for a private conversation, his apology was offered to the other guests, but he wished to begin the series of interviews he planned regarding Rackham's capture and trial immediately. He knew that Candy would be a great source of background for the coming interviews. They were in a deep conversation for almost an hour.

Mr. Pettigrew, oddly enough, was instantly drawn to the Thumper. Pettigrew leaned forward into the conversation with some enthusiasm; Mr. Pettigrew was excellent company when in his cups, despite his tendency to giggle. When the Thumper leaned forward as well, I knew Pettigrew was on to something.

I was left alone with my thoughts for a few moments, and then a movement, and a soft but commanding voice caught my attention.

"A gold guinea bought me a brief meeting with my daughter today," Mr. Cormac said as he pulled up a chair in front of me, "She told me that both she and Mary are indeed pregnant, no question about it.

"At tomorrow's session, the midwives will confirm their pregnancies and execution of the sentences will be stayed until they will have given birth." He raised a hand to silence me. "This gives us nearly five months, as they are both due in May of the coming year. I mean to save my daughter, Mr. Tanner." His eyes flashed fire.

Again the hand…I learned quickly that Mr. Cormac got right to the point, right away.

"My Anne spoke very highly of you, Mr. Tanner, in terms of your character, courage and integrity — she told me also of the many comforts that you have provided for her, as well as for your wife — I am most grateful to you, sir, most grateful indeed."

I studied the man before me as he spoke. His voice carried the lilt of Ireland. It was quietly forceful; he was a man who was used to being listened to; and so I listened.

"I wish to meet with you privately, and confidentially, Mr. Tanner. My little brigantine, *Constant,* arrived not an hour ago. She is berthed at my customary slip not 100 yards from here; you will know her by two lanterns set by her gangplank. I wish you to join me aboard her tomorrow after the evening gun, say four bells of the first watch, for a frank discussion of the means required to save my daughter...and your wife."

"Sir Charles is a fine man, and he will do what he can to save my daughter and your wife. He will undoubtedly importune the Governor to allow me custody of Anne's child when it is born, rather than have the child condemned to a life of poverty, however gentle the foundling hospital at St. Catherine might be.

"He will most certainly keep your name out of the matter, for to bring you into the issue would be of grave danger to you, and a palpable embarrassment for him. He will, I know plead on behalf of both women, that their sentences be transmuted, and that they be transported as bond servants to one of the American colonies. In the end it will come to nothing, I fear. My daughter and your wife will face the gallows. Now, Mr. Tanner, I do not wish to simply have custody of Anne's child, I want my daughter, and my grandchild at home in Carolina with me."

He finished his glass of wine, and continued.

"Myself however, I am not such a fine man as Sir Charles, I am accounted as a gentleman only as I carry a legal degree. I am indeed a very roughhewn man, and I am used to making things happen as I wish them — or need them — to happen, and I will do *whatever* must be done in order to save my girl.

"Anne, of course, is being, as always, a most willful and determined child. She is my Pearl of great price however, and she will not leave the prison without Mary, she has said as much to me today, and thus, Mr. Tanner, you and I are bound one to the other."

With that, he simply got up and walked away to join Pettigrew and the Thumper.

Pettigrew induced Woodley to tell stories of his days as a pugilist in the English country fairs. Those Englishmen who lived in these islands were hungry for news and stories of the homeland; it helped them to maintain a sense of connection to the home island, and to the more 'homely' aspects of English country life. Woodley, with his naturally gregarious personality and broad North Country accent was a wealth of amusing — and some outrageous — stories.

His interview with Captain Johnson finished, Candy joined in with his observations, and his history as a 'student' of Woodley. The evening ended most convivially an hour or so later, with a toast to the King, and to stout English hearts across the world.

Candy and I were berthed together in a very comfortable guest cabin, which was part of Captain Johnson's personal suite. I heard four bells of the middle watch as I drifted into sleep. I dreamed of Mary again, this time as I had seen her in the firelight of that last night in the Forest with the Maroons, glowing and radiant in the flickering light, her eyes, her smile… at four bells of the morning watch a cabin boy was sent to rouse us.

Promptly at 9 am, Friday November 29, the court was reconvened and the first order of business for the court, after the formalities, was the report of the midwives who were assigned to examine Mary and Anne's claims of pregnancy. The two midwives agreed, and reported that both women were indeed 'quick with child," and that their subsequent questioning, and careful examination, had led them to propose that both women became pregnant in about mid August, and that both women could be expected to give birth sometime in the first weeks of May of the coming year.

The court then ordered both women for appearance, and when they were brought forth the president of the court addressed them.

"You Anne Bonny and you, Mary Reede, spinsters, have upon examination both been found to be with child. According to English common law the bastard children within you are innocent of the crimes of which you have both been found guilty, and are thus protected from the just sentence of this court, delivered severally upon you in the court's most recent session."

"Thus in accordance with English common law, you Anne Bonny and you, Mary Reede shall be returned to whence you came, and shall be held at his majesty's prison at Santiago De La Vega until such time as ye shall have given birth to your bastard children.

"The sentence of this court condemning you to be hanged for the crime of high piracy is here-by stayed until such birth, and then shall be carried out within 48 hours after the birth of said bastard children. The said bastard children shall then be given over to the care of the foundling hospital of St. Catherine's parish."

With this finding Captain Johnson rose to leave the court, motioning Candy and I to accompany him. When we were outside he drew both of us aside, and away from the large crowd drawn up to receive news of the two now famous female pirates, and their fate.

"I will be speaking to the Governor at the close of court today"; he said to me. "I will make arrangements with him for me to interview as many of Rackham's remaining crew as I may wish to. I am of course most interested in speaking with Mary and Anne," he turned to address Candy, "I would like you, Mr. Jones, to accompany me on the interviews with Quick and the others, and John," he continued with a smile, "I wish you to accompany me on my interviews with the women."

My heart jumped into my throat knowing that I would at last see Mary again.

That night I went for a walk on the docks to stretch my legs, and arrived at the *Constant* for my requested meeting with Cormac — promptly — the fourth bell of the watch still ringing as I mounted the gangplank.

I was met at the gunwale by a handsome well appointed mature black man, with deep kindly eyes, and I made him to be a man in his early 50s. he carried himself proudly and spoke in that soft drawl common to the southern colonies of America.

"Good evening and welcome aboard the *Constant* suh," he said with a bow and a broad smile. "You must be Mr. Tanner. Master William is waiting for you in his cabin suh, if you'd be so kind as to follow me down. My name is Joseph. I work directly for Master William, if there's any way that I can be of service to you suh, please let me know."

The *Constant* was a trim, clean and well-maintained brigantine, her lines promised speed. She had after all made excellent time to Jamaica, considering that she had to make sail a tide later than the *Elizabeth.* Joseph led me aft to the quarterdeck and down the captain's hatchway, abaft the bitnacale, to William Cormac's private cabin.

The man Joseph knocked on the cabin door and announced that Mr. Tanner had arrived. Cormac was already standing to greet me when Joseph opened the door for me. There was another gentleman present with Cormac.

He was a very well dressed and professional looking man, of medium height, solidly built, and frankly looking a bit like a boxer. He had a broad barrel chest and a solid powerful look to him that reminded me a bit of Candy, and Woodley.

"Mr. Tanner, welcome sir, please make yourself at home," Cormac said, "this is Dr. Tomas Escheverra one of my associates and friends here in Jamaica. Tomas, along with his private practice, is also involved with the foundling hospital of St. Catherine's parish, and is often called upon for medical treatment of prisoners at the prison in Santiago De La Vega. Thomas, this is the Mr. Tanner that I spoke to you of, the husband of my daughter's friend Mary Reede."

"John," he used my given name for the first time, "Dr. Escheverra will be instrumental in the plan that will be laid out for the rescue of my daughter, and your wife. Now please help yourself to some refreshment as we await the arrival of our other guest."

There was a very nice Claret, a strong American rye whiskey, a delightful American cheddar style cheese, fresh ships bread, fresh Island fruit and a black sweet coffee.

I kept myself to the coffee and some fruit as we waited. At Cormac's insistence I took a small measure of the rye whiskey, it went like a signal rocket to my stomach, I choked a bit on it and gasped out… very fine…choke… quite smooth… to the rollicking laughter of both men.

After a few moments of light conversation there was a tap on the door and at Cormac's response the man Joseph appeared in the doorway with a smaller figure in the shadows directly behind him.

"Ah, I see that my other guest has come aboard," Mr. Tanner, he said, "I believe you are acquainted with Mr. Sackett? He comes to me with the highest possible recommendation from every damned source I spoke to, including my daughter and Mrs. Tanner."

I turned quickly about and was overjoyed to see Trinket's wide smile. He was dressed in his usual manner, being the loose serviceable apparel of a sailor, but the quality of the cloth he wore was much better then hitherto. I rose to greet him with a happy little laugh and we embraced. At that moment I knew the plan, whatever it might be, was in the best possible hands.

"Ah laddie," said Trinket, "as Queen Nanny said we are bound together you and I, and I am overjoyed to see ye, and to give aid to you and the lasses in this matter. Rest assured, John, that I too have looked into what is said of Mr. Cormac and the good doctor," at this he gave a small nod to our host, "they are both as they claim and appear to be, and we are gathered here tonight for serious business. I promise ye, John, that only death will keep me from returning Mary to your arms, and of course the little firebrand — Cormac laughed — safely to her father."

I saw Trinket as well take only the strong coffee and a ships biscuit. We four then drew chairs together around the small table behind which Cormac sat, and after a bit of light chatter between Dr. Escheverra, Trinket and me, William Cormac drew our attention with a cough.

"Gentlemen," he said in that commanding manner that was his native tongue, " I am confident that the notoriety of even this case will fade away over the ensuing months. The Governor is intent that all the waters appertaining to his Governorship should be swept clean of pirates. This will work greatly to our advantage, for it will result in scores of trials. And hangings? Lord, possibly by the hundreds. There will be massive piles of paper where in some documents might simply… disappear.

"Our other advantage lay in the pecuniary interests of men who are poorly paid, subject to the arbitrary dictates of their betters, have no opportunity to better themselves, and who almost invariably have taken upon themselves 'other mouths' to feed.

He took along drought of the whiskey and then leaned forward.

"Dr. Escheverra has provided me with a list of those guards and officials within the prison whom he believes would be most receptive to filthy lucre, his list includes, to my great joy, Mr. Foster, the provost Marshall himself, who apparently has some expensive and not socially acceptable habits to support.

He refreshed his cup of the rye whiskey and took a bite of bread, indicating to all of us to refresh ourselves as we wished, and then continued.

"On April 28 next, my brigantine the *Constant* will come in on the evening tide, which my sailing master assures me — using the arcane mathematics known to sailing masters — will be at 6 p.m. She will anchor a cable off shore at the mouth of Kingston harbor, and will be brought about and readied to up anchor and away on the ebb. There will be an experienced midwife aboard her to service the ladies should they come to the term during the course of our journey to the Carolinas.

"After the evening gun at full dark, four picked men of my crew, and four 'other' men of my hire, will bring our launch to my normal slip on the Kingston dock. Mr. Sackett, and Mr. Tanner will meet them there. The launch will have swivels mounted fore and aft, and all these men will be heavily armed. The four 'other men' will as well bring with them sufficient additional firearms and grenadeos so that if the circumstances require it they may blast their way in and then release and arm every damned condemned pirate in that Godforsaken hell hole.

"Make no mistake gentlemen," he continued, his voice rising, "It is my intention to bring out my daughter — and your wife Mr. Tanner — peacefully by acts of simple bribery, that is the plan in place; but by God entertain no doubt that I will bring them out by fire, force of arms and chaos if necessary. I will not leave this island again without my girl."

We three sat as transfixed, savoring the raw power of the man. Cormac recharged his cup

"Now immediately upon their landing, Mr. Sackett will take charge and lead these four 'other' men to the prison by a good common wagon which he will have purchased, and have hired a team of fast horses, and a dependable teamster to manage withal. The four men of my crew will remain with the launch. They will be prepared and armed to play hell with any pursuit if need be.

"The main gate of the prison compound will have unfortunately not have been secured properly, and our party should be able to enter the quadrangle with ease. Mr. Sackett will lead the party into the prison proper; he will have been previously well acquainted with its layout by Dr. Escheverra. The single bribed sergeant of the guard, when he has observed our entry into the quadrangle, will find matters in another area of the prison to concern him.

"He will have left his keys on his desk. Dr. Escheverra will have visited the prison the day prior in order to deliver the agreed 'packages," and to confirm in which cell the women are being held. Mr. Sackett, and one of the other men will move quickly to the ladies cell, release them and bring them out to the wagon as quickly and quietly as possible.

"My further orders to those men whom I will have sent for the release of my daughter are simple: If need be they are to blow the damned gate open, subdue the guards by force, take the keys, and as they move down the cells to release the women, they shall begin releasing newly armed and desperate men into the equation… in passing they are to use a grenadeo to destroy the office of the perfidious Mr. Forbes. I sincerely hope that it does not come to such a pass, but all contingencies must be covered.

"In either case the wagon will then carry the women and the company back to the wharf, at a reasonable pace if there is no alarm and pursuit, at best possible speed if there is. Now if there is an alarm and pursuit I expect you, Mr. Tanner, to be ready to take charge of my men at the dock and to see that the wagon and the launch are protected once they come up on the wharf, and all parties discharge to the launch. The launch will proceed at all possible speed to the *Constant,* which will be on alert and ready to immediately hoist anchor and make for the open sea."

"The *Constant's* hull will have been freshly scraped when I come in April, all her sail will be new best Bristol… for I will wish her to have her maximum sea legs. She is quite a speedy, and a very weatherly, little vessel; she used to be a slaver, and their stock in trade is speed.

"She will also have been rearmed with a dozen four pounders, and manned for the voyage by experienced men, in the event that we may need to discourage a Coasta Garda vessel or two as we escape Jamaican waters."

"God willing we will leave Kingston that day with no alarm having been sounded, and I expect us to be well away at sea before the hue and cry sounds.

"I'll now entertain any questions."

Chapter 25
Spanish Jack

The quartermaster rang six bells of the middle watch as Trinket and I left the *Constant* together that night. There had been only a few questions regarding the plan voiced, none of them consequential to its outcome, they mostly regarding details of time and distance. Cormac answered them all clearly. When we were well along the way on the dock, I turned to Trinket and asked him the question that gnawed on Candy and me for the past month.

"Trinket, did Vasquez deliver us to Barnett?"

"That's a fair question considering the circumstances. To be honest, I cannot say that it was not discussed. Barnett and Hornigold, what can I say of them? Both of them the most experienced, respected and feared of privateers. They know the game — inside and out — they know who is who, and who does what, and with who. They put the fear of God into everyone on the coast which wasn't a simple honest fisherman.

"They got on Rackham's scent right off, and after Ocho Rios they began to shut down the coast as they trailed him. Every vessel stopped, every slip, every wharf and landing visited, every vessel there searched, many of them scuttled right where they lay, or seized for prize money. A lot of folks were very unhappy.

"I, that is, we cleared the point just in time to be greeted by the flash and the roar as the *Kestrel* was taken. We come about right quick I assure you, and we beat our way out of there in all sorts of a hurry, sure every minute that we'd come upon old Hornigold prowling nearby. Very near run thing in all, if we had made contact with you first and then Barnett come up … well, we wouldn't be talking like this.

We parted when we drew up to the Elizabeth's berth, we embraced and once again I swelled with confidence knowing that this man, and friend, was heartily involved in Mary's rescue. I watched fondly as he continued up the wharf with that peculiar gait common to those used to walking on a rolling deck.

Early the next morning, back aboard the *Elizabeth,* a cabin boy woke me and summoned me to Captain Johnson's private office. I responded with alacrity, still tucking my shirt into my britches as I entered his cabin.

"John," he said matter-of-factly, "clean yourself up proper, my cabin boy is preparing a bath and suit of clothes for you; he will queue your hair as well — I need you to be very shipshape this morning. We will breakfast together, and you will then accompany me today on a visit to the prison, as a member of my staff. We are there to begin interviews with all of the surviving members of Rackham's crew. I believe we'll start with the ladies" — my heart jumped into my throat — "their stories will be the thing of legend, when the history of these times is written."

I saw a sly little smile twist his mustache.

We entered the Prison courtyard at 10 a.m. the Provost Marshal himself greeted Sir Charles in the obsequious manner common to those public servants who know that there is nowhere further upward for them, unless they have garnered praise and approbation from influential men such as Sir Charles. After pleasantries we were given over to a Sergeant of the guard, and two guards; I noticed that their uniforms — such as they were — were worn and shabby; they wore the uniform of poverty, despite their shiny buttons.

Customarily, any visitors to the prison were thoroughly searched, their names and habitations noted, their interest in the person being visited was noted, and their visit closely monitored by a guard; there was no direct contact allowed, and no whispering, or 'secret signs' were allowed.

These rules of course do not apply to a Knight of the Garter and a Member of Parliament, nor to his staff. Captain Johnson made it very clear that the presence of a guard would inhibit the prisoner being interviewed. He wished to interview, unaccompanied in the cells, so that the prisoner might see that there was no guard in view, and thus more readily give a true accounting of his actions.

Captain Johnson gave me clear instructions regarding the visit with Mary and Anne. I was to sit quietly behind him and take notes on his conversation. I was to make note of any such items as dates, places or unusual occurrences. He was sincerely interested in the stories of their lives. He truly sensed the emotional bonds involved between the three of us, and felt that my presence would put them both at ease.

“You will need to show restraint,” he said. “I will arrange for a private visit between you and Mary, you may rest assured, but for now this visit must be exactly what it purports to be, the visit by a Knight of the realm, and his special secretary, for the purpose of personally interviewing convicted pirates and writing a narrative report to the Lord High Admiral on the particulars of piracy, and of the men who choose to be pirates; as well as of his privately observed effectiveness, or lack thereof, of certain policies of suppression,” he paused, and chuckled, “I thought Foster would fall over when he saw the warrant that I carry from his Lordship.

Mary burst into tears when she first saw me; there was a little gasp and the trembling in her otherwise erect posture, but her face, twisting and her eyes overflowing. I composed and controlled myself in the same way that a man must when he is under fire. From the corner of my eye I noticed Anne throwing her hands up to her face to cover her emotions.

The tension of the scene was not lost on Captain Johnson; I saw his face twitch. The captain was indeed a fine man, a kind man. I could see that that he was deeply moved. He looked at me, then looked to Mary, then back to me, and then turned away from us. He interposed himself between Anne, and Mary and me so that no one could see us. Mary and I rushed to each other’s arms, and we were able to at last embrace again.

A cough from the captain brought us back to the business at hand. Captain Johnson asked each of them several questions as I sat behind him as instructed. I will admit that I was of absolutely no use to him that day, what notes I did take, were incoherent and disorganized. I had eyes and attention only for my love, and we two spent most of the time simply drinking in each other’s face. Another brief embrace, a kiss, and a whispered I love you and the visit was over. I was in a daze and remember little of what transpired afterwards.

The next morning Candy and I were called for breakfast with Captain Johnson. He greeted us warmly as always and after breakfast he informed us that a packet had arrived late in the previous day, carrying a summons for him, and delivered by Pettigrew, and that he would needs sail on the evening tide for Cadiz.

“Candy, you shall sail with me. I will want to interview you further as we make for Cadiz. I will depend upon you to inform me fully on the now infamous Captain Rackham, as you have indeed sailed with him twice. There was little of any real interest to be learned from the rascals that are the remnant of his crew, and so I look to you. At Cadiz we will rendezvous with Captain Lovewell and the *Rachel.* I believe that Captain Lovewell will offer you the second mate's berth at that time.

"Now John," he turned his attention to me, "I have informed Mr. Forbes that from today you are to have freedom of access, as my special secretary, to the women prisoners, as his Lordship has a special interest in their cases — I know you will not abuse it — You will continue to make notes, and report on all further visits made after the *Elizabeth* has sailed. Mr. Pettigrew will collect them and forward them to me via packet. I may in fact send to you, through him, particular questions his Lordship would like answered.

"I've informed Mr. Forbes that you would be visiting the prison fortnightly, and that he should extend the same courtesies to you, as my special secretary, as he would to me." He paused with a little smile. "I also informed him that I would be attaching to my reports a complementary letter regarding the prison and his administration thereof. He is a man who knows which side of the bread the butter is on and will accommodate you as I wish.

"I've arranged a suite of rooms for you above Mr. Pettigrew's office on Monk Street. I will have your things transferred there today. Mr. Pettigrew has also refreshed the 100-pound purse available for your comforts.

"The final matter I need to discuss with you John, is Mary." I set forward in my chair betraying nothing with my face, although my stomach churned with each mention of her name, "I have spoken at length with the Governor regarding the women, encouraging him on two occasions to mitigate their sentences to transportation to the northern colonies; he frankly would not hear of it.

"The last time I spoke with him on the matter, he had before him a report from a Lieutenant Laws of his majesty's sloop of war *Happy.* Noted in the report was an act of particularly extreme and brutal piracy committed against his most Catholic Majesty's galleon *Santa Maria Oloroso* off the coast of Columbia, by a vessel closely matching the description of Rackham's schooner *Kestrel.* Only the quick thinking of a wounded young Lieutenant, left for dead, saved the few survivors from a treacherously set fire aboard the plundered vessel, 'dreadful, heartless carnage' are the very words the Governor used.

"The report also concludes that it was the very same vessel that fired upon his majesty's sloop of war *Happy,* resulting in extensive damage to the sloop, and the serious wounding of several of his majesty's seamen. Short of an act of parliament, there is nothing to be done; I'm sorry, very sorry indeed for you. I can only hope that it will be some comfort to you, to be able to bring some comfort to her in this extreme.

I knew that this fine man had done everything within his power to help Mary. I also realized the great kindness he was doing for me. He could as well have ordered me to ship out with him, as I was his employee, or he could've left me to my fate as a refugee on the island, but he chose to make it possible for me to comfort Mary over these final months with my love. His purse, and his gracious assignment to me, would enable me to have contact with Mary that I would not have available to me otherwise.

"When this dreadful business is… finished, I wish you to return to Bristol, your parents long to see you. I have work for you, and I can promise you an excellent berth. Mr. Evans at the Albion yards has also inquired about you as well; there is a real future for you when you return home.

That very night I walked down the dock four berths to the *Constant.* I gave my name to the mate on watch, and in a very short time the man Joseph came to greet me in the warmest possible fashion.

"Mr. Tanner, Mr. Tanner suh, so good to see you again," he said, "Mr. William is very pleased that you have come by, and wants me to bring you to his cabin immediately.

Cormac was positively thrilled with the recent development.

"You'll have access under the aegis of a Knight of the realm, God love us. Escheverra can now deal exclusively with Forbes, he treats him for an…unfortunate condition, and thus has access to him in the most private and intimate of circumstances, well away from the prison itself. Important documents must be lost, that is the crux of it, and now you my friend can assume the tedious business of bribing of the guards.

With this he pulled a cord hanging close by his desk, and in the moment the man Joseph knocked lightly and stepped into the cabin.

Cormac spoke briefly with him by the door; I could not hear their conversation except to know that Cormack gave an instruction.

He turned his attention once again to me. "The *Constant* will make sail on the morning tide, when you leave tonight Joseph will hand you a fat purse containing 50 of pieces of eight, and a gold sovereign. Each time you visit you are to press a piece of eight into the hand of the sergeant assigned to that wing of the prison; his name is Marcos. You will make your last visit on April 20 next, on that visit you will deliver the remainder of the purse to him, and tell him that on April 28 the wagon will come with the other sovereign promised to him."

My heart was light that night when the carriage deposited me at Pettigrew's building Number 24 Monk Street. Pettigrew was very happy to see me, most gracious, and after a glass of wine together I retired upstairs to a very comfortable bedroom, with a sitting room overlooking the street.

Following both the instruction of Captain Johnson, and the instruction of my heart I visited Mary and Anne fortnightly. And according to Cormac's instruction always pressing a piece of eight into the hand of the sergeant of the guard who escorted me to their cell.

It was always the same man, Marcos.

On our first visit together, under the guise of taking notes I wrote a very brief message and turned my pad so that Mary could read: *On the evening of April 28 Trinket will come for you and Anne. Documents will disappear and you will both be free.* I tore the note up immediately and placed it in my pocket as Mary's eyes swelled with tears.

Knowing Mary's story intimately, I was able to write of it in detail to Captain Johnson from memory, and thus Mary's and my time together was spent most in speaking of the future that we both wished for, and longed for. It would be impossible of course for us to return together to England, and so we began to discuss where in the world we could make our life together. She was enthralled by my description of the little New England harbor town of Boston and we decided that the Massachusett Bay colony would be our goal.

Mary did share with me a droll story regarding Anne playing the mermaid to distract the watch on deck, when Rackham and the crew stole the French packet schooner *Crécerelle* out of Port Au

Prince harbor a short month prior to taking the *Rachel*, her French name translated to *Kestrel.*

My interviews — in the strict sense — were thus confined to Anne Bonny and her story, and her father's story.

Anne's father was a successful solicitor in the port city of Kinsale, in county Cork on the extreme southeastern coast of Ireland. He was also a married man when Anne's mother Mary Brennan came to work for the family. His position in the city, and in the future politics of the city seemed assured; he was a respected member of the bar, well married with a successful practice.

William Cormac had a very passionate affair with Mary Brennan, which inevitably led to Anne's bastard birth in 1702; the identity of the father was unquestionable. The then Mrs. Cormac promptly filed suit for divorce on grounds of adultery and fornication. It was a truly scandalous affair, and a great shame to the woman. In revenge for Mary's part in her shame she planted silverware in Mary's private things, and had her convicted of theft. Mary Brennan and her child were transported to the Carolina colonies, Mary as a purchased bondservant, Anne as a bastard child dependent.

William Cormac threw everything in Ireland to the wind, followed Mary to the Carolinas and bought her bond. They were married shortly thereafter. He was a faithful husband, and deeply loved his Mary until her untimely death in 1713. Her mother's death at such an early age, Anne turned 12 that year, seemed to unleash all of the rebelliousness of her spirit, and its wildness. Her father spoiled her outrageously, she being the only connection left to him of his beloved wife.

She told me that only the calming presence of her friend and confidant, her father's freed man whom she called 'uncle Joseph," kept any peace in the home. Until at last her father, when she was 16, sought to betroth her to the son of a neighboring plantation. I knew instantly that I had met the same Joseph, still in her father's service aboard the *Constant*

She chose instead, in her wild foolishness, to clandestinely marry and run off to sea with a Charles Town roughneck, a 'chinless weakling' — as she called him — named James Bonny. His desire was to be a pirate, and so to New Providence in the Bahamas they went. Her father promptly disowned her, in order to save his property from any claim by his now 'son-in-law."

James Bonny turned out to be every bit the spineless nitwit her father warned her he would be, having neither the stomach nor the brains to be a pirate. So he became an informant for the new Royal Governor Woodes Rogers, whose mandate from the king was to rid the Bahamas of pirates. Rogers was an iron man himself being once a very successful privateer captain, and up to the task. The King's pardon was offered to all who would forswear their piratical ways and return to peaceable pursuits. Many, including my friend Candy, took the pardon and lived up to it. Many others took the pardon but later spurned it — to their peril, others refused it and sailed away. The Bahamas were no longer and never again the haven for piracy.

Anne met John Rackham, recognized a real man when she saw one and fell in love.

Rackham confronted her 'husband' with his perfidy and threatened to kill him, Anne pleaded with Rackham for his useless life. James Bonny saw fit to actually threaten them with a divorce suit for adultery. Rackham laughed in his face, gave him 100 pounds to purchase Anne from him, and told him that if he ever saw his face again he, Rackham, would shoot him down like the dog he was.

Anne joined Rackham aboard his newly stolen sloop the *William,* and that very night they sailed from New Providence and never returned. Anne began to dress and act the part of the man. This was done in part to placate his crew, who in their superstition were not happy about a woman being aboard. In part the change was also made as part of Anne's bold and rebellious nature.

Sunday April 20, 1721 was my last visit to the prison prior to the expected date of deliverance the 28th. As instructed I handed Marcos the remainder of the purse, and informed him quietly of the appointed date. Other then our introductions on the first of my visits, and civil greetings on the remainder of the visits, these were the first words we had together, he assured me but everything would be as it should be when the wagon arrived for the women.

Mary did not look well that day, her face was sallow and her eyes had an unusual brightness to them; I noticed also that Anne seemed to hover a bit.

"Are you not well my love," I asked her.

"I shall be right enough. When we have slipped this foul place and I can breathe free air again, sea air, with you dearest.

She took my hand and placed it upon her stomach, I felt our child move within her.

We held each other quietly for a long time on that last visit.

I returned to Pettigrew's and began work on the final report that I would give him to forward to Captain Johnson. I felt pangs of guilt frankly, as I had indeed imposed upon the freedom that he gave me as his agent secretary. I used that freedom for my own end, that being to circumvent the law — possibly by violence — in order to save my wife. I endeavored over the next week to send through to him as complete and detailed a report on, and biographies of both Mary and Anne as possible.

I have been gratified to see that so much of the report that I sent through to Captain Johnson for the attention of the Lord High Admiral has been printed for general consumption in his already famous book: '*A General History Of The Robberies And Murders Of The Most Notorious Pyrates."* Published at London in '24.

The *Constant* arrived at sunset of April 28, directly after the evening gun. She dropped anchor just inside the harbor mouth, under the guns of Fort Charles. Her bow to the open sea. She fired, and was returned the prescribed salute.

The night was the new moon, and there was a low mist building all across Kingston Harbor that dark night. One could just make out faint lights from atop Fort Charles across the bay as the cutter came cleanly and quietly up to the appointed wharf shortly after dark. A leader line was thrown up to us, and Trinket and I drew up a ship's rope ladder, tying it off to a piling. No words were spoken.

The four men who climbed out of the cutter, and came quickly and quietly up the ladder were as dark and muffled as the night itself. They wore dark browns, dark grays, only, and on their heads black Monmouths. I sensed that their bearing and their movements were practiced and military, like one would expect from Marines or such. Cormac had engaged very serious looking men in case of trouble.

Each mounted the ladder effortlessly, and as they came to the deck I could see that they were very fit men indeed. Each one carried a brace of pistols on clips on a broad black belt, a short sword, and a large bag over the shoulder; every bit of metal that I could see had been smoked so that there was no reflection. Each man gave me a hard look and a brief nod and then reported straightways to Trinket at the wagon. After some moments of hushed discussion the men climbed into the wagon, and Trinket walked over to me.

"John, I expect no trouble tonight. Cormac has proper greased the capstan very nicely, but if there is trouble, Cormac, as he said, is prepared to take the women out by force if necessary. These four men are ready to do what may needs be done. They are a set of Cuban brothers as came recommended by Jorge — by this he meant Vazquez — they will do nothing 'less I set them loose, and then they are right fierce ugly dogs, forsooth. They are prepared, each one of them, to arm four released prisoners, and they carry grenadeos enough to blast their way in if needs be.

"Now if it comes to trouble, you'll know of it soon enough. The sound of us blowing — he laughed — the damned gate off of the prison will carry thus far at night I'm sure." At that he stopped, and then began again very seriously, "should you hear that John, ye are to take charge of these men, and set up here to give us good cover when we round yonder onto the dock. There are a dozen charged muskets in the launch, and the murderers are charged with buckshot, and there are two spare pots loaded… now God be with us, for mercy is what we bring."

With that he slapped my shoulder, and then walked quickly to the wagon. He sprang up beside the teamster as if jumping to the shrouds, and then with a soft 'git' the wagon clattered down the wharf at a businesslike pace, one that would raise no notice, or alarm to an observer.

The wagon chosen was a common one, the sort that regularly brought goods and people from the docks of Kingston the 14 miles to Santiago De la Vega, and return. A good four hours were assumed for the round-trip, barring unforeseen circumstances. There was nothing for us to do except settle in to wait, relaxed but vigilant.

In a couple of hours the night turned more quiet about us. The vessels in the harbor begin to go to sleep, the laughter and the voices slowly ceasing, the bump and scraping of gangplanks being drawn up and secured, and the ringing of the ship's bells muffled by the thickening fog.

Just as the tide began to turn I heard the fog muted clatter of the wagon as it turned onto the wharf. There was no pursuit so therefore the wagon came briskly, but not in an obvious rush. The crew of the launch were immediate in their actions, the oars were readied and space made ready and cleared for the oncoming seven people, eight with myself. I can hardly describe my excitement.

The wagon pulled up short at the slip and as there was no alarm or pursuit a more relaxed attitude was taken by the four men in the launch as they cleared and prepared for the journey back to the *Constant.* I found it odd that Trinket remained seated beside the teamster, and seemed to just stare blankly ahead.

The wagon disgorged one, two, three, four hard man who had not needed to fight their way in and out of the prison after all, and then a fifth figure, smaller and muffled with a cloak, it was Anne…

I looked behind her into the now empty recesses of the wagon, a cold hand at my heart

"Where is Mary," I asked.

"She is dead, John," Trinket replied in a flat emotionless voice, "God give you peace."

I remembered Trinket's promise that only death would keep him from delivering her to my arms.

Anne Bonny rushed to me at that moment and then clasped herself tightly against me, she was wailing and catching her breath. "Oh John. Oh John, oh John," She kept saying, "Mary died of the fever — Spanish Jack, Escheverra called it, the yellow fever — this very morning. She had been ill all week, we thought it was due to her pregnancy, the fever raged upon her yesterday and in the early hours of this morning…I was with her, to the very end, and held her as she died, she spoke your name at the last — oh! I cannot speak of it. She burst into sobs.

"She was so happy with you, that week in the mountains, she spoke to me so often of it, she loved you so — you're such a good man, John, oh I'm so sorry I, I can't — words fail me" She held me close and tight against her, I could feel her body shaking, then I felt my own shaking as we clung to each other.

"I must go to her," I remember saying in a dead voice, as if it another spoke through me.

"T'will do ye no good lad," it was Trinket at my side, "ye kenna, as she's been moved to the tombs at St. Catherine's, she'll be buried in the pauper's field of the church grounds tomorrow morning. A good proper Christian burial is all this world has left for her. Poor darling lass… "Lass?," he repeated, "if ye'd had a dozen as good men aboard the *Kestrel* that morning"… his voice trailed off.

"Then I shall be there with her in the morning," I said, my body felt cold.

"Oh no, John no," cried Anne, "come away with us now, Trinket is leaving with us, Candy is gone and you will have no friends left upon this island. Come away to Carolina with us. Daddy I know has work for you. I know Mary would want you to go away with us. She would want you to be safe and cared for. What will you do here now? Oh do come away with us.

I heard a longing in Anne's voice, and I saw softness in her eyes that I'd never seen before. I saw clearly that she wished to care for me.

"I cannot, Anne. I wish you Godspeed, but I must be where she is till the last.

I turned then and bid a most affectionate farewell to Trinket.

"Remember," he said to me, "what Nanny said, we are not done one with the other.

I pressed a piece of eight into the hand of the teamster for passage back to St. Catherine's Parish as the launch pulled away from the wharf and made for the *Constant.*

I arrived at the tombs for St. Catherine parish just before dawn, and let Mary know that I was there. At first light a party of graves keepers arrived, and after finding an open spot began to dig. They were perhaps half an hour or so in digging the grave, laughing and joking amongst themselves the while, which is common to men who do such work.

Shortly after they finished preparing the gravesite, two guards and a now familiar Sergeant from the prison arrived at the tombs; a priest and two acolytes accompanied them from the parish. The tombs were opened, and a canvas wrapped form strapped onto a board was brought forth; I choked off my shaking sobs.

Mary was indeed given a good Christian burial. The last rites and prayers were read over her, and special prayers added for the soul of our innocent child who had perished with her; no one took notice of the weeping man in the morning shadows under the trees.

Later, when the graves keepers had finished their work and left, I walked over and knelt beside Mary's grave. It was marked solely by a small squared off flat rock only a little bigger than a man's hand pressed into the dirt at the head of the grave. It was the soft white limestone common to the island and unmarked.

I took it up, and with my clasp knife I carved her name deeply upon it: Mary.

I replaced the stone, and then pressed a shiny piece eight into the earth, where I thought her heart might be. I sat there beside her grave for quite a long time, till darkness fell, and spoke to her. I promised her I would never forget her, and I never have.

With Pettigrew's help I found a vessel bound out of Kingston for the port of Boston in the Massachusett Bay colony on May 15 of 1721. Arriving there on July 4, 1721.

As the vessel cleared Fort Charles, I looked to our larboard toward Plumb point, and saw at least what was left of Jack Rackham, for the last time.

He was shapeless and black, and he hung in a cage by the sea.

Epilogue

Charles Towne
Carolina Colony
Autumn 1727

Her name is Mary Constant Cormac. She is named in honor of her deceased grandmother Mary, and her mother's best friend Mary Reede. Her middle name honors the vessel upon which she was born on May 10 1721.

Her last name, Cormac, is that of her grandfather William Cormac. She is so named because her grandfather would not have the name of Bonny attached to his beloved granddaughter.

Her mother is Anne Bonny, her father was John Rackham, late pirate of Jamaica.

She is a very precocious, loving and fearless little girl of six.

She is as 'bold and bright as a shiny brass button' her mammy Jemma always says; she is also very beautiful, like her mother.

Her hair is a rich chestnut, like her mother's, with coppery highlights. She has a long slender and sensitive face, with high cheekbones and deep-set penetrating blue eyes, like her father.

She loves the sea, and the boats, and the bustle of activity at the dock — mammy Jemma once had told her that she was 'ocean borned," her momma giving birth to her at sea on grandpa's boat.

She loves all the nice men that she meets when her grandpa and her momma bring her down to the docks to see one of grandpa's boats unload. And when they bring her to the dock she always gets to wear the little blue linen jacket, and the bright red sash and bonnet that she loves.

She loves the sound of the gulls too, and she always brings them some of mammy Jemma's corndodgers — though she eats some of them herself because they are so good.

She loves mammy Jemma

She loves as well to hold a piece of corndodger between her fingers, with her arm upstretched, and wait for one of the gulls to swoop down and take it with a bold cry.

It makes her laugh.

She always runs ahead in her excitement.

“Come along back now, Mary,” Anne called out to her, “Grandpa and I wish to go into the warehouse first, you can see uncle Joseph there honey.”

She loves uncle Joseph.

CPSIA information can be obtained
at www.ICGtesting.com
Printed in the USA
BVOW09s1331191117
500830BV00004B/195/P